Praise for #1 *New York Times* bestselling author Sherryl Woods

"Sherryl Woods gives her characters depth, intensity, and the right amount of humor."
—*RT Book Reviews*

"Sherryl Woods writes emotionally satisfying novels about family, friendship and home. Truly feel-great reads!"
—#1 *New York Times* bestselling author Debbie Macomber

"Woods is a master heartstring puller."
—*Publishers Weekly*

Praise for Jo McNally

"With witty characters and only a small amount of drama, *Slow Dancing at Sunrise* is an entertaining and charming story that will appeal to readers of small-town romances."
—*Harlequin Junkie* on *Slow Dancing at Sunrise*

"Readers will be charmed by this sweet, no-nonsense Christmas romance full of genuine emotion."
—*Publishers Weekly* on *Stealing Kisses in the Snow*

With her roots firmly planted in the South, #1 *New York Times* bestselling author **Sherryl Woods** has written many of her more than one hundred books in that distinctive setting, whether it's her home state of Virginia, her adopted state, Florida, or her much-adored South Carolina. Now she's added North Carolina's Outer Banks to her list of favorite spots. And she remains partial to small towns, wherever they may be.

Sherryl divides her time between her childhood summer home overlooking the Potomac River in Colonial Beach, Virginia, and her oceanfront home with its lighthouse view in Key Biscayne, Florida. "Wherever I am, if there's no water in sight, I get a little antsy," she says.

Sherryl loves to hear from readers. You can visit her on her website at www.sherrylwoods.com, link to her Facebook fan page from there or contact her directly at Sherryl703@gmail.com.

Jo McNally lives in coastal North Carolina with one hundred pounds of dog and two hundred pounds of husband—her slice of the bed is very small. When she's not writing or reading romance novels (or clinging to the edge of the bed), she can often be found on the back porch sipping wine with friends while listening to great music. If the weather is absolutely perfect, Jo might join her husband on the golf course, where she tends to feel far more competitive than her actual skill level would suggest.

She likes writing stories about strong women and the men who love them. She's a true believer that love can conquer all if given just half a chance.

#1 *New York Times* Bestselling Author

SHERRYL WOODS

ONE TOUCH OF MOONDUST

**HARLEQUIN
BESTSELLING
AUTHOR
COLLECTION**

HARLEQUIN®
BESTSELLING
AUTHOR
COLLECTION

Recycling programs
for this product may
not exist in your area.

ISBN-13: 978-1-335-91877-2

One Touch of Moondust

First published in 1989. This edition published in 2020.

Copyright © 1989 by Sherryl Woods

A Man You Can Trust
First published in 2019. This edition published in 2020.
Copyright © 2019 by Jo McNally

This edition published by arrangement with Harlequin Books S.A.

For questions and comments about the quality of this book,
please contact us at CustomerService@Harlequin.com.

Harlequin Enterprises ULC
22 Adelaide St. West, 40th Floor
Toronto, Ontario M5H 4E3, Canada
www.Harlequin.com

Printed in U.S.A.

CONTENTS

ONE TOUCH
OF MOONDUST

Sherryl Woods

For Lucia Macro,
who sees beyond my blind spots and always
finds the heart of the story, with thanks for
her editing skill, her patience and her humor.

Chapter One

Gabrielle came to a halt in the middle of a cracked sidewalk richly decorated with dramatic and colorfully executed graffiti. She checked the address she'd marked in the paper against two numbers that dangled precariously upside down beside a dilapidated building's front door. If the empty space between them had once been filled by a seven, then this was in fact "Recently Renovated Brownstone." Apparently the renovations were less recent than hoped for.

Tucking her chilled hands in the pockets of her coat for warmth, she regarded the faded facade, dirt-streaked bay windows and dingy, peeling trim with a sense of resignation. It was a very long way from Park Avenue. Taking a deep breath of the brisk fall air, she wrapped her fur coat more tightly around her and stepped into the dreary foyer.

It had possibilities, she decided, viewing the muddy tile floor and dull brass fixtures with a critical eye. The construction looked sound enough and she'd be willing to bet that the apartments all had hardwood floors. She seemed to recall a chimney on the outside, which meant there were fireplaces. Yes, it definitely had possibilities, she thought with a vague sense of anticipation, the first she'd felt in weeks.

In fact, a few months earlier when her career on Wall Street had been ascending at a dizzying pace, she might very well have bought the whole place and restored it as a promising investment. Now, with no brokerage house work to be found for a talented but still very junior financial analyst, she could barely afford the advertised bargain rent. In fact, if she didn't make some career decisions soon and find another job, she'd be forced to retreat to her family home in South Carolina and live on humble pie for the rest of her life. It was not an alternative she cared to endure.

Gritting her teeth with determination, she began climbing the endless, creaking steps to apartment 4B, where the smell of fresh paint was wafting through the open door. She considered that an encouraging sign after the dinginess and disrepair below.

Gabrielle tapped on the door and waited. The hammering sounds coming from deep inside the apartment didn't let up. She knocked harder and called out. The pounding stopped.

"Yo," a husky masculine voice responded cheerfully. "Be right with you, sweetheart."

Sweetheart? Gabrielle's vivid imagination immediately supplied an image to go with that impertinent voice: a well-muscled, catcalling construction worker atop steel beams overlooking Fifth Avenue. He'd be rugged, impervious to slights and persistent. She'd walked past the type half a dozen times a day and they'd always made her want to check to see if her slip was showing. When this man emerged a moment later she was startled to see how accurately he fit the image. She was also startled to discover that in this case her slip was the last thing on her mind. The man quite simply took her breath away.

Bold blue eyes examined her with a disconcerting, leisurely thoroughness. As if on cue, impudent lips emitted an approving whistle. Light brown hair, still streaked with highlights from the summer sun, waved in casual and charming disarray. Faded, paint-spattered jeans clung to narrow hips and muscular thighs. Despite the chill in the air, a shirt hung open, revealing a chest covered with coarse brown hair that arrowed provocatively downward. Gabrielle was torn between clutching her coat more protectively around her and stripping it away from her suddenly burning flesh. She settled for trying to stare him down.

The attempt failed miserably. He laughed, an all-too-knowing gleam in his eyes.

"So," he said, amusement lacing through his voice,

"what's a sophisticated lady like you doing in a place like this? Slumming?"

Detecting sarcasm rather than humor in the remark, she had to bite back an instinctive angry retort. He had an apartment. She needed one. It was no time to look around with the hauteur of Bette Davis and declare, "What a dump," much less deliver a lecture on manners to the hired help.

She held up the paper instead. "I've come about the apartment. May I see it?"

With a wide smile punctuated by dimples, he gave a grand, sweeping gesture. "Be my guest."

Gabrielle stepped cautiously inside and took a slow survey of the empty room. She had difficulty registering the apartment's features because the man stood right behind her, watching her every move. Where she went, he followed, first with his eyes, then by ambling along behind. Since he couldn't possibly be concerned about theft, she had to assume he was doing it to rattle her.

It was working. Quite well, in fact. She tried to shake off the feeling with common sense. With her whole life off-kilter, the last thing she needed was an instantaneous physical attraction to a man of apparently limited means and ambition. A handyman, for heaven's sake. The members of the Junior League of Charleston would die laughing at the notion of Senator Graham Clayton's daughter having palpitations over a handyman.

"Do you know anything about the building?" she asked when she'd seen the living room and two tiny bedrooms. She'd been right about the fireplace. It was small, but suggestive of cozy winter evenings. She was less hopeful about the floor. It was wood all right, but paint-spattered, scuffed and marred by several generations of spills. It would require extensive elbow grease, sanding and quite possibly a miracle to restore it.

"What did you want to know about the building?"

"When was the last time an exterminator was here?"

He shrugged doubtfully. "There's always a can of Raid."

One blond brow arched significantly. "I see." She glanced once more around the empty living room. "The ad said furnished."

"It will be."

"When?"

"Tomorrow. Maybe the next day. Whenever I get finished with the work."

The man obviously had a careless disregard for timetables. To a woman whose calendar had always been carefully scheduled in fifteen-minute increments such a blasé attitude was both irritating and irresponsible. "When exactly will it be available?" she persisted. "I'm facing a deadline."

"An anxious client?"

She stared at him blankly. "Client?"

"You're a real estate agent, right? If you want to buy, it's not for sale. If you have someone who wants to rent, I'd prefer to deal direct. Sorry, no agents."

"I'm not in real estate. I'm looking for myself. To rent," she amended, in case he was worried that she was planning to buy the property and fire the help—starting with him.

Instead of putting his mind at ease, though, she seemed to have astonished him. "You actually want to live here yourself?"

"Why not?" she said defensively, though she knew perfectly well what he meant. "It's an apartment. I need a place to live."

"Try Park Avenue."

"I did," she admitted ruefully. "The price is right here."

"So," he said, conducting a more thoughtful survey, "the lady's down on her luck." There was little sympathy in his voice, only mild curiosity.

She drew herself up with dignity and tried to wilt him with a haughty stare. "Temporarily."

The stare had no discernible effect. "Does that mean you'll be moving out the minute you get a few bucks together?"

She considered lying, but figured he'd never believe her if she did. There was a disconcertingly astute gleam in his eyes—one that was all too typical of corporate sharks.

"Yes," she said finally.

"Then why would I want to rent to you?"

"I'm here. I've got the money." At least for the first month, she amended to herself.

"This is New York, sweetheart. You're not the first person to stop by and you won't be the last."

"Are you holding out for the highest bidder?"

"Maybe. What're you offering?"

The speculative look in his eyes brought a flush to Gabrielle's normally pale complexion. This time she did settle her coat more protectively around her and headed for the door. In the past few months she'd sacrificed just about everything but her pride and her dignity. She wasn't about to lose those, as well.

"Never mind," she said on her way out. "I don't think this would work out."

He caught up with her before she could reach the door. "I'm sorry," he said with what sounded like total sincerity. She studied his expression, assessing him as she might a prospective investor. His eyes, for once, were serious, which did the strangest things to her ability to breathe. He touched her sleeve. "Please. Accept my apology. If you want the place, it's yours."

"Why?"

"I've been through a few rough times myself."

The suddenly sympathetic, contrite demeanor made her extraordinarily suspicious. Leopards rarely changed their spots in the blink of an eye. This leopard was also shifting his weight uneasily from one foot to the other. She waited for his next move.

"There is one thing you should know about first, though," he said finally.

"Which is?"

"The bathroom."

Despite herself, she grinned at his cautious tone. "I'm familiar with the concept. I assume this one has all the usual amenities."

"More or less," he said, intriguing her as he beckoned and headed toward the opposite end of the living room. "Through here."

She walked into a narrow kitchen with peeling wallpaper and yellowed linoleum and came to a halt, her mouth dropping open. "I hope that's a planter," she murmured, staring at the large, claw-footed ceramic tub in the middle of the room, then at her guide. He was laughing.

"Nope. That's the tub all right. It's more convenient to the stove in here."

"The stove?" she repeated weakly.

"In case the hot water runs out and you…"

"I get the picture. Where's the rest of it?"

"It?"

"The bathroom."

"Through that door."

Deciding it wouldn't be wise to take anything else for granted, Gabrielle peeked through the door. Thankfully there were no more surprises. The sink and toilet appeared old, but functional—she checked just to be sure—and the room was clean.

Now she was the one hesitating. She had finally accepted the idea that her current budget wouldn't allow for luxuries, but a tub in the kitchen? Still, she thought of the long list of depressing, unsatisfactory apartments she'd already seen. With all its flaws—and she wasn't minimizing them—this was still far and away the best.

"Okay," she said eventually, if reluctantly. "I can live with this."

"There's one other thing."

She felt her heart sink. The way he'd said that told her it was even more ominous than having to take her bath in the middle of her kitchen. "What?" she said with a weary sigh.

"If you're in a hurry to move in, you might have to deal with a roommate."

Her eyebrows shot up. She gave him a hard stare. He looked decidedly uneasy again, which was unnerving in a man of his apparent self-confidence. "A roommate? You mean it's already rented?" She felt oddly disappointed.

"Not exactly."

"Well, it's either rented or it's not."

"Actually it's just temporarily occupied."

"Does this have anything to do with the sleeping bag I saw rolled up in one of the bedroom closets?"

He nodded. "It's mine."

That was definitely a problem. "When will you be moving out?"

"In a couple of months, as soon as I can get the apartments downstairs finished, but it's okay. We could share the place until then. It has two bedrooms and I'd promise to stay in mine."

He crossed his heart dramatically, then treated her to that wide, high-voltage smile. Obviously he meant it to be friendly and reassuring. He had no idea that it set her pulse to racing in a way that normally indicated such crises as imminent stock market crashes or a dramatic fall in the value of the dollar. If there had been a chair in the room, she would have collapsed into it. She refused to sit in the tub.

"This isn't such a good idea," she said. It was an eloquent understatement. It was a horrible, impossible, not-to-be-considered-for-an-instant idea. "I'll have to keep looking."

"Where will you go?"

"I don't know. Someplace."

"Can you stay where you are?"

"Not after Saturday."

"Is there a friend you can move in with?"

She thought of several who'd offered, all of them part of the fast-paced, well-heeled world she was leaving behind. "No."

"Can you afford a hotel?"

For the first time she heard a note of compassion in his voice. She sighed. "No."

"Then think about my offer. Come see the garden before you decide," he encouraged, holding out his hand. Gabrielle ignored it and he jammed it into his pocket. The snub didn't faze his upbeat mood as he enthused, "It's a little ragged now, but in the spring with tulips and crocuses and forsythia in bloom, it'll be magnificent. At least that's what my father says and he's got a green thumb that's known all over Long Island."

Gabrielle felt a ridiculous twinge of doubt. She was a sucker for a garden. Always had been. The Clayton house in South Carolina had been surrounded by azaleas and roses with an extravagantly colorful and overgrown English country garden in back that had been her personal domain.

"I'll take a look," she said finally. "But I don't think it will change my mind. I've never had a roommate, not even in college."

Left unspoken was the fact that she'd never lived with a man under any circumstances. Where she came from it still wasn't considered proper, especially for the daughter of a highly recognizable politician. Goodness knows, her relationship with her former fiancé had been proper. Which, she admitted ruefully, was probably part of the problem. With Townsend Lane she hadn't even been tempted to commit a casual indiscretion, much less have a sizzling affair.

She followed her prospective roommate downstairs, through a narrow hallway and onto a tiny stoop. What she saw made her smile in a way that she hadn't smiled in a very long time. A bit of sunshine stole into her heart.

The tiny, walled-in area had flower beds along the fringes. Now they were jammed with a haphazard display of chrysanthemums, marigolds and zinnias in yellows and oranges and reds. A wrought-iron table and two chairs fit tidily into the middle. The whole garden was shaded by a huge maple tree next door, its leaves already turning to the fiery shades of autumn. It was charming, utterly and irresistibly charming.

"What's the rent?" she asked finally. Perhaps if she concentrated on the business aspects of the transaction, she wouldn't be quite so vibrantly aware of the fact that she was committing herself to living with a man she'd met less than an hour earlier. It would be a practical decision under the circumstances, a way to stretch her remaining savings. She waited for his response to see just how far she could make those last dollars go.

"We can work it out."

"Will I have to sign a lease?"

"What for?" he asked. "You've already told me you have every intention of breaking it."

It was an unexpected plus. There would be no arguments when the time came for her to move back out.

"And we're strictly roommates? You have your own room. I have mine. We share the kitchen. Right?" An image of the tub popped into mind. "We have a schedule for the kitchen," she amended.

Apparently the same provocative image lurked in his mind, too, because he grinned. "If you say so."

She took another look around the garden, then held out her hand. "Then I guess we understand each other Mr....?"

He enfolded her hand in his much larger one and held it just long enough for the calluses and warmth to register against the chilled softness of her own flesh.

"Reed," he said in a slow, deliberately provocative way meant to emblazon the name on her memory. "Paul Reed."

She swallowed hard. "And I'm Gabrielle Clayton." It came out sounding disgustingly breathless.

"Gabrielle, huh? Quite a mouthful for such a little bit of a thing. Why don't I call you Gaby?"

She felt her control slipping away and inserted the haughty edge back into her voice. "Gabrielle will do just fine. Ms. Clayton would be even better."

"So, Gaby, when do you want to move in?"

She gave him an icy stare. It was going to be a very long month. Or two. "As soon as possible."

"Will Friday be okay? I should be able to get the basics taken care of by then."

She supposed if she was about to walk straight into danger, it was better to get it over with. "Perfect," she said without the slightest tremor.

"One last thing," she said as she went to the foyer. "For as long as we're sharing the place, we split the rent fifty-fifty."

"That's really not fair. I'm inconveniencing you. I'll take care of the first month. After that you pay the full rate."

She toyed with the temptation, then dismissed it. Being in this man's debt could lead to all sorts of potentially explosive misunderstandings. "Fifty-fifty."

He shrugged. "If that's what you want."

"And the same with the utilities."

"Okay."

"And you call me Gabrielle."

He grinned. "We'll have to work on that one."

He followed her onto the front stoop and watched as she started down the steps. She felt his gaze burning into her.

"Have a nice week," he said just then. The husky

note in his voice sent a delicious shiver down her spine before he deliberately taunted, "Gaby."

Paul Reed, she decided as she marched off to the subway station, was a very irritating man. Since that was the only real certainty to come out of the morning, she was stunned that she'd put up so little fuss about living with him even on such a temporary basis. She was not an impetuous woman. While working on Wall Street had demanded a certain amount of risk-taking, her decisions were always well-informed, not reckless. So why on earth had she agreed to move in with a man like Paul Reed, a man who made her usually sensible head spin? During the subway ride back to Manhattan, she told herself he'd caught her in a weak moment, with little money and a lease that was about to expire. She even blamed it on the zinnias.

Now, after a blast of cool air and a little distance, she was thinking more clearly. That knot of uncertainty in her stomach was sending a message. She ought to listen to it. She would call and cancel their agreement. No, forget calling. His voice would sizzle across the phone lines and she'd agree to something else ridiculous. It was far more sensible not to show up. It would teach him a valuable lesson about good business. He should have insisted on a lease. He should have asked for references, a deposit. Quite possibly he'd considered the fox coat adequate. If only he knew. It was the last thing of value she owned and she could very well be forced to hock it if things didn't turn around soon.

Pleased with her decision to forget all about the

apartment in Brooklyn and about Paul Reed, she pulled the classified ads out of her purse and began to search for another, more suitable apartment, one with a tub where it belonged and no overwhelmingly masculine roommate. But before the subway even crossed into Manhattan, her spirits sank. She could not bear the thought of looking at another dump. The brownstone which, like her, was at a turning point in its life seemed increasingly attractive. And Paul Reed, she decided, she could manage.

"How bad could it be?" she murmured under her breath, hoping for a stronger sense of conviction. It was only for a month after all. Four weeks. She'd handled stock portfolios worth millions. She'd dealt with avaricious, rakish men. She could handle anything for four weeks, even a man like Paul Reed. Starting Monday she'd double her efforts to find a new job. Within a month or two at the outside, she'd be back on her feet and back in Manhattan.

An image of Paul Reed's bold, impudent smile danced across her mind. The subway suddenly seemed much warmer. Doubts flooded back more vividly than ever.

It was the balance in her checkbook that took the decision out of her hands. When it came right down to it, there was no choice at all. It looked as though Friday would be moving day. She'd just buy a very sturdy lock for the bedroom door.

Now why did you go and do a stupid thing like that? Paul asked himself repeatedly after Gabrielle had left.

Oh, sure, he needed the money if he was to keep this restoration on schedule and make the monthly payments on the brownstone, but he could have insisted that she wait another month before moving in. He could even have volunteered to move downstairs with his sleeping bag. He'd lived like a vagrant amid the rubble up here for weeks now anyway. Instead he'd managed to manipulate her into sharing the place with him. Was he suffering from some need to torment himself? Hadn't he learned anything about the unbreachable differences between the classes while he'd been growing up on Long Island? He'd been the housekeeper's son on an estate the size of a country club. It had kept him on the fringes of high society all of his life. The women he'd met had been vain, shallow and spoiled. He'd learned the hard way that they were unsuited to anything but the most pampered way of life.

He slammed a nail so hard it shook the door. Gabrielle Clayton belonged in a place like this the way diamonds belonged in the Bowery. She probably wouldn't last half as long as diamonds did in that neighborhood, either. It would give him a certain perverse satisfaction to watch her try to adapt to a life-style she quite obviously considered beneath her.

He'd seen the way she looked at him, too, as if he were no better than a lazy, unambitious handyman. Too many people had looked at him just that way. It was about time he taught one of them a lesson about quick judgments and superficial values.

But why Gabrielle Clayton? a voice in his head

nagged. He grinned ruefully. That answer was obvious to anyone who took a good, hard look at her. With her honey-blond hair, delicate bone structure and slight Southern accent, she was a sexy bundle of contradictions wrapped in fur. Scarlett O'Hara and the Ice Maiden all rolled into one. She had the kind of wide, dangerous eyes that could tempt a man to the edge of hell. There wasn't a healthy, competitive male alive who wouldn't want to explore the possibilities, to try to ignite a flame that would warm that cool exterior, that would put laughter on those sensuous lips.

All he had to do now was make sure he wasn't the one who got burned.

Chapter Two

Her parents!

What on earth was she going to tell her parents about this move? Gabrielle thought with a dawning sense of horror as she listened to her mother cheerfully rattling on about the tea party she'd attended the previous afternoon in one of the gracious old houses overlooking Charleston Harbor.

"I do so love that part of town. I don't know why your father won't consider moving. I suppose it's because this old house has been in his family for generations. I'm all for preserving family history, but is it necessary to live in it? Oh, well, if he won't, he won't. Did I mention that Townsend was there?"

When Gabrielle didn't respond, her mother prodded, "Gabrielle, dear, are you there?"

"What?"

"Is something wrong, dear?"

"No, of course not, Mother." She injected a note of cheery bravado into her voice. "Everything's just fine. What were you saying about Mrs. Lane's tea party?"

"I was telling you that Townsend stopped in. He asked how you were," she said pointedly.

"That's nice."

"Don't you want to know how he is, dear?"

"Not particularly."

"Gabrielle!"

She rolled her eyes. "I'm sorry. Of course, I want to know how he is."

"He misses you, dear. I'm sure of it, even though…"

"Even though what, Mother?" she responded on cue.

"Well, I wasn't going to tell you, but since you ask, he's been seeing Patricia Henley."

"That's nice. I'm sure she's much more suited for life with Townsend than I ever was. She actually likes those awful horses of his."

There was an audible gasp on the other end of the line. "Gabrielle, what is the matter with you? It's not like you to be so sarcastic."

"I wasn't being sarcastic. Townsend is happiest on the polo field, as you perfectly well know. Patricia adores horses. She's been riding since she was five."

"We gave you riding lessons," Elizabeth Clayton said stiffly, her voice filled with hurt.

"And I hated them. You didn't fail me, Mother," she said more gently. "You and Father offered me an opportunity to learn all of the social graces. Can I help it if I preferred the *Wall Street Journal*?"

It was a tedious and all-too-familiar conversation. It did, however, serve as an excellent delaying tactic. Any minute now her mother would hang up in a huff.

Coward! The accusation nagged at her. "Mother," she began, interrupting further news of Townsend. "Mother, I really do have to go. I'm busy packing."

"Packing? Where are you going, dear? You haven't mentioned a trip. Are you coming home?" she inquired, her voice suddenly excited. "Oh, it will be so good to see you. Your father and I miss you terribly. We worry about you up there in that awful, dangerous city."

Guilt was now added to cowardice. "Actually, no, I'm not coming home. I'm…" *Blurt it out, Gabrielle!* "I'm moving."

"Oh, are you? It's about time." Whatever disappointment her mother was feeling that Gabrielle was not coming home was now tempered by swift and obvious relief. "I've always thought that apartment of yours was much too small. Whoever heard of living in a single room? I don't care if it is on Park Avenue, that apartment doesn't suit someone of your background. Why, the closet in my bedroom is bigger than that."

That was certainly true enough. It had been specially built to accommodate Elizabeth Clayton's designer wardrobe, which included enough hats to supply every woman who turned out for the annual Fifth Avenue Easter Parade. It was not that her mother was a frivolous woman. She simply needed the trappings to feel secure in Charleston's more elite social circles, from which she'd once been excluded. Gabrielle had learned long ago to tolerate the excesses, since her father actually enjoyed them. It gave him frequent opportunities to indulge his still-beautiful and adoring wife. He'd learned to his chagrin that similar gifts were wasted on his daughter. She preferred lessons in financial management and subscriptions to business magazines.

"The new apartment is larger," Gabrielle said cautiously, hoping that would be enough information to appease her mother's curiosity. If her mother even suspected the existence of a man like Paul Reed, she'd be on the next flight to New York, clucking over her endangered chick.

"Two bedrooms in fact," Gabrielle added.

"How wonderful! Your father and I will come for a visit soon, now that you have room for us. Tell me all about it. Where is it? Is it a new building, one of those skyscrapers? I'm sure the view must be quite spectacular."

"We'll talk about it later," Gabrielle hedged, already regretting the impulsive disclosure. She couldn't very well explain that the second bedroom was going to be very much occupied or that the building predated her birth and quite possibly her mother's. Mentioning that it was in Brooklyn would definitely arouse more discussion than she could possibly cope with.

"It will take me a while to get settled and do some decorating." *Talk about understatements.* "I have to go now, Mother. Give my love to Dad. I'll call you soon."

"But, dear, you haven't given me the new address or phone number."

"I'll call you with it later. The phone's not even installed yet. Bye, Mother. I love you."

She hung up quickly, before her mother could force her to divulge any more details. Her mother could have been used by the military. She had ways of extracting the most personal disclosures when you least expected it. Once, right in the middle of a conversation about Gabrielle's high school geometry homework, she'd gotten her to confess that there had been boys at Melinda Sue Wainwright's slumber party. She still didn't know how her mother had done it. She'd learned, though, that it was best not to prolong a conversation with her mother when she was trying to protect any intimate secret.

She wondered if she could avoid talking to her at all until after this sojourn in Brooklyn ended.

On Friday morning Gabrielle took a last look around her elegantly furnished studio apartment on Park Avenue. She was going to miss the thick gray carpeting, the glass-topped dining-room table, the outrageously expensive leather convertible sofa, the mahogany wall unit that hid stereo, television, VCR and compact disc player. She was even going to miss the dreadful modern print that hung in the tiny foyer.

She had rented the apartment at the height of her all-too-brief success on Wall Street, at a time when she'd been thumbing her nose at her protective family. After seeing her very first Manhattan apartment, another studio with a less pricey address, they'd begged her to come back to Charleston. They'd reminded her that she could live there in style as a member of high society. She would not have to eat her dinner perched on a sofa, her plate on a coffee table that barely came up to her kneecaps. She definitely would not have to sleep on that very same sofa. There were nights when she couldn't find one single comfortable spot on that two-inch mattress that she was tempted to do as they asked.

However, had she returned they also would have expected her to marry stuffy, rigid Townsend Lane, who was destined for greatness, according to her father. Her refusal to set a wedding date had disappointed them. She doubted if it had had any effect on Townsend at all. He'd barely noticed her when she was there. He'd taken her breaking off of the engagement with his usual cool disinterest and gone off to Palm Beach to play polo with Prince Charles.

If her parents had considered her breaking up with Townsend foolish, they found her business ambitions unladylike in the extreme. Women in the Clayton clan were supposed to inherit wealth—as her father's sweet, but mindless sisters had—or marry it, as her mother had. They weren't supposed to set out to attain it for themselves. She had disgraced them by doing just that, first with a Charleston brokerage house, then by moving to New York where she could avoid their disapproving, bewildered looks.

After the fuss they'd raised about her leaving home, she had sworn to make it on her own. Even at the outset in New York, she'd refused all their offers of money. She had weathered one stock market crash, only to lose her job a few weeks ago in a subsequent belt-tightening. Unfortunately there were plenty of other stockbrokers and analysts in similar straits, all fighting over the same few openings. Her savings had dipped precariously low. Even so, she knew she couldn't go home again. She would suffocate under all that well-meaning interference. Ten minutes at home and she would revert to being six again, instead of a cool and competent twenty-six.

She pressed the button on the intercom that connected her to the lobby and requested a taxi. It was an extravagance she could ill afford, but she refused to tote her belongings all the way to Brooklyn on the subway. Besides, it would take at least five trips just to get them downstairs. She refused to make twice that many trips back and forth to Brooklyn. She convinced herself that in the end, the taxi would be more cost-effective.

In the lobby she said goodbye to the aging doorman, who'd taken to watching out for her. He had the manners of a well-trained butler, all icy propriety, with a glimmer of affection that dared to show itself in little kindnesses.

"Now you be careful, miss," he said when he'd tucked her into the front seat of the cab after helping the driver to load the trunk and back seat with luggage and boxes. "Stop by now and then."

"Thank you, Robert. I will. You stay inside on rainy days now. You don't want your arthritis acting up. Next time I get over this way, I expect to see pictures of that new grandson of yours."

The washed-out blue of his eyes lit up. "You can be sure I'll have a whole collection of them by then," he said. "Goodbye, miss."

"Goodbye, Robert."

As the cab pulled away, she was surprised to discover a tear rolling down her cheek. She brushed it away and watched until Robert went back inside and the building disappeared from view.

Thankfully the cabdriver, a burly man about her father's age, wasn't the talkative kind. He left her to think about endings and beginnings and all that went on in between. She was feeling gut-wrenchingly nostalgic all of a sudden. The driver, Mort Feinstein according to the ID tag located on the glove compartment door, glanced over occasionally. Gabrielle caught the growing concern in his expression and avoided meeting his gaze directly.

As they drove into the neighborhood of the new apartment, the driver's concern turned to alarm. He pulled to the curb in front of number six-blank-two and stared around disapprovingly.

"It's not safe," he decreed.

"No place in this city is safe. I'll use locks."

"And stay inside? You shouldn't walk down the streets. Take a look around."

"Please, no lectures. Just help me unload my things."

"You're a nice girl. I can tell you're from a fine family. What would they think, they should see this?"

"They won't see it."

"You know what I mean. What you want, you want your father should have a heart attack, he finds out you're living in a neighborhood you can't go out in even in daytime?"

"It's not that bad," she said, getting out and slamming the door. She opened the back door, began removing things from the back seat and piled them up on the sidewalk. Still shaking his head, the taxi driver began getting the suitcases out of the trunk.

"You stay here," he said. "I'll take them inside. What floor?"

"Four."

He rolled his eyes.

"I'll help," she volunteered.

"If you help, who'll watch? Stay."

Just then Paul emerged from the building. His jeans were just as faded and just as snug as the ones he'd had on when they'd met, but he had buttoned his shirt either in honor of her arrival or in concession to the near-freezing temperature. He smiled at her, a slow, breathtaking smile that made her wish for a minute that he was her lover and that they were embarking on a mad, passionate affair.

Without saying a word, he took the full load of luggage from the taxi driver. Mort looked him over carefully, then nodded. He turned to Gabrielle. "Maybe it'll be okay."

"What was all that about?" Paul asked when the taxi finally had pulled away and they'd hauled everything up to the fourth floor landing.

"He doesn't think I should be moving into this neighborhood."

Paul opened his mouth. She spoke first. "I don't care to have this discussion with you, too."

"Fine." He nudged the door open with his foot and stood aside for her to enter. She found…chaos. At least she hoped that's what it was. Surely it couldn't be his idea of furnishings.

A sofa that sagged dangerously in the middle had been shoved against one wall. Two chairs in a similar state of disrepair were situated haphazardly in the middle of the room. None of the pieces matched. An orange crate had been placed in the midst of this unlikely arrangement. A mayonnaise jar filled with marigolds had been plunked in the middle of it. As a gesture of welcome, it was a nice touch. As decor, it was frightening. She was terrified to look in the other rooms. Squaring her shoulders resolutely, she walked down the hall.

Each bedroom had a twin-size bed with a mattress that dipped in a way that set off desperate warning signals in her back. There was a scarred four-drawer dresser in each room. Each had a jar of marigolds on top. At least he was consistent, she thought with a sigh.

She dropped her suitcases in the room with the least offensive bedspread—pink chenille with a minimum of tufts missing. She would have to use the tiny dressers in both rooms and both closets for her clothes. She might not have her mother's acquisitive nature, but she did own more than two dresses. Maybe Paul could at least keep his clothes downstairs while he worked on the apartment.

When everything had been dragged inside, she turned to Paul. "If you'll just give me my keys now, I'll start settling in and you can go on doing whatever you were doing before I arrived."

He dropped the keys in her hand, picked up more of her bags and hauled them down the hall.

"Thanks, really, but I can manage the rest of this," she protested.

"No problem. Until we get these things out of the way, we'll just be stumbling over them."

"Don't you have work to do downstairs?"

"Not today. I took the day off so I could welcome you properly."

Gabrielle was just picking up a box of dishes when the seductive undertone to his words registered. She dropped them. The crash of Limoges didn't even faze her. "Welcome me?"

"Yeah," he called over his shoulder. "I'm glad you like the pink room. I figured you would. I'd already put my stuff in the other room."

"Why would you want to welcome me?" she said, regarding him suspiciously. "We have an arrangement. That's all. You come and go as you please. I come and go as I please."

He grinned at her. "Does that mean you don't want lunch?"

Before she could say a strenuous no, her stomach rumbled. "Okay. Fine. Lunch would be good. We can iron out the details of the arrangement and make a schedule for the kitchen."

"Whatever you say."

In the kitchen there were more marigolds on the counter. A bottle of wine had been opened, an omelet pan was on the stove and she could smell French bread warming in the oven. Her mouth watered. She tried not to notice that the wallpaper was still peeling.

"Is there anything I can do?"

"Nope. It's all under control, unless you'd like to pour the wine."

"Sure. Where are the glasses?"

He nodded toward the cabinet to his left. "Up there."

She found four jelly glasses with cartoons on them and a stack of plastic cups. Well, why not? The wine would taste just as good from a glass with little yellow Flintstone characters on it as it would from her Waterford. She selected the two that matched and poured the wine, then handed Paul his glass.

"Shall we have a toast?" he asked, glancing over at her.

"To what?"

"Roommates." His gaze lingered on her until she felt heat rise in her cheeks. Her heart thumped unsteadily. "And friends."

Before she could protest, he tapped his glass to hers and sipped the wine. "It may not be French, but it's not bad."

Gabrielle wondered at the defensive tone, then taunted back, "I prefer California wines myself." She grabbed two mismatched plates from the cupboard and turned around to set the table…only there wasn't one.

"Where…?"

"We'll have to eat in the living room, unless you'd like to go outside. I think it's warm enough today for the garden, if we stay bundled up. The sun's just getting around there."

The garden. Perfect. Just the thought of it brought a smile to her lips. "We'll go outside."

She loaded up everything she could carry and went

downstairs. Paul followed minutes later with the steaming food. When they'd finished the cheese and mushroom omelets, the entire loaf of French bread and a bowl of grapes, he slid lower in the chair, stretched his powerful legs out in front of him and stared at her as he sipped his wine.

"You should spend more time outdoors," he said finally. "You're too pale."

"Haven't you heard? The sun is bad for your skin."

"Use sunscreen and moderation. It'll put a little color in those cheeks. You could add a couple of pounds, too. You've probably been starving yourself."

"I have not been starving myself, thank you very much, and my figure is no concern of yours."

"I'm the one who has to look at it."

"You don't have to. In fact, I'd prefer it if you didn't. Remember our deal."

"Our deal was that I'd stay in my own room at night. There were no restrictions on what I'd do during the day."

"Which brings us to something very important. We need to set a schedule."

"I don't do schedules." The response was deceptively soft and pleasant. She had a feeling it hid a mulish personality.

"If this is going to work, we have to have a schedule," she said firmly. "You can't just come barging into the kitchen when I'm…" She could not bring herself to complete the thought.

"Fixing breakfast?" he offered with a grin.

She scowled. "No, dammit. When I'm taking a bath."

She struggled for a businesslike demeanor. "Now, it seems reasonable that I have the use of the kitchen in the morning, since I have to go out on job interviews. You probably like to bathe at the end of the day anyway. So that should work out nicely."

He was shaking his head.

"What's wrong?"

"I take two baths a day. Morning and night."

"Why?"

"Habit."

"Break it."

"Two baths."

It was hard to argue with cleanliness. "Okay, fine. Take your damn bath in the morning. Just make sure you leave me some hot water and be out of the kitchen by seven-thirty."

"I eat breakfast at seven-thirty."

"Where? In the tub?"

"At the counter, standing up. Toast, cereal, eggs and coffee."

"That's not healthy. You need to sit down and digest your food properly. You can eat your breakfast in the living room."

"But I always…"

"If you want your morning bath, you will eat your breakfast in the living room."

"That's blackmail," he retorted.

"That's compromise," she growled.

He grinned. "Okay."

She regarded him suspiciously. "You're agreeing?"

"I just said I'd do it, didn't I? Who's going to do the dishes?"

"We're each going to do our own."

"That means I'll have to come back into the kitchen, while you're..."

Oh, dear heaven! "Never mind," she said, gritting her teeth. "Leave the dishes. I'll do them."

"Then what do you want me to do to even things out?"

"Nothing."

"I'll fix lunches for both of us," he went on as if she hadn't spoken.

"I won't be home for lunch."

"You can take it with you."

"I prefer to eat in restaurants."

He tilted his head knowingly. "Can you afford to do that right now?"

"No," she admitted reluctantly.

"Fine. Which do you prefer, peanut butter or tuna fish?"

"Yogurt."

"On a sandwich?"

Patience, Gabrielle. Have patience! "No. In its own little container. I'll pick some up when I go to the store."

"Don't you think we should go to the store together? For the next few weeks, I mean. If we combine groceries, we'll both save. Right?"

She supposed it did sound practical. "Okay. We'll make up a list when we go back upstairs."

"Who needs a list? We'll just go and get whatever appeals to us."

"That's inefficient and expensive. We'll end up with

things we don't really need and we'll forget some of the basics."

He stared at her solemnly. "You need to loosen up. Do you put everything in your life on little lists?"

"Not everything," she said stiffly. He was, however, remarkably close to the truth. She didn't have much patience with wasted motion.

"That's a good way to miss out on what's important."

"It works for me."

He shrugged. "If you say so. Now there's one thing we haven't talked about."

"Which is?"

"Guests. What do we do if we want to have someone over?"

"You mean like a date?" The mere thought of it raised all sorts of awful possibilities she hadn't considered. She supposed a man like Paul would date a lot. She also imagined he wouldn't leave those dates at their own front door with a chaste peck on the cheek. The thought stirred a little agony of uncertainty deep inside her. She met his amused gaze.

"Yes, a date," he said softly.

"Can't you wait until you move into your own apartment?" she grumbled.

"I'm willing to compromise here, but let's not go nuts about it. Don't you date?"

"Of course, I do, but it won't kill me to meet my dates in a restaurant for the next few weeks."

"And after?"

"After what?"

"After dinner?"

"We'll each go to our respective homes."

"Sounds sensible." The way he said it, it sounded like a death sentence. He cast a meaningful look at her. "I'm not that sensible."

"Fine. If you are unable to curb your male hormones for a few weeks, just let me know and I will arrange to be out for the evening."

"For the night," he corrected.

Of course, it would be for the night. She seethed. "I will not be kept out of my own bed for an entire night."

"I don't mind, if you don't," he said easily. "I guess that settles everything."

"Yes. I guess it does." Why had all this talk of dates left her feeling empty and alone all of a sudden? She enjoyed living alone. She was perfectly capable of entertaining herself. She had her collection of CDs and tapes, her videos of her favorite movie classics, and a stack of unread books. Let Paul Reed go out tonight. Every night, for that matter. She'd be just fine. It would be good to have the apartment to herself...until he came home with these dates of his.

She stood up suddenly and began snatching the dishes off the table.

"Something wrong?" Paul inquired innocently.

"Of course not. What could possibly be wrong?"

"You seem upset."

She slammed the dishes right back on the table. "I am not upset. Nothing is wrong. I am going upstairs to unpack, if you don't mind."

She stalked away from the table, then turned back. "Thank you for the lunch," she said politely.

He was grinning. In fact he looked rather pleased with himself. "You're welcome," he said softly.

To her unreasoning fury, she heard the quiet lilt of his laughter as she stormed up the stairs. This was going to be the longest damn four weeks of her entire life.

Chapter Three

Paul couldn't sleep, not with those provocative sounds emanating from Gabrielle's room next door. Apparently she'd taken him at his word and had invited a date over on her very first night. So much for all of those self-righteous protests of hers.

In an attempt to give her some of the space she so obviously wanted, he'd spent the rest of the day away from the apartment. He'd hoped, on his return, that she would be settled in and that his own rampaging hormones would have quieted down. At first he'd been relieved that she was already in her room with the door closed. He wouldn't have to put his libido to the test. Then, as he'd stripped off his shirt, he'd heard the soft music, the low, intimate murmur of voices. Something had knotted painfully inside him.

Retreating to the kitchen for a beer, he'd told himself it didn't matter. Gabrielle Clayton was a roommate, a source of income. That was it. He had absolutely no personal interest in what she did with her evenings. He told himself it was good that he saw her for exactly the kind of woman she was from day one. He told himself to go to bed and forget all about her.

Fat chance!

He stared at the ceiling, his imagination running rampant. The messages it sent to his body were not restful. He flipped on his own radio, found a station playing quiet, soothing music…all about romance. Why didn't somebody just play lullabies at night? He turned the dial and found a classical station. The music was soft and just as romantic, but at least there were no words. He closed his eyes, thought about the lulling rhythm of waves against the shore and felt the tension in his body begin to fade at last.

Then, just about the time he finally began to drift off, he heard the start of a rhythmic thumping from next door. He groaned and buried his head under a pillow. It didn't shut out the music or the other far more tantalizing sound.

What in the hell was she doing in there? Never mind. He knew what she was doing. He could picture it all too vividly, her long legs sleek and bare, her golden hair spilling across the bed, her body slender and urgent.

He groaned and debated getting another beer. At this rate she'd drive him to alcoholism within a week. Telling himself it was his own fault was no comfort at all. Telling himself there was absolutely nothing he could do about it without seeming like a meddling, jealous jerk didn't quiet his tightly strung nerves, either. Telling himself he could not possibly survive an entire night of this torture motivated him to get out of bed, yank on a pair of jogging shorts and risk humiliation by pounding on Gabrielle's door. He acted quickly, before he could think about the consequences.

"Keep it down in there," he yelled, then stomped back toward his own room.

With surprising speed for someone engaged in such heated activity, she flung her door open and stepped into the corridor. He hadn't counted on that. It stopped him right in his tracks, unable to do any more than stare at her as his pulse throbbed. Her face was flushed, her hair mussed. Her chest was heaving. His entire body tightened in immediate response. Knocking on that door had been the second stupidest damn mistake of his entire life, topped only by inviting her to live here in the first place. If listening had been torment, witnessing her sensual arousal was pure agony.

"I'm sorry," she said breathlessly. "I had no idea you could hear me. I didn't even realize you'd come home."

"I'm not surprised," he said.

Apparently the sarcasm escaped her. She continued to regard him with wide, innocent eyes. "I couldn't sleep," she explained, "so I had my radio on for a while, but it didn't help. Then I got to thinking about how I've been missing so many aerobics classes and, since I couldn't sleep anyway, I thought I'd just run through the exercises. I'm sorry if the tape woke you."

As the significance of her explanation sank in, Paul

felt his entire body go slack with relief. "Aerobics?" he said, hoping that the grin spreading across his face wasn't nearly as silly as it felt. "That's what you were doing in there?"

"Of course. What did you think?" Her eyes widened, then sparked with amusement. She bit back a chuckle. "You didn't?"

He stared back indignantly, still fighting his own grin.

"You did, didn't you? You thought I had someone in there." Then she began laughing, the first genuine, honest emotion he'd ever seen from her. It was a glorious sound. She peeked at him and started chuckling all over again.

"Okay," he grumbled. "So I got it wrong. Just go back to bed."

She swallowed back another laugh with effort. "I told you. I can't sleep."

"Count sheep."

"It doesn't work."

"Try reciting the names of all the states and their capitals."

"I want to sleep, not test my memory. If I miss one, I'll be up the rest of the night trying to remember it."

"I'm sure the aerobics won't help. Your blood's probably pumping so fast right now, it'll be hours before you settle down. Try some warm milk."

"We don't have any. We never did get to the store today." She smiled at him enticingly. "Since you're awake, too, we could play cards."

"Bridge, I suppose?"

"Poker."

He hesitated. The idea of playing poker with a half-dressed woman in the middle of the night held a certain appeal. Too much appeal. If he had a grain of sense, he'd go out for the blasted milk instead. "Do you have any cards?"

"Of course," she said, going immediately to a box that had been carefully labeled with every item in it.

"That much organization is probably illegal. When you move, you're supposed to lose things."

"Who says?"

"It's a law of nature or something." He led the way into the living room and gestured toward the orange crate. "You deal. I'm getting a beer. Want one?"

"Beer sounds good."

That surprised him, but he made no comment. Nor did he say much when she displayed an extraordinary knack for knowing when to hold her cards and when to fold 'em. When she folded for the fifth or sixth time in a row, Paul grew frustrated.

"Why not play the hand out?"

"It's always better if you know when to cut your losses."

"We are not playing for the rent money. Hell, we're not even playing for matchsticks."

"If you get out of the habit of playing like you mean to win, it'll get you in trouble later."

"And who taught you that bit of wisdom?"

"My father. He swears it's how he made his first million."

"His first million?" Paul repeated with a dry inflection. "Exactly how many does he have now?"

Gabrielle shrugged sleepily and took another sip of beer. "Ten. Twenty. I don't know. He doesn't think it's important for women to know those things."

"If your father has all that money, why are you living here?" Paul asked, thoroughly bemused. He'd known Gabrielle was classy, that until very recently she'd had some money, but he'd had no idea just how much.

"Because *I'm* almost broke," she explained patiently.

"But your father—"

Her chin set stubbornly, though the effect was lost in a yawn. "That's his money," she said, continuing to shuffle the cards.

It finally dawned on Paul that there was some sort of pride at stake here. "Your father doesn't know you're running out of money, does he? How long before the next trust fund check comes through?"

"What trust fund check?" She put the deck of cards down in front of him. "Cut."

Still perplexed, Paul did as she asked. So there was no trust fund, he thought as she dealt. Yet she didn't seem to be estranged from her family. The fondness she felt for her father had been unmistakable in her voice. She had quoted him not with irony, but with respect. Figuring out the complexity of the relationship was something he decided to leave for another time.

They played a few more hands before he got up and went for another beer. When he came back into the living room, she was sitting on the floor, legs tucked under her, her head resting on the orange crate.

"Gaby?"

She gazed up at him with sleepy eyes and a suggestion of a smile on her lips. All at once playing poker and her family's elusive financial dealings were the last things on his mind. He tried to tell himself the swift sexual reaction was perfectly understandable. He hadn't fully recovered from that earlier misinterpretation of the noises in her room. He reminded himself sternly that he had no personal interest in Gabrielle Clayton beyond her ability to pay the rent.

Then he made the mistake of picking her up and carrying her back to her room. She snuggled. The woman curled up in his arms, buried her face against his neck and smelled like some exotic flower. He wanted to drop her onto her bed and escape just as quickly as he possibly could. Instead he put her down gently, then stood watching her, wondering at the vague tightening in the pit of his stomach. This woman wasn't cool and distant. This woman wasn't a snob. She was warm and vulnerable and desirable. And he needed to get very far away from her very fast.

The room next door wasn't nearly far enough. Gaby might have been sleeping peacefully in her own bed, but she made her presence felt in his dreams. He blinked awake to incredible loneliness and throbbing memories.

Well, hell, he thought, staring at the ceiling for the second time that night. He might have been tempting fate by inviting her to share this apartment. He might even have hoped that the chemistry between them would prove irresistible. But he hadn't planned on feeling this tender protectiveness at all. In fact, quite the opposite. He'd been absolutely certain that daily doses of her disdain would fuel his natural aversion to women who thought they were too good for the average man. Instead she hadn't been in the apartment twenty-four hours and already his carefully erected wall of preconceptions was cracked at the foundation. It made for a very long night.

Gabrielle did not want to get out of bed. It was Saturday morning. From the brightness of the sun slanting through the window, she judged it to be a beautiful day. But Paul was very likely to be in the next room and she wasn't sure she was at all prepared to go another round with him.

Every one of their encounters had disturbed her in some indefinable way that went well beyond irritation. Their latest, in fact, was a dim but decidedly pleasant memory. She recalled the strength of his arms around her, the gentleness of his touch, the oddly haunted look in his eyes when he'd thought she'd been with another man. She wasn't sure which was likely to be more difficult to face, the impossible man she'd first met or the tender one who'd helped her through the night. Such uncertainty had a tendency to make her cranky.

Finally she dared a trip to the bathroom. Fortunately Paul didn't seem to be anywhere in the apartment. In the bathroom, however, she was reminded emphatically of his presence. She found his damp towel laying on the floor, his razor beside a sink dotted with specks of dark hair and his T-shirt on the door handle. The intimacy it suggested sent a little shiver dancing along her spine. That made her mad, though admittedly out of all proportion to the seriousness of his transgression. It also helped her to put that single incident during the night into its proper perspective once and for all. She was rooming with an inconsiderate slob, not some knight in shining armor.

She cleaned the sink, washed up, dressed, picked up his belongings and tore open the door with every intention of dumping the items in the middle of his bed. She hadn't counted on practically tripping over him. He was lying in the middle of the kitchen floor, his very bare upper body partially hidden in a cabinet. Unfortunately quite enough was exposed to tease her imagination. She dropped his things on his stomach and heard a muttered exclamation, a thump and then a curse.

He emerged rubbing his head and peered at her balefully. "What's the story?"

"There is one bathroom in this apartment."

"How observant of you to notice," he retorted, responding to her admittedly nasty mood. "What's the problem?"

"I will not clean up after you."

"You don't have to."

"Well, we sure as hell don't have a maid to do it."

"Right again."

"I will not live in a pigsty."

He carefully removed the assortment of items on his stomach, holding them up for inspection. "I'd hardly call one towel, a razor and my underwear the makings of a pigsty."

"It's a start."

"Come on, Gaby, loosen up. I'm used to living alone. We'll have to work out the details as we go along. I'll buy a medicine chest for the razor. I'll install a towel rack later. As for my underwear, if that disturbs you…" he began with a leer.

"It doesn't disturb me!" She was practically shouting.

He grinned. "Then why are you shouting?" Paul couldn't resist chuckling at her furious expression. It was good to see yet another break in that cool, controlled facade of hers. In fact, if it weren't so dangerous to his own equilibrium, he might make that his immediate goal, seeing to it that Gabrielle Clayton exchanged what had apparently been a rather uptight existence for something a little more carefree. Even now her frown wavered uncertainly. He had a feeling that now that she'd told him off, she wasn't quite sure what to do next. Politeness dictated an apology, but her mood obviously did not.

"Come on," he said, putting aside his wrench and his common sense. He got to his feet and held out his hand.

She regarded him warily. "Where?"

"We're going to brunch."

He caught the quick flash of interest in her eyes before she shook her head. "We can't. There's too much to do around here."

"It can wait."

"I cannot live in total chaos."

"You can work twice as hard on a full stomach."

"I don't have money to throw away on brunch when we can cook right here."

"I do. Besides, there's no food in the refrigerator except for some cheese that's turning green."

She swallowed hard at that. "Okay. But we're room-mates. We go dutch or not at all."

"Not this time. We're celebrating."

"What?"

"Our first fight."

"It's not our first," she said with the beginnings of a smile. "We've been arguing since we met."

"Then it's time we called a truce." He grinned at her. "Over brunch."

She caved in sometime between his deliberately provocative description of fresh-squeezed orange juice and the promise of waffles and warm maple syrup.

"One hour," she agreed finally. "No more."

"Relax, Gaby. If you eat too fast, you'll get indigestion. Isn't that what you told me yesterday?"

"An hour," she insisted, glaring again.

"Do you want to time it down to the second?" he inquired, offering her a view of his watch. She scowled back, yanked on her jacket and descended the stairs like a queen on her way to court.

"Where are we going?" she asked, turning back at the corner to wait for him.

"I thought you knew," he retorted. "You're leading the way."

She slowed her steps and grumbled, "Don't you ever hurry?"

"Not if I can help it. Stress is bad for you. Don't you ever slow down?"

"You can't afford to in my business."

So, he thought, she really hadn't been taking money from her father. "What is your business?" he asked, envisioning an elegant boutique on Madison Avenue struggling against exorbitant rents and fickle tastes.

"I'm a stockbroker."

Stunned, he simply stared at her.

Oblivious to his astonishment, she bit her lip. "Actually, I was a stockbroker. Now I seem to be having trouble convincing people of that."

Paul tried to reconcile his first impressions with reality. "Were you any good?"

"I was damn good."

"So why'd they fire you?"

"Who says they did?"

"You don't seem like the type of lady who'd walk away from a sure thing with no prospects in sight." And yet, in many ways, that was exactly what she'd done when she'd left the family nest.

"You think you have me all figured out, don't you?"

"Not really," he said honestly, gesturing to a crowded deli at the same time. "Is this okay?"

"Fine."

He gave his name to the hostess, then turned back to Gabrielle. "Well? What happened?"

"Okay, I was fired." The sparks in her eyes dared him to make fun of her for that. "Not because I wasn't good, though. It's just that there were dozens who were better and who'd been there longer."

"If the business is all that tight, what makes you think it'll be any better at another brokerage house? You could work your tail off and end up out of a job again, right? All through no fault of your own."

She shrugged, her expression resigned. "It's a risky business."

Curious about her unemotional tone and the flat, empty look in her eyes, he said, "Why do you do it?"

"I trained for it. It's what I do. You hammer and paint. I sell stocks and bonds."

"Why?"

She ignored the question as they were finally led to a table. As soon as she was seated, she buried her face behind the menu. It didn't take a genius to figure out she was avoiding the question. As soon as their orders had been taken, Paul persisted. "Why, Gaby? What is it about the stock market that turns you on? Is it the money, the power, the risks? What?"

Her gaze narrowed defensively. "You sound as though you disapprove of making money."

"Hey, what's to disapprove of? Money's great and it's none of my business what you do with your life. I just see a woman who's existing on nervous energy, who can't sleep at night, who's living in an apartment she considers to be not much better than a slum—"

"I never said that."

"It's in your eyes, sweetheart. They're the windows to the soul, remember. They'll give you away every time."

She immediately looked chagrined. Rudeness apparently was inconceivable to someone of her unfailingly polite Southern upbringing. Every time she crossed the boundaries of what she considered polite conversation, she looked guilty. And apologized.

"I'm sorry," she said, right on cue.

"Hell, you don't have to be sorry on my account. I like where I am. I like who I am. What about you? What does it take to make you happy, Gabrielle Clayton?"

"Success," she said instantly, but that trace of uncertainty was back in her eyes.

"How do you measure success? By the number of shares of stock you've sold? By the size of the portfolios you handle? By the takeovers you've manipulated? When you played Monopoly, were you only happy when you'd bought up all the real estate?"

She looked uncomfortable with the question. "I wanted to win, if that's what you're asking. Don't you?"

"Sure, but I only compete with myself. I don't have to conquer the world."

"We're all entitled to different goals."

"Don't patronize me, Gaby."

She flushed guiltily again. "That's not what I was doing."

"Wasn't it? I'm sure you think it's just terrific that I'm content when the paint goes on smoothly. Isn't it nice that Paul can be happy with so little?" When she started to deny it, he shook his head. "Those eyes again, sweetheart. They say it all."

"And what about your eyes?" she snapped back. "You've jumped to a few conclusions about me, too. Rich. Spoiled. What else, Paul? What labels did you stick on me at first sight?"

He slumped back in the booth and grinned ruefully. "Touché. Maybe we ought to start all over again without any preconceptions."

"Why?" she asked softly. "In a few weeks I'll be out

of your life. What we think of each other won't matter at all."

"Are you so sure of that?" he responded just as quietly, not sure why he was so quick to defend the possibility of a future for them.

He saw the heat rise in her cheeks, caught yet another glimmer of uncertainty in her eyes. "Never mind. We've gotten entirely too heavy for an outing that was meant to relax you. Let's play hooky for the rest of the day and just have some fun."

"But the apartment, all those boxes, you promised to get the medicine chest and the towel rack…"

He heard the token resistance in her voice, saw the wavering resolve in her eyes and wondered how long it had been since she had allowed herself the simple pleasure of an afternoon off.

"Tomorrow will be soon enough, Gaby."

A spark of irritation flared in her eyes and something else, a surprising wistfulness. It confirmed his suspicion about the lack of stolen moments she'd captured for her own joy. He played to that tiny hint of vulnerability.

"Please," he coaxed, "Gabrielle."

Chapter Four

Despite its brightness, the sun hadn't taken the crystal sharp bite out of the fall air. Gabrielle shivered as they strolled toward the subway entrance at Paul's favored leisurely pace. Seeking warmth, she poked her icy hands into the pockets of her denim jacket. She should have worn the fox coat, but it would have looked out of place with her jeans and sweater. It would also have underscored the vast differences between herself and Paul. His idea of style seemed to consist of clean jeans, an unrumpled shirt and a sheepskin jacket that was several years removed from the sheep.

"Come on," he said, apparently noticing the effect the brisk air was having on her. "It's freezing out here. I'll race you."

Gabrielle's prompt protest was lost as he took off

with the loping, natural stride of an athlete. She sputtered indignantly, but was too much of a competitor to ignore the challenge. By the end of the block, the cold air hurt her lungs and her side ached, but she was filled with the strangest sense of exhilaration. Her whole body felt alive with anticipation.

Paul grinned at her and she found herself smiling back, suddenly more lighthearted than she'd felt in years. It was a beautiful day, her housing problem was temporarily resolved and until Monday there was not a thing in the world she could do about finding a new job. Paul was a handsome, sexy companion with a sense of humor. Why not enjoy this day, this moment?

"That run put some color in your cheeks," he said approvingly.

She shook her head with feigned impatience. "What is this fixation you have about my coloring? Did you have aspirations for being a doctor?"

"No medical hopes at all," he said, taking a slow step toward her. Gabrielle's breath caught in her throat as he reached over, caught a strand of her hair and tucked it behind her ear. The unexpected gesture startled her with its tenderness. His rough knuckles grazed her cheek and sent warmth flooding through her.

"It's not your coloring," he said, his intent gaze lingering. "It's your health I'm worried about. You don't take care of yourself properly."

"And you still want me to ride the subway?" she retorted. She was teasing, but she was unable to hide the slight catch in her voice.

"Now, with me, you're perfectly safe," he promised in a voice that could have seduced a saint.

Their gazes collided. Her pulse beat erratically and she wondered just how true his statement about her safety actually was. The instinct to run was powerful, the temptation to stay even stronger.

They spent the rest of the day exploring Paul's New York. It wasn't the same part of the city Gabrielle had grown used to seeing. Instead of the elegance of Lincoln Center, they wandered through the colorful seediness of Chinatown. The narrow, crowded streets smelled of garlic and ginger and incense. Shop windows were jammed with displays of gaudy trinkets side by side with graceful Oriental antiques. In one, buried beneath worthless porcelain vases, Gabrielle spotted a small silk rug, its colors muted by age, its fringe tattered in spots. Despite its worn appearance, it appealed to her sense of proportion and color.

"Oh, Paul, it's perfect," she exclaimed.

"For what? A dust rag? It's decrepit."

She glared at him. "No more than our apartment building."

Only after the words were out of her mouth did she realize that she'd actually sounded proudly possessive about the still shabby Brooklyn apartment they'd shared for less than twenty-four hours. From the quizzical expression on Paul's face, she knew he'd noted the slip of her tongue.

"Really, don't you think it would be perfect for one of the bedrooms?" she said hurriedly.

He looked skeptical, but said agreeably, "If you want it, get it."

Once inside the store, however, the price daunted her. It would put a significant dent in her savings, though from what she knew of Oriental carpets, it was not outlandishly high. Making a quick calculation in her head, she made a decision. She told the smiling proprietor she would pay him half what he was asking.

"No, no. Not possible," he said, his expression suitably horrified. "Price firm. No discount. It is very valuable. Fine silk. Good workmanship."

Gabrielle examined the rug closely, then dropped the edge in exaggerated disgust. "It needs repairs. I will have to pay at least half what you're asking just to clean and restore it."

He could hardly deny the truth of that. Reluctantly he knocked the price down by a fourth. Gabrielle glanced at Paul and saw the amused quirk of his lips.

"Another fifty dollars and we have a deal," she said with finality.

The man looked as though she were trying to rob him. "No, no, lady. That is too much."

Gabrielle sighed heavily. "Okay," she said, and started for the door. She took one last, longing look at the carpet. Then she noticed Paul's dismayed expression, just in time to keep him from intervening. She grabbed his hand and dragged him purposefully toward the exit before he could offer to pay exactly what the man was asking in a misguided attempt to please her.

"But—" he protested.

"Don't you dare make an offer," she whispered. He stared disbelievingly, but kept quiet.

They were in the street when the proprietor caught up with them. "Okay, lady, we make a deal."

She gave Paul a smug smile and followed the man back inside. When she'd written her check, he rolled and wrapped the carpet with loving care before handing it over to Paul to carry.

She held in her delight until they reached the corner, then turned and grabbed Paul's arm in excitement. "Can you imagine? He actually sold that carpet to me for a fraction of what it was worth."

"But you said…"

She waved aside his obvious confusion. "I was bargaining."

Paul shook his head in astonishment. "You really must have been good on Wall Street. I'd never have guessed from your expression that you were cheating that poor old man."

"I wasn't cheating him," she explained patiently. "He probably got it for even less than that. He knew what he had to get to make a profit and I guarantee you, I didn't get him below that."

"But you will still have to pay for cleaning and repairing it."

"Don't be silly. I'll hang it over a tree limb and beat it. I can stitch up the fringe myself."

Paul stared at her, openmouthed.

"What's wrong now?"

"You. In the first place, I would never have expected

you to be satisfied with anything less than brand-new and top of the line."

"You have a lot to learn about the value of antiques," she countered.

He ignored the barb. "Okay, but I definitely would never have imagined you bargaining over the price of something."

"How do you think rich people stay that way?"

He rolled his eyes. "Fine. I'm sure you learned those tactics at your daddy's knee along with poker, but the idea of your sitting down with needle and thread completely boggles my mind."

She grinned at him then and adopted her most Southern accent, the one that called to mind hamhocks, black-eyed peas and grits. She laced it with the sweetness of honeysuckle. "Why, Paul, honey, don't you know we gentlewomen always learn sewing and piano along with the social graces."

He winced. "Sorry. I did it again. Is there anything about you that fits the image or can I anticipate constant surprises?"

"You won't be surprised, if you remember I'm Gabrielle Clayton, not Scarlett O'Hara or Faye Dunaway in *Network*."

A fleeting frown gave away his guilt. She wondered which of the personae he found the more disconcerting—the Southern belle, born to the manor, or the sharp-witted career woman. Or perhaps it was the seemingly contradictory blend of the two. Whichever it was, he tried to cover his confusion by quickly pointing her in the direction of a bakery in Little Italy. "As a reward for your success, you get coffee and dessert."

The thought of food so soon after their huge brunch held no appeal. Normally her breakfasts consisted of coffee and half a grapefruit, her lunches of yogurt and her dinners of fish and a salad. She frequently forgot all about one or more of those. Today she'd already eaten more calories than the three meals combined. "Not for me," she said. "I'm still stuffed."

He pulled her inside the warm, fragrant bakery anyway and led her straight to the display case. "Maybe you can resist one of these sinfully rich, chocolate cannoli, but I can't. I have to give in to temptation once a day or I feel I've failed to live up to my image as a hormone-driven rogue."

The pointed rejoinder, reminding her that she'd made a few snap judgments of her own, shut her up.

Paul picked out the creamy pastry, then compounded the temptation by ordering capuccino. "Sure you don't want some?"

"No. Absolutely not. Just a cup of black coffee."

"It's bad for your nerves. How about decaf?"

She looked at the waitress. "Black coffee, loaded with caffeine."

The waitress glanced deferentially at Paul, earning a scowl from Gabrielle. "Whatever the lady wants," he confirmed. "But bring two forks, just in case."

Seated, with the cannoli in front of her, Gabrielle's resistance diminished considerably.

"Try it," Paul urged, cutting into the pastry. Chocolate and cream puffed out the ends. She swallowed hard. He held the bite in front of her. Her mouth watered. "Come on. We'll walk it off."

Challenged by determined blue eyes, she took the bite at last, slowly licking the cream from her lips. It was heavenly. "Mmm."

"Another one," he tempted.

"No, really." But with the taste lingering on her tongue and Paul's eyes still intent on hers, her usually indomitable willpower faded. Before she realized it, she'd eaten the entire cannoli. She glanced at the empty plate and blinked guiltily. "Oh, dear. I'm sorry."

He laughed. "For what? They have more." He signaled the waitress for another order. "You sure you won't want your own this time?"

"Very funny. I wouldn't have eaten the last one, if you hadn't tempted me."

"Are you that susceptible to temptation?" he inquired with a devilish gleam in his eyes.

"Only before four o'clock in the afternoon on the fourth Saturday in months that begin with O."

He glanced at his watch and gave an exaggerated sigh of disappointment. "I'll mark my calendar for next year." Grinning, he sat back, sipped his capuccino and studied her. "What would you like to do now?"

She hesitated, uncertain of his interests or his budget and aware of a surprisingly strong desire to accommodate both. Usually she scoured the weekend events listings in the papers on Friday, then planned exactly how she would spend her all-too-rare free time. It was about as spontaneous as the ticking of a clock.

"It's up to you," she said, experiencing a daring sense of excitement that was all out of proportion with the innocence of the situation.

"How do you feel about art?" he asked, taking her by surprise again.

"Modern or classical?" she replied enthusiastically. She'd taken one art history course in college to fulfill what she'd considered to be a totally frivolous requirement. She'd enjoyed the class far more than she'd expected to and once in New York had indulged the fascination with regular visits to the museums and galleries. She was on the invitation list for the openings of all major showings.

"Take your pick," Paul offered. "We can go to the Metropolitan or the Museum of Modern Art or we can go to a couple of places I know."

She was instantly intrigued by the prospect of discovering what type of art interested him. "The places you know," she said at once.

He smiled his approval, then led the way to Soho, where each gallery's art was more wildly imaginative than the one before.

"Well," he said thoughtfully as they stood in front of a sculpture made of clock and auto parts. It was called *Ride to the Future*. Gabrielle recalled the reviews. One critic had described it as "banal and lacking in excitement."

"What do you think?" he inquired with what she assumed had to be feigned solemnity.

"You can't be serious." She stared at his face for some indication he was merely teasing her. He met her gaze evenly. "My God, you really are serious."

"That's right. Don't just dismiss it. Tell me what you really think of it."

"I think…" She walked around the display, viewing it from all sides and perspectives, trying very hard not to be influenced by what she'd read or her own taste for far more traditional works. This was definitely not Michelangelo's *David*.

"I think it's an interesting concept," she concluded finally, trying to squirm off the hook.

"Well executed?"

"I suppose." She couldn't keep the doubt from her voice.

"But not to your taste?" he said at once.

She sighed and admitted reluctantly, "Definitely not."

She waited for some expression of disdain for her lack of daring. Instead he nodded in satisfaction. "Good. I thought it looked like a piece of junk, too."

Gabrielle was startled into laughter. "I thought you loved it."

Amusement lit his eyes. "I know. I wanted to see how politely you could decimate it."

"For a minute there I was terrified you might be the artist."

"Trying not to insult the artist, huh? You succeeded admirably. My favorite word when I get invited to these shows is *interesting*. It's amazing how many inflections you can give that word to convey everything from approval to dismissal."

"*Fascinating* is good, too. Or how about, *I've never seen anything quite like it before.* Delivered solemnly, it's very effective."

Their amused gazes caught, sparks danced and the laughter slowly died between them. "Amazing how much we've already found we have in common," Paul said with a disturbing mixture of satisfaction and defiance in his tone.

"Amazing," she echoed softly, when what she really felt was fear, not amazement. Already she was struck by the sense that this man could turn her life in a totally unexpected and dangerously fascinating direction. He wasn't easily intimidated. Nor was he fitting neatly into the niche she'd carved for him. And when he looked at her, every bit of common sense ingrained in her since birth fled.

She reminded herself staunchly that she was in control, that the parameters of their relationship had been clearly drawn. They were short-term roommates, nothing more. And Paul, she sensed even after their short acquaintance, was an honorable man. Satisfied that their bargain was unbreachable, she relaxed her guard again.

It was nearly midnight when they got home, after eating spicy Mexican food in Greenwich Village and drinking far too many margaritas.

Gabrielle felt just as exhilarated as she had in the morning and slightly tipsy. She couldn't recall the last time she'd had so much uninhibited, unstructured, spurof-the-moment fun. Nor was she feeling particularly guilty about it. How extraordinary!

"Thank you," she said as they stood in their darkened living room.

Impulsively she stood on tiptoe to brush an appreciative kiss across Paul's lips. In the hushed silence she suddenly heard the pounding of her heart, the sharp intake of his breath. Then she looked into Paul's eyes and saw the unmistakable darkening of desire, felt her own blood race. As their breath mingled, she knew if she touched the warmth of his lips, even just this once she'd get burned. There were limits, even in the midst of magic. The idea that they could remain simply roommates, that their emotions would remain impassive, fled with the blink of an eye. The sense of destinies irrevocably entwining overcame her again.

Paul's well-muscled body, tight with tension, was suddenly too tempting, too overpowering. Shaken, she backed away a step, the friendly kiss abandoned as a very bad idea.

"You're running again, Gaby," he said with heart-stopping accuracy.

"Gabrielle," she said with a touch of her old defiance.

His lips curved into a faint smile. He ran a finger along her jaw. "Gabrielle," he said in a whisper so soft it caressed as gently as a spring breeze. Her resistance turned to liquid fire as he moved toward her. Her whole body trembled in anticipation.

"You promised," she said with a broken sigh as he bent closer. Still, despite the nervous plea, her lips remained parted for the kiss, waiting, longing. The mere sensation of anticipation was one she'd denied herself for too long. It sang through her veins.

At her protest, though, a shadow passed over Paul's features and he straightened slowly, reluctance etched on his face. "So I did."

He settled for running his fingers through her tangled, wind-tossed hair, the light touch grazing her cheeks. Her body ached from the tension of wanting more and knowing that satisfaction of that need would be wrong for both of them.

The expression in his eyes was regretful as he whispered, "Sweet dreams, Gabrielle." Then he turned and went straight to his room without a backward glance.

Paul's body was hard and charged with the urgency of his desire to claim the woman who slept in the next room. In just a few hours curiosity had slipped into fascination and was quickly turning into something much stronger. It wasn't supposed to have been this way, but he should have known it would be. He'd always wanted things that weren't his to take.

It had been hellish for a small boy to discover that the toys his friends took for granted would never be his. His mother had been a housekeeper, his father a gardener. Honest, kind, hardworking people, they had loved him all the more because he had come along late in their lives.

Because of his parents' jobs, he had grown up on a huge estate on Long Island. His playmates had been the children of the manor, children just like Gabrielle Clayton. No matter how hard he'd tried to be one of them, though, they were always just beyond his reach. He wore their cast-off clothes and he dreamed their dreams. But for him those dreams were unattainable. At age five, the differences had been insignificant. By twenty they'd torn at his gut. That was when he'd realized with irrevocable and heartbreaking finality that Christine Bently Hanford would never really think of him as anything more than the son of the hired help.

It had taken him ten years away from there to get over the anger, to find his own niche, to become comfortable with who he was and what he wanted out of life. Envy and bitterness had faded, replaced by contentment. Or so he had thought until Gabrielle had appeared on his doorstep. Was he still trying to capture the unattainable? To prove he was good enough? If that's what he was doing, he was being unfair to himself and to her.

Then again, maybe she was just a lady who was going through the same sort of identity crisis that had torn him apart ten years ago. He'd learned to live with reality, rather than fantasy, to find satisfaction in what was, rather than what he wished life could be. Maybe he could teach Gabrielle the same lesson.

And then what? Could they live happily ever after? Not likely. That happened only in storybooks, where Cinderella was swept away by the handsome prince. No one ever wrote about what happened when the prince woke up to reality and found out Cinderella was no princess.

This story—his and Gabrielle's—would end now, before anyone got hurt. He smiled in the darkness, his lips touched with irony and the sensible finality of the decision.

Famous last words.

Chapter Five

With a disconcerting sense of déjà vu, Paul awoke to the thumping of furniture. He smiled. Then a sudden crash from the room next door was followed by a surprisingly extensive barrage of colorful words. Paul would have sworn Gabrielle Clayton had never heard that particular vocabulary at home, except possibly during one of those infamous poker games. He leaped out of bed and ran for the door, stopping just in the nick of time to tug on a pair of gym shorts.

When he got to Gabrielle's bedroom, he pushed on the door, but it wouldn't budge. He panicked, pounding on the door. "Gaby, are you all right? What happened in there?"

There was no response.

"Gaby?"

"Go away," she muttered finally, sounding thoroughly disgruntled.

"Gaby, sweetheart, open the door," he pleaded more gently. He suspected the persuasive tone was about as wasted on Gabrielle as it would have been on a three-year-old who'd locked herself in the bathroom. "I just want to make sure you're okay."

"I am perfectly fine," she growled. "Just go back to sleep."

Paul's panic began to recede in the face of her spirited responses. Now he was simply curious. "How can I possibly sleep when it sounds like war has erupted in the room next door? Do you need any help?"

"No. I can handle this."

"Handle what?"

"I'm just rearranging things a little."

"With dynamite?"

"Very funny."

"That furniture's too heavy for you to manage alone. Wouldn't you like a little help? Open the door."

He heard her mumble something and suspected it was another of those words. "What did you say?"

"I said I can't open the damn door."

"Why not? Is it locked? I have a spare key. I'll slide it under the door."

"It's not locked."

"Is it stuck?"

"No, dammit."

Amused by the mixture of irritation and fierce pride he detected in her voice, he inquired lazily, "Well, if it's not locked and it's not stuck, what's the problem?"

"The bed's in front of it."

He chuckled.

"Don't you dare laugh."

"I'm not laughing," he swore, fighting the urge to do exactly that. "Just move the bed."

"Oh, for heaven's sake, don't you think I would if I could?" she snapped.

Paul bit back another laugh. "Gabrielle, exactly what is wrong in there?"

"I was trying to put down my new rug," she began after a lengthy pause. Her voice trailed off forlornly. That odd note in her voice concerned him as nothing else had. Gabrielle Clayton forlorn? Defeated by an inanimate object?

"And," he encouraged.

He could practically hear her taking a deep breath before she said in a rush, "I moved the bed and then the chest fell over and now I'm sort of trapped in here."

Any desire to laugh died at once. "Under the damn chest?" he demanded, his voice rising in panic again.

"Sort of," she said softly. "Oh, hell, I was so sure I could do this on my own."

"Just wait there," he said soothingly before he realized the utter absurdity of the order. Of course she would stay right where she was. What else would a woman with most of her bones crushed do?

Without giving it a second thought, he raced through the apartment, down the steps and around the building to the fire escape. He was halfway up when the icy metal against his bare feet registered. Suddenly he realized exactly how ridiculous he must look climbing a fire escape in gym shorts on a morning when the temperature could not possibly be much above freezing. It wasn't something he had time to worry about, though. Gabrielle might even be going into shock. She'd sounded pitiful and frail there toward the end, when she'd finally admitted she was trapped. That tone of voice was definitely unusual for her.

He reached the bedroom window and tried to lift it, peering through the glass for some sign of Gabrielle under the hodgepodge of furniture. He saw bare toes and a slender calf. He followed the curve of her leg upward, trying not to linger over it, and encountered—the chest of drawers, on its side. Only the fact that a corner had snagged the edge of the bed on the way down had kept it from landing on top of her with its full weight. His breath caught in his throat and his heart seemed to stop right then. The silence inside that room seemed particularly ominous. Impatient with the stuck window, he shattered the glass, oblivious to the cuts on his hand.

At the sound of glass breaking, Gaby shouted at him. "Don't you dare come in here and bleed all over my new carpet."

His heart began pumping again.

"Did you hear me?" she called out. "No bleeding."

He grinned at the feisty warning. She must be improving. "I heard, but I don't give a damn about your carpet," he said, feeling suddenly more cheerful. "Just stay still until I can get to you. I have to be careful where I step because of all the glass."

"Aren't you wearing shoes?"

"Sorry. I didn't take time to stop and dress formally. Think of this as a come-as-you-are party."

"What are you wearing?" she asked curiously.

"Shorts," he said curtly.

"That's all?" She definitely sounded better. In fact, she sounded downright perky.

"Be thankful I'm wearing those. At least it's probably enough to keep the neighbors from calling the cops about the crazed nudist on our fire escape. Now before I lift this chest up, does anything hurt?"

"Mostly my pride."

"Sorry. I'm afraid you can't afford any just now."

He lifted the chest up slowly, making a frantic grab for the drawers as they slid forward. He just barely kept them from tumbling out on top of her.

Once the piece of furniture was righted and out of the way, he saw that she'd been trapped not so much by the weight of the chest as by that damnable carpet. It was wrapped halfway around her, pinning her arms to her sides, raising all sorts of interesting possibilities. He knelt down beside her, trying very hard not to stare at the rounded swell of her breast peeking from the top of a very sexy nightgown. That view fueled those possibilities more effectively than matches and gasoline.

"You're not dressed," he said, his choked voice laced with surprise and sudden uncertainty. His mind was screaming *off-limits* so loudly his head hurt. It wasn't the only part of his body responding to the intriguing combination of sensuality and indignation before him.

"I hadn't planned on having company," she retorted

dryly. "I might add that my body is covered more adequately than yours."

Paul had a horrible feeling that was all too true. Fighting embarrassment and desire and a whole new meaning of panic, he freed her from the carpet with swift, trembling fingers, then shoved the bed aside. He noticed that she seemed to be holding her breath, her eyes wide as they met his. A man could get lost in those eyes.

"Get dressed," he ordered brusquely as he left the room.

"Aren't you going to help me clean up the mess?" The laughing request followed him down the hall, daring him to stay. He wondered how often Gabrielle was tempted to play with fire.

"Later." Perhaps after he'd taken vows of celibacy.

He went back to his room, grabbed his clothes and practically ran through the apartment to the bathroom. En route he regarded the tub balefully and promised himself that he would install a shower in every one of the apartments the minute he had the money…even if he could only supply it with cold water. That was all he was likely to use for the next few weeks anyway.

Gabrielle was filled with confusion as she watched Paul storm off. She hadn't realized at first that he really was furious. Otherwise she would never have teased him after he'd come to her rescue. Why on earth had he gotten so upset? She certainly hadn't meant to get trapped in her room. And, given time, she probably could have extricated herself. She hadn't damaged the battered old furniture, for heaven's sake. And how much could it cost to replace a pane of glass?

Of course, the swift reversal of his mood from concern to testiness might have had something to do with the highly charged atmosphere between them. Even she had to admit that it was incredibly disconcerting to keep tripping over their physical attraction. She had not been immune to the flying sparks just now. Her own pulse was just beginning to settle back into its normal rhythm.

Well, there was nothing to be done about that except to ignore it. They simply couldn't allow another quiet, intimate moment like last night's to occur. Of course, if this morning was any indication, perhaps they shouldn't be together in the same room—even in broad daylight. If Paul truly felt that uncomfortable in her presence, then maybe he should consider moving downstairs.

That decided, she put on her jeans and a soft rose-colored sweater before venturing into the kitchen to make coffee. She heard Paul swearing in the bathroom. When he threw open the door and caught sight of her at the stove, he just glared and stomped on past. Moments later she heard the front door slam.

"I guess he doesn't want breakfast," she muttered, searching through the refrigerator for something edible. She poked at a loaf of bread that was definitely past its prime. There was a package of luncheon meat that had dried out and curled on the edges. In fact, the only thing that appeared to have been purchased more recently than the Stone Age was a bottle of catsup. She sighed and settled for the coffee.

Paul returned before she'd taken the first sip of her

coffee. He was carrying the Sunday paper and a bag, which he dropped on the orange crate. "Bagels," he announced abruptly. "If you want one."

"Thank you."

"Any coffee left?"

"On the stove."

"Thank you. Do you want any more while I'm getting it?"

"No, thank you."

The politeness was beginning to grate on her nerves. She grabbed the front section of the paper and hid behind it. Bad as they were, the headlines were less depressing than the awkward wariness between the two of them.

Still, when Paul returned, she said politely, "Did you want to see the front section of the paper?"

"No. I'll read the sports section first."

"Fine." When she'd finished, she reached for the rest of the paper. Her hand collided with Paul's. Startled, they both looked up as if they'd made contact with a live electrical wire. "Sorry," they said simultaneously.

Gabrielle wondered if all relationships went through cold wars like this, wars that erupted for no apparent reason and sizzled with tension. She opened her mouth to force a confrontation, but Paul's forbidding expression silenced her. Now wasn't the time. Instead she got to her feet, took her dishes into the kitchen and washed them. As she was heading back to her room, Paul called to her. She walked to the doorway.

"Yes."

"Sorry. I shouldn't have snapped at you earlier."

"No problem," she said. When he turned back to the paper, obviously satisfied that the matter was concluded, she went on down the hall, torn between puzzlement and irritation. The apology had acknowledged the situation, but it certainly hadn't resolved it. Her own failure to pursue the matter was an indication of how thoroughly out of her element she felt.

As the morning went on, Paul's mood didn't improve, though eventually he did come down the hall to help her move the furniture back into place and sweep up the shards of glass. As they worked they exchanged a minimum of conversation, all of it exceedingly polite. When they'd finished, he pulled on his jacket and headed for the door.

"Where are you going?" she asked, then remembered it was none of her business. "I just meant in case someone calls."

"I'm going to get new glass for the window."

"Then let me give you some money."

"I broke it. I'll pay for it."

"You broke it on my account."

"Forget it, Gaby. Just sit down and relax. Read the paper or something."

"What about groceries?"

"What about them?"

"Shouldn't we go to the store today? Or would you rather I go alone?"

He sighed heavily. "Get your coat. We might as well go now."

She opened her mouth to remind him that they hadn't made a list, then clamped it shut again. If they forgot something, they'd get it later. In his present mood Paul was unlikely to want to discuss the relative merits of green beans versus broccoli before he'd even reached the produce section.

At the store Paul grabbed a shopping cart and steered it deftly through the narrow, crowded aisles to the dairy case on the far side of the store. "We'll work our way back."

"But we should do this last," she protested.

"Why?"

"It'll spoil."

"Not unless it takes you all afternoon to shop."

She glared at him. "Okay. Fine. What do you want?" she said as she grabbed a package of butter and a triangle of Brie. He picked up a block of cheddar cheese and a tub of margarine.

"Eggs?" she asked.

"Yes."

She reached for brown eggs. He shook his head adamantly. "Eggs are supposed to be white."

"You don't eat the shells," she reminded him. "What's the difference?"

"If there's no difference, then you might as well get the white ones."

She picked up a half dozen of each, then stalked off to the cereal section. She had a box of oat bran in her hands when Paul arrived with the cart.

"What's that?" he inquired suspiciously.

"Oat bran. It's good for your cholesterol."

"I eat cornflakes."

"Can't you just try this?"

"I have always eaten cornflakes."

Gabrielle threw up her hands in resignation. "Fine. If this is some nostalgic thing for you, we'll get cornflakes."

Suddenly his lips twitched. She felt the first tiny break in the tension.

"I suppose you have a thing about bread, too." She recalled that the loaf in the refrigerator had once been white. He nodded. She sighed. "We'll get white and whole wheat."

As they approached the meat section she said, "What about dinners? Do they have decent fish here?"

"Beats me."

"What do you eat?" she began, then held up a hand. "Wait. Let me guess hot dogs and steak."

He grinned. "What else?"

"You're going to die before you're forty."

"As long as I don't do it while we're sharing the apartment, it shouldn't bother you."

"Couldn't we make a deal for the next few weeks? I'll do the cooking and you'll try whatever I prepare."

He glanced down at the groceries they'd already collected. "Okay," he said finally. "But none of those funny looking green things."

Gabrielle's mind went blank. "Funny looking green things?"

"You know, they look sort of like a cactus."

"Artichokes?"

"Yeah. That's it."

She bit back a laugh. "Okay. No artichokes. Anything else?"

"No fish eggs."

"I wouldn't dream of wasting caviar on you."

"And we go out for pizza one night a week, so I won't starve to death."

Laughing, she held out her hand. "It's a deal."

After an instant's hesitation, he took her hand. "Deal," he said softly, his gaze locked with hers. It was not a look meant to be shared over raw hamburger. It spoke of candlelight and white damask napkins. Or maybe satin sheets.

She knew without any explanation that the truce had to do with far more than artichokes and caviar. Paul, a man whose life had probably been quite simple only a few days ago, was struggling to find the right balance for their complex and confusing relationship. That handshake was his renewed commitment to try.

But despite the pact in the grocery store, the day continued to have moments of high tension, moments when a glance threatened to turn into far more, moments when a casual remark took on added meaning. Paul's edginess communicated itself to her until they were practically tiptoeing around the apartment to avoid offending each other.

Finally Gabrielle retreated to her room and sat down with the classified ads. Moments later she heard Paul leave the apartment. Her heart sank to the pit of her stomach, but she forced herself to concentrate on the ads. She already had two interviews lined up for the following morning. Both were for jobs she'd heard about by word of mouth. Still she looked, circling one or two that she'd at least call about.

"And what if these don't pan out?" she said aloud. "How long are you going to wait before taking Paul's advice and looking for something different?"

One more day, she promised herself finally. If Monday's meetings and calls failed to result in at least a strong possibility of a job offer, she would turn elsewhere. To remind herself of the commitment, she folded the classified section and placed it prominently where she couldn't miss it, propped against the mayonnaise jar of flowers that had barely survived the morning's calamities with petals intact.

She decided it was time to replace them. A visit to the garden might also soothe her frazzled nerves and keep her out of Paul's way. If he was going to growl around like an angry bear, it was definitely wise to stay out of his path.

Unfortunately he found her.

"We need to talk," he began at once, sitting down in the chair opposite her. He picked up one of the flowers she'd cut and began stripping it of its petals.

"Okay," she agreed cautiously, moving the remaining flowers out of reach. "What about?"

"Our..." He hesitated, refusing to meet her eyes. "Our arrangement."

"Does that include an explanation about why you've been in such a foul humor ever since this morning?"

"You noticed?" he said with a touch of wry humor.

"That doesn't necessarily qualify me for a Ph.D. in psychology. So, what's the story?"

"We have a problem."

"Already? I've only been here two days."

"That's long enough."

Gabrielle drew in a sharp breath. The response was hardly unexpected, but disappointment began somewhere deep inside and settled around her heart. "Are you suggesting that I leave?"

He hesitated far too long before answering. "No," he said finally. "I asked you to move in. I certainly don't want to turn right around and throw you out." He sounded very stoic. She wanted to throttle him. In fact she might have, if he hadn't looked quite so miserable and confused. "It's just that we have to reach some sort of understanding."

"About what?"

"This relationship."

"That's easy. We don't have one." The remark was glib, but there was considerably less conviction in her voice than she would have liked.

"Exactly."

She didn't pretend to misunderstand the all-too-adamant response. "I think I see what you're getting at. Every now and then our bodies take over and pretend they haven't gotten the message that we're off-limits to each other, that we're coming from different places, heading in different directions. Is that it?"

"Yes. I mean you're an attractive woman. A man would have to be dead not to respond to you, even though he knows it's an impossible situation."

"And you are far from dead," she concluded.

"Exactly."

"Would it help if I wore baggy clothes?"

He grinned at that. "I don't think so. I have a feeling you could wear a gunny sack and I'd see right through it. So to speak," he amended.

"Any other suggestions?"

He stared at her helplessly, then shook his head.

She considered their situation analytically. Normally it was something she was very good at. "Maybe we're going about this all wrong. Maybe we should just get this right out in the open. You're attracted to me. I'm attracted to you. We both know we shouldn't do anything about it, so that makes it forbidden and, therefore, all the more interesting."

He held up a hand to interrupt her. "There's only one problem with that particular logic. Taken to its natural conclusion, we should just go right ahead and explore the possibilities and see where these feelings take us."

Gabrielle swallowed hard. The idea had far more merit than she cared to admit. Every time she glanced at Paul's strong hands, she recalled the magic in his most casual caress. She glanced at them now and her skin burned. "I see what you mean," she said shakily. "You think we'd be in even more trouble than we're in now."

"I know it," he said with such conviction that she smiled.

"Okay, I'm open to suggestions." She leaned forward, eyes wide, and propped her chin in her hand.

Paul's eyes widened and he leaned away from her hurriedly. "Don't do that."

"What?"

"Look so damnably inviting. You could tempt a man to ruin with that look."

She did laugh at that. "If something's going to happen between us, it will be with our mutual consent, right? Since you want to keep this strictly platonic and so do I, we should have no problem. We're not a couple of lusty kids with no sense. It should be even easier beginning tomorrow. You'll be back at work. I'll be job-hunting. We probably won't even see each other."

He seized on her logical, unemotional comments with transparent relief. "Absolutely. That's right." He got to his feet looking far more relaxed than he had when he'd joined her a half hour earlier. She was surprised he didn't hold out his hand to be shaken. He was even whistling when he went back inside.

So, she thought when he had gone, it was all out in the open. Discussed and resolved exactly the way it should be between two rational, mature adults who knew a mistake when it stared them in the face.

Now all they had to do was live with it. And that was complicated by the realization that with every hour that passed, she was having more and more difficulty recalling why she and Paul were so terribly wrong for each other. It sure as hell didn't have anything to do with artichokes. She didn't like them, either.

Chapter Six

In the morning their unemotional, carefully conceived plan went wildly awry.

Still half-asleep and suffering from a splitting morning headache that she blamed totally on Paul's seductive invasion of her dreams, Gabrielle wandered barefooted into the chilly kitchen. She began running water for her bath, only dimly aware that there seemed to be plenty of hot water. Yawning, she slipped off her robe and climbed into the tub, sinking slowly down into the luxurious warmth. She slid lower, sighed and rested her head against the back of the tub. Some of the tension began to ease in her shoulders and neck.

The she heard a door open. The bathroom door! Not five feet away. And only one person could possibly be opening that door at this hour of the morning, unless a particularly fastidious burglar had stopped in to shave.

"Paul, don't you dare come into this room!" Admittedly overly hysterical and definitely wide-awake, her screech echoed off the walls and made her head throb even more.

The door slammed shut, the noise like a shotgun blast reverberating through her head. She prayed he was on the far side of it.

"Dammit all, Gaby, we had a schedule."

He had retreated. But even through the door, she could hear that his indignation was tempered by a slight breathlessness. Apparently her warning shout hadn't been quite in time to prevent a very thorough look at her unclad body. The temperature in the kitchen seemed to warm by several degrees, setting her cheeks aflame.

"I forgot it," she said with unaccustomed meekness as embarrassment washed over her.

"It was your schedule. You wanted me out of the kitchen by seven-thirty. It is now seven-twelve."

"Okay. So I didn't look at the clock. Are you going to kill me over eighteen measly little minutes?"

"I wouldn't if I were anywhere other than trapped in this bathroom. Get out of the tub. You'll have to finish your bath later, after I've had mine."

She did not want to get out of this water, now that she was in it. She knew instinctively that there was not enough hot water in the entire building to give her a second bath this temperature. "Give me ten minutes. That's all."

"Out," he repeated with stubborn insistence. "You're on my time."

"Five minutes," she bargained, reaching hurriedly for the soap.

"Forget it. I have to get to work. I'm already running late. I might as well forget about my own bath. I'll be doing good just to make it across town. I am coming out now."

It occurred to her that for a man she'd pegged as irresponsible, he was suddenly awfully conscious of time management. Under the circumstances, the turnaround seemed extraordinarily suspicious.

"Don't you…" She began the warning with haughty indignation. It failed her as she heard the latch click. She stared at the opening door with a growing sense of incredulity and dismay. He was actually coming out. Wearing a towel and a frown. Her heart thumped unsteadily. His arms and shoulders were every bit as muscled as she'd imagined. His stomach… well, never mind. His stomach was much too low and definitely too bare for a lady to be studying.

Then she considered her own predicament. She glanced down. There were no bubbles in this water. No frothy covering. Not even a bar of soap floating on the surface. Come to think of it, there wasn't even a towel nearby. She hadn't been nearly alert enough to remember to bring one. Towels belonged in bathrooms. Then, again, so did tubs. Logic aside, the fact of the matter was that there probably wasn't a decent covering within twenty or thirty feet. In his current belligerent mood, she certainly couldn't count on Paul to supply one…except perhaps for the one he was wearing and that would create far more problems than it solved.

"Paul Reed, if you're going to insist on walking through here, then you can at least close your eyes," she said imperiously, lifting her gaze—very hurriedly—to clash defiantly with his. It was a tactic she'd seen her mother use with extraordinary success with everyone from her father to the gardener. They, however, had not reacted with the same amusement that played about Paul's lips.

"If I close my eyes, I'm liable to trip and join you in that water," he pointed out, clearly unimpressed by the command in her tone. In fact, he looked as though he was beginning to enjoy her discomfort.

She switched to a heartfelt plea. "Then look at the counter. That'll guide you right out of here. Please."

It was only after he'd done just that with her watching him warily, that she realized she was essentially trapped in the kitchen—in the damned tub—until he left the apartment. Of course, she could retreat to her room soaking wet, leaving a trail of water for Paul to complain about and wearing a silk robe that, when wet, would reveal almost as much as it concealed. Or she could break down and request a towel.

She was still debating the relative merits of the alternatives when she heard a sharp intake of breath behind her. She held her own breath for the impatient outburst that was sure to follow.

"Dammit, Gaby, aren't you out of here yet?"

She sank lower in the now murky, icy water. She wanted very badly to respond to the exasperated tone.

She wanted almost more than anything to tell him exactly where he could go with his badgering and his self-righteous indignation. She wanted to lambast his insensitivity to her predicament. She wanted to remind him of how any gentleman would have handled the situation.

The fact remained that she needed a towel and there wasn't a gentleman in sight.

"If you'll bring me a towel, I will be happy to get out of your way," she said, substituting stiff formality for angry charges.

To her surprise he did exactly as she asked without a murmur. When he returned, however, he lingered just a shade too long in the doorway. The ragged sound of his breathing warned her of his presence nearby. He was either dramatically out of shape or he'd paused to take in the view. She'd seen his well-toned muscles and bet readily on the latter. He was gawking again. Despite the rapidly cooling water, her skin burned under his slow, thorough surveillance. She recalled the smoldering deep blue of his eyes in the moonlit living room on Saturday night, the quickening then of his breath and her pulse.

Finally she heard his footsteps, soft and coming heart-stoppingly close. Unless his nobility was far stronger than she had any reason to credit him with, he could see quite clearly the tightening of her nipples just below the surface of the water, the bare plane of her belly, the shadowy triangle of hair below. Swallowing hard, she held out her hand for the towel.

"I'll hold it for you," he said thickly.

They both knew it was not a gentlemanly gesture.

Far from it. It was temptation. It was daring all sanity. But short of staying stubbornly right where she was so Paul could witness the deepening rose of a blush in her cheeks and God knows where else, there seemed to be little alternative.

Furious, yet undeniably intrigued by the sensations rocketing through her, she shot a quick peek up. The indiscreet glance caught the visible rise and fall of his chest, saw the lines of tension at the corners of his mouth, the blatant hunger in his eyes as he caught her gaze and held it for an eternity.

Just when Gabrielle thought he'd stolen her breath forever with something as simple as a look, he closed his eyes and murmured something that sounded like a cross between a curse and a sigh of regret. He dropped the towel and left, slamming the front door behind him. The sound echoed through her soul.

Surrounded by deafening silence, Gabrielle trembled violently at the nearness of her escape. *Their* escape. She dressed hurriedly and left the apartment with a sense of urgency, trying to leave behind the undeniable thrill of pleasure she had felt for one all-too-brief, maddening moment under his hot, longing gaze. With pesky, troubling persistence, it followed her, creating distraction in its wake.

She remembered her all-important briefcase midway to Manhattan. She snagged her last pair of expensive hose on a torn subway seat she would ordinarily have been alert enough to avoid. She filled out the first two-page job application with visibly shaky handwriting that bore little resemblance to her usual firm script.

For a few panicky seconds she couldn't recall her new address. During her first interview, she found herself staring blankly at her prospective employer, unable to recall his name or his question, but remembering Paul's face all too vividly.

The interview ended shortly afterward with a non-committal and unpromising handshake. For the first time in her life Gabrielle found herself ordering a drink with lunch. She downed the martini in two quick gulps and was tempted to order another. Only rigid self-discipline and the prospect of that two o'clock inter-view kept her from it. She never touched her salad. Her thoughts in turmoil, she ripped the crisp French roll into a mound of crumbs, then stared at the resulting mess in astonishment.

In the ladies' room, she examined herself in the mir-ror and caught the confusion in her eyes. No man had ever taken her so much by surprise. No man had ever breached her defenses so skillfully, though many had tried. Worse, Paul wasn't even trying. He was as shaken as she was by the attraction that warred with an incom-patibility so basic only a fool would ignore it. If ever their common sense failed simultaneously, however, she had no doubt the resulting explosion of desire would be thrilling beyond imagination. Sadly, their broken hearts would be destined to lie in the ultimate rubble of that explosion.

If she were wise, she would move out now. She would take an offer of temporary shelter with one of her friends and make Paul Reed nothing more than a distant memory. Without a doubt, she knew she should go while there were no wounds to heal. And yet...

The hammer slipped, missing the nail and leaving a semicircular gash in the expensive mahogany paneling. Cursing, Paul glared at the offensive hammer. It wasn't his. His was at home, left behind with all of his other tools in his frantic race from the apartment that morning. Rather than returning for them and risking yet another disconcerting encounter with Gabrielle, he'd been borrowing what he needed from the men he'd hired to work with him on this renovation job in an increasingly swank section of Brooklyn Heights.

Still muttering under his breath, he yanked out the few properly placed nails that held the damaged strip of wood, then tossed it aside. He was about to replace it when he heard a nervous cough.

"Uh, boss?"

Only one of his workers respectfully called him "boss." He turned to stare into the concerned eyes of the skinny, blond eighteen-year-old he'd been training as a carpenter's assistant. His own expression softened. Underneath the often cocky demeanor and bitter cynicism, Mike was a good kid. He'd just needed somebody to believe in him, not unlike Paul himself had at that age.

"What's up, Mike?"

"Don't you think maybe you ought to take a break?" he said cautiously.

The comment sounded suspiciously like advice. From a snot-nosed kid no less. Paul's hackles rose.

"Why?" he said. The retort was unnaturally soft. It should have been taken as a warning.

Unused to such subtleties, Mike persisted. "It is time for lunch."

"Then take it," Paul said in a dismissive tone that would have sent a lesser man scurrying. Mike's pimpled chin tilted defiantly. He even risked taking a step closer. A tiny spark of approval flared inside Paul as he waited for the counterpunch.

"You coming?" Mike said hopefully.

"Not now."

Mike drew in a deep breath, but his gaze never wavered. "Maybe you should."

Exasperated, Paul scowled.

"I mean," Mike persevered. "You've already ruined five strips of this stuff this morning." He poked a scuffed work boot at the stack of discarded boards. "At this rate, the job's going to cost you money."

Paul found himself staring at the pockmarked wood as if he had no idea how it had gotten there. He sighed heavily, then grinned. "You may have a point," he admitted finally. "You grab the lunches and I'll run down the block and pick up some soda."

Mike held out one black pail, identical to Paul's own. "I've already got my lunch. I couldn't find yours."

Of course not, Paul thought with wry acceptance. It was still at home in the damned kitchen. Not far from his tools. Even closer to the spot where he had very nearly lost his head and seduced Gabrielle Clayton at seven thirty-two this morning.

Tomorrow he would put the tools and his lunch by

the front door the minute he got up. Tomorrow he would be out of the apartment by seven-fifteen and not one second later. Maybe even seven o'clock. Tomorrow, if he was lucky, he would avoid temptation altogether.

Tonight was another story.

Gabrielle's day improved only to the extent that she actually did get home without taking the wrong subway, leaving her purse behind or getting mugged. Beyond that, it could be counted as one of the worst days of her life. The two interviews she'd had—and the others that hadn't panned out—convinced her that she would never work as a broker again. Despite her promise to herself that she would take this as a clear sign to move on to a new challenge, her spirits were at an all-time low.

It didn't help to open the door and see that horrible hodgepodge of furniture Paul had collected. Without removing her coat, she flipped through the yellow pages, whirled around and went back out.

Two hours later, her mood vastly improved, she was back again, stumbling awkwardly up the front steps with her purchases, dumping them in the foyer and collapsing on the bottom step. Listening to the sound of music and hammering, rather than being nervous as she'd expected to be, she was simply grateful that Paul was home to help. She shouted at the top of her lungs to be heard over the noise.

The hammering paused, though some rock tune she didn't recognize blared on. She didn't hear the opening of the apartment door over the din, but she looked up in time to see Paul peer over the fourth floor banister.

"Thank goodness," she said with heartfelt relief.

"What?" He held his hand to his ear to indicate he couldn't hear her.

"I need your help," she shouted.

"What?"

She shrugged and pointed at the collection of items in the foyer, then gestured for him to come down. He approached her slowly with the wariness of a man who expected anything but a friendly reception. He stayed a careful three steps from the bottom, as if he expected to need a head start back up.

"What's all this?" he asked cautiously, staring at the two badly scarred tables and the large bag from a neighborhood hardware store.

"It's for the apartment," she said excitedly, determined to put the morning's awkwardness behind them. "Aren't they absolutely perfect?"

"For what?"

"End tables, of course. And I saw this really wonderful sofa. It was an incredible bargain, but I couldn't figure out how to get it home and I decided you might want to take a look at it, too, before we get it."

"Why are you doing this?" He looked thoroughly baffled.

"What?"

"Furnishing an apartment you have no intention of staying in more than a few months."

"Because I'm not sure I can stand looking at what's in there now, even for a few months."

He regarded the tables skeptically. "If you don't mind my saying so, these don't appear to upgrade the quality of the decor by much. How many layers of paint do you suppose are on here?"

"Six," she said readily. At his surprised glance, she grinned. "I counted when I was chipping my way down to the natural wood. I think it may be cherry. Come on. Help me get them upstairs."

"How did you get them this far?" he asked, stacking them on top of each other.

"They didn't walk by themselves, I can tell you that."

He regarded her incredulously, from the fox coat to the tips of her two-inch Italian heels. "And you carried that bag, too? How far did you lug this stuff?"

"Not far. I found the tables in this perfectly marvelous secondhand store about fifteen blocks from here. I picked up the rest at that hardware store a couple of blocks over."

Paul was staring at her as if she'd just declared an ability to lift a moving van by the tips of her fingers. "Are you nuts? Why didn't you call for help?"

"For heaven's sake, it wasn't that far. I had to stop a lot, though," she admitted.

"You and your idiotic streak of independence," he muttered in disgust. "It was far enough to strain your back."

"My back is fine."

"It won't be in the morning."

"That will be my problem, won't it?"

"Not if it means you'll want to soak it in a hot tub," he retorted, staring at her meaningfully. "Call next time, okay?"

"Okay," she said very softly. The gruff concern combined with the all-too-fiery memories to make her miss a step. She stumbled and only her sharp reflexes kept her from tumbling backward down the stairs. The near-accident snapped her back to reality. She concentrated very hard on reaching the apartment without further embarrassment, then on placing the tables in precisely the right spot. When Paul had them exactly where she wanted them, she nodded in satisfaction, finally taking off her coat and tossing it across the sofa.

"I knew they would work."

"They do, don't they?" Paul said, sounding pleased. "What about the paint?"

Oblivious to her designer suit, Gabrielle knelt down and began pulling cans of paint stripper, pads of steel wool, protective gloves and a container of tung oil from the bag. "The man at the hardware store assured me this was everything we'd need."

"We?"

She gave him her most winsome smile. "You'll have to help. I don't know anything about stripping furniture."

"Neither do I."

Stunned, she stared up at him. "Are you sure?"

A faint smile tugged at his lips. "Very."

"But you put it on. You should know how to take it off."

He shrugged. "It sounds logical when you say it, but the reality is that I have never stripped a piece of furniture in my life. I have occasionally used a blow torch to melt paint off certain things."

She frowned. "I don't think that would be good for the tables."

"Probably not," he agreed with a wry expression.

"Okay. That's a little bit of a problem, but it's certainly not insurmountable. How hard can this be? There are directions on the cans."

"Gaby, I love your enthusiasm, but we can't do this now. I have work to do downstairs. I want to get another apartment rented by the first of the month."

"Can't you leave it just for tonight?" she said, unable to hide her disappointment. "You worked all day. What kind of boss do you have?"

She watched in astonishment as he burst into laughter. "The best, actually. I work for myself."

"Well, I know you're a carpenter, for heaven's sake. And you paint. And who knows what all, but you do take jobs."

"Of course," he said. "That's where I was all day. I'm in the middle of the renovations on a house in Brooklyn Heights."

She absorbed that news. It didn't conflict dramatically with anything she'd said. "Then this is a second job?"

"This?"

"Here. Managing this building and fixing it up."

He shook his head and said with the sort of patience usually reserved for overly inquisitive children, "No, Gaby. I own this building."

She stared at him blankly, trying to absorb the implications. "But…"

"But what?"

"I thought you were just a…" Now that she knew differently, she couldn't bring herself to say exactly what she had thought.

"Don't blame me, if you jumped to a conclusion."

"You let me do it," she accused, feeling a curious mixture of betrayal and pleased astonishment. "You let me go on thinking that you were just some sort of common laborer."

The words slipped out before she had time to censor them. She recognized the mistake the instant she looked into Paul's eyes. The blue sparked with fury.

"I beg your pardon," he said with an iciness that froze her straight to the marrow in her bones. "There is nothing *common* about giving a good day's work for a good day's wages, no matter how *lowly* some people might consider the task."

"I didn't mean that," she said miserably.

"I can't see any other interpretation. When you thought I was no more than a *common laborer*," he said, apparently determined to humiliate her by throwing her own ill-considered words back in her face, "was that what kept you out of my bed? Does everything change now that you know I own property and have a bank account that doesn't provide for frills, but keeps a roof over my head? Does it, Gaby?"

She stood up and met his furious glare evenly. "I'm sorry. I'm sure it must seem that I'm the worst sort of snob, but you're deliberately misunderstanding."

His gaze was unrelenting. "Am I really? What's held you back then?"

"Because we're not right for each other," she said,

knowing the argument sounded weak. There were literally hundreds of reasons two people might not be right for each other. She hadn't given him one of them.

"I'm not good enough, isn't that what you mean?"

"No," she protested, but deep inside she knew that was exactly what she'd thought.

He ran his hand through his hair. "For God's sake, Gaby, don't lie about it. What's the point?"

The point was that she didn't want him to know how shallow she was capable of being. Unfortunately it seemed he already knew it. "You knew what I thought all along, didn't you?" she said finally. When he didn't answer, she raised her voice, needing to share the anger and the blame. "Didn't you?"

He sighed wearily. "Yes. At least I suspected it."

"Then why didn't you correct the mistake then? Why did you let it come to this? Did you enjoy making a fool of me?"

"I'm not the one who did that. You did it all by yourself. You used superficial values to judge me, label me and tuck me away." He grabbed her arms and held on so tightly that she had to bite back a gasp. She refused to admit to the pain, which she was certain was no greater than the anguish she saw in his eyes.

"I'm a man, Gaby. An individual who has a thousand different facets to his personality, just like you do." Their gazes clashed, hers repentant, his blazing with anger and frustration.

"Dammit," he swore softly, his hands dropping to his side. He seemed to be biting back something, restraining himself.

Gabrielle rubbed her arms and waited for the explosion to go on. When it didn't, she said, "You might as well go on."

"No."

"Don't stop now. You're on a roll. Then, again, maybe I should remind you of the niche you've put me in and exactly how many times I've proven you to be mistaken. Don't tell me you didn't expect to have a rich prima donna, a real spoiled brat on your hands. You have a real hang-up when it comes to money. Even I can see that."

He sighed. "Okay, you're not the only villain in this piece. That's all the more reason we should stay as far away from each other as we can get. We seem to bring out the worst in each other."

Gaby refused to let that lie go unanswered. "Not always." At his shocked and disbelieving look, she added, "At least not for me."

"What are you saying?"

"All day today I've been remembering the way I felt this morning. You never even touched me and yet I felt as though I were the most desirable woman on the face of the earth. I felt a fire inside that I'd never felt before."

"That's lust, Gaby. We've never even tried to deny that we feel that. I ought to know. I came damned close to forcing myself on you in there this morning."

She shook her head and smiled. "Don't even try to turn what nearly happened here today into some sort of ugly scenario with me as the poor victim. I wanted you, just as much as you wanted me."

"It's not enough, Gaby. For this to work, we need

mutual respect and we've just established that it doesn't exist. Our bodies may be in perfect harmony," he said, a bitter note of regret in his voice, "but our heads are in different worlds."

Gabrielle wanted to protest, but there was far too much truth in what he said. If they were to find their way to something real and meaningful between them, they would have to start over. The prospect might have seemed insurmountable were it not for one thing.

"What about our hearts?" she responded finally, reaching out to touch his chest. He trembled as her fingers lingered over the spot where his heart thundered at a revealing pace. "What about those?"

Paul's eyes widened at the softly spoken taunt, but she didn't wait around for an answer. She picked up her coat and left, not sure where she was going, only certain that she wanted to be far from here when she began to cry.

Chapter Seven

Paul stared at the door as it slammed behind Gabrielle, instinctively noting that the frame seemed a little loose on top. He automatically went for his hammer and a handful of nails as he pondered her exit line.

What the hell was she talking about? Had she been trying to suggest that this thing between them amounted to love? That was crazy. They barely knew each other. In fact, until tonight they'd both apparently been influenced—subconsciously at least—by fairly negative first impressions, the kind that did not inspire love or anything remotely akin to it.

Then, again, maybe that's what someone of Gabrielle's background had to think in order to justify a sexual relationship. Which, he noted ruefully, they didn't

even have. Perhaps in her circles, she even had to justify desire.

Well, she could call it anything she liked. Personally, he thought lust or chemistry was a pretty adequate
label. It was possible to lust after a total stranger—a
lady with a pair of shapely legs, for instance, or one
with long red hair that flashed fire in the sunlight. But
you sure as hell couldn't love someone you didn't even
know. If tonight's argument had told him anything, it
was that he and Gabrielle knew as much about each
other as two people who happened to sit on neighboring bar stools. They'd both been talking for days, but
obviously neither of them had been listening.

And that, he decided, was something he couldn't do
a damn thing about until she came home. He went back
down to work on the third floor apartment. The sooner
it was finished and rented, the sooner he could complete
the second floor unit and then, finally, his own on the
ground floor. Then there would be some space between
him and Gabrielle, assuming she hadn't already moved
on long before that. That prospect wasn't something he
cared to think about at all.

At first, tonight, seeing the excitement that lit her
eyes when she'd come in, his stomach had knotted.
He'd been convinced that only a new job would spark
that high-voltage smile and guileless enthusiasm. When
he'd seen the two tables and realized that, for the moment, she intended to stay—job or no job—he'd been
overwhelmed by relief and a vague sense of victory. It
was as if those tables represented a sort of commitment.

It made what had happened afterward all the more

confusing. How, in the midst of the teasing and laughter over those tables, had things gotten so intense and so wildly out of control? One minute they'd been talking about paint, putting it on and taking it off. It certainly should have been less volatile than a similar discussion about clothes, for instance. Still, the next minute accusations and countercharges were whizzing through the air aimed at hurting.

No matter how hard he tried, he couldn't account for Gabrielle's motives. To be honest, though, he understood his own all too well. In part at least, he'd been releasing years of pent-up emotions, blaming her for long-ago slights, protecting himself from the pain of another rejection. He'd set out to achieve emotional distance at a time when physical space wasn't possible. What had almost happened this morning had shown him the need for that.

Gabrielle had been gone nearly an hour when he heard the downstairs door open, then the heavy tread of slow, tired footsteps. He held his breath as the steps approached the third floor, then went on. He sighed. Apparently there would be no confrontation again tonight, no resolution of the earlier argument. Maybe it was for the best. Perhaps in the morning, with clearer heads, they could get at the real problems between them. He felt slightly guilty over his relief at the reprieve.

Working with renewed concentration on the new kitchen cabinets, he was startled when he turned and found Gabrielle standing in the doorway. She'd changed out of her tailored-for-success business suit into jeans and a surprisingly faded sweatshirt that dipped unevenly at the neckline and bagged everywhere else. She'd never looked sexier or more approachable. If he kept looking at her, it would shatter his control. He turned back to the cabinet, fitting a corner together with careful precision, then tapping a nail into place.

"What happened here tonight?" she said softly. The uncertainty in her voice was enough to tie his gut into knots all over again. He couldn't look at her. If he did, if he saw the slightest hint of vulnerability in her eyes, he would take her in his arms and they would both be lost.

"We both found out we'd been living in a dreamworld. Reality set it." He kept his voice deliberately cool, determinedly nonchalant.

"I don't think so." The crisp note of conviction surprised him.

"So what do you think happened?"

"I think we were getting too close. I think you were feeling things you didn't want to feel and you set out to destroy those feelings."

His head snapped around at that. He hadn't credited her with mind-reading and wasn't about to admit to her skill. "Where the hell would you get an idea like that?"

She was not the least bit intimidated by his gruff tone. "It's the only thing that makes sense. You admitted that you'd known all along that I had doubts about getting involved with you, so all that garbage about my being a snob was hardly news. You used it, though. You took something we hadn't even put to the test…"

"Your attitude…"

"Was based on a misperception."

"Does that make it any less unconscionable?"

"Oh, for heaven's sake, you're every bit as hung up on the class distinction as you accuse me of being. Is being a reverse snob one bit better than being a snob? I resent that label, anyway. It's not the money itself or the lack of it that creates incompatibility. Even two rich people often develop even more dramatically different life-styles, make far different choices because of the restrictions or size of their bank account."

"You went to Harvard. I went to the school of hard knocks. Is that what you mean?"

She grinned. "In a way."

"That's a wide chasm to bridge."

"Maybe."

"I tried it once before and it didn't work," he admitted, surprising himself with his candor. He'd never told anyone about Christine. His parents had guessed, of course. They had even tried to warn him the relationship was a mistake. He'd ignored the warnings.

"Why didn't it work?" Gabrielle asked.

"She was rich. I was poor."

"Was it really that simple?"

He thought about Christine, really thought about her for the first time in years. Nothing about her had been simple.

"She liked to be where the action was. If her friends were skiing in Switzerland, that's where she wanted to be. If they were on a cruise in the Mediterranean, she couldn't wait to join them. She went to every charity ball in the city, every club opening, every major art exhibit. It all cost money and I didn't have it. The few times I went with her it was a disaster. She and her crowd talked about places and people I'd never even heard of. At first I was a curiosity. But it didn't take long for her to figure out that the novelty had worn off and I didn't fit in."

"So she dumped you?"

"Something like that," he said. It was a calm, unemotional description of something that had once been devastating. Even now he couldn't recall it without a surge of anger and humiliation.

"Were you really that happy with someone so different?" He tried remembering exactly how it had been ten years ago on the day when he'd had to admit it was over. He and Christine had spent the weekend sailing with her friends in Newport. Lulled by the sun and the ever-present pitcher of vodka and tonic, he'd felt oddly detached. He'd listened to the gossip that substituted for meaningful conversation. He'd watched Christine spend an entire day worrying about her tan line. And he had been incredibly bored. Still, that night he had been caught up in years of powerful feelings again. He had proposed. What a mistake it would have been if she'd said yes.

Suddenly he grinned at Gabrielle. "That's amazing. I just realized that I was bored to tears. For ten years I've been hating myself for not being able to fit in, only to discover I'd hate being like that crowd."

"Does that mean we can put my family background aside from now on?" Before he could answer, her gaze clashed with his. He read the challenge that was in her eyes long before it crossed her lips. "Do you want me, Paul?"

He'd thought he'd prepared himself for anything, but he was stunned by the direct question. His body responded before he could begin to find the right words for an answer.

"Yes," he said finally.

"And I want you."

"Which doesn't resolve the real problem," he reminded her, ignoring the sudden tightness of his jeans across his abdomen. "Come here."

She stepped into the room. He hesitated, then put his hands around her waist and lifted her up to sit on a completed section of the counter. He stepped between her splayed knees, his hands sliding down to rest on her thighs. It took everything in his power to leave the contact between them at that.

"Gaby, what you just said makes a lot of sense. Just because your family has money doesn't mean you're at all like Christine. But you are the kind of woman who's bound to have certain expectations in a relationship. I can't promise you anything right now. I'm just beginning to get on my feet financially. My goals aren't extravagant or earthshaking, but I don't want to lose sight of them. It took me a long time to become comfortable with who I am. Now that I am, I don't want to start dreaming impossible dreams."

"Am I an impossible dream?" she said quietly, her clear eyes meeting his, then becoming shadowed by doubts. Her gaze dropped to his chest.

"Right now, yes." When she tried to interrupt, he said, "I know you're not the same shallow person Christine was. But you *are* confused and vulnerable. You're searching for answers for yourself and your future. If we become involved now, you could stop looking. Remember that Robert Frost poem about the road not taken?"

Surprise flickered in her eyes. Then she nodded.

"It was all about choices, Gaby. Unless I'm very much mistaken, tonight you don't think you have any and it terrifies you. Gabrielle Clayton has probably always had the world at her feet. She could choose any direction for her life and with a snap of her fingers, it was hers. You're facing now what I faced years ago. You can set almost any goal in life you want, you can work like hell to attain it, you can even have money and power behind you, but there are absolutely no guarantees of success. The satisfaction has to come in making the effort." He sighed, wondering if he was only talking in circles. "Am I making any sense?"

"Too much," she said with weary resignation. "I'm just not sure what it has to do with us."

He searched for the right words. He wanted her to understand that his decision was for now, but perhaps not for always. No guarantees, though. No commitment. And only a suggestion of hope.

"When—if—you and I get together, I want it to be because you have options again. I want you to feel strong and in control of your life, to know every road that's open to you. And then, if you choose to be with me, it will be because we both know it's what you want and not the desperate act of a woman who's afraid to be alone."

She listened thoughtfully, but frowned at the end. "I am not desperate," she said heatedly.

He grinned at the sign of renewed spirit. "Good. Then you won't mind waiting a while, until we both know exactly what we want."

"I'll mind," she said. "But you're right. Waiting makes a lot more sense."

Just to make sure he diminished temptation, he changed the subject. Something had put her into this strange mood tonight and he needed to understand what it was. "Want to tell me what happened on those job interviews today?"

She met his gaze, then looked away. "Not particularly."

He pressed the issue. "Were they that discouraging? Had they already hired someone?"

"No."

"Then maybe they'll call tomorrow."

She shrugged indifferently. "Maybe."

Puzzled, he probed for an explanation for her negativity. It was totally out of character for a woman who was normally optimistic, direct and determined. She had not made that climb on Wall Street by accepting defeat so readily. "Didn't you like what they were offering?"

"It wasn't that," she admitted with obvious reluctance. "In fact, the jobs were fine. So were the benefits packages."

"What about the people?"

"They were okay, I guess."

"What then?"

"I'm not sure I handled myself that well in the interviews. I just couldn't get it together somehow."

"Why?" He watched the blush creep into her cheeks and felt a pang of guilt. "It wasn't because of what happened this morning, was it?" The shade of pink deepened to rose. "Oh, Gaby, I'm sorry."

She gave him a faint smile, obviously meant to reassure. "Don't worry about it. At first I blamed it on being distracted by that, too, but I think it was more than that."

"What?"

She hesitated a long time before answering, staring at the floor when she finally did. "I think I was bored by it all." She glanced up, her expression filled with astonishment at the admission. "Can you imagine? I fought like hell to get to New York, to make it on Wall Street, then I come to one little hurdle in my career and I'm suddenly bored. Do you suppose I'm trying to find an excuse for failing?"

"Nope," he said with certainty. "I've suspected for some time now that the enchantment was past. With your drive, you'd have found another Wall Street job by now, if you'd really been looking. Besides, I don't think you're the kind of lady who needs excuses. I think you've come to a turning point. Instead of being down, you should be excited."

"Right. I have exactly fourteen hundred dollars left in my bank account, no job prospects in sight and credit card bills coming in every day. I'm thrilled."

"Focus on the good side. You're opening yourself up to new possibilities. Take something temporary, if you feel you have to. Borrow from your parents."

"Never," she said adamantly.

"Why not?" he said, struck by the fire in her quick response. "Wouldn't they give you a loan?"

"Sure. With strings."

"Such as?"

"Move home to Charleston, take up my rightful place in society, pour tea until my wrist aches, marry someone with exactly the right pedigree no matter how boring and start the cycle all over again in a new house." She shuddered. "No way."

He grinned and applauded.

"What was that for?"

"You've made your first choice."

"I made that one when I left," she said, dismissing it as any sort of big deal.

"Times change. The stakes change. The choice you made tonight is not the same one you made when you left for New York. Give yourself a little credit."

He wanted to kiss away the doubts, but knew it would be sheer folly to risk touching her at all. He'd been entirely noble for the last half hour. He'd meant every word he'd said about giving her time to find her way. But he'd realized something about himself along the way. He wanted Gabrielle Clayton in his life far more than he'd admitted up to now. He'd simply been afraid to acknowledge the feelings that were growing in him. And, despite all his talk about freedom of choice, he was going to do everything in his power to see that she stayed right here.

Everything short of seduction, he amended. For now. Which meant he had to get her out of this room at once.

"Go," he said, his voice suddenly husky. "Get some sleep."

"Can't I help? I'm lousy with a hammer, but I could paint or something."

The offer tempted, not because it would speed the work, but because it would keep her close. His noble intentions weren't etched deeply enough for that. "Not tonight. It's late. If you want to do some work in here tomorrow, I'll bring the paint down for you."

To his amazement, she actually seemed excited at the prospect. She dropped down off the counter, then gave him a quick peck on the cheek before starting from the kitchen. In the doorway, she paused and looked back. "Thanks for the pep talk."

"No problem."

"You realize, of course, that you're shattering another stereotype."

"What's that?"

"The ruthless, unsympathetic landlord."

"Wait until you miss your first rent payment," he said with mock ferocity, enjoying the burst of laughter that lingered long after she'd gone upstairs.

Over the next few weeks Gabrielle came to accept that her life was changing dramatically. She hadn't reached a decision about what sort of job to look for, but Paul had given her a short-term alternative. He'd offered her free rent in exchange for helping him with the painting in the remaining apartments. She'd protested the exchange, but he'd shown her figures to prove that he was getting the better part of the bargain.

The arrangement had a couple of side benefits, as well. She had time to continue haunting secondhand shops and fabric stores to complete the work on their place. And she got to spend time with Paul. They were together every evening, sharing sandwiches or home-made soup and, occasionally, pizza or Chinese take-out. Each day she learned something new about him, something that made her respect grow and her desire mount.

The fact that he pointedly kept his distance only escalated the heated longing that assailed her at the oddest moments. Her gaze would linger on his fingers as they clasped a wrench and her imagination would soar. She'd wipe a speck of paint from his cheek and her flesh would burn. Her body was in a constant state of repressed excitement but her thoughts were, surprisingly, calmer and more serene than she'd imagined possible.

On the day she finally finished the work on their apartment, she planned a surprise celebration. She'd even calculated the effect a bottle of wine might have on their wavering resolve. It was obvious that for the past week it had been difficult for Paul to say good-night and go off to his own room. One night neither of them had gotten any sleep because neither would make the first move to break off the conversation that was punctuated by laughter and increasingly heavy-lidded looks of longing.

Gabrielle set the refinished oak dining-room table with her best china and crystal. She polished her silver candlesticks and added a small bouquet of the last flowers from the dying garden. She'd capitulated to Paul's secret passion for thick, rare steaks and bought two of the best the butcher had. She'd made her own dressing for the salad and snapped fresh green beans. She had even made an apple pie. From scratch. She'd spent the whole afternoon peeling apples and rolling the dough for the double crust. Still warm, it was sitting on the kitchen counter now, the tempting cinnamon scent wafting through the apartment.

After her bath, she dressed in wool slacks and a soft sweater with a cowl neckline. She brushed her hair until it shone with warm golden highlights, then added a light touch of makeup.

At dusk, her anticipation mounting, she lit a fire in the fireplace and sat down to wait. As the room darkened, her spirits sank. Worry replaced excitement, followed by indignation, then deepening concern, then fury. It was after midnight when he finally arrived.

Paul took in the spoiled dinner and Gabrielle's scowl at a single glance. She bit her lip to keep from shouting at him like a fishwife. She would be calm. She would be reasonable. She would listen. And then she would heap guilt on him until he was drowning in it.

"What happened? Your date didn't show?" he said.

The man actually seemed to feel sorry for her. Either he was incredibly obtuse or he was a master at acting the innocent.

"Something like that," she said coolly, very proud of her control. "Where have you been?"

"I had dinner with a friend."

"I see." She couldn't keep the edge out of her voice, though she'd sworn at least a dozen times during the evening that she wouldn't give him the satisfaction of knowing that he'd hurt her.

He sat down in the chair opposite her, looking perplexed. "I have the feeling I'm missing something here. Are you mad at me?"

She stared at him, then shook her head. "Paul Reed, you cannot possibly be that dumb." So much for staying cool. "I spent thirty dollars on steaks and wine," she snapped. "You bet your life I'm mad at you."

He picked up the half-empty cabernet sauvignon bottle. "Apparently the wine didn't go to waste."

"Don't change the subject."

"I wasn't aware that's what I was doing."

"Couldn't you have called?"

Paul sighed. He'd stayed out on purpose tonight because it was getting so he couldn't bear being in the same room with Gabrielle and keeping his hands off her. He wanted to explore the satin texture of her skin, to set her flesh on fire. He wanted those velvet-brown eyes to smolder with the heat of his touch. If he'd had any idea she was sitting in front of a fire waiting for him with wine and food, he'd probably have stayed out the rest of the night. His good intentions had withstood about all the temptation they could handle. Even now his fingers trembled from his effort at restraint. He wanted badly to caress the lines of tension on her face until they eased.

He sighed again and closed his eyes. When he opened them, he said, "Okay. I guess we'd better talk this out."

"Please, don't do me any favors," she said sarcastically. He winced under the direct hit.

"I'm sorry if you went to all this trouble for me, but you didn't mention you were going to do it," he said reasonably.

She shot him a look of pure disgust. "It was supposed to be a surprise. You've come home every night since I've been here. You have been downstairs hammering or sawing or painting by no later than five-thirty. You've stayed at it until midnight. How was I supposed to know that tonight would be the one night in a month you'd find something better to do?"

Paul couldn't think of a single adequate response for her logic. Feeling a nagging hunch that he was playing dirty, he tried putting her on the defensive. "We're roommates, Gaby. We both agreed it was for the best right now. I shouldn't have to check in with you."

She stared at him, absorbing the low blow. "I'm not crazy about the definition of our relationship, but don't even roommates deserve consideration?"

Her chin was tilted defiantly, but there were huge tears clinging to the corners of her eyes. She looked so forlorn that he muttered a curse and went to her. Overcome with guilt, he took her chin in his hand and met her gaze.

"Of course they do. And I am very sorry I spoiled your evening."

Suddenly her bottom lip quivered and one tear rolled freely down her cheek. Paul thought he could bear anything but her crying, especially when he felt responsible for her pain.

To prevent a second tear from following the first and then a third and on and on until his own heart broke, a kiss seemed to be the only answer. He seized it far too readily.

Just one, he promised himself as his mouth claimed hers, slowly savoring the touch of velvet against fire.

Just a fleeting taste of her lips, he vowed again, his tongue discovering the salt of tears and the tang of wine.

Just a brief offering of warmth and tenderness and understanding. Just to keep her from crying. Just between friends.

Of course, it wasn't enough.

Chapter Eight

For a man who was all hard angles and gruffness, Paul seduced with surprising gentleness, Gabrielle decided as he kissed away her tears. She wasn't sure what she'd expected, but it hadn't been these slow, tender caresses that melted every last bit of icy anger and left her gasping for more. The persuasive, eager touch of his lips, so long in coming, was like a taste of heaven. She wanted to linger there forever, surrounded by this astonishing sense of contentment.

"Gaby," he murmured, breaking away far too soon, just when she was getting used to the sensuous warmth of his mouth. "We can't do this."

"We can," she said, pressing her mouth against his to assure his silence. Her tongue declared a daring assault on his firmly closed lips, until they parted on a groan of pure pleasure. Desire welled inside her, filling her with an aching sense of need. The faint scent of sawdust and paint and masculinity seduced as effectively as any heady man's cologne of musk or spice. This powerful attraction between them was no longer something to talk about or even think about. It was time to feel, to let their emotions lead them for once.

Though Gabrielle had never been more certain about her own desires, more ready to listen to her heart, Paul fought this latest kiss. Her own senses heightened, she recognized his struggle to do the right thing in the tense set of his shoulders, his rigid stance. The marines would have approved of that stance. She could imagine the desperate, rational argument being waged in his head as his skin burned beneath her touch. That kind of determined logic required bold tactics. A shudder swept through him as she slid her hands beneath his shirt.

"Gaby, no." This time the protest was breathless and far less emphatic.

She lifted her confident gaze to meet his troubled expression and smiled. "Yes."

"You've had the better part of a bottle of wine. You don't know what you're doing."

She experimented with proving otherwise. She pressed her body closer to his, trailing kisses along the side of his neck, then running her tongue along the shell of his ear. A soft but distinct moan of pleasure rumbled deep in his throat. She grinned in satisfaction. "Oh, really?" she said demurely.

He scowled at her. "I was not referring to your technique."

"That's nice," she said, beginning to unbutton his shirt. Now that she was getting the hang of this, she was thoroughly enjoying it. He grabbed her hands.

"Gaby! Enough!"

She stared into eyes that glittered dangerously. "Okay."

He regarded her suspiciously, then nodded and released her. Her gaze never left his as she reached out and ran one finger lazily along the zipper of his jeans. After his first startled gasp, his jaw clenched and he swallowed convulsively. The determined look in his eyes wavered. His body's response beneath her daring touch was unmistakable.

"Damn you," he said softly, his breathing shallow.

"You don't mean that," she said, refusing to back away. Her confidence surged more powerfully than it had in weeks.

Finally Paul's hard, unblinking expression softened to one of wry acceptance. "No. I don't mean it," he said, his arms pulling her close. She could feel the ragged whisper of his breath across the top of her head.

"I don't want this to be a mistake," he said.

"It isn't," she said with astonishing certainty. If anything, Paul's doubts and restraint had proved that to her. He respected her and that was every bit as important as loving her.

She had yet to define her own feelings clearly, but she recognized that they were stronger and more powerful than anything she'd known before, a blend of friendship and desire that might very well become love. But the relationship needed intimacy to grow, to mature into something lasting. Whatever happened in the future, tonight's risk was one that had to be taken.

His hands cupped her face, the pads of his thumbs playing across her lips as he studied her intently. Gabrielle felt her heart thundering against her ribs as she waited. Finally he nodded, then lowered his mouth to hers again in a gentle promise.

When the kiss ended, he kept the promise, scooping her into his arms and carrying her through the darkened apartment to her room. He reached for the light switch, but she shook her head.

"There's a candle."

When he'd lowered her to the bed, he lit the candle, filling the room with the scent of lavender. Then he turned and started for the door.

"Paul?"

"I have to protect you. I'll be back," he promised.

Her heart filled to overflowing at this further evidence of his caring. Her trust was not misplaced. This was right. As she waited for his return, her stomach muscles tensed in anticipation of his joining her on the bed. Her pulse was beating to a sensual cadence. Then, as the narrow mattress sank beneath his weight, her skin tingled at the brush of denim and flannel against her flesh.

Expecting no more than urgency and a swift claiming from this first time together, Gabrielle instead found herself caught up in a slow building of passion. Paul teased and tempted and explored, waiting for sensation to subside before finding new ways to drive her wild with desire. She'd never imagined this exquisite tension, the urgent need to reach a peak of pleasure beyond all experience. He played her body as expertly as a long-time lover, but with the reverence of a man receiving an incredible gift for the first time. He lingered and tasted and stroked until fire consumed any remaining doubts for either of them.

His skin became slick beneath her anxious touch. His muscles tensed to steel as he moved to claim her at last. There was one unbearably slow thrust that startled her with its promise of yet more pleasure. She gasped as he withdrew, then began to fill her once again.

She heard his faint, startled exclamation of her name as if from very far away, then sensed that he was hesitating. Her body protested at the delay. Instinctively her legs circled his back and her hips rose in search of a heat that ignited her own passion.

She was vaguely aware of Paul's anguished moan as he plunged into her again. There was an instant of pain that took her by surprise and then was gone as their bodies adapted to a natural rhythm as old as time. Just when she thought she'd reached the highest peak of excitement possible, he led her on, flames of pure sensation firing her blood. And when passion exploded through her body at last, joy radiated through her heart at the unexpected sense of fulfillment.

The delicious tension slowly subsided. She opened her eyes to find Paul staring at her. "Okay?" he said, brushing damp tendrils of hair back from her face.

"More than okay." Rapture lingered as an incredible sensation of well-being.

"Why didn't you tell me?"

"Tell you what?" she said, rubbing her fingers across the stubble that darkened his jaw. The sandpapery, masculine texture sent shivers dancing through her.

"That you'd never been with a man before."

"Does it matter?" she said, feeling oddly defensive at a moment when she wanted to indulge herself in far sweeter memories.

He smiled. "Not in the way you're apparently thinking. I could have made it better for you, though."

"I doubt that," she said, a wry inflection in her voice.

Grinning slightly, Paul ran a finger across her lips. "Thanks for the flattery, but really, why didn't you say anything?"

"It's not exactly something you announce on a first date."

"This is not a first date. We've been living together for weeks now."

"Platonically."

"Barely," he said dryly.

She scowled at him. "If you want to get technical. But I still say this is our first date."

"At what point did it become a date and not just another night at home? When you decided to fix a fancy dinner? When I inadvertently stood you up? Or when you began to seduce me?"

He had a point, though she couldn't imagine why he felt the need to belabor this. Being a virgin at her age might be unusual, but it wasn't exactly a crime.

"Okay," she said grumpily. "Even tonight wasn't a date, which is all the more reason for me to have kept my mouth shut about my lack of experience. Why does that bother you so much? I thought men got all macho and tingly knowing that they were the first. Didn't I get it right?"

"Don't get testy. You got it very right. I was just surprised. You're a beautiful, desirable woman. I can't believe you've never had a serious relationship."

"Actually, I was engaged."

"And you never..." he began incredulously.

"If you'd met Townsend, you'd understand. It was a very formal engagement. Until I met you, I had no idea of the meaning of the word desire."

"I'm glad I was able to broaden your vocabulary."

All of a sudden there was an odd tension in his voice that puzzled her. It didn't fit with the tender aftermath of glorious lovemaking. "What's wrong?"

"Tell me the truth, Gaby. Was this just an experiment? You'd certainly gone out of your way to set the scene, right down to the candle by the bed. Did you decide it was time to discover your own sexuality and pick me because I was in the neighborhood and struck you as being an adequate stud?"

Shocked by the crude assessment of what had just happened between them, she sat up in bed, clutching the sheet across her breasts. She felt embarrassed and cold and incredibly empty inside.

"I really must not have gotten it right, if you think that," she said, her voice flat. "I never said I didn't have opportunities to hop into bed with other men. I said I'd never had these feelings before." She glowered at him. "*You* inspire them. I don't know what they mean or the full ramifications of tonight, but I wanted this to happen between us because it felt right. Now I have to wonder if it wasn't an awful mistake."

Paul winced as if she'd slapped him. He reached out to touch her, but she shrugged off his hand.

"I'm sorry," he said. "I should never have said that. Maybe I said it because I was feeling guilty about my own motives. God knows I've wanted you from the very first moment you walked into this apartment. Up until now I've had sense enough to keep my hands off."

"You don't have any reason to feel guilty for taking what I offered, only for making it seem ugly and cheap." She allowed her point to sink in, then sighed. "Paul, I don't regret what happened tonight."

"That's not what you said a minute ago."

"I was furious at you a minute ago for trying to ruin something very special."

The tension seemed to drain from his body at last. She saw the spark of heat flare in his eyes and recognized it. "Maybe I should try to make it up to you," he suggested in a voice that sent fire sizzling through her veins all over again.

"Maybe you should."

When Paul woke in the morning, he was surprised to find that he was alone in Gaby's bed. During the night, he'd gotten accustomed to waking up and finding her nestled close beside him. Sometimes he had contented himself with just watching her sleep, filled with an overwhelming sense of possessiveness. More often, he'd needed to touch her, to feel the satin of her skin as it warmed beneath his fingers. And on more of those occasions than he'd dreamed possible, she had come awake to his touch, returning it with sleepy pleasure, until they'd wound up clinging together in passion yet again.

He stretched, got out of bed and without bothering to pick up his scattered clothes went in search of Gabrielle. He heard her before he found her, her voice low and edged with a note of nervousness he'd never heard before. He walked into the living room, where she was curled up in the corner of the sofa talking on the phone. She glanced up at him, her eyes widening as she took in his state of undress. He went over and dropped a light kiss on her forehead, then sat down across from her, feeling not one bit guilty about his blatant eavesdropping. He wanted to know what had put the tension in her voice and the frown on her forehead.

"Yes, Daddy. Of course, everything is all right. You don't need to worry about me."

Paul watched as she swallowed hard. A blush crept into her cheeks. "The job is going just fine."

Startled, he simply stared at her. She refused to meet his gaze.

"Of course, I know I can count on you and Mother. If there were anything wrong, I would tell you. I have to go now, Daddy. There's someone at the door. I'll talk to you again next week. No, really. I'll call. I'll give you the phone number next time. 'Bye."

She pushed down the button to break the connection, even before she replaced the receiver. She still didn't look at him.

"What was that all about?"

"Just checking in with my parents. If I don't call once a week, they get a little crazy."

She started to get up.

"Don't leave."

She sat back down, looking guilty and thoroughly uncomfortable.

"You haven't told them about your job yet, have you?"

"You were sitting right here. You know I haven't."

"Or about where you're living?"

Her chin rose defiantly, then she sighed. "No."

"Why not?"

"They'd worry."

"It sounds to me as though they're already worried."

"If you knew my parents, you'd realize that it's a perpetual state of mind."

"Then why not tell them the truth?"

"Because they'd start pressuring me to come home. I'm not up to it."

"Are you afraid you'd give in and go?"

"Of course not."

"Then tell them. I could tell from the sound of your voice that the deception is beginning to take a toll on you. Get it out in the open. Let them know that you're doing just fine, that you're getting your life back together, making decisions about what you want to do next."

"And how do I explain you?"

He grinned. "Now that's an interesting question."

"Dammit, I'm serious. If they find out I am living with a man, they won't wait around to find out the circumstances. My father will be up here with a shotgun."

"Is that really what you're afraid of? You don't seriously think your father will shoot me unless we traipse off to the nearest chapel."

"Cathedral," she corrected. "Senator Graham Clayton's daughter would only get married in the fanciest cathedral around, with an entourage and trappings that would make the royal weddings in England look like they were thrown by paupers."

"Senator Graham Clayton?" Paul repeated in a voice that was admittedly choked. The man's name was synonymous with conservative politics and old-fashioned family values. A shotgun would probably be too good for a man who was sitting around naked chatting with his daughter. He'd probably string him up from a tree in Central Park and not necessarily by his neck. "I think I see the problem."

A faint grin flitted across Gabrielle's face. "I thought you would."

"I still don't like the idea of your lying to him. If he finds out what's happened before you tell him yourself, it will only upset him more."

"How is he going to find out? He's too busy keeping the whole country on the straight and narrow to worry about one wayward daughter."

"What if he tries to call you at work?"

She stared at him, her expression horrified. "Oh, damn," she whispered softly.

"Obviously that's not something you'd considered. What if one of your friends up here tries to track you down by calling your family? You've pretty much dropped out of sight. It's not unthinkable that they'd assume you'd gone back to South Carolina."

"You're a real bundle of good news this morning, aren't you? Why aren't you still asleep?"

"I missed you," he said evenly. "Now stop changing the subject."

"I don't want to talk about this," she said stubbornly.

"Fine, but you'd better think about it. Delaying the inevitable is only going to make it worse."

He left her sitting on the sofa, staring out the window.

Senator Graham Clayton. He couldn't get the name out of his head as he dressed and went downstairs to finish painting the living room of the apartment that would soon be his. If last night had complicated his relationship with Gabrielle, this morning's revelation had given new meaning to the word. He might be considered a suitable addition to the family of some pleasant, middle-class politician whose name wasn't recognized beyond his own state, but he no more belonged in Senator Clayton's reportedly idyllic family than he did in Buckingham Palace.

"How many coats of paint are you going to put on that spot?" Gabrielle asked, interrupting his panicked thoughts.

He stared blankly at her, then at the wall. Sure enough he'd been running the roller over the exact same square for the last ten minutes. "I guess I wasn't paying attention."

"I hope you weren't down here panicking about the shotgun."

His expression must have given him away because she sighed heavily. "I knew it. I knew the minute you found out about my family, you'd start building your defenses right back up again. I can just hear that brain of yours clicking through all the reasons why we're unsuited and magnifying them out of all proportion."

"You have to admit the stakes are a lot higher than I'd realized."

"Stakes? The only thing at stake here is whether or not you and I care about each other. I can't speak for you, but I'm falling in love for the first time in my life."

Paul felt his heart stop then start again at a faster beat. He shook his head adamantly. "You can't do that."

"Who says?"

"I do. It won't work."

"It was working well enough a few hours ago."

"Don't remind me."

She walked toward him until they were standing practically toe to toe. He felt as though he were suffocating.

"I think I have to," she said softly, before curling her fingers into the hair at the back of his head. His scalp tingled and the sensation danced straight down to his... Oh, hell, he thought weakly as her lips claimed his with a possessiveness that captured his breath and robbed him of all sensible thoughts. For a woman who'd been relatively inexperienced twenty-four hours ago, she was catching on quickly.

Sparks danced in her eyes when she released him. "Remember that the next time you get any crazy ideas about going back to being my pal."

Paul refused to let a little thing like an unbridled libido destroy his common sense, which had been strengthening with a vengeance ever since that phone call. He had to find some way to remind Gabrielle of exactly how mismatched they were. They'd been living in isolated, idyllic harmony here for several weeks now. She hadn't been forced to face what his world was really like, how vastly different it was from her own.

"I've been thinking," he began, still sorting through possible ways of introducing her to reality. "This apartment will be finished in a few days now. Maybe we ought to show it off."

She regarded him suspiciously. "Where did that come from?"

"It's just an idea. I mean why not have a party? You can meet some of my friends. I can meet some of yours. We've worked hard to get this place in shape. It's time we celebrated."

"Under normal circumstances, that would make perfect sense. Why do I have this feeling that there's a catch in there?"

"Because you have a suspicious nature?" he suggested cheerfully.

"With good cause," she retorted. "Are you trying to prove something to me?"

"What would I be trying to prove?" He concentrated very hard on dipping the roller into the paint, then spreading it onto a new section of the wall. He could not look into her eyes.

"That we mix like oil and water."

He swallowed hard. "How would a party show that?"

he asked innocently. "It's just a bunch of people getting together for a good time."

"Exactly. So don't get any crazy ideas that your friends will offend me so deeply that I'll stop wanting you or that my friends will be such snobs that your friends will hate them. In fact, I will go so far as to bet you that this will be the very best party you have ever been to."

Paul had a feeling he'd gone about this all wrong. Gabrielle was now determined to make this stupid party work and she would do it, if she had to invite the symphony and the New York Rangers to entertain the divergent crowd. He didn't even need to wait for Senator Clayton to show up with his hanging noose. Right now, he had all the rope he needed to hang himself.

Chapter Nine

Despite her avowed self-confidence, Gabrielle felt trapped and more than a little worried. She had no choice now but to treat the upcoming party as a challenge. She knew perfectly well that Paul expected it to be a disaster, maybe even hoped it would be. She also knew that their future hinged in some twisted, obscure way on its success. While she resented having her fate tied to something so superficial, she accepted the situation, gritted her teeth and set out to prove Paul wrong.

Thankfully, being a politician's daughter had equipped her to play hostess at almost any kind of event from a Fourth of July picnic in a town square to a gala at the country club. She'd campaigned in factories and bowling alleys as readily as antebellum estates. She could make polite small talk with people she'd never

seen before and would never see again, leaving each
one convinced they were indelibly etched on her memory. It was easy enough to convince herself that unless
Paul dragged in homicidal maniacs, she could main-
tain her aplomb.

In addition, planning a party for thirty people in her
own home should be a piece of cake. She'd learned from
a master. Her mother approached entertaining with the
skill of a tactical expert in a military command post.
Gabrielle knew all about guest lists and food quanti-
ties and wine selection. What she didn't know about,
of course, were the tastes of Paul's friends.

It was the unknown factor, combined with the stakes,
that gave all of her careful planning an edge of panic.
A full week before the Saturday night party, she found
herself filling a grocery cart with six different beers—
imported and domestic, light and regular—because she
had no idea which one Paul's friends might like. She
bought pâté and little quiches at a gourmet French bakery, then in a frenzy of uncertainty added bags of po-
tato chips and pretzels to the menu. She polished her
silver, then decided to use Paul's stainless steel flatware.
She went through the closet and picked out a basic designer dress suitable for any occasion, then changed her
mind and dragged out comfortable jeans and a hand-
knit sweater.

Unless she asked him a direct question, Paul virtu-
ally ignored the preparations. On Saturday his contribu-
tion was a trip to the corner for ice, which he dumped
in the tub—before she'd had her bath. At her scowl of
displeasure, he took it back out and stored it in the al-

ready crammed refrigerator. Later, as he returned the ice to the tub and added the assorted six packs of beer, she caught him grinning.

"What's so funny?" she asked, glowering. She was in no mood for amusement at her expense.

"You could open a bar with this variety."

"If you'd offered any suggestions, I might not have had to buy a little of everything."

"My friends will drink whatever's available. Won't yours?" he inquired.

"Go to hell."

The evening was certainly getting off to a stellar start, she thought as she put the finishing touches on a clam dip surrounded by chilled vegetables. Even the disparate guests were likely to get along better than the host and hostess. She absentmindedly snapped a carrot stick in two, then threw the pieces into the trash in disgust.

"Gaby."

"What?"

"This is not worth having a nervous breakdown over."

"Isn't it? You're hoping everyone will have a rotten time, just so you can say I told you so and move out of here with a clear conscience."

He came up close behind her and slid his arms around her waist. The fresh, tangy scent of his after-shave teased her senses. "No. I'm not."

"You are." She turned around in his embrace so she could read his expression. "And I want your friends to like me. I really do, but if they don't, it shouldn't have anything to do with what's happening between us. I'm not worried about what my friends think of you."

"Aren't you?"

"No."

"How many of your friends did you invite?"

"Okay. I only invited a few, but I don't have that many close friends here anyway. Ted and Kathy were the only couple I got really close to and Jeff was an office pal. They're the only people I've stayed in touch with. And no matter what you think, I am not a believer in the old adage that you can judge a person by the friends he keeps. People develop relationships—and marriages, for that matter—for all sorts of reasons."

"I know that," he said with a sigh.

Despite the reassuring words, the tone wasn't convincing. Gabrielle's feeling of dread returned as she turned back to the arrangement of carrot and celery sticks. Paul left to put music on the stereo.

When the first knock came at the door, she tensed and wondered exactly how long she could get away with taking refuge in the kitchen. Despite the fact that she was never more than three feet from the stove, the quiches burned because she forgot all about them as she tried to hear how things were going in the living room.

She was on the verge of tears, infuriated by her own silly retreat, when Paul returned to the kitchen for beers for the first arrivals.

"What's wrong?" he asked at once.

"I burned the quiches."

"There's enough food in there to feed all the homeless in Manhattan. Don't worry about the quiches. Just come on out."

She shook her head.

He stared at her. "Why not? I thought you were going to stop worrying about how well everyone got along and just enjoy this party. I thought you wanted to prove something to me tonight."

She glared at him. Talk about throwing down the gauntlet or hoisting her with her own petard. The man had a particularly nasty habit of throwing her words back in her face.

"Let's go," she said determinedly, aware that there was an unmistakable note of doom in her voice.

Once in the living room she noticed that people actually seemed to be enjoying themselves. Jeff Lyons, who was handsome, funny and gay, was discussing racketball with one of Paul's friends. Ted and Kathy waved from across the room, where they were talking to a young blond man she recognized as a member of Paul's work crew. A beautiful woman with spiky black hair and a studded leather jacket over her denim miniskirt was enthusiastically describing her latest art exhibit to a rapt woman in a Norma Kamali original. Since Gabrielle didn't recognize either one of them, she assumed they were both friends of Paul's. Apparently his own social circle contained an eclectic mix.

So, she thought with the first flicker of relief, it wasn't going to be so awful. People weren't sorting themselves out into his friends and hers with an obvious chasm in between. Maybe she'd been right all along. She allowed herself a small, triumphant smirk before going to introduce herself to the artist. She seemed like a likely person to begin with. They would at least have art in common.

She had barely given her name when the artist's heavily made-up dark brown eyes widened to the size of a Kewpie doll's. "So you are the one. I'm so glad to finally meet you. I'm Theresa. Paul tells me he brought you to see some of my work."

An unfortunate image of auto parts entwined with clocks came to mind. Tongue-tied with astonishment, Gabrielle stared at her. "Yes," she said finally. "It was…"

Theresa laughed. "Don't bother trying to be polite. My work falls into that love it or hate it category. Maybe if I did something a little more mainstream, I wouldn't be broke all the time." She shrugged indifferently. "What's money, though, as long as I have my artistic integrity intact?"

"Money pays the bills," the owner of the Norma Kamali outfit said. "Maybe you should just marry wealth the way I did. I can paint what I want without worrying about critical or popular success."

"Don't pay any attention to all that cynical talk," Theresa said. "Maureen is also crazy in love with the man in spite of his millions and her work is now selling for 2500 a canvas. By the way, Gabrielle, Paul was telling us you're responsible for the decor in here. It's fantastic. You have a real eye for color and proportion."

Gabrielle tried to survey the room with an objective eye. It was better than before, but hardly the stuff of an interior designer's dreams.

"I'm glad you like it," she said cautiously, wondering how much simple politeness had contributed to the compliment.

"I do. Did it cost a fortune? I know I'm being terribly nosy, but when you've lived in a dump like mine, this looks wonderful. I'd give anything to have my place fixed up like this, but most of my money goes right back into art supplies."

"Actually, I did this on half a shoestring."

Maureen looked surprisingly impressed. "How? I just paid a fortune to an interior designer and the results aren't half as interesting. My apartment looks exactly like twenty others on the Upper West Side."

Basking in the apparent enthusiasm, Gabrielle described her forays through the secondhand stores and fabric shops. "Actually, it was fun. I refinished the furniture myself. It's not exactly professional caliber work, but there's a sense of adventure in discovering what's under all the grime."

"It looks great to me," Theresa said enthusiastically. "I don't suppose you'd like to take on a client. You'd have to work with a pretty limited budget and we'd have to negotiate your commission, but I'd love to see what you could do with my place."

The idea intrigued her. "What exactly would you need to have done?"

"Everything," Maureen said fervently before Theresa could respond. "How an artist can live in that dreary place is beyond me. I'd be painting in black and gray. Come to think of it maybe that does explain your sculpture."

"Very funny. As you can see, Gabrielle, I do need help. Paul volunteered to come over sometime and help me paint, but I haven't even had time to pick out a color scheme."

"Thank God," Maureen said. "Her idea of subtlety is purple and orange."

Gabrielle laughed. "I suppose I could take a look at your place and see if I get any ideas. I wouldn't want to charge you for it, though. I have some time right now and I enjoy digging around for bargains."

"Oh, no," Theresa said. "This is business. Don't sell yourself short. Turning an empty space into a warm, inviting home is a talent. I insist on paying you for it."

Just then Jeff came over. She introduced him to the two women, then after a promise to call Theresa about the decorating, she began circulating, checking the food, greeting newcomers. She finally made her way to Paul, who was chatting enthusiastically with Ted and Kathy. To her surprise they were discussing the construction of the apartments. Ted was amazingly knowledgeable.

"I was just telling Paul that Kathy and I have been looking for a place just this size," Ted said, after giving her a kiss. "We want to move before the baby comes."

"But you have a wonderful apartment," she protested. Paul's arm settled around her shoulders. She was surprised at how right the gesture felt and how casually Paul had made it. Perhaps he was beginning to relax with the success of the evening, too. She glanced at Ted, trying to judge his reaction, but he seemed far more interested in examining the quality of the woodwork.

"A wonderful, expensive, small apartment," Kathy corrected, rubbing her hand over her expanding belly. "It's not big enough for us *and* the baby. I'm not going to be working for at least a few months after the baby is born and with the market slow right now, we don't want to get in over our heads financially."

"You could rent one of these, if you're interested," Paul said. Gabrielle stared at him in astonishment. The second and third floor were already rented. The tenants were moving in December first. The only empty apartment was Paul's on the ground floor. He'd intended to move in next week. They hadn't discussed what their living arrangements would be after that. This was the first indication she'd had that Paul was actually thinking that they should continue living together.

"I could show you the one that's available," he offered now.

Kathy's eyes lit up. "I'd love to see it."

"But don't you think it's a little too far out?" Gabrielle said, still feeling that a move that had turned out to be so right for her might be very wrong for Ted and Kathy. "The neighborhood is still in transition. It's not what you're used to."

"But it's on the way up, not down," Ted countered. "I noticed that as we were driving over."

"But you should be thinking of buying, not pouring your money into rent," Gabrielle said, not sure exactly why she was fighting the idea of having these two lovely people as neighbors when they were clearly enthusiastic about the prospect.

"Right now all the property we like is out of our

price range. I'd rather rent someplace like this for a while, so we can build our savings," Kathy said. "Ted, let's go look."

"I'll stay here," Gabrielle said, watching as Paul led them away. He and Ted were already exchanging ideas for further development of the neighborhood. Astonishing, she thought as she watched them go.

She was in the kitchen when they came back. Kathy's face was alight with excitement. "It's wonderful," she enthused. "The second bedroom will be perfect for a nursery. We're going to talk about it some more, but I think we're going to take it."

She hugged Gabrielle. "I have to get home and put this soccer kicker inside me to bed, but thank you so much for inviting us over tonight. It's been far too long since we've seen you. It would be fantastic to have you and Paul for neighbors."

"Yes," Gabrielle said, feeling numb at the speed with which events seemed to be taking place. Decisions had been made tonight she hadn't been consulted on and couldn't begin to understand.

It wasn't until all the guests had left and Paul was stretched out on the sofa that she had a chance to think about her reaction to the prospect of having Ted and Kathy living downstairs.

"Come sit with me," Paul said.

"I want to get some of this mess cleaned up."

"It can wait. I want to talk to you."

Sighing, she went to join him. He pulled her down into his lap, his arms around her waist. The increasingly familiar sense of belonging crept over her as she leaned back against his chest.

"I thought the evening went well," he said, his fingers idly stroking her stomach.

"Yes."

"Why so down, Gaby? I thought you'd be gloating. It all worked out, just the way you expected it to. I like your friends. You like mine. Nobody was standing in judgment of anyone else."

"It was all very civilized," she agreed testily.

"I thought it was better than that. People actually seemed to be having fun. Our lives are blending together."

"I suppose."

He kissed the back of her neck. "Then what's the problem?"

"How can you rent that apartment to Ted and Kathy?" she blurted finally. "It's all wrong for them."

"How do you figure that? They want two bedrooms. It has two bedrooms. They want a moderate rent. I'm asking a moderate rent. The garden even gives them a place for the baby to play."

Unexpected tears welled in her eyes. "How terrific for them," she said.

"Gaby! Don't you want them here?" He sounded confused and dismayed. "They're your friends. I thought you'd love the idea of having them nearby."

"It's not that," she said, recognizing that she was babbling incoherently, but not sure exactly what the real problem was.

"That was supposed to be your apartment," she said finally.

She heard Paul's sharp intake of breath. "I see. I didn't realize you were so anxious for me to move downstairs."

"It's not that, either."

"Are you upset because I just assumed you'd want me to stay up here with you?" he asked patiently.

"No. It's…it's the garden." The minute she'd said it, she felt absolutely ridiculous, but she knew it was the truth. She loved that garden. She'd been waiting for the day in the spring when it would be blooming just beyond their living room window.

"What?" Paul said, clearly baffled.

"I wanted the garden to be ours."

"It is ours."

"No. It will be theirs."

"Did you want us to move downstairs? Is that it?"

She smiled shakily. "Silly, isn't it? I guess that is what I wanted. We worked on that apartment together. I picked out the paint and the Formica for the kitchen. I sanded those floors. I thought of it as ours."

"But you worked so hard to decorate this one. I guess I thought you'd rather stay here. I can always tell Ted and Kathy that this is the one for rent."

"That's dumb. This is a perfectly wonderful apartment and you're right, we have gotten it fixed up just the way we wanted it…except for the tub in the kitchen, that is. And Kathy shouldn't have to climb all those stairs."

"Does that mean it's okay with you, if we rent to them?"

"Yes."

His fingers stroked even more possessively across her abdomen. "I'm glad it matters to you where we live," he said softly. "But the main thing is, we're still going to be together. I have to admit that we got past a big hurdle tonight."

Yes, she thought, allowing herself to indulge in a feeling of contentment at last. That was one thing that had come out of tonight. They were together, bound more inextricably than ever.

"I had a talk with your friend Theresa," she told him. "She wants to pay me to help her decorate her place."

"That's great. Are you going to do it?"

"I thought it might be fun. At least it'll keep me busy until I finally decide what I want to do."

"Maybe this is what you should be doing with the rest of your life," he suggested slowly, as if trying to gauge her reaction. "You enjoy it. There's a need for it."

"Don't be silly. This is just a one-shot deal. It'll keep me from going crazy until I find real work."

"Maybe," he said, but there was a more hopeful look in his eyes than she'd ever seen before.

"You really think this could be the answer for me, don't you?"

"Think about it. You seemed awfully happy when you were fixing this place up. You were excited every time you discovered some treasure buried in a second-hand store. Isn't that what a career should be? Something that's fun, as well as lucrative?"

"But this is more like a hobby."

"Only because you've treated it that way. It doesn't have to be. It could be good for us, too."

She drew in a deep breath. "What do you mean?"

"It's something we could do together. It would be a natural. You could think up some jazzy little name for the business, even print up cards. When I do jobs, people are always asking me if I know anyone who does decorating for less than an arm and a leg. We could specialize in low-cost but very classy renovations."

"You might be right. It would put us on an equal footing," she said thoughtfully, unaware of Paul's sudden tension.

"Meaning?"

"It would put an end to this hang-up you have about me being better than you."

Paul pushed her aside and stood up, his expression furious. "Dammit, you just don't get it, do you?"

"What's wrong?" she asked as he paced around the room, raking his fingers through his hair.

"Can't you see that this has nothing to do with putting us on an equal footing economically? I want you to be happy. If going back to a brokerage house, putting in endless hours and developing ulcers in a quest for a six-figure income makes you happy, then go for it. My ego can stand it if you make ten times what I do. I love you, Gabrielle. I'm not trying to own you."

Breathless and wide-eyed, she stared at him. "You love me?"

He stopped pacing and stood gazing down at her. "I suppose I do," he said as if the thought had just made itself very plain for the first time.

A soft smile began slowly, then blossomed across her face. That warm, melting feeling played havoc with her senses. "Then why are you so far away, when you could be down here holding me?"

After a hesitation that went on so long it almost frightened her into thinking he was having second thoughts, he moved back to her side at last. She knew as his lips came down hard on hers that simply saying the words did not assure them of an easy time of it from now on, but it was a start. With their feelings out in the open, they could finally begin to make decisions about what was best not just for them as individuals, but for the two of them together. It was unlikely that they would always agree, but they were learning the art and rewards of communication and compromise.

For now, though, his mouth was hot and urgent against hers and problems that might creep up in the future were the last thing on her mind.

Chapter Ten

Gabrielle found that decorating Theresa's apartment was an entirely different challenge from selecting the pieces for her own place. The artist's bold personality required more vibrant colors, more unorthodox accessories. Her search for the right things led to the discovery of even more stores that stocked inexpensive used furniture, carpet remnants and even cast-off, unrestored antiques.

She came home every day exhausted, but filled with enthusiasm. Her once well-manicured nails had long since chipped and broken so badly that she had to keep them short and unpolished. She usually had tiny spatters of paint on her eyelashes or the tip of her nose. She rarely dressed in anything fancier than jeans. Her hair was usually pulled back into a simple ponytail. Her arms were constantly sore from hauling her finds home to be repaired and then to Theresa's. Equally filthy and bone-weary, she and Paul fought over the hot water in the evening, more often than not sharing the old-fashioned, oversize tub and a bottle of wine as they talked about their days. She'd never looked less sophisticated or felt a greater sense of contentment in her life.

One night Paul found her already deep in scented bubbles, the kitchen filled with a pattern of soft colors cast from a beautiful Tiffany lamp she'd spent the afternoon cleaning up.

"I like the atmosphere," he said quietly, standing in the doorway.

Her skin tingled just from the heated expression in his eyes. "Join me," she suggested.

Without taking his eyes from hers, he dropped his toolbox on the floor and began stripping off his clothes. The sheepskin jacket fell first, followed by his plaid flannel shirt. He tugged his T-shirt from the waistband of his jeans, then lifted it over his head, baring an expanse of chest matted with dark whorls of hair. Work boots were kicked off, then socks tossed aside. His fingers lingered at the snap on his jeans, his eyes filling with amusement as he teased her with a deliberate delay.

Gabrielle took a slow sip of wine and watched, her heart thumping unsteadily in her chest. Lord, the man was gorgeous. She wondered if there would ever be a day when the sight of him didn't set off sparks deep inside her. He stripped off the jeans at last, then the jockey shorts as her breathing set a pace just short of ecstasy.

He slid into the tub, his legs stretched intimately

alongside hers. Pink and aqua lights danced across the bubbles.

"Where'd you find the lamp?"

"Hmm?" she murmured, reluctant to shift to a more impersonal mood.

"The lamp," he said, grinning.

She tried to tamp down her wildly vivid imagination, which was far removed from lamps. "Down near the Bowery." Her voice still had a whispery quality.

He stared at her, horrified. "Gaby, I don't want you going down there."

The delicious mood vanished at once as his sharp tone registered. "It's safe enough in the daytime," she said, then added pointedly, "it's certainly not that much worse than this neighborhood."

Her stubborn independence had become a frequent source of minor irritation to him. He was beginning to learn, though, that his objections only caused her to dig in her heels. She restrained a grin now as he reluctantly swallowed more protective advice.

"Are we keeping the lamp?" he asked finally, conceding the argument. "It doesn't look like it would fit with what you've been getting for Theresa."

"No and it doesn't really fit with what we have here, either, but the price was too good to pass up."

"Maybe that's because some of the glass is missing."

For a man who'd bought a run-down building and envisioned these wonderful apartments, he was amazingly short-sighted about potential when it came to her finds. "Obviously," she agreed. "But last week I found a woman who does work with stained glass. I think she'll give me a deal on fixing it. I'm taking it over tomorrow."

"And then what?"

"And then I'll have it in case I ever need it."

Paul grinned. "Need it for what?"

She splashed water at him with her foot. "Stop pushing. I haven't decided yet about the business."

"Haven't you?"

"Paul, there might never be another soul who wants to hire someone just to shop the secondhand stores for them."

"I have a customer now who's interested," he said nonchalantly, gazing up at the pattern of lights on the ceiling as if her response weren't of the slightest interest to him. It was one of his more infuriating methods for manipulating her.

"If you're not too busy," he added. "I've told him you're pretty booked."

Her curiosity was instantly aroused, just as he'd known it would be. She deliberately ran her foot down his chest to get his attention.

"Okay, don't stop now, you rat. Who is it? What is the place like? What kind of look is he after? What sort of budget does he have?"

He met her gaze with feigned surprise. "I take it you're interested after all."

"Don't smirk. I'll talk to him."

"Not just him, Gaby. Don't you think it's time you named this business and printed up cards? I'll bet those stores you've been patronizing would even hand them out for you."

She considered the possibility thoughtfully. The idea was beginning to intrigue her more than she'd been willing to admit. "They might," she conceded.

"Then why are you hesitating? Are you afraid of failing? You have a sound business mind. You must see that the opportunity is there, if you want it. You'd be offering a unique service. I'm sure Theresa will spread the word and I have plenty of customers who'll jump at the chance to have someone decorate for them at a reasonable cost."

"I suppose you're right, but what if I get bored with this, the way I did with Wall Street? So far it's been fun, but I've only done our place and Theresa's."

Paul captured her foot and kissed her toes. His fingers massaged away the last of the soreness and the kisses sent waves of heat spiraling through her. It was a fantastic distraction.

"Then you'll do something else," he said when she'd almost forgotten the question. "It's not as if this will require a major capital investment that will be at risk. How much can business cards cost? You don't have to worry about inventory or the overhead of office space. You don't even have to buy a fancy wardrobe. Your expenses will be at a minimum."

"My parents—"

"Have nothing to do with this decision," he said firmly. "Besides, don't they want you to be happy? They'll probably be thrilled to hear that you've started your own business."

Gabrielle had her doubts about that. They might approve of her operating a discreet, exclusive antique store in the center of old Charleston. But they would die of shame if they ever saw the run-down places she visited to find her bargains. They'd also probably hire a body-guard to trail around after her.

But she could not live her life for her parents. She'd known that when she'd left South Carolina and it was no less true now. She finally gave free rein to the excitement that had been building inside her ever since they'd first discussed the idea. She grinned at Paul. "Let's go for it."

"I assume you're referring to the business," he said as his fingers trailed a blazing path up her leg. Her breath caught in her throat.

"That, too," she said in a voice suddenly slowed by desire.

"Want to talk about the details?" he inquired as he did something particularly magical to the back of her knee.

"Later," she murmured weakly.

"Smart woman. It's nice to know that your priorities remain in order now that you're a career woman again," he said as he lifted her from the tub and carried her down the hall. She was too busy running her tongue along the rivulets of water on his neck to reply.

Second Chances, despite certain personal distractions that occasionally took precedence, turned into a flourishing business. Paul and Gabrielle had more work than they could handle. The commissions weren't huge, but the satisfaction was tremendous and working with Paul gave her new respect for his talent at renovation.

He did caring, conscientious work and his customers appreciated it.

On a personal level, their lives had meshed so completely that she couldn't imagine a future without Paul. She'd found her ideal mate, a man who was strong and supportive and caring, in the most unlikely place of all. She was still in his arms early one morning when she received a frantic phone call from Ted.

"What on earth is wrong?" she asked at once. "You're babbling. Slow down. Is it Kathy?"

"No. It's you. You're going to kill me."

The genuine panic in his voice made her very nervous. Ted was the calmest man she'd ever met. "Would you please just tell me what's wrong?"

"It's your parents."

Oh, hell. "What about my parents?"

"They're here."

Shock and dismay swept through her. "Here? In New York?"

"Yes, in New York." He took a deep breath, while Gabrielle's breath stopped. "Actually they're in this office. I got in a few minutes ago and they were already here waiting for you."

"At seven-thirty?"

"Gabrielle, you used to be in the office by seven," he reminded her. "They expected to find you here."

"What have you told them?"

"I haven't said anything yet, except that I'd try to reach you. No one else had the nerve to tell them you didn't work here anymore."

She swallowed hard. "Do you think they've figured it out?"

"Not yet, but they're beginning to guess that something's wrong. Your father's pacing and I've seen that expression before. It's the one he had on his face when he lost the vote on that health care amendment. I can't stall them much longer. They wanted me to give them your new number."

Paul had remained silent up until now, but he suddenly took the phone from her hand. "Ted, what's the problem?"

While Gabrielle pulled her knees to her chest, wrapped her arms around her legs and shivered uncontrollably, Paul extracted information from Ted. She was barely listening. This was her worst nightmare come true. She should have told her parents weeks ago. She could have sent a letter. She could have done almost anything except what she'd done, which was to hide from the truth in Brooklyn. She'd been living in a make-believe world.

She tuned back into the phone call just as Paul said, "Fine. Send them over."

"No," Gabrielle yelped, grabbing for the phone. "Ted, you can't send them here. Tell them I'll meet them at the Waldorf or the Plaza, anyplace they like in an hour. I need to explain things to them."

"You can do that here," Paul said quietly.

She saw the ominous look in his eyes, the stiff set of his jaw and flinched. This was something she couldn't give in about, though. She had to see them alone. She could not expose Paul to an outpouring of their anger and dismay. She could not risk their disdain of the life she and Paul had built together. Once she'd explained, told them how well things were going for her now, how much she loved Paul, maybe it would be okay. They weren't unfeeling ogres, for heaven's sake.

Clenching the phone so tightly her hand hurt, she repeated, "Tell them I'll meet them."

They agreed on the Palm Court at the Plaza at nine. She hung up, more shaken than she'd ever been in her life. Not even her announcement of her plan to move to New York had terrified her like this.

"If you do it this way, we don't have a chance," Paul said.

"It's the only way I can do it. I have to prepare them."

"For what? Your great come-down in life? Me?"

"I don't mean it like that," she said miserably.

"How do you mean it? What you're doing sounds exactly like what someone who's ashamed of her life would do."

She looked at it through Paul's eyes and understood why he felt that way. "Please, try to understand. I just want it to be perfect when they meet you. I'll explain everything and then I'll invite them over for dinner tonight. Is that all right?"

He nodded reluctantly. "I suppose that will have to do."

She slid her arms around his waist and rested her head against his chest. "I do love you."

He sighed heavily. "I know, Gaby. I'm just not sure it's enough."

Gabrielle walked into the Plaza with her shoulders squared and her head held high. Only she knew that an army of butterflies had been allowed to fly free in her stomach.

She saw her parents at once. Her father's steel-gray hair, florid complexion and ramrod straight posture were unmistakable. Her mother looked like an exquisite doll beside him. She was patting his hand, a familiar gesture that usually meant her father was about to explode and her mother was trying to forestall it. As she approached, her mother's face flooded with relief.

"Gabrielle, darling, here you are at last."

She bent over to give her mother a kiss. "I'm early," she said in response to the implied criticism. She felt herself regressing automatically to six-year-old status and pulled herself together.

"You know your father. He has absolutely no patience. He was furious when we got in last night and he realized we wouldn't be able to reach you until this morning. Then when you weren't at the office... Well, thank heavens, that nice young man was there."

"Ted." Gabrielle looked at her father and saw the affection in his eyes that counterpointed his scowl. She gave him a kiss. "Hi, Daddy. Why didn't you let me know you were coming?"

"How the hell were we supposed to do that?" he grumbled. "It was a last-minute thing. You know I don't approve of personal calls at work and you haven't seen fit to give us your new phone number."

"Sorry, Daddy," she said, sitting down gratefully and grabbing a menu before she could start wallowing in apologies. "Have you ordered yet? I'm starving."

"No, dear. We've been waiting for you."

"Why weren't you in the office, Gabrielle?" her father demanded. She'd wondered how long it would take for him to get to the point, but she still wasn't prepared for the question.

"You've been fired, haven't you?" he said when she didn't respond.

"Yes," she said, meeting his gaze evenly. This was it. The next few minutes would decide once and for all if she was a grown-up, independent woman or a coward.

Her mother gasped. "Darling, why didn't you tell us? We would have helped. Your father has contacts, I'm sure."

"I didn't want to use Daddy's contacts. I knew I could handle things myself."

"But what are you doing for money? That's why you moved, isn't it? You were running out of money. Oh, dear heavens, Gabrielle, you're not living in some awful place with cockroaches, are you?"

Gabrielle grinned despite herself. "No. Actually the apartment is quite nice. It's a renovated brownstone in Brooklyn."

Her mother turned pale at that. She'd barely accepted the idea of Manhattan. Brooklyn was beyond her imagination. None of her friends ever visited Brooklyn. They rarely got beyond the Plaza and Fifth Avenue.

"Is it safe?" her father demanded at once.

"Safe enough. And…" She couldn't meet their eyes. "Actually, I have a roommate."

"Another stockbroker?"

"No."

"One of your friends from school?" her mother said hopefully.

"No. It's someone I met when I first moved in." She'd gotten this far. She might as well go for the rest. "It's a man and I'm very much in love with him. He's a contractor. He does renovations."

"Oh, my," her mother said, waving her napkin to stir a breeze. She did look ready to faint. Gabrielle encouraged her to take a sip of water.

"I'm fine, dear. It's just that this is such a surprise."

"Shock would be more like it," her father growled. "Who is this man? What do you know about him? What's his family like? I hope you've looked at his background very carefully, Gabrielle. A woman in your position can't be too careful. It would be just like some con artist to take advantage of you because of me."

"Actually, Paul didn't even know you were my father until quite recently. He wasn't wild about it."

"What!" Her mother was aghast. "Why on earth not?"

"Because he's a wonderful, sensitive man. He sensed that you would disapprove of him because he's not rich and powerful. I'd like it very much if you would help me prove him wrong. I'd like you to come to dinner tonight."

"Like hell we will," her father said. "I do not condone your living with a man, no matter what his financial status, without being married. It goes against everything I stand for."

"I'm not asking for your blessing, Daddy," she said with quiet finality. "This is what I want. You can either accept it or not. It's your decision. I'll understand if you feel it would put you in an uncomfortable position politically."

"Now, Gabrielle," her mother whispered in a shocked tone, instinctively reaching out to pat her husband's hand. "Your father is worried about you, not his political career."

"Then please come tonight," she said again. "I really think you'll like Paul, if you give him a chance."

"Is he keeping you?" her father said bluntly.

Gabrielle swallowed her fury and managed to say politely, "No, Daddy. We've started a business together. I'm earning my own way."

"What kind of business could you possibly do with a contractor?"

"We'll tell you all about it tonight. Will you be there?"

Her mother cast a look of entreaty toward her father. "Please."

He sighed heavily, then said with obvious reluctance, "Okay. We'll be there."

Once the shock of her news wore off, they spent the rest of the meal catching up on other gossip from home. Gabrielle gave them her address, then went home to prepare a dinner that hopefully would soothe her father into a more receptive mood.

It might have been better, she thought later, if she'd fed him tranquilizers. From the minute her parents walked through the door, the tension was so thick it would have taken an ax to chop through it. Everyone was so incredibly polite, she felt like choking.

Her parents found her apartment *quaint*. The word was said with a slightly disdainful sniff. Paul congratulated her father on a recent victory in the Senate. She knew it was for a bill with which he violently disagreed, but he kept his own opinion in check. Her mother found Paul *charming*. That was said with a subtle lift of her eyebrows, meant to be seen only by her father. Naturally Paul saw it as well and the lines of tension around his mouth deepened. And then there were the less than subtle comments about Townsend, how devastated he was over the broken engagement, what a wonderful future he had, how often his family inquired about Gabrielle.

The final blow for Gabrielle came when they pointedly wondered when she'd be coming home to stay. It was as if they hadn't heard a single word she'd said that morning.

Shocked and infuriated by the blatant rejection of her life with Paul, she said, "I'm not coming home. I thought I'd made that clear this morning."

"But, dear, you can't go on living this way," her mother said, twisting her napkin nervously.

"What way is that, Mrs. Clayton?" Paul said.

Gabrielle heard the restrained fury in his voice and waited for the explosion. Her mother, however, hadn't been a politician's wife for thirty years for nothing.

"Paul, it's not that we don't appreciate your giving Gabrielle a place to stay," she said, immediately reducing his status to that of Good Samaritan. "Nor is it that we think your apartment isn't lovely. You've done an interesting job of fixing it up."

There was that word, Gabrielle thought with a groan. *Interesting*.

"Actually, your daughter is responsible for the decor,"

Paul replied with obvious pride. "She's becoming quite a success as a decorator."

Her mother looked startled. Gabrielle shot a guilty look at Paul. "I hadn't told them about the business yet."

"I see," he said heavily.

Gabrielle heard the defeat in his voice, but had no idea how to reassure him short of turning the dinner into a family shouting match. She listened to her father's patronizing remarks and her mother's weak attempts to pacify everyone and saw Paul fighting to remain calm.

"Perhaps I'd better leave," Paul said finally. "I'm sure you have things you'd like to discuss without an outsider present."

"Paul," Gabrielle protested helplessly as he grabbed his jacket and strode to the door.

"We'll talk later," he said curtly. "Good night, Mr. and Mrs. Clayton."

Gabrielle watched Paul go and knew the greatest fear she'd ever known, greater than losing her job, greater even than losing her family's support. And it made her blazing mad, at her parents and most of all at herself. Paul had chosen to act charitably and ignore her parents' rudeness, rather than fight back. She should have had the courage to defend not only him, but their relationship.

"How dare you?" she said, turning on her parents the minute Paul had left.

"What did we do?" her mother asked in seemingly genuine bewilderment.

"You've just spent most of the evening putting Paul down. Putting both of us down. Even after Paul mentioned our business, you weren't interested enough to ask about it. You've just confirmed for him what he's always feared, that he's not good enough for me." She gulped back a sob. "Well, you're wrong. He is good enough. He's better than either one of you."

Her mother gasped and her father looked more furious than she'd ever seen him.

"Young lady, you will apologize to your mother and me at once."

"I will not. You have been unforgivably rude to a man I love."

Her mother seemed to rally. "Darling, we certainly never meant to insult Paul."

"Gabrielle knows that," her father said. "The man has to understand that we're just looking out for your welfare. Now Townsend—"

"I don't want to hear one more word about Townsend," she snapped. "You say you just want the best for me. Has it occurred to either of you yet that what I have right now might be the best for me? Have you been paying any attention at all to what's been going on here tonight? I've never been happier. I love Paul. I hope to God he loves me enough to forgive your behavior. This is where my life is now, not in Charleston and certainly not with Townsend."

Her father reached for her hand. Without the bolstering effect of his anger, he looked older. To her amazement he even looked a little bit afraid. "Gabrielle, honey, your mother and I just worry about you. This isn't what we envisioned for you."

"It's not what I envisioned, either, but Paul is what's

best for me. I've never been more certain of anything in my life. He's encouraged me to discover who I really am, rather than to rebel against what I don't want to be."

"What about Wall Street? You were so dead set on that once," her father reminded her.

"Maybe it was because I knew you and mother would hate it. I saw the life you had in mind for me, married to Townsend, spending my days doing dull, boring, predictable things and I reached out for the one thing that I knew was more exciting. I always envied you going off to work every day, while mother had to stay at home."

"But I love being at home," her mother protested.

"I know you do," Gabrielle said more gently. "And I guess that's what we all need to realize. Each of us is entitled to make our own happiness, whatever it is. Mine is with Paul, with this new business of ours."

"You really are sure about this, pet?" her father said, squeezing her hand. He searched her eyes for an answer.

"I really am."

"Then I suppose that will have to be good enough for me. We'll wait with you until Paul comes back. We'll explain that we were wrong."

One thing about her father, when he'd been convinced of something, he gave it his full-fledged support. She got up and kissed him. "Thank you, Daddy, but no. I think we'd better be alone. I'll call you in the morning. Maybe we can get together again before you leave."

"I'd like that," her father said. "I'd like to get to know this man you love. He must be something for you to care this much."

"He is, Daddy. He's pretty special."

Her parents left then amid more apologies and promises to be available for any plans she and Paul wanted to make with them.

Left unspoken was Gabrielle's greatest fear: that the apologies might be too late, that Paul might not come back to her at all.

Chapter Eleven

When Paul left the apartment, he walked aimlessly for a while, then got into his car. His stomach was in knots. He couldn't think straight. Only once before in his life had he felt this lost and defeated and furious. Not since he and Christine Bently Hanford had stood under a starry sky, and she'd stared at him in astonishment as she laughed at his proposal. He had felt like such a fool. In all these years since that humiliating night, he had never felt such gut-wrenching inadequacy. He had avoided any situation, any person likely to put him at such a disadvantage again.

Until Gabrielle. Until this beautiful, vulnerable woman had come along and convinced him that what they had together could survive anything. But not this, he thought angrily. Gabrielle's parents had dismissed him as casually as they might a servant. Worse, he had tolerated it, which didn't say much for his character or for his sense of self-worth. How would Gabrielle ever respect him after this?

Without realizing where he was headed, he found himself on his way to Long Island. Maybe there were answers to be found in the past. Maybe he needed to link these two failures in his mind in order to walk away from Gabrielle with his dignity intact.

One thing he knew for certain after tonight: he had to walk away. He would not allow her to be subjected to the kind of pressure her parents had exerted tonight. It wasn't fair to expect her to give up so much for a life with him. She ought to go back to Townsend and all the advantages she could have in Charleston.

He turned into the gate of the Hanford estate and drove to his parents' cottage without once looking in the direction of the main house. The cottage lights were still on, which meant his mother was probably up knitting while his father slept in an easy chair, a book open on his chest. He glanced in a window at the familiar scene and smiled. It gave him an odd sense of continuity.

He tapped on the door and heard his father's startled, "What's that?"

"I'll get it, John. Put your shoes on." His mother opened the door a crack and peeked out. "Paul!"

Her round, wrinkled face lit with pleasure and she enfolded him in plump arms. She smelled of talcum powder and a vague hint of cinnamon. She'd probably baked a coffee cake for the Hanfords' breakfast, he thought, recalling how Christine had loved it. As a child she'd often stolen a portion from the breakfast table for him, then they'd shared it as they sat side by side in the tree house his father had built for them in a giant oak.

His father was on his feet now, moving more slowly than he'd remembered. Years of kneeling on cold, damp ground had made his knees stiff. "Boy, what brings you out here at this hour on a weeknight? Everything okay?"

"Give him a minute to settle down," his mother chided. "Come into the kitchen. I've just baked a coffee cake. We'll have that and I'll make a fresh pot of coffee."

"What will the Hanfords do in the morning, if we eat their breakfast?" Paul asked.

"They'll get oatmeal. It's better for Mr. Hanford anyway," she said, giving him a conspiratorial grin.

Within minutes they were settled around the kitchen table as they had been a thousand times in the past. It was where family decisions were always made, amid good food and gentle love.

"Work going okay?" his father asked, probing carefully.

"Fine, Pop. I have more business than I can handle." He hesitated, then added, "I'm working with someone now."

"Oh?"

He began, then, to tell them about Gabrielle and Second Chances, about the jobs they'd done, about her talent and enthusiasm.

"She's more than a business partner, isn't she?" his mother asked with her incredible perceptiveness. "You're in love with her."

He grinned ruefully. "It's that plain?"

"It is to me. You don't come home talking about casual friends with that special gleam in your eyes. You haven't looked that way since…" She broke off uneasily.

"Since Christine. You can say it, Ma."

"You're better off without her. Surely you see that, son," his father said. "She'd have brought you nothing but misery. She was spoiled rotten by her daddy. Maybe that wasn't her fault, but it turned her into a user. She took from you without paying no mind to your feelings. She deserves that empty, cold marriage she's found herself in."

It was not the first time Paul had heard references to Christine's unhappiness, but he found that at last it meant nothing. He simply felt sorry for her, as he would for anyone trapped in an impossible situation of their own making.

"Are you going to marry this Gabrielle?" his mother asked.

"I don't think so, Ma. She's…she's a lot like Christine."

His mother gasped softly and frowned. His father looked just as worried. "Now, son, you're too old to be needing advice from me, but I've got to warn you—"

He held up his hand. "It's okay. You don't need to say it. I met her parents tonight and I think I finally realized why it wouldn't work. She'd be caught between us."

His mother stirred her coffee, her expression thoughtful. "Does that mean you think she's in love with you?"

"She says she is."

"But you said…"

"When I said she was like Christine, I didn't mean she was selfish. I just meant that she comes from the same kind of privileged background. Her father's Senator Graham Clayton, for God's sake. He could hand her the world on a platter."

His parents exchanged another worried glance. "But she's satisfied with what you can give her?" his mother asked quietly.

"She claims she is, but *I* can see it's not enough. She deserves all those things she can have if she goes back to South Carolina. Until tonight I'd been able to ignore the fact that I was denying her things that should rightfully be hers."

"If you walk out of her life, do you honestly think that's what she'll do? Will she go home?"

He stared at his mother and thought of Gabrielle's determination to make her own way, her absolute refusal to consider going back or even accepting help from home. It was a perspective he hadn't considered. "No. I don't suppose she would."

"Is she smart?"

He grinned at that. "A hell of a lot smarter than I am at times."

"Then she wouldn't do something dumb like staying with you, if she thought it was wrong for her, now would she?"

He laughed and suddenly the doubts began to dissipate. "I don't suppose she would."

"And she's smart enough to recognize a decent, caring man?"

He stood up, pulled his mother from her chair and swung her around. "Thanks, Ma."

He bent down and gave his father a kiss that left a startled but pleased look on his face. "If this works out, I want you to come to dinner with us on Sunday."

"No ifs. It will work out. You bring her here," his mother countered. "I'll make pot roast."

"No. I want you to sit back and enjoy a meal for a change. Besides, you haven't seen the apartment since we fixed it up." He grinned at his father. "And I think Gabrielle would love your ideas for the garden. It seems she aspires to a green thumb. She's got bulbs scattered all over the place and can't decide where to plant them. If we don't get them in the ground soon, I'm liable to cook them for dinner one night by mistake."

"If you want to make us really happy on Sunday, you'll announce your engagement. I'm ready for some grandbabies to take care of."

"I'll do my best, Ma."

He drove home with a silly, expectant grin on his face. He and Gabrielle were going to work this out. He would do his best to win over her parents, but he wasn't marrying them.

Marrying?

Well, hell, wasn't that what this was all about? He'd been half-crazy in love with the woman from the first minute she'd appeared on his doorstep with her fox coat, stubborn chin and vulnerable eyes. He admired her strength and honesty. He thrilled to her sharp wit. And he cherished her gentleness. The images that flashed through his mind now weren't of a sophisticated, stylishly dressed woman, but of Gabrielle with paint on the tips of her eyelashes, hands that smelled of turpentine and a smile that grew at the sight of him. Yes, marrying was definitely what this was all about. He was whistling when he went up the stairs at 2:00 a.m., the future as clear to him and as filled with promise as it could possibly be.

The only light on in the apartment was the Tiffany lamp in the kitchen. He found Gabrielle in her bed, her cheeks still damp with tears. Had they been for him or for the life she'd given up?

Filled with wonder by her beauty, he gazed down at the hair spread across the pillow like threads of gold. He traced the full curve of lips still pouty from the urgent kisses he'd stolen before her parents' arrival. Such a passionate, giving lover. He'd never imagined such ecstasy was possible, not for anyone, much less him.

But, despite the optimism he'd felt with his parents and on the long ride home, he wondered fleetingly if he was wrong. Could this really last? After the initial period of adjustment, he and Gabrielle had lived together in almost perfect harmony for these past weeks. But he'd always felt the arrangement was temporary. It was as if she was simply on loan to him, as if she could be taken away at any instant and returned to her rightful place in the world.

Suddenly he wanted, no, *needed* a commitment. Until now Gabrielle had been the one in search of new goals and possibilities. He had encouraged the search, but done very little to assure his own place in her future. Tonight had changed that in some immeasurable way. The link between them, always unspoken, but always at the center of his thoughts, had to be forged now into something lasting. If he lost her after this, he knew with absolute certainty that he would never find a replacement to equal her.

He brushed her cheek with a gentle caress, then slipped from the bed. He needed movement to keep pace with his thoughts. He glanced into his own sparsely furnished room and wondered if he'd ever be able to sleep there alone again. He wandered through the living room, touching the tables she had refinished with such love, the sofa she had spent days cleaning until the fabric was almost as bright as new. He paused at the round oak table, still set for a dinner that had very nearly caused him to run from the one thing that would make his life complete: Gabrielle's love.

He touched the china, the crystal, the silver, the linen napkins. All bore the unmistakable mark of wealth and good taste. Yet Gabrielle had seemed perfectly content for all this time with cheap plates and stainless steel utensils. She had adapted to his life-style with an ease and willingness that astounded him now that he saw this new evidence of what she'd been used to. Even more remarkable was the fact that with the trappings of money so close at hand, she had never once imposed them on him. Until last night, when she had wanted to do something special for the all-important first meeting between him and her parents.

His own compromises had been far less. In fact he'd done nothing to change his way of life to accommodate hers. If anything, he had taken advantage of her loss of income as a way of keeping her his economic equal. Consciously or unconsciously, he had been testing Gabrielle, waiting for her to fail, waiting for the moment when she railed at their modest life-style and demanded more. It made him sick to think how unfair he'd been.

So, tell her, he thought, staring out the window. Expose your own vulnerabilities for a change. Ask her to get married and see if she'll run or stay. It was, of course, the ultimate test.

As he peered into the darkness, telling himself it might be too soon to talk about a lasting, forever kind of love, too risky to make plans for the future, he saw the first flakes of snow drifting down. For the first time in his life, he saw them not as the promise of back-breaking chores, but as a hint of magic and beauty that had to be shared.

He went back to the bedroom, sat on the edge of the bed and shook Gabrielle gently. "Wake up."

A smile played across her lips, but her eyes remained tightly shut.

"Gaby."

"Mmm."

"Wake up. I want to show you something."

"You're back," she murmured with quiet surprise.

"I'm back," he confirmed.

"I'm glad." Her hand, still warm from resting beneath her cheek, crept into his and clung. Then she sighed contentedly and closed her eyes again.

"Sweetheart, wake up."

"Is it morning?"

"No."

She blinked, tried to focus her gaze, then patted his cheek. "Go back to sleep."

He shook his head and grinned. He went back into the living room where he'd tossed his jacket across a chair. Then he came back and pushed open her window. He wrapped the covers securely around Gabrielle and scooped her up in his arms. She nuzzled against his neck, murmuring her contentment. The brush of her lips against his skin almost made him forget his goal. It would be very easy to climb back into bed with her and go about waking her in an entirely different way.

But tonight was about more than their bond of physical love. It deserved a special kind of magic. Holding her tightly, he stepped out onto the fire escape.

The blast of cold air snapped her awake at once. She stared around blankly, her gaze finally locking with his. "Paul, what are we doing on the fire escape in the dark?" She glanced down, her eyes widening. "When I'm only wearing a blanket?"

"You'll see," he promised evasively.

"Are you planning to throw me off the roof?" she inquired calmly as he began climbing up the fire escape.

He grinned. "Not unless you give me any problems."

She nodded, yawning sleepily and nuzzling closer. "Good."

When they were on the roof, he stared around at the scattered lights, the inky sky, then lifted his face for the soft touch of snowflakes melting against his skin. "Look up," he told Gabrielle.

She held her head back and gazed at the sky. When the first snowflake caressed her cheek, she touched the spot with an expression of dawning understanding. Her eyes sparkled with delight as the snow began to fall more heavily.

"It's snowing," she said softly, her tone filled with awe. "The first time this winter."

Paul shook his head, feeling a stirring of amazement and happiness deep in his chest. "It's moondust."

She grinned at the whimsical statement. "There's no moon."

"Of course not," he explained patiently. "It's inside, being chipped into millions of specks of moondust. It only happens on special occasions."

"Oh, really," she said, laughing. "Which occasions are those?"

His gaze met hers and the sparks began to blaze, sparks so hot they endangered the snow. "When two people fall in love."

She gasped softly and her eyes filled again with wonder. "Oh, Paul. It's going to be okay after all, isn't it?"

Her lips sought his, warm and pliant and moist from the kiss of the moondust. There was magic in the kiss, a spell that dared him to go on, the words whispering across her mouth. "Marry me, Gabrielle."

Her answer was in the soft moan of pleasure, the hungry demand of her lips on his, the teasing invasion of her tongue.

"Is that a yes?" he asked, breathing heavily.

"Yes."

"We'll have problems," he warned.

"Never."

He'd never heard a more unrealistic claim, but he

loved her optimism. "We'll work them out," he corrected. "I may never be able to give you what you're used to. There won't be diamonds, just moondust."

"This," she said, curving her arms around his neck. "This is what I want to get used to. I was so afraid I'd lost you tonight. Do you have any idea how much you've given me, how empty my life would be without you?"

"I've given you?" he repeated incredulously.

"Of course. Hopes, dreams, belief in myself. Not to mention that I've never before been swept from my bed in the middle of the night to see the first snowfall."

"I should hope not."

"Don't make jokes. This is the most romantic proposal any woman could ever have. Our children will be awed and amazed that their practical, down-to-earth father did it."

"Our children?" he said weakly, thinking that his first cautious step was quickly turning into a race toward the future. He felt as though he'd put one tentative toe into an ocean and been caught up by the tide.

"They'll be beautiful," she promised, apparently captivated by the idea. "They'll be smart and creative. Very creative."

"Obedient?" he asked hopefully, the prospect beginning to take on a certain appeal for him, as well. His mother would be ecstatic.

"Stubborn," she said ruefully.

"No doubt. At the risk of sounding like I'm rushing things, how soon do you plan on expanding our family?"

"Well, it does take time," she said with just a hint of

regret. "I can't just go to the store in the morning and pick out two or three."

He chuckled. "I do know where they come from."

She touched his cheek. "From nights like tonight."

Emotion crowded his chest. Joy sang through his veins. He swallowed hard. "God, I love you."

"Show me, then. Take me inside and show me."

Inside, with the magic of moondust swirling around them, they found that little corner of heaven where dreams become reality.

Paul awoke in the morning to the touch of something very cold against his lips. His eyes snapped open to find Gabrielle kneeling on the bed beside him, her hands filled with snow. He grinned. "If you're planning to do what I think you're planning to do, forget it. I'm bigger and stronger and I will get even."

"It's moondust, remember? I'm saving it."

"It will have a very short life expectancy curled up in your hand like that."

Her expression sobered. "Will our love melt the same way someday, Paul?"

He pulled her down beside him. "No. Not if we don't let it."

"But you almost left me for good last night, didn't you?"

"Almost," he admitted. "But not because of anything you did. Not even because I didn't believe in our love."

"My parents?"

"Yes. They threw me. I realized how much I was asking you to give up."

"It's my decision, Paul. Yours and mine. My parents will learn to live with whatever we decide."

"I told you last night, I'll never be able to match the life you've left. Our children won't be wearing designer diapers and going to fancy preschools that teach piano to two-year-olds. Can you really accept that?"

"Designer diapers? Piano lessons?" she repeated incredulously. "That's really what's been worrying you, isn't it?"

His silence was answer enough. She went on. "Darling, if what I grew up with was so irresistible, do you think I would have left it? The only thing important for a relationship and for kids is love and the commitment to do the very best we can. We have that."

His hands caressed her cheeks as he searched her eyes. They were glowing with the truth of her love. "Then I guess there's just one thing left to do," he said.

"What's that?"

"Set a wedding date."

She threw herself into his arms. "I do love you," she said, dropping kisses over his face.

He swallowed hard, torn between laughter and desire. She tilted her head and stared at him. "This is a very serious moment in our lives, Paul Reed. What's so funny?"

"Your moondust is melting down my back."

An impish light flared in her eyes as she moved behind him. "We certainly won't want to lose any of that," she said seriously as her tongue set out to capture every drop.

"Umm, Gaby," Paul said as a shiver sped down his

spine. "Do you think we might want to keep some of this moondust in the freezer? It may be hard to come by in August and I'm definitely beginning to see several interesting uses for it."

She tangled her bare legs with his and ran her hands provocatively down his chest. "We can always use our imaginations."

Paul closed his eyes and absorbed the wicked sensations. She was right, he thought before giving himself entirely over to her touches. The moondust would always be with them and, if treasured, like diamonds it would only increase in value with time.

* * * * *

A MAN YOU CAN TRUST

Jo McNally

This book, with a Genuine Good Guy as a hero,
is dedicated to the memory of
a Genuine Good Guy—my dad. He was quietly,
yet fiercely, devoted to the people he loved.

I love and miss you, Dad.

Chapter One

The resort parking lot was quiet.

That was hardly surprising, since it was seven o'clock on a Monday morning.

But Cassandra Smith didn't take chances.

Ever.

She backed into her reserved spot but didn't turn the car off right away. She didn't even put it in Park. First, she looked around—checking the mirrors, making sure she was going to stay. Pete Carter was walking from his car toward the Gallant Lake Resort. He waved as he passed her, and she waved back, then pretended to look at something on the passenger seat as she turned off the ignition. Pete worked at the front desk, and he was a nice enough guy. He'd offer to walk her inside if she got out now. And maybe that would be a good idea. Or maybe not. How well did she really know him?

Her fingers tightened on the steering wheel. She was being ridiculous—Pete was thirty years her senior and happily married. But some habits were hard to shake, and really—why take the chance? By the time she finished arguing with herself, Pete was gone.

She checked the mirrors one last time before getting out of the car, threading the keys through her fingers in a move as natural to her as breathing. As she closed the door, a warm breeze brushed a tangle of auburn hair across her face. She tucked it back behind her ear and took a moment to appreciate the morning. Beyond the sprawling 200-room fieldstone-and-timber resort where Cassie worked, Gallant Lake shimmered like polished blue steel. It was encircled by the Catskill Mountains, which were just beginning to show a blush of green in the trees. The air was brisk but smelled like spring, earthy and fresh. It reminded her of new beginnings.

It had been six months since Aunt Cathy offered her sanctuary in this small resort town nestled in the Catskills. Gallant Lake was beginning to feel like home, and she was grateful for it. The sound of car tires crunching on the driveway behind her propelled her out of her thoughts and into the building. Other employees were starting to arrive.

Cassie crossed the lobby, doing her best to avoid making eye contact with the few guests wandering around at this hour. As usual, she opted for the stairs instead of dealing with the close confines of the elevator. The towering spiral staircase in the center of the lobby looked like a giant tree growing up toward the ceiling three stories above, complete with stylized copper leaves draping from the ceiling. The offices of Randall Resorts International were located on the second floor, overlooking the wide lawn that stretched to the lakeshore. Cassie's desk was centered between four small offices. Or rather, three smaller offices and one huge one, which belonged to the boss. That boss was in earlier than usual today.

"G'morning, Cassie! Once you get settled, stop in, okay?"

Ugh. No employee wanted to be called into the boss's office first thing on a Monday.

Blake Randall managed not only this resort from Gallant Lake, but half a dozen others around the world. It hadn't taken long for Cassie to understand that Blake was one of those rare—at least in her world—men who wore their honor like a mantle. He took pride in protecting the people he cared for. Tall, with a swath of black hair that was constantly falling across his forehead, the man was ridiculously good-looking. His wife, Amanda, really hit the jackpot with this guy, and he adored her and their children.

Blake was all business in the office, though. Focused and driven, he'd intimidated the daylights out of Cassie at first. Amanda teasingly called him Tall, Dark and Broody, and the nickname fit. But Cassie had come to appreciate his steady leadership. He had high expectations, and he frowned on drama in the workplace.

He'd offered her a job at the resort's front desk when she first arrived in Gallant Lake. It was a charity job—a favor to Cathy—and Cassie knew it. It took only one irate male guest venting at her during check-in for everyone to realize she wasn't ready to be working with an unpredictable public. She'd frozen like a deer in headlights. Once she moved up here to the private offices, she'd found her footing and had impressed Blake with her problem-solving skills. Because Blake hated problems.

She tossed her purse into the bottom drawer of her desk and checked her computer quickly to make sure there weren't any urgent issues to deal with. Then she made herself a cup of hot tea, loaded it with sugar and poured Blake a mug of black coffee before heading into his office.

He looked up from behind his massive desk and gave her a quick nod of thanks as she set his coffee down in front of him. Everyone knew to stay out of Blake's way until they saw a cup of coffee in his hand. He was well-known for not being a morning person. He took a sip and sighed.

"I was ready to book a flight to Barbados after hearing about the wedding disaster down there this weekend, but then I heard that apparently *I*—" he emphasized the one-letter word with air quotes "—already resolved everything by flying some photographer in to take wedding photos yesterday, along with discounting some rooms. Not at *our* resort, but at a *competitor*. I hear I'm quite the hero to the bride's mother, but I'll be damned if I remember doing any of it."

Blake's dark brows furrowed as he studied her over the rim of his coffee cup, but she could see a smile tugging at the corner of his mouth. The tension in her shoulders eased. Despite his tone, he wasn't really angry.

"The manager called Saturday looking for you," she explained. "Monique was in a panic, so I made a few calls. The bride's mother used the son of a 'dear family friend' to organize the wedding, instead of using our concierge service. The idiot didn't book the rooms until the last minute, and we didn't have enough available, which he neglected to mention to the bride's mom. Then he booked the photographer for the wrong date." She smiled at the look of horror on Blake's face. "We're talking wrong by a full month. It was quite a melodrama— none of which was our fault—but the bride is some internet fashion icon with half a million followers on Instagram. So we found rooms at the neighboring resort for the guests we couldn't handle, and convinced the wedding party to get back into their gowns and tuxes for a full photo shoot the day *after* the wedding, which was the fastest we could get the photographer there. Mom's happy. Bride's happy. Social media is flooded with great photos and stories with the resort as a backdrop. I assumed you'd approve."

Blake chuckled. "Approve? It was freaking brilliant, Cassie. That kind of problem-solving is more along the lines of a VP than an executive assistant. You should have an office of your own."

She still wasn't used to receiving compliments, and her cheeks warmed. When she'd first arrived, she'd barely been able to handle answering calls and emails, always afraid of doing something wrong, of disappointing someone. But as the months went by, she'd started to polish her rusty professional skills and found she was pretty good at getting things done, especially over the phone. Face-to-face confrontation was a different story.

This wasn't the first time Blake had mentioned a promotion, but she wasn't ready. Oh, she was plenty qualified, with a bachelor's degree in business admin. But if things went bad back in Milwaukee, she'd have to change her name again and vanish, so it didn't make sense to put down roots anywhere. She let Blake's comment hang in the air without responding. He finally shook his head.

"Fine. Keep whatever job title you want, but I need your help with something."

Cassie frowned when Blake hesitated. "What is it?"

"You know I hired a new director of security." Cassie nodded. She was going to miss Ken Taylor, who was retiring to the Carolinas with his wife, Dianne. Ken had taken the job on a temporary basis after Blake's last security guy left for a job in Boston. Ken was soft-spoken and kind, and he looked like Mr. Rogers, right down to the cardigan sweaters. He was aware of Cassie's situation, and he'd made every effort to make sure she felt safe here, including arranging her reserved parking space.

"Nick West starts today. I'd like you to work with him."

"Me? Why?" Cassie blurted the words without thinking. She laughed nervously. "I don't know anything about security!"

But she knew all about *needing* security.

Blake held up his hand. "Relax. I'm not putting you on the security team. He'll need help with putting data together and learning our processes. I need someone I can trust to make sure he has a smooth transition."

"So... I'm going to be *his* executive assistant instead of yours?" Her palms went clammy at the thought of working for a stranger.

"First, we've already established you're a hell of a lot more than my EA. And this is just temporary, to help him get settled in the office." Blake drained his coffee mug and set it down with a thunk, not noticing the way Cassie flinched at the sound. "He's a good guy. Talented. Educated. He's got a master's in criminal justice, and he was literally a hero cop in LA—recognized by the mayor, the whole deal."

A shiver traced its way down Cassie's spine. Her ex had been a "hero cop," too. Blake's next words barely registered.

"I'm a little worried about him making the shift from the hustle of LA to quiet Gallant Lake, but he says he's looking for a change of pace. His thesis was on predictive policing—using data to spot trouble before it reaches a critical point." That explained why Blake hired the guy. Blake was all about preventing problems before they happened. He did *not* like surprises. "It'll be interesting to see how he applies that to facility security. His approach requires a ton of data to build predictive models, and that's where you come in. You create reports faster than anyone else here."

Cassie loved crunching numbers and analyzing results. She started to relax. If Blake wanted her to do some research for the new guy, she could handle that.

"I also want you to mentor him a bit, help him get acclimated."

"Meaning…?"

"Amanda and I are headed to Vegas this week for that conference and a little vacation time. Nick's going to need someone to show him around, make introductions and answer any questions that come up. He just got to town this weekend, and he doesn't know anyone or anything in Gallant Lake."

"So what, I'm supposed to be his babysitter?"

Blake's brow rose at the uncharacteristically bold question.

"Uh, no. Just walk him around the resort so he's familiar with it, and be a friendly face for the guy." He leaned forward. "Look, I get why you might be anxious, but he's the director of security. That's about as safe as it gets."

Her emotions roiled around in her chest. She hated that her employer felt he had to constantly reassure her about her safety. Yes, the guy in charge of security *should* be safe. All men should be.

"Cassie? Is this going to be a problem?" The worry in Blake's eyes made her sit straighter in her chair. What was it Sun Tzu wrote in *The Art of War*? The latest in a long line of self-help books she'd picked up was based on quotes from the ancient Chinese tome.

Appear strong when you are weak…

"No, I'm sure it will be fine. And the data analysis sounds interesting. Does he know…?"

"About your situation? No. I wouldn't do that without your permission. I only told Ken because you'd just arrived and…"

She was hardly strong now, but she'd been a complete basket case back then.

"I understand. I don't think the new guy needs to know. I don't want to be treated differently."

Blake frowned. "I don't want that, either. But I do want you to feel safe here."

"I know, Blake. And thank you. If I change my mind, I'll tell him myself." She was getting tired of people having conversations about her as if she was a problem to be solved, no matter how well-meaning they were. "When will I meet him?"

"He's getting his rental house situated this morning, then he'll be in. I'm planning on having lunch with him, then giving him a quick tour. He dropped some boxes off yesterday. Can you make sure he has a functioning office? You know, computer, phone, internet access and all that? I told Brad to set it up, but you know how scattered that kid can be."

Two hours later, Cassie was finishing the last touches in West's office. The computer and voice mail were set up with temporary passwords. The security team had delivered his passes and key cards—his master key would open any door in the resort. Brad, their IT whiz, had been busy over the weekend, and a huge flat-screen hung on one wall. On it, twelve different feeds from the security surveillance room downstairs were scrolling in black and white. It looked like a scene straight out of some crime-fighter TV show.

A familiar voice rang out in the office. "Hel-lo? Damn, no one's here."

Cassie stepped to the doorway and waved to Blake's wife. "I'm here!"

Amanda Randall rushed to give Cassie a tight hug. Cassie *hated* hugs, but Amanda got a free pass. The woman simply couldn't help herself—she was a serial hugger. She was also Cassie's best friend in Gallant Lake. They'd bonded one night over a bottle of wine and the discovery they shared similar ghosts from their pasts. Other than that, the two women couldn't be any more different. Amanda was petite, with curves everywhere a woman wanted curves. Cassie was average height and definitely not curvy—her nervous energy left her with a lean build. Amanda had long golden curls, while Cassie's straight auburn hair was usually pulled back and under control. Amanda was a bouncing bundle of laughing, loving, hugging energy. Cassie was much more reserved, and sometimes found her friend's enthusiasm overwhelming.

"I brought chocolate chip cookies for everyone, but I guess you and I will have to eat them all." Amanda held up a basket that smelled like heaven.

"You won't have to twist my arm. Come on in and keep me company."

Amanda followed her into the new guy's office.

"Wow—this is some pretty high-tech stuff, huh?" Amanda walked over to the flat-screen and watched the video feeds change from camera to camera. One feed was from a camera in front of Blake and Amanda's stone mansion next door to the resort. The private drive was visible in the view from above their front door. "I really need to talk to Blake about those cameras. I don't like the feeds popping up in some stranger's office."

"Hasn't resort security always been responsible for the house, too?"

"I was never crazy about that, but Blake insisted. And it was different when it was Paul, whom I'd known from the first week I was here. And then Ken. I mean, he's like having a favorite uncle watching over the house. But some hotshot ex-cop from LA watching me and the kids coming and going?" Amanda shuddered. "I don't think so. Have you met him yet?"

"Who?"

"The new guy? Superhero cop coming to save us all? The one who has my husband drooling?"

"No, I haven't met him yet." Cassie set a stack of legal pads on the corner of the desk, opposite the corner Amanda now occupied as she devoured a cookie. "What do you know about him?"

"What *don't* I know? He's all Blake talked about this weekend. 'Nick is so brave!' 'Nick is so brilliant!' 'Oh, no! What if Nick doesn't like it here?' 'What if Nick leaves?'" Amanda acted out each comment dramatically, and Cassie couldn't help laughing. "But seriously, he *really* wants this guy to work out. You know Blake—he believes in preventing problems before they happen, and that wasn't Ken's strong suit. He's so anxious for this guy to be happy here that he actually suggested we skip our trip to Vegas so he could be here all week for *Nick*! That was a 'hell no' from me. We haven't been away together without the kids in ages."

Amanda finished off the last of her cookie, licking her fingers. "And this girl is ready to par-tay in Vegas, baby! Whatcha doin'?"

"Blake said Nick dropped off these boxes. I'll unpack them, and he can organize later." Cassie pulled the top off one of the boxes on the credenza. It was filled with books on criminal science and forensics. She put them on the bookshelves in the order they were packed. Police work was usually a life's calling. What made this guy walk away from it?

She stopped after pulling the cover off the second box. It contained more books and binders, but sitting on top was a framed photo. She lifted it out and Amanda came around the desk to study it with her.

It was a wedding portrait. The tall man in the image looked damned fine in a tuxedo, like a real-life James Bond. His hair was dark and cropped short, military style. His features were angular and sharp, softened only by the affectionate smile he was giving the bride. Her skin was dark and her wedding gown was the color of champagne. Her close-cropped Afro highlighted her high cheekbones and long, graceful neck. She was looking up at the man proudly, exuding confidence and joy. Cassie felt a sting of regret. When was the last time anyone thought that about her?

"Wow—are those two gorgeous or what?" Amanda took the silver frame from Cassie and whistled softly. "I wonder who it is." She turned the frame over as if there might be an answer on the back.

"I'm assuming it's Nick West and his wife."

"No. Blake told me he's single."

"Maybe she's an ex?"

Amanda rolled her eyes. "Who keeps photos like this of their ex? Maybe it's not him at all—could be a brother or a friend. But if it is Nick, he's hot as hell, isn't he?"

Cassie took the picture back and set it on a shelf. "I hadn't noticed."

"Yeah, I call BS on that. There isn't a woman under the age of eighty who wouldn't notice how hot *that* guy is. You'd better be careful, especially now that you're living in the love shack."

"The *what*?"

"Nora's apartment—we call it the love shack. First it was her and Asher. Then Mel moved in there and met Shane. And now *you're* there, so…"

Cassie's aunt had sold her coffee shop in the village to Amanda's cousin Nora a few years ago but still worked there part-time. The apartment above the Gallant Brew had been a godsend when it came vacant shortly after Cassie's arrival. But a *love shack*?

"I don't believe in fairy tales. And even if Nora's place *did* have magic powers, they'd be wasted on me." She started to pull more books out of the box, but Amanda stopped her.

"Hey, I'm sorry. I don't mean to push you. Sometimes my mouth gets ahead of my brain. But someday you're going to find someone…"

Cassie shook her head abruptly. "That ship has sailed, Amanda. I have zero interest in any kind of… whatever." She glanced back to the photo and studied the man's dark eyes, sparkling with love for the bride.

Her heart squeezed just a little, but she ignored it. "I can't take the chance. Not again."

"Not every guy is Don. In fact, there are millions of guys who *aren't* Don."

Amanda meant well, but they were straying onto thin and dangerous ice here. Cassie had wedding photos, too. They were packed away somewhere, and they showed a smiling couple just like this one. She'd been so innocent back then. And stupid. She was never going to be either again.

"Look, I have a ton of work to do, and this guy—my *coworker*—is going to be here any time now. No more talk about love shacks and hotness, okay?"

Amanda stared at her long and hard, her blue eyes darkening in concern. But thankfully, she decided to let it go. She picked up the basket of cookies. "Fine. I have to finish packing for the trip anyway. I'll leave these out on the coffee counter." She started to walk away, then spun suddenly and threw her arms around Cassie in an attack hug. "We leave in the morning, but we'll be back next week. If you need anything at all—*anything*—you call Nora or Mel and they'll be there in a heartbeat."

Cassie bit back the surprising rebuke that sat on the tip of her tongue. She was fed up with everyone hovering and fretting, but she knew it was her own damn fault. How many times had she called Amanda those first few months, crying and terror-stricken because of a bad dream or some random noise she heard? Sure, she'd changed her name and moved about as far away from Milwaukee as she could get, but Don was an ex-cop with all the right connections. That's why she kept a "go-bag" packed and ready at her door. She took a deep breath, nodded and wished Amanda a safe and fun trip. But after she left, Cassie was too agitated to sit at her desk. She ended up back in Nick West's office, unpacking the last box.

A little flicker of anger flared deep inside. It had been nudging at her more and more lately, first as an occasional spark of frustration, but now it was turning into a steady flame. She wanted her life back. She wanted a life where she could rely on herself and stand up for herself. She looked at the wedding photo again. She wanted a life where she smiled more. Where she didn't jump every time someone...

A shadow filled the doorway.

"Hey! Whatcha doin' in here?"

Chapter Two

Nick West knew he'd startled the woman, but he was just trying to be funny. It was a *joke*. He figured the auburn-haired stranger would jump, then they'd both have a good laugh as he introduced himself. Humor was always a good icebreaker, right?

He never figured she'd send a stapler flying at his head.

He managed to swat it down before it connected with his face, but it ricocheted off the corner of his desk and smacked him in the shin.

"Ow!" He hopped on one leg. "Damn, woman! I was just kidding around." He rubbed his throbbing shin, unable to keep from laughing at the way his joke had backfired on him.

But the woman wasn't laughing. She was wide-eyed

and pale, her chest rising and falling sharply. Her eyes were an interesting mix of green and gold. Her hair was a mix, too—not quite red, but more than just brown. It was pulled back off her face and into a low pony-tail. She was pretty, in a fresh-scrubbed, natural way. Then he noticed her hand, which was clutching a pair of scissors like she was getting ready to go all Norman Bates on him.

The desk was still between them, but he raised his hands as if she was holding a loaded gun. He'd already seen how good her aim was.

"Whoa, there! Let's dial it back a notch, okay? I'm Nick West and this is my office… I think. Am I in the wrong place?" The thought didn't occur to him until he said it out loud. Shit. Had he just burst into some woman's office and scared the bejesus out of her? What if this was the boss's wife? He'd heard Randall's wife was involved in the resorts somehow. Even if it wasn't her, traumatizing a coworker wasn't a good way to start his first day here.

The hand holding the scissors lowered and color came back to her previously white knuckles. She lifted her chin, but it trembled, and there was genuine fear in her eyes. It made him feel like a jerk.

"Look, I'm sorry. I was kidding around. I do that sometimes."

"You scared the hell out of me, and you did it on purpose!" Those green-gold eyes flashed in anger. "Is that how you plan on introducing yourself to everyone here? Because I've got news for you—it won't go over well." She reached up to push her hair behind her ear and took a steadying breath. "This *is* your office, Mr. West. I'm Cassie…um… Smith, and I'll be working with you. I was setting up your desk."

Great. He'd never had a secretary before, and he'd just traumatized the first one he got. *Smooth move, West.* He grunted out a short laugh, rubbing the back of his neck as he tried to figure out how to fix this mess.

"Let's rewind and start over, okay? You're my first secretary." He stopped when her eyes narrowed. "What? What'd I say wrong now?"

"I am *not* your secretary. I'm Mr. Randall's executive assistant, and I'll be supporting you with some of your projects. I'll provide data. I'll run reports. But I don't take dictation and I won't be fetching your damned coffee."

Well, well, well. The jumpy lady had a backbone after all. Nick knew how to be a good cop. He had no damned clue how to be a good executive.

"Not a secretary. Got it. Like I said, I'm new at this corporate thing. In LA, I had a dispatcher and a desk sergeant. Something tells me you'll be closer to the latter." He nodded down to her hand. "I'd be a lot happier if you'd put those down."

Cassie looked down and appeared surprised to see the scissors still in her hand. She dropped them to the desk like they were burning her.

"Sorry," she mumbled. She continued to look down, lost in thought.

Her body language was all over the place, causing his cop's sixth sense to kick in. First she was jumpy and defensive. Then proud and outspoken. And now, as she apologized, she visibly shrank. He didn't like timid women. They reminded him of victims, and he'd had his fill of victims. But then again, victims didn't fling staplers at people's heads.

"Don't apologize," he said. "That was a juvenile thing for me to do. I gotta remember I'm not in a police precinct anymore." And he'd never be in one again. He rubbed his thigh absently. Shoving that thought aside, he flashed her a rueful grin. "I'll probably need your help monitoring my corporate behavior."

She nodded, not returning the smile, but straightening a bit. "I don't like practical jokes, but I'm sure you'll do fine here. It's a good group of people, and they like to have fun."

Interesting. She said *they* like to have fun, not *we*. He looked around the office. He'd barely noticed it yesterday, just dropping off his boxes and checking in to his room to crash after the long cross-country drive. The view of Gallant Lake was sweet. The giant flat-screen on the wall with all the changing camera feeds was even sweeter. He saw the photo on the bookshelf and blinked. Jada. It was her death that chased him out of LA and into this new life. The picture was a reminder of how quickly good things could go bad.

A large hand clamped down on his shoulder from behind, and Nick restrained himself from spinning around swinging. Old habits were hard to break. In this case, it would have been especially bad, since it was his new boss.

"Sorry I missed your arrival, Nick. We had a guest giving the desk staff a hard time about the five movies on his room bill. Turns out his ten-year-old has a thing for superheroes and didn't realize movies are fifteen bucks a pop." There weren't many men who could make Nick tip his head back and look up, but Blake Randall was one of them. He was a few years older than Nick, but he had no doubt Randall could hold his own in a physical challenge. Blake spotted Cassie on the other side of the desk. "Oh, good, you've met Cassie. You're going to want to treat this girl right because she's the one who can make or break you, man."

Nick met Cassie's gaze. Her moods were as changeable as her eyes. Now that Blake was here, she was clearly more relaxed.

...she's the one who can make or break you...

Even after Blake's warning, Nick couldn't resist teasing her.

"Oh, don't worry, Blake. Cassie's made quite an impression already." Her eyes narrowed in suspicion. "She's already throwing things... I mean...*ideas*...at me." Her hands clenched into fists, and he was surprised his skin wasn't blistering under the heat of her glare. "She even took a stab at trying to define her job responsibilities."

Blake was oblivious to the tension buzzing in the room. "Trust me, there is no way to define her job duties. Cassie's always surprising you by doing more than expected." Nick's smirk grew into a wide smile.

"Yeah, she's full of surprises. Oh, look, the stapler fell off the desk." He bent over to pick it up from where it had landed earlier. He couldn't help wondering if exposing his back to the woman, with scissors still nearby, was a good idea. "We don't want the boss to think you were throwing things at me, now, do we?"

"No, we don't." She watched as he set the stapler on the desk. Her voice was cold as ice. "But Blake knows me well enough to know I'd never launch an unprovoked attack."

Nick looked up in surprise. *Touché.* She was playing along. He winked at her, and a little crease appeared between her brows.

Blake chuckled behind him. "I can't imagine Cassie throwing things at anyone." Her cheeks went pink, but Blake didn't seem to notice. "Come on, Nick, let's grab lunch and I'll make some introductions. Would you like to join us, Cass?"

"No, thanks. I have work to do. You and Mr. West go ahead and…"

"Mr. West?" Blake looked at Nick and frowned. "We're on a first-name basis up here, Nick."

"No problem. Cassie and I were joking around earlier and she's just trying to get a rise out of me." Now it was her turn to be surprised. She looked at him and her mouth opened, but she didn't speak.

For the first time, Blake seemed to pick up on the undercurrent of…something…that was swirling around them.

"Really?" He looked at Cassie with clear surprise. Apparently she wasn't known for cracking jokes. She gave Blake a quick nod and smiled. It was the first smile Nick had seen from her, and it was worth waiting for, even if it was aimed at someone else. Her whole face softened, and her eyes went more green than gold.

"You two go on to lunch, and let me get back to work, okay?"

His curiosity was definitely piqued. Cassie Smith had a story.

On Thursday morning, Cassie was still trying to put a finger on her riled-up emotions. It started before Nick West's arrival, so she couldn't place all the blame on him for this low rumble of frustration and anger that simmered in her. In no mood to deal with her tangled hair, she pulled it into a messy knot on top of her head and frowned at the mirror. Simple khakis, sensible shoes and a dark green Gallant Lake polo shirt. Practical attire for a busy day. She was giving Nick a tour of the grounds today and wanted to be able to keep up with his long strides.

The man was always in motion, leaving her constantly on edge. He paced when he talked and bounced when he sat. He had a foam basketball that he tossed around his office when he was alone in there, and it drove her crazy. Yesterday she'd moved her computer so her back was to his door, trying to avoid the distraction of the ball flying through the air. Nick started laughing the minute he walked into the office and saw the new arrangement, and laughed every time he walked by. *Jerk*.

She went downstairs in the loft apartment and poured herself a cup of tea, adding three spoonfuls of sugar. She usually joined Nora in the coffee shop before heading to the resort, but Nora had her hands full watching Amanda and Blake's teenaged son and toddler daughter this week. Mel might be down in the shop, but it was more likely Amanda's other cousin would be enjoying her coffee with her fiancé on the deck of their waterfront home. So Cassie fixed herself a bagel and sat at the kitchen island, feeling almost as restless as Nick West.

Ugh! She'd known the man only three days, and he was in her head constantly. His big laugh when he was kidding around with employees—who all seemed to adore both him and his practical jokes. The way he started every conversation with a booming "Hey! Whatcha doing?" The way he rapped the corner of everyone's desk sharply with his knuckles every time he passed it. Except hers. After the first time he did it and she'd squeaked in surprise, he'd left her desk alone.

But she hadn't managed to stop his infuriating running joke of putting her stapler—the bright blue one she'd flung at him on their first meeting—in a different place every day. Monday afternoon she'd found it on her chair. Tuesday, it was next to the coffee maker. And yesterday, when she attended a meeting in the surveillance room with Nick and the entire security staff, the blue stapler was sitting on the circular console that faced the wall of monitors. She spotted it immediately and turned to glare at him, only to find him laughing at her. *Ass.*

Sure enough, when she walked into the office later that morning, the stapler was sitting next to a small vase of daffodils on her desk. Wait. Where did the daffodils come from? The sunny flowers were in a simple vase, which on closer inspection turned out to be a water glass.

"They reminded me of you, slugger."

Nick West was leaning against the doorway to his office. He'd taken his jacket and tie off and rolled up the sleeves of his dress shirt. That was his usual uniform during the day. He always looked ready for action.

"Excuse me?"

"You know—sunny and bright and happy?" He was baiting her. Yesterday, he'd asked her why she was so serious all the time. Deciding the misogynistic question didn't deserve an answer, she'd walked away, but she should have known he wouldn't drop it. She dropped her purse into a drawer and clarified her comment.

"I was referring to the 'slugger' part."

"Well, you've got pretty good aim with that arm of yours, and you're a fighter. Slugger seems to fit you."

Cassie's breath caught in her throat. He thought she was a *fighter*?

"And what should I call *you*? Ducky, for how fast you dodged the stapler?" He gave her an odd look, somewhere between surprise and admiration. Then his face scrunched up.

"Ducky is a hard pass. Let's stick with Nick."

She looked at the flowers. "Please tell me the director of security didn't *steal* these flowers from the garden in front of the resort."

Nick winked at her. He was a big winker. She did her best to tell herself those twinkling brown eyes of his had no effect on her. "They actually haven't left the property, so at best, the director of security has just *misappropriated* them. I think they look nice there, don't you?" She rolled her eyes.

"I'm sure a cheating accountant thinks misappropriated funds look *nice* in his bank account, too, but that doesn't make it any less a crime."

He barked out a loud laugh. "And here I thought I left all the attorneys back in LA. You missed your calling." He turned back to his office, but stopped cold when she called out.

"Oh, Mr. West?" His exaggerated slow turn almost made her laugh out loud, and she hadn't done that in a long time. He admittedly had a goofy charm. "Don't forget the stapler. You seem to prefer mine to the one you have in your office, so maybe we should switch." She picked it up and tossed it gently in his direction, surprised at her own moxie. He was equally surprised, catching the stapler with one hand. She nodded at the daffodils. "And thank you for the stolen goods."

He gave her a crooked grin. "Just following orders. Blake told me to treat you right, remember?"

Cassie rolled her eyes again and turned away, ignoring his chuckle behind her.

A couple hours later, Nick was surprisingly all business during their tour of the grounds, jotting notes on his tablet and snapping pictures. It was a gorgeous early May day, warming dramatically from earlier in the week. A breeze raised gentle waves on the lake, which were shushing against the shoreline.

They started by walking around the exterior of Blake and Amanda's home, a rambling stone castle named Halcyon, then worked their way down the hill past the resort, all the way to the golf course that hugged the shoreline. The entire complex, including the residence, covered over one hundred acres, and by lunchtime, Cassie felt as though they'd walked every one of them.

She rattled off anecdotes as they walked. Nick's security staff had been showing him around all week, but Blake instructed her, in his absence, to give Nick a tour that included the *stories* behind the business. This place, with lots of help from Amanda, had changed Blake's life. He wanted his employees to understand its importance. Nick listened and nodded, busy with his notes.

She told him the history of Halcyon and how close the mansion had come to being destroyed, along with the resort. The rebirth of the resort, thanks to Amanda's designer eye and Blake's hotel fortune. The coinciding growth of the town of Gallant Lake, where most of the employees lived and many guests shopped and dined. The upscale weddings the resort specialized in, often for well-heeled Manhattanites. And the new championship golf course, already home to several prominent charity tournaments.

He glanced at her several times as they headed back from the golf course, but she was careful not to make eye contact. His chocolate eyes had a way of knocking her thoughts off track. The waves were larger now that the wind had picked up. Above them was the sprawling clubhouse, a stunning blend of glass and timber, with a slate tile roof.

"Where's the best place to launch a kayak around here?"

"What?"

"I want to get my kayak in the water this weekend,

and my rental doesn't have a dock yet. Does the resort have a launch site?"

Cassie stopped walking and looked at him, brushing away the stray strands of hair that blew across her face. She knew her mouth had fallen open, but it took her a moment to actually speak.

"You're asking *me* about kayaking?"

"You live in a mountain town. You must do *something* outdoors. Are there mountain bike trails here? Places to rock climb?"

Her chest jumped and it startled her so much she put her hand over her heart. That had been dangerously close to a laugh. She shook her head. "You are definitely asking the wrong person. I'm sure those things exist around here, but I don't know anything about them. You should ask Terry at the front desk—he's outdoorsy."

"Outdoorsy?" His shoulders straightened. "I'm not 'outdoorsy.' I enjoy outdoor activities. There's a difference."

"And that difference would be?"

Nick stuttered for a minute, then rubbed the back of his neck. "I don't know. But it's different, trust me. You've never kayaked here?"

"Uh…no. My idea of a good time is curling up with a book and a cup of tea."

He shook his head. "Well, that's just sad. I'll think of you tomorrow night when I'm out on the water taking in the scenery and you're stuck at home reading some boring book."

She turned away and started walking. "I'm working tomorrow night."

"Yeah? On a Friday night?"

"There's a big wedding this weekend, and the rehearsal dinner is tomorrow. One of our events people is on vacation, so I'm helping our manager make sure everything runs smoothly."

"The manager is Julie, right? I spent yesterday afternoon with her. She seems on top of things." Cassie nodded. Julie Brown was nice. If Cassie was sure she'd be staying in Gallant Lake, they'd probably be better friends. But she couldn't afford to get too comfortable. Nick, walking at her side, shook his head with a smile. "Blake wasn't kidding when he said you don't have a defined job description—you're everywhere."

"I'm wherever I'm needed. *That's* my job description."

He studied her intently, then shrugged.

"Hey, if you'd rather work than join me on the water, that's your loss."

This laughing whirlwind of a man was making her crazy. Because for just a moment, she wondered if it really *would* be her loss if she didn't go kayaking with him.

She quickly dismissed the thought. Her in a kayak with Nick West? Not happening.

Chapter Three

Nick leaned back in his office chair, turning away from the security feeds to watch Cassie through the open door. She was on the phone with someone, typing furiously and glancing at the schedule on the tablet propped up on the desk by her computer. The woman could seriously multitask. Was she the calm, cool professional he saw right now? Or was she the meek woman who'd flinched when he'd dropped a pile of papers on her desk this morning? Was she the woman who got uptight if there were more than a couple people in a room? Or was she the woman he saw yesterday, giving him a tour of the property with pride and confidence?

He'd checked her employee file—a perk of his job title. The information was pretty thin. She'd been here only a few months. She'd managed an insurance office in Milwaukee for a while but had been unemployed for over a year before moving here six months ago. Not exactly a red flag. She could have been going to school or job hunting or whatever. She'd clearly won Blake Randall's confidence, but she didn't give off a sense of having a lot of confidence in herself. Instead, Cassie seemed all twisted up with anxiety. Unless she was busy. Then she was cool and...controlled. It was as if being productive was her comfort zone.

She hung up the phone, then immediately dialed someone else. Her back was to him, ramrod straight. Her auburn hair was gathered in a knot at the base of her slender neck. He wondered what she'd look like if she ever let that hair loose. She was dressed in dark trousers and a pale blue sweater. Sensible. Practical. Almost calculatedly so. He grimaced. This was what happened when you spent eight years as a detective—you started profiling everyone you met.

"Margo? It's Cassandra Smith, Mr. Randall's assistant. Did you see the email I sent you last week? I didn't receive a reply and thought perhaps you missed it..."

Nick's eyes narrowed. There was an edge to Cassie's voice he hadn't heard until now. She was a whole new person. Again. He picked up his foam basketball and started bouncing it off the wall by the doorway. He smirked when Cassie stiffened—the fact that she hated his throwing the ball around was half the fun of doing it.

"Yes... Well, if Mr. Randall saw these numbers, he'd definitely be concerned... Right. And if Mr. Randall is concerned, he might be on the next flight to Miami for a conversation... Exactly. The restaurant is consistently selling less alcohol than they're ordering every week. That inventory has to be going somewhere... What's that?... Oh, I see. The bartender had his own family restaurant and was ordering a little extra for himself? I'm assuming he's no longer employed with us?" She was scribbling furiously on a notepad on her desk. "You know, Margo, you have access to the same reports I do, so you may want to start reading them more closely... I'm sure you will. I'm glad we had a chance to talk... Yes, you, too. Have a great weekend."

Nick moved to the doorway while she talked, working her diplomatic magic with the Miami manager. As she hung up, he leaned against the doorjamb and started to clap slowly. Being Cassie, she just about jumped out of her skin, spinning in her chair with a squeak of alarm. He really was going to have to be more careful around her.

"Sorry, I couldn't help but overhear. Those were some good people skills, Cassie. I'm impressed, but since I'm responsible for loss management, I'm also concerned. Do we have a problem in Miami?"

Color returned to her cheeks and her chin lifted. "Not anymore. I saw the discrepancy last week. It was only a case or two here and there, but it's something the hotel manager should have spotted herself. She won't be ignoring any more of the reports I send out."

"And you really weren't going to tell Blake? Or me?" That might be taking her job responsibility a step too far. She stuttered for a moment, then met his gaze with the slightest of smiles, causing his chest to tighten in an odd way.

"It happened before *you* arrived, and I told Blake the minute I saw it."

Nick replayed the conversation in his head. Cassie let Margo believe Blake wasn't aware, but she hadn't actually stated that. Clever girl.

"Bravo, Miss Smith." She shrugged off the compliment, as usual. "Are you still planning on working the rehearsal dinner tonight?"

"Yes. It will probably run like clockwork as usual, but with Blake out of town and one of our managers off this week, Julie doesn't want anyone thinking they can slack off." She checked the time on her phone. "I should probably get down there. Have fun kayaking."

Nick nodded and wished her a good evening, not bothering to tell her he wouldn't be paddling on the water tonight after all. He'd be sitting in the surveillance room with Brad, learning how everything worked in there. Turned out Brad was in IT and also worked security on the weekends.

Three hours later, his head was spinning with all the information Brad was throwing at him. Nick was comfortable with technology, but remembering which control moved the images from the smaller monitors up to the large wall monitors mounted around the room, which control sped up or reversed the feeds, how to copy a feed to the permanent drive rather than the temporary one that saved them for only fourteen days... It was enough to make his head hurt. And to have it rattled off to him by some geeky kid barely out of college didn't help his mood any.

There were digital cameras all over the resort, both

in the public areas as well as in all the employee passageways and the kitchen. He'd spotted Cassie repeatedly. She seemed to be everywhere behind the scenes tonight, clipboard in hand, watching all the action. She'd changed into a crisp white shirt and dark slacks to match the rest of the staff. She didn't interact with a lot of people. He saw her speaking with the manager, Julie. Then she'd been with Dario, the head chef, gesturing toward the plates being prepared.

He'd seen that pattern with her before—if she knew and trusted someone, she was relaxed and looked them straight in the eye when she spoke. But if she wasn't comfortable with someone, her body language was completely different. She avoided both eye contact *and* conversation. She kept her body turned at a slight angle instead of facing them directly. Was she just painfully shy, or had something happened in her past to make her this way? Nick leaned back in his chair, chewing on the cap of his pen and scanning the monitors.

He spotted her a little while later, heading across the lobby toward the side door, purse slung over her shoulder. She was heading home. He frowned and checked the time. It was after ten o'clock and she was alone. They had cameras in the lots, but he'd noticed most of them were trained on customer parking, not the employee lot. He stood and shook Brad's hand.

"This has been a great session, man. Thanks. But I think I'll call it a night." He looked around and frowned. "You're on your own tonight?" Brad was a good kid, but he looked like a younger version of Paul Blart, the mall cop. Nick had doubts about Brad's ability to handle the type of situations that could come up when a wedding crowd got to drinking. "You've got my mobile number, right?"

Brad laughed. "I'm not alone. Tim's on vacation, but Bill's out doing the first night check on doors and gates." The team made the rounds to all exterior access points to the buildings three times every night. Nick nodded and left the room, waiting until he got to the hallway before closing his eyes in frustration.

Bill Chesnutt was even older than Ken Taylor had been. The guy was a retired marine, but he'd retired a *long* time ago. So basically they had Paul Blart and Andy Griffith watching over the resort on a Friday night. Perfect. He was going to need to make some changes here, but he didn't want to rock the boat too early. He'd have a sit-down with Blake when he returned and discuss the options—better training, better people or both. He headed out the side door toward the employee parking lot.

Cassie was walking in the next row over from him, head down and looking tired. There were nowhere near enough lights in this damn lot. Nick headed in her direction, making a mental note to talk to the employees about using a buddy system to walk to their cars after dark until he could get more lights out here. This might not be the streets of LA, but there were bad guys everywhere.

Nick walked up behind Cassie, not happy that he was able to get this close without her noticing. She should be more aware of her surroundings. He was only a few feet away and she didn't even know…

In the blink of an eye, Cassie spun and swung her fist at him. He dodged just in time, and something glinted in the light. Her car keys were sticking out between her fingers. That would have left a mark if she'd connected. She was digging in her purse with her other hand.

He barely had time to register what was happening before the pepper spray hit him in the face.

Chapter Four

"Agh! Son of a *bitch*! What the hell is wrong with you? God *damn* it, that hurts!"

Cassie watched in horror as Nick West covered the side of his face and doubled over, yelling in pain and letting out a string of curse words.

"Oh, my God. I didn't know it was you!" She stepped forward to help, but her lungs started to burn and she couldn't get a good breath. She started coughing, her chest burning. Still hunched over, Nick grabbed her arm, spinning her around and shoving her away with a hand to her back.

"What are you…?"

"Get away from me!" Nick's growl was rough and loud. "Get away!"

He was angry. He *pushed* her. She immediately fell back on a practiced reaction.

"I'm sorry…"

That wasn't what she was thinking. She was thinking Nick was an idiot to frighten her like that. But before she could take back her apology, coughing overtook her. Tears ran down her face.

"Damn it!" Nick's hand wrapped around her wrist and he dragged her to the grass along the dark edge of the lot. Then he propelled her even farther away from the cars, sending her stumbling. He was bent over, looking up at her with one eye tightly closed, like the Hunchback of Notre Dame. Rage burned in that one open eye. His voice was tightly controlled. Almost calm.

"Stay back. You inhaled some of your own pepper spray. Hell, Cassie…" He dropped to his knees, raising his hands to his face but not touching them to his skin. "Water…"

She dived back into her bag and pulled out a water bottle. She started to hand it to him, then realized he couldn't see her. "Turn your face up toward me, Nick. I'll pour the water."

He tilted his head. "Just the left side…" She poured the water slowly over the side of his face, and he took a deep, ragged breath. She did the same, noticing her lungs didn't feel like they were in spasms any more.

"What were you thinking, sneaking up on me like that? I thought you were kayaking." He didn't answer, just sat on the grass, his head between his knees, both eyes tightly closed. A low, steady groan was the only sound he made. She sat next to him. "I was only defending myself…"

Sun Tzu said it perfectly. *Invincibility lies in defense.*

His whole body went rigid and he raised his head, glaring at her with his right eye. The left side of his face and neck were bright red in the glow of the parking lot light, his left eye tightly closed.

"*Defending* yourself? I could write an entire training manual on what *not* to do from your performance just now." He closed his good eye and grimaced. "Damn, that hurts."

Cassie was caught between sympathy and anger. Anger seemed easier. "A training manual, huh? Since you're doubled over in pain right now, I'd say I did a pretty good job of rendering you harmless."

Before she could blink, Nick's hand snaked out and grabbed her wrist, yanking her almost onto his lap. His face was so close to hers that she could smell the pepper spray on his skin. She was too stunned to scream, but her heart felt like it was going to leap straight out of her chest.

"Do I look *harmless* to you right now, Cassie? If I'd been an attacker, you'd be dead, or worse. I could have forced you into your car and…" He growled to himself and released her with another curse, driving his fist into the ground at his side. "You did *everything* wrong. You let me get too close. You used the keys first when you should have used the spray. The keys-in-the-fingers trick only works when you're in close hand-to-hand combat, which should be your *last* resort. You took so long getting the pepper spray that I would have had your purse away from you before you could reach it."

Nick picked up the water bottle and poured what was left down the side of his face and neck. "You gave me time to turn away, so you didn't completely incapacitate me. And then, instead of running when you had the chance, you stepped forward, right into your own cloud of pepper spray, and nearly incapacitated *yourself.*" He turned to focus his good eye on her. "So, yes. A whole training manual. On what *not* to do."

Cassie stared at the dark ground, focused on bringing her pulse under control. Nick had been careful not to hurt her when he'd grabbed her, but he'd still frightened her. On purpose. She'd hate him for it if it weren't for the truth of what he'd said. If he had been some random attacker—if he'd been *Don*—she would have been a victim. Again.

"Why are you armed with pepper spray? Did something happen to you?"

She didn't look up.

"Yes. Something happened."

"Here?"

She shook her head, her body trembling so badly she didn't trust her voice. The only sound was his wheezing breath. He finally cleared his throat.

"Okay. Something happened. Somewhere." His voice was gravelly from the pepper spray, but it was calmer than it had been a few minutes ago. "And you wanted to protect yourself. That's smart. But you need to do it *right.* I'll teach you."

Her head snapped up. He was doing his best to look at her, even though his left eye was still closed.

"What are you talking about?"

"I'll teach you self-defense, Cassie. The kind that actually works."

"Are you talking karate or something? I thought the pepper spray…"

"It's a tool, but you need more than that. If some guy's amped up on drugs, he'll just be temporarily blind and *really* ticked off." He picked up the pepper spray canister from the grass at her side. "This stuff will spray up to ten feet away. You never should have let me get so close before using it."

"I didn't know that."

"Exactly." He grimaced and swore again. "I need to get home and dunk my face in a bowl full of ice water." He stood and reached a hand down to help her up. She hesitated, then took it.

"Are you okay to drive, Nick? Do you want me to…"

"I'm fine. I'm only a couple miles from here, and I have one functioning eye. How about you?"

She was rattled to the core and definitely wouldn't get any sleep tonight, but one of her favorite things about Nora's place was that there were few places for anyone to hide in the wide-open loft. She always parked her car right next to the metal stairs that led to the back entrance. "I'm good. Don't worry about me."

Nick walked slowly to his Jeep, still cradling the side of his face with one hand. She felt bad that he was suffering, but she also felt a tiny spark of pride.

Maybe she hadn't fought back successfully, but she'd *fought*. That was something, right?

Nick went into the office for a few hours on Saturday morning, but there was no sign of Cassie. He should have been relieved, considering she about killed him with that damn pepper spray the night before. Instead, he felt a nudge of disappointment, and more than a nudge of concern.

Something happened.

One of the reasons he wasn't a cop anymore was that he'd run out of patience with victims. He looked at Jada's wedding photo on his shelf. No, that wasn't completely true. He'd run out of patience with victims who didn't help themselves. Who willingly *allowed* themselves to be victims. That's why his partner was dead. If Beth Washington hadn't gone back to her husband, Jada would still be alive.

But Cassie had armed herself with pepper spray and she hadn't hesitated to use it. She'd used it *badly*, but she'd used it. It was a good thing she was so bad with the stuff—at least she'd blinded him in only one eye.

He slid his notes from his time with Brad into a manila folder and put it on the corner of his desk to review on Monday. Blake Randall would be back in the office, and Nick's orientation period would come to an end. He looked forward to getting down to business. But first, he needed to finish unpacking and get himself settled in the small house he'd rented on Gallant Lake. He was getting sick of living out of cardboard boxes.

It was weird not seeing Cassie sitting at her desk

when he left the office. He wondered if she'd take him up on his offer to teach her self-defense. She didn't need to become a Krav Maga expert to protect herself. But she was so damn jumpy and twitchy about everything. She'd have to lose that spookiness to be effective at self-defense, which was all about outthinking the enemy. Nick frowned. He didn't like the thought of the quiet brunette having enemies. Especially the kind who drove her to have such a quick trigger finger on a canister of pepper spray.

The heavy blue stapler sat on the corner of her desk, just begging to be hidden somewhere. Maybe he should leave her alone, especially with the boss coming back next week. But what was the fun in that? He set the stapler on the windowsill, tucking it behind the curtains that were pulled back to show the view of Gallant Lake and the surrounding mountains. Maybe he'd get out in the kayak tomorrow if the nice weather held.

But he woke the next morning to the sound of rain pounding on the metal roof. Kayaking was out of the question. He slid out of bed and opened the blinds on the window facing the water. Looked like a good day to do some shopping for the basics he needed to fill his pantry and refrigerator. He liked to cook healthy meals, but this transition week had seen him settling for far too many pizzas and frozen dinners. Time to get back on track. But first, there was an interesting-looking little coffee shop in Gallant Lake that he'd been meaning to try, and this was a hot-coffee sort of morning.

Apparently lots of people felt the same way, because the Gallant Brew was busy. As he stood in line, he studied the local artwork that lined the brick walls. A large bulletin board was filled with fliers about local events—a quilt show at the library, a spring concert at the elementary school, a senior travel group meeting at one of the churches. Slices of a small-town life he had no idea how to navigate.

His rising sense of panic settled when he saw the notice from the Rebel Rockers climbing club. The group was advertising a spring multipitch climb at the Gunks. The famous Shawangunk Ridge was known to be one of the best rock-climbing sites in the country, and a group climb like this would be a great way for him to learn his way around the cliffs. He'd get to know some local climbers, too. He tore off one of the paper strips with a phone number on it. Maybe this wouldn't be such a bad place after all.

There was a collective burst of female laughter from the back of the shop, and one of the voices sounded oddly familiar. There were two women bustling behind the counter, trying to serve the large group ahead of Nick. One was older and tall, with a long braid of pewter-colored hair. The other was petite, with dark hair and a bright smile. She said something over her shoulder toward the hallway that disappeared into the back of the shop. That's where Cassie Smith stood, juggling a large cardboard box in her arms.

The shorter brunette was filling a metal pitcher with frothy steamed milk, her voice rising over the hiss of the high-tech espresso maker. "Just set those mugs in the kitchen, Cass. I had no idea how low we'd gotten. You're a lifesaver!"

"No problem. I'll go get the second box for you."
Cassie, dressed in snug jeans and a short pink sweater
that teased a bit of skin at her waist, turned away. Hot
damn, her auburn hair was swinging free this morning,
falling past her shoulders thick and straight. The box
struck the corner hard as she turned. Her grip slipped,
and she threw a knee up to keep the box from hitting
the floor as she tried to regain control.

Nick was there in three long strides, grabbing the
box away from her. To his surprise, both women at the
counter rounded on him like he'd gone after Cassie
with a machete.

"What the hell do you think you're doing?" The older
one slammed the cash register shut, ignoring the protest
of her customer and heading his way with fury in her
eyes. The petite one was less confrontational.

"Sir, you can't be back here…"

"Nick?" When Cassie spoke his name, both women
stopped.

"You *know* this guy?" The taller woman looked him
up and down, clearly unimpressed with what she saw.
"I've never seen him in here before."

"He works at the resort, Aunt Cathy. He's okay." She
reached for the box. "I'll take that."

Nick shook his head. "It's heavy. Tell me where you
want it."

She opened her mouth as if to argue, then recon-
sidered, pointing to the kitchen. "Anywhere in there.
Thanks." He set the box down on the stainless steel
counter in the tiny kitchen, then turned to face her.

"That's too heavy for you to be carrying."

"Apparently not, since I managed to carry it down a long flight of stairs just fine. I didn't steer very well, that's all." She turned away and headed down the hallway, then looked over her shoulder at him in confusion when he followed. "What are you doing?"

"You said there was a second box. I'll get it."

She turned slowly, her right brow rising.

"No. You won't."

Nick shook his head in frustration. "We can stand here and argue about it as long as you'd like, but I *am* going to carry the other box down. If you'd bumped that one into the wall on the stairs, you could have fallen and broken your neck. Do you care anything at all about your own safety?"

"Seriously? I pepper-sprayed you in the face Friday night. I think that shows how much I care about my safety."

"Yeah? You still haven't agreed to my offer to help you learn how to protect yourself. And you're fighting me about carrying a box of coffee mugs when you know damn well I'm right." His voice rose slightly on those last words, and she stepped back. Her voice, on the other hand, dropped so low he barely heard her.

"I'm sorry…" Her brows furrowed as soon as the words came out, as if she hadn't expected them.

"You don't have to be sorry, Cassie. Just be smart. And accept help when it's offered. Come on…" His hand touched her arm and she flinched. What the hell? Was she *afraid* of him? He dropped the "cop voice" Jada always used to give him hell for and raised his hands in innocence. "Hey, I'm trying to be a nice guy here. Leave the door open. Tell your aunt to call the cops if we're not back down here in five minutes. Do whatever you need to do, but I think you know in your heart you're safe with me. And Cassie?" He waited until she made eye contact with him, eyes full of uncertainty. "Bring some comfortable clothes to the office tomorrow. We're going to hit the workout room and you're *going* to learn some self-defense moves."

Chapter Five

I think you know in your heart you're safe with me...

It was Thursday, and Cassie couldn't stop rolling Nick's words around in her head. There wasn't a man in the world she considered safe. Maybe Blake Randall, but as her employer, he held an awful lot of power over her. She trusted him, but he wasn't exactly "safe." There was a difference.

She hadn't felt afraid when Nick stepped inside her apartment Sunday morning to take the second box of mugs from where Nora had them stored in the laundry room. She'd felt...uneasy. On edge. His presence, with his loud, confident, king-of-the-world attitude, seemed to suck all the air out of the place. He was true to his word, taking less than five minutes. He'd taken the mugs downstairs, accepted a free to-go cup from Nora as thanks, then left with barely a nod in her direction.

She pulled the office curtain aside and picked up the hidden stapler. It was the second time this week Nick had used that hiding spot. He was slipping, probably distracted now that Blake was back from vacation and grilling him about his plans for this resort as well as setting up a travel schedule to visit the other Randall Resorts International properties during the next quarter.

But Nick hadn't forgotten his promise to teach her self-defense, no matter how many times she tried to tell him it wasn't necessary. On Monday, he'd pointed to his face and said "pepper spray" to remind her of her so-called failure. Today would be their second session, and he'd warned her things were going to get more challenging. On Monday, he'd basically lectured her about judging proximity—when to use pepper spray (six to ten feet), when to use car keys in the fingers (within a foot) and when to go for the crotch kick (only if there's body-to-body contact). He explained the thumbs-to-the-eyeballs trick for if the struggle was up close. She'd objected, doubting she could press on someone's eyeballs, and he said the move was for life-or-death situations. She'd been in that type of situation more than once with Don. Yeah, she'd have gladly put his eyes out if she could have.

She heard the elevator ping down the hall, followed immediately by the sound of male voices echoing loudly in the hallway. Nick was telling a story about some would-be thief they caught nude in a chimney in LA. She braced herself just as the door to the office suite flew open. Blake was in the lead, laughing and giving her a quick nod before heading to his office. Right on his heels were Brad from IT and Tim from security, and bringing up the rear and laughing the loudest was Nick. The onslaught of noisy men set off all of Cassie's alarms, but she'd taken a deep breath before their arrival and managed to flash them a smile. Brad and Tim waved and greeted her before following Blake, but Nick stopped at her desk, a furrow of concern appearing between his brows.

"Everything okay?"

"You mean other than being invaded by what sounded like the entire second fleet? Yeah, I'm fine." She thought she'd managed to hold on to her bright smile, but he clearly didn't buy it.

"Sorry about that. I wasn't thinking."

She wasn't sure what to do with his apology. It wasn't something she had a lot of experience with when it came to men. Before she could come up with a response, Blake stuck his head out of his office door.

"You coming, Nick?" He frowned when he saw Nick leaning over Cassie's desk. "What's going on?"

"I was just apologizing to Cassie for the racket we made. I've gotta grab my file on the lighting I was looking at for the parking lots, and I'll be right in." Nick headed into his office, but Blake stayed put.

"Did our noise really bother you?" he asked.

"No, no. Of course not." Her face warmed.

"Then why was Nick apologizing?"

She busied herself moving papers around on her desk. She didn't want Blake fretting about her.

"I have no idea. Honestly, everything's fine."

Blake watched her for another moment, then shrugged and turned away. Before she could relax, Nick strolled out of his office with a file in his hand. He slowed as he passed her, his voice low and just for her ears.

"Five o'clock in the gym?" Worried that Blake might still be listening, she nodded, not even looking up. Nick reached out and knocked over her stapler with his finger as he passed, causing her to jump.

She reached for the stapler with a roll of her eyes.

"West!" Blake shouted from his office. "Come on, man!"

Nick gave her a playful grin. "Later, slugger."

The door to Blake's office had barely closed when Amanda Randall arrived, tanned and smiling. She set a paper bag on the corner of Cassie's desk.

"I'm betting you haven't had lunch yet, right?"

Cassie reached for the bag eagerly. Amanda was a great cook, which had never been Cassie's strong point. "No, but something tells me I'm going to have lunch now."

Amanda sat in one of the chairs by the window. "Only if you like roast beef sandwiches with cheddar cheese and horseradish sauce. Hey, the girls and I are going to the Chalet tonight for pizza. Wanna join us?" As much as Cassie liked "the girls"—Amanda's cousins Nora, who owned the coffee shop, and Melanie, who owned a clothing boutique in town—she had another commitment tonight that she was oddly reluctant to cancel.

"I can't, but thanks anyway."

Amanda, for all her blond curls, baby blue eyes and bubbly demeanor, was a smart and intuitive woman. "Can't? Or won't? I don't like the thought of you sitting alone in that apartment all the time. Being a hermit isn't good for you."

Being a hermit kept her safe, but she didn't bother reminding her friend of that. Amanda's assumption that she was turning into a recluse, while true, still rankled.

"I actually have plans tonight." She regretted the words as soon as she said them. Now she was going to have to explain something she wasn't sure she even understood.

"I'm sorry… What? You have *plans*? What kind of plans?"

She stalled by taking a bite of the sandwich. "Oh, wow, this is delicious…"

"Yeah, yeah, I know." Amanda took the arm of Cassie's chair and turned it so they faced each other. "Now tell me about these 'plans' of yours."

She glanced at Blake's closed door and lowered her voice. "I'm…meeting with Nick West at five o'clock." She took another bite of the sandwich, watching the speculation in Amanda's eyes.

"Meeting him for…?"

"A training session of sorts." More sandwich. The heck with stalling. The sandwich was really just that good.

Amanda leaned back in her chair, crossing her legs and folding her arms.

"Honey, I have two children. One's a teenager and

one's a toddler. They will both tell you that I always sniff out the truth no matter how long it takes, so you may as well spill it."

Cassie set the sandwich down on a napkin, nodding in surrender.

"He's teaching me self-defense."

Amanda's mouth and eyes went round simultaneously.

"Nick West? Nick West, the hot security guy?"

"Shh! He's in Blake's office, for God's sake."

Amanda lowered her voice, but not her astonishment.

"Nick West is teaching you self-defense? As in, really teaching you? One-on-one? Or is this some class he's offering?"

"It's a…private class."

"Holy shit, what happened to you in the week I was gone? You're going to let a hot hunk of man show you self-defense moves? Let him touch you? Learn to throw him down on the floor? Of course, now that I've met the guy, I wouldn't mind throwing him down myself!"

"It's not like that. And you're married. To Nick's boss."

"Hey, just because I'm married to the sexiest man I know doesn't mean I'm *blind*. But I'm more interested in what *you* think. The guy just got here, and you've become such good friends that you're okay engaging in hand-to-hand combat with him? All sweaty, up close and personal? That's not the Cassie I left in Gallant Lake last week." Her smile faded. "Wait, did something happen? Are you doing this because Don did something?"

Cassie was so caught up in the thought of "up close and personal" that she almost didn't answer. And when she did, she once again shared more than she'd intended.

"I pepper-sprayed him."

"Who? *Don?*"

"Of course not! *Nick.* He startled me in the parking lot last Friday night and I hit him with pepper spray. He was somewhat critical of my technique."

Amanda's look of horror quickly slid into one of great amusement. "You pepper-sprayed the new head of security? Here at the resort? That's priceless! Does Blake know?"

"Not from me. And I doubt Nick's bragging about it, since it didn't end well for him."

"So you assaulted the man and he responded by generously offering to give you private self-defense lessons? Why?"

And that was just one of several hundred-thousand-dollar questions, wasn't it? Why was Nick offering to help her? Why had she agreed? And would there really be sweaty, up-close contact in the process? And how exactly did she feel about that?

Nick had been in the resort's third-floor workout room for a full fifteen minutes with no sign of Cassie. Looked like she was going to blow him off. He was half hoping she *would* quit. Offering private lessons was a bad idea on a couple of levels. It was probably considered unprofessional—it showed favoritism, or something. It could be taken the wrong way, for sure. Was it creepy? Forward? She didn't seem any more interested in him than he was in her, though. She was a looker, but he'd never been drawn to meek women.

He moved from the treadmill to the free weights. He should have told her to go take a class or read a book or a dozen other things besides offering to train her personally. After all, while she was at work, his security team would keep her safe. And when she wasn't at work, it was none of his business. If she didn't show up today, he'd urge her to go find a gym somewhere and relieve himself of the responsibility. He'd learned with Jada that getting involved in solving someone else's problems only led to heartache.

There was a movement near the door and he looked up to find Cassie watching him, her eyes dark and unreadable. Her hair was pulled back into her usual ponytail. She wore a baggy gray sweatshirt over black leggings, with a pair of sneakers that looked new. So she'd been paying attention on Monday when he told her those old canvas flats were not going to cut it for actual exercise. That was good. It meant that, despite her skepticism, she was taking this seriously. Which meant there was no good way to get out of teaching her what she needed to know.

He set the weights down quietly, conscious of her aversion to loud noises.

"You're late."

Her cheeks flushed pink. "I had a last-minute call, and then I had to change. I'm sorry…" Her brows furrowed that way they always did when she said those two words. As if they were acid on her lips. Her shoulders straightened. "But I'm here now, so we should get sweaty... I mean...busy."

He laughed at her stammered words. "Sweaty, huh? We can do sweaty if you want, but I think we should take it slow. I want to show you some basics today that you won't need a lot of strength for."

"You're the instructor."

"You know, it wouldn't hurt for you to get sweaty once in a while." Her eyes went big and he laughed again. "I meant you should start some strength training and maybe some running. The stronger you are, the more confident you'll feel, and the more effective you'll be."

She scoffed. "Running? You think I should start *running*? I don't think so."

"If not running, then find something you enjoy that will give you some cardio and strength. Go hiking, or mountain biking, or anything. I'm telling you, Cassie, the more you move, the better you'll understand your body, and the better you'll be at defending yourself. Not to mention it's just healthy to do."

She looked at him for a long moment before shaking her head. "I'm not looking to become some health nut or kickboxer. Let's stick to the plan. Teach me the basics."

"You need to warm up first. Give me fifteen minutes on the elliptical."

"Why?"

"As you said, I'm the instructor. And you're my little grasshopper, so hop on that machine and show me what you got."

She obeyed, but not happily. "I don't understand

what this has to do with self-defense. I'm not going to be able to elliptic away from someone." After only a few minutes, she was puffing for air and grimacing. Her legs were probably already cramping. She was in worse shape than he'd thought. He grabbed a fresh bottle of water from his bag and handed it to her. She came to a stop.

"If you can't make it five minutes on this machine, you aren't going to be able to do diddly against an attacker. You think you can fight a man the size of me or bigger? When you're standing there wheezing at me after doing basically nothing?" He didn't let her reply, grabbing the bottle from her hands and gesturing to her to get moving. "Okay, new plan. You hit this room every morning, and you get on the elliptical and go until you can't go anymore. Eventually, you'll be going thirty minutes or more, and you'll thank me for how great you feel."

"Don't…hold your…breath…"

It was ironic, listening to her talk about breath when she didn't have any. He gave her a wide grin.

"Okay, let's review while you're warming up. I'm an attacker. I'm six feet away and coming at you. What do you do?"

"I…use the…pepper spray…" She huffed out the words between gasps for air.

He shook his head. "Do you have pepper spray in your hands right now?"

She shot him a glare. "No!"

"Then forget it. If the perp is within twenty feet and running at you, you don't have time to dig in your purse for pepper spray. Same with a gun. Unless it's in your hand at that point, it's useless."

"I don't…want a…gun."

He rubbed the left side of his face. "Yeah, you're dangerous enough with pepper spray. I hate to think what you'd have done the other night with a handgun. So what do you do?"

"Scream?"

He shrugged. "Meh. It's not a bad thing, but it's not going to save you unless you're lucky enough to have the dumbest bad guy in the world and he's attacking you in a public place. Try again."

"Hit…him?"

"Where? With what?"

"I don't… Oh, shit… I can't…do this." She stopped moving. "Okay, maybe you're right about my conditioning." A soft sheen of sweat covered her face. "I'd hit him with my fist."

"Yeah?" Nick folded his arms on his chest. "Show me a fist."

She did what so many inexperienced fighters do. She folded her fingers over her thumb and into a fist.

"Do you intend to hit me as hard as you can with that fist? Maybe right on my jaw?"

She looked at her fist, frowning, as if she knew this was a trick question. Finally she nodded, but without conviction.

"Cassie, if you hit me hard with your hand folded like that, you'll not only break your damn thumb, but you won't hurt me at all. Go ahead, get off the elliptical and take a swing in my direction. Punch at my hand." He saw the doubt in her eyes. "I won't let you hurt yourself. I'm just trying to show you how limited your motion is with your hand like that."

She took a swing, hitting the flat of his hand, but he didn't offer any resistance, letting his hand come away.

"Okay. Now make a fist with your thumb *outside* your fingers, like this." He clenched his hand in a fist, releasing it the minute he saw her skin go pale. Shit. She'd seen a man's fist before. He swallowed hard. "Show me."

She did as he asked. He took her hand and moved her thumb, then curled her wrist so her knuckles were forward. "Now hit my hand. And put some oomph behind it. Start with your body low and rise up into the punch."

Her first attempt wasn't half-bad. Her next few were better, as she started to grasp the concept of lowering her center of gravity and propelling upward with her body, not just her small fist. When she actually connected with his hand with enough force to send it snapping back, she flashed him a wide grin.

"I did it!"

"You did. But throwing a punch is going to be your last resort. You need to know how to do it, but honestly, unless you connect with the guy's nose, or maybe the center of his chest, you're not going to stop him. He'll return the punch and it'll be lights out for you unless it's an eighty-year-old mugger."

Her eyes narrowed in on him. "So I can't use pepper spray and I can't scream and I can't punch. What do I do, just stand there?"

His curiosity got the best of him.

"What happened to you, Cassie? Were you assaulted? Mugged?"

She stepped back and visibly shrank before his eyes, shoulders dropping, head lowered, gaze fixed on the floor by his feet.

"I don't want to talk about it." His chest tightened at some of the darker possibilities.

"I get that, but it would help me to know what's driving your fear."

She stared at the floor so long and so intently he wouldn't have been surprised if smoke started rising from near his feet. He'd done enough interrogations to know that it was human instinct to fill a silence with words. He *could* wait her out, but she wasn't a perp. He opened his mouth, but she beat him to it, painting a picture he was hoping not to see.

"I was in a parking garage. At night. He came from between two cars. I was checking my phone and he was on me before I knew it." Her voice was monotone, like a robot reciting a programmed recording. "That's all you need to know."

"That's why you're so vigilant now. And jumpy."

Her head snapped up. "I'm not that jumpy."

"Says the woman who threw a stapler at my head and pepper-sprayed me in the face."

A trace of a smile tugged at her mouth.

"Okay. I'm jumpy. And I hate it."

He nodded, considering the best way to come at this problem. The "problem" at hand being Cassie's fear. He'd deal with the problem of his physical reaction to her vulnerability—a trait he generally abhorred in women—when he was alone and could think more clearly.

"Look, if a guy is coming at you with the intent to do you harm, you need to fight. Show him you mean business. Plant your feet wide and solid, like this." He took up a fighter's stance, and she did her best to mimic it. "Get in his face. Make noise. Fight like hell, and fight dirty."

"You said not to scream."

"No, I said it probably wouldn't do any good. But I'm not talking about screaming. I'm talking about *noise*. Aggressive noise. Have you ever watched karate or judo or even tennis?" She nodded. "Did you notice how some players make loud noises as they're swinging? Even if they're just chopping a wooden board? That sound makes them feel more powerful. It's more like a roar than a scream, and you can learn to do that once your confidence gets better."

He stepped up in front of her, hating the way she shrank back, but not reacting to it. She was going to have to get used to this. "When the attacker is up close and personal, look to find a weak spot."

"You mean his balls?"

He barked out a laugh. "No, that's another lesson, when I'm wearing protection. Look at my face. What are my weak spots there?"

She studied him intently, and he did his best not to fidget under her examination. There was something about her gaze that made him energized and restless. Uncomfortable and excited at the same time. The sensation kicked him way outside his comfort zone.

"You told me about the eyes already."

"What else do you see that's vulnerable?"

"Your nose?"

"Right. But here's the key—don't swing at it from the side. Come at it from below, with the heel of your hand slamming up against it. Picture yourself driving his nose right into his skull. It'll hurt like hell, and it could give you a chance to break free. Like this." He took her hand and pressed it against the base of his own nose. And damned if he didn't have the crazy urge to kiss the palm of her hand. He shook it off and tried to stay focused. "But just like the punch, put your whole body into it. Think of every move as your only shot." She pressed against his nose and he grinned at her. "We won't be practicing that one. At least not on me. Now what else do you see that's vulnerable?"

Her eyes darkened when her gaze fell to his mouth. He did his best to ignore the stirring he felt below his waist. It was a normal response to a pretty woman studying his mouth, right?

"Yes, the mouth can be vulnerable. It's not the best place to start, but lips are tender. Pinch, bite or smack him with your elbow, like this." In slow motion, he swung his elbow out and stopped an inch from her mouth. "If you've got room to swing, use your elbow before you use your fist. It's harder and more likely to do harm without hurting yourself in the process. What else?"

"I don't know. That's about it, right?"

He moved his hands to each side of her face and gently tugged on her ears. Her eyes met his, and it took all his focus to stay on topic. "No one likes having their ears yanked. And if you really latch on and pull, the guy will be screaming. If you're in close contact and your hands are free, don't hesitate to pull on those ears as hard as you can." He released her ears, but his fingers lingered, brushing back her hair and stroking the tender skin of her neck… *What the hell?* He pulled his hands back and stepped away from Cassie. She looked as confused as he felt. But she hadn't stopped him. Interesting. He cleared his throat.

"Yeah…so…that's about it, I guess…for tonight…um…" Nick couldn't believe his own voice. He was babbling. Nick West, tough cop, was *babbling*. And all because he'd touched Cassie's warm, soft skin with the tips of his fingers.

Color flooded her cheeks as she blinked and looked away. "Yes. Of course. That gave me plenty to…um…think about… Thanks." She turned and grabbed the small canvas bag she'd dropped by the door.

He regained some composure once she turned her back on him. "Hey, don't forget about the elliptical in the morning."

She looked over her shoulder, her hand on the door handle. "Tomorrow's Friday."

"Yeah? And? No excuses, girl." He nodded toward the machine. "You need to make yourself stronger, Cass. Give yourself a fighting chance. You owe yourself that much."

Chapter Six

Cassie stood outside the door to the Chalet for a long time. A really long time.

Amanda had been relentless about Cassie getting out more, threatening to drop off a dozen cats at the apartment to complete her transition into a little old crazy cat lady. Amanda knew why Cassie was leery of going out, getting attached to people, exposing herself. But Cassie knew she had a point. When Julie Brown invited her to the weekly gathering of resort employees at the local bar tonight, as she did almost every week, she'd surprised them both by agreeing.

Maybe it was Nick's king-of-the-world attitude rubbing off on her. Her self-defense classes had morphed into strength and agility training over the past few weeks. He'd been horrified by her lack of conditioning and athleticism, which she'd never seen as a problem. But the time he forced… No, that wasn't fair… The time he *encouraged* her to spend on the elliptical had proved his point. She'd had no stamina at all. She absently rubbed her lower back. She was paying the price with a host of sore muscles, but she was also starting to feel a little more confident. A little stronger, both physically and mentally. He was challenging her, and surprisingly, she liked it.

She could hear the band playing country rock, and the hoots and hollers of the patrons inside. Some of them were her coworkers. Julie. Tim. Brad. Josie from the restaurant. It was the innocent sound of people having a fun Friday night in a small town. Nothing to worry about. But she hadn't thought there was anything to worry about in Milwaukee either, that night she went out to have fun with some coworkers and ended up in intensive care.

It was the anger of that memory that propelled her forward. This was *not* Milwaukee. She steeled herself and stepped inside. She could do this. She had to do this. She had to start living again.

Julie ran over, laughing in a high-pitched voice that suggested she'd already had more than a few drinks. "Cassie! Oh, my God, I'm so glad you came tonight! It's turned into quite a party." Julie waved her arm vaguely in the direction of the U-shaped bar. "It's one of those nights when everyone invited actually showed up, even *you*!"

Cassie recognized most of the people gathered on one side of the bar. Mostly front desk staff. And one tall, dark-haired man at the corner of the bar, watching her with a wry smile over the rim of his beer glass. Nick West. What was he doing here? Trying to prove he was one of the guys? She frowned. That wasn't fair. Maybe he was just trying to make friends in a new town.

Julie followed Cassie's gaze and nudged her shoulder.

"I know, right? The girls have been practically killing each other to take that empty stool next to him, but he said he's saving it for a friend. We're all hoping that friend is as hot as Nick is, without the I'm-your-boss baggage."

"He's not my boss." Cassie said the words to herself, but Julie managed to hear them in the noisy bar. Maybe Julie read lips.

"That's right, you both report to Blake. Are you interested?"

"What?" Cassie forced herself to look away from Nick and met Julie's speculative gaze. "Interested? I'm not interested in any man. Been there. Done that."

Got the scars to show for it...

"One and done, huh? He must have been a doozy." Julie linked her arm through Cassie's. "Come on, let's get us some drinks."

Cassie did her best not to make eye contact with Nick when they walked past, but he made that impossible when he stood and greeted them.

"If you gals are looking for seats, you can have these two." He gestured to the bar stool he'd just vacated and the one beside it.

"I thought you were saving it for someone."

Nick looked directly at Cassie. "You're someone."

Julie looked back and forth between them with a grin. "Okay, then. Thanks!"

Having Nick here set her plans to *slowly* start a social life a little off balance. This was no longer a gathering of employees having fun. This was Nick West, and she was never on her best footing when he was around. For one thing, he made her snarkier than usual.

"Sitting at a bar seems a little tame for you, Mr. West. I'm surprised you're not out climbing a mountain or hunting wild boar with your bare hands."

His right brow arched high, making a direct hit on her heart. "And I'm surprised you're not curled up in a bathrobe with a book of pretty poetry and cup of tea, Miss Smith."

He had no idea how tempting that idea was. "That actually sounds lovely. You might want to try it sometime."

He grinned. "Are you inviting me to a private poetry reading?"

She tried to picture the two of them sitting by the big windows in her loft, reading quietly and glancing at each other warmly as they sipped their tea. Her reaction to the vision was visceral, with her entire body heating and a shiver of some unknown emotion tracing down her spine. She forced herself to laugh lightly but wasn't sure if it sounded genuine at all. This was a game she wasn't used to playing.

"I think there's as much chance of that happening as there is of the two of us going mountain climbing together."

Julie chimed in, looking delighted. "Oh, my God, you two are adorable together!"

She and Nick both looked at her in surprise, speaking in unison.

"We're not together!"

Julie waved her hand dismissively. "Whatever. You're both so serious at work, but here you are being all teasing and flirty and it's… It's cute. That's all."

Nick glanced around, and it burned Cassie to realize he might be wondering if any other employees thought he was being "cute." Probably not a trait the head of security wanted to be known for. And she'd started it all with her sarcastic comment.

"I'm… I'm sorry." She closed her eyes, furious with herself for saying those two words so often. "I should probably…" She started to slide off her seat, but Nick stopped her with a hand on her hip. He moved his hand away as soon as she stopped, but she could still feel the warmth of it.

"No, don't go. And stop with the damn apologizing." His voice dropped for her ears only. "You do that way too much." His gaze locked on hers, and she swallowed hard. Yes, she apologized too much. It was a survival tool she hadn't managed to shake. His eyes softened. He leaned against the bar, his chest only inches from her back, his breath blowing across her neck as he spoke. "What'll you have to drink, ladies?"

Julie held up her glass. "Chardonnay for me, thanks."

Cassie managed to nod and speak without stuttering. "Sounds good. I'll have the same."

Nick caught the bartender's attention and placed the

order, chatting with the guy as he filled their glasses. That was Nick. Outgoing. Full of life and laughs. Her total and complete opposite. Their drinks were delivered, and Nick moved on down the bar to talk to Tim. Cassie was relieved. She didn't want to be rude to the guy, but she also didn't want to hang out at a bar with a man who made her body tingle in dangerous ways.

Everyone started to mingle back and forth, and within an hour, there was a cluster of resort employees standing around Julie and her. People were laughing and jostling each other, and some even took to the dance floor when the music started. Cassie couldn't relax completely, but she did her best, laughing along with everyone else at the stories being told. She didn't have any funny stories of her own to share, but no one pressed her. Most gave her a quick look of surprise when they saw her, but no one made a big deal of her first outing with them.

Julie was telling a story about the woman who tried to tell her the rottweiler she had stuffed into her wheeled dog carrier was within the resort's fifteen-pound limit for pets. Cassie excused herself for the ladies' room, located beyond the dance floor and down a darkened hall. The back of her neck prickled as she stepped into the hall, and her hand automatically reached for her bag. Damn it. She'd left the bag, and her pepper spray, on her chair. She pulled her shoulders back and scolded herself for being paranoid. She couldn't live the rest of her days afraid of being around people. As Nick said, there were ways of being smart that would keep her safe without needing weapons or an armed guard. She just had to focus on her surroundings and be prepared. She locked the bathroom door quickly.

She saw the man as soon as she stepped back out into the shadowy hall. He was behind her, near the men's room. Waiting. He smiled when she glanced his way. She was in a small-town bar with friends. It wasn't likely he was an actual threat. But being alone with him in this hall with the music blaring so loudly that no one would hear her scream was not a wise thing. And self-protection was all about acting wisely. Cassie straightened.

Never look like a victim.

Nick had repeated those words a dozen times in the past few weeks. *If you look like a victim, you're a temptation someone might not be able to resist.* It wasn't about dressing or looking a certain way. He was trying to make the point that a distracted, weak-looking woman was exactly what bad guys were looking for. A smart bad guy would think twice about approaching an alert woman with a bold stride and a don't-mess-with-me expression, even if she was faking it. As Sun Tzu said, *all warfare is based on deception.*

She gave a quick, polite grin to let the man know she saw him and turned toward the dance floor, acting far more unconcerned than she felt. Then she felt his hand on her arm. She swallowed her panic and tried to pull away, but he didn't release her.

"I saw you laughing with your friends at the bar. You're pretty. Wanna dance?" His words rolled into each other just enough to tell her he was drunk. As much as her heart was screaming *Danger! Danger!*

her brain told her there was no threat to his words. He wasn't out to hurt her. He was a drunk guy on a Friday night looking for a dance. All the same, she curled her hand into a proper fist, just in case. She struggled to come up with an appropriately noncommittal smile.

"Thanks, but no. Now if you'll excuse me..." She tried again to tug her arm away from him, but he wasn't giving up. The booze had clearly given him a shot of confidence in his ability to woo a woman in the bathroom hallway. *Damn it, please give up!*

"Aw, come on, babe. Just one dance. And after that, you can walk away if you want..."

Her spine went rigid with defiance. She was so tired of being ordered around. Of being told what she could and could not do. There was no attempt to smile this time around.

"Actually, I can walk away from you right now, *without* dancing. And that's what I'm going to do." She planted her feet firmly, imagining herself lowering her center of gravity as Nick taught her to do. Then she pressed the heel of her hand against the guy's chest and pushed, pulling her arm free. He stumbled back a step, eyes wide in surprise.

"Okay. Okay. You're one of those independent women. I dig it. But, honey..."

He reached for her, but before she could decide how much pain this drunk deserved to feel, he was gone in a blur of dark color that came from behind her. She heard the thump of the guy's back hitting the wall, and the whoosh of air that escaped him at impact.

"You want to walk out of here under your own

power?" Nick West growled the words through clenched teeth as he leaned on his forearm, which was braced against the guy's chest. "If so, I suggest you keep your grabby-ass hands in your pockets and find an exit *now*."

The drunk nodded quickly, and Nick stepped back. The man scooted past Cassie without even glancing in her direction. Leaving Cassie alone in the dark hallway. With Nick. Which suddenly felt far more dangerous than before.

"What do you think you're doing?" She was surprised at the edge of anger to her voice, and Nick seemed to be, too.

"I *think* I'm saving your ass from the drunk dude who just ran off." Nick frowned. "Did he hurt you?"

"No! I didn't need your help, Nick. I had it under control."

"He had you by the arm. Out of sight in a dead-end hallway. I swear to God, woman, you seem determined to put yourself in harm's way…"

"I freed my own damn arm, and he was just a drunk." She lifted her chin. "And now I'm in that lonely hallway with *you*, so what's the difference?"

"The difference is you know *I'm* not going to drag you into one of these closets and hurt you. You didn't know that about him. But you're right—you did free your own arm. Without me." The corner of his mouth quirked up into a crooked grin. "Wonder where you learned that trick?"

He was fishing for compliments. When she didn't answer right away, he rubbed the back of his neck, glancing over his shoulder at the crowded dance floor, where people were stomping along to a line dance. Her sense of fairness finally kicked in.

"Yes, I'm a good little student." She looked around, chagrined to realize she hadn't noticed the other doors in the hall, one labeled "office" and the other labeled for "employees only." The drunk *could* have pulled her into one of those rooms and no one would have known. Except Nick, who'd apparently followed her. Looked out for her. She lost more of her anger. "Now you know why I stay home and read books. I don't have to fight my way to and from the restroom when I'm home by myself."

Nick stepped closer, and her back brushed the wall as she tried to retreat.

"Maybe not, but sitting around alone, doing nothing, is no way to live." He shuddered. "I'd go stir-crazy."

She couldn't help smiling at the thought of always-restless Nick sitting in an easy chair with a book in his hand. "Maybe we both live the lives best suited for us. You charge after adventure, and I read about it."

The timbre of his voice changed, lowering in volume and increasing in intensity.

"Maybe the proper balance is somewhere between our two extremes."

She nodded. "You might be right. Maybe we could help each other out with that."

There was something about this guy that made her blurt out her thoughts before she had a chance to digest them.

"What are you proposing?"

"What? Oh…um…nothing. It was just a random thought. An observation more than an invitation."

She needed to get out of here. She wasn't used to this type of banter with a man, and she wasn't good at it. All this push and pull, advance and retreat, was a mysterious dance she'd never done before. After all, Don always made sure there were no obstacles to her being attracted to him. He'd paved the way and groomed her to rely on him. But Nick didn't do that. Nick kept her guessing, left her wondering if he wanted to be around her or if she was nothing more than a pest. She started to turn away but stopped when Julie walked into the hallway, carrying Cassie's purse.

"There you are! I thought you left and forgot this… Oh…" Julie noticed Nick's presence and her eyes went wide. "What's going on, guys?"

Nick moved a bit farther from Cassie, but his eyes never left hers. "We were just talking about helping each other out with a few things."

Julie looked speculative. "Out *with* or out *of* a few things?"

"Oh, my God, don't be ridiculous!" Cassie felt her cheeks warming. "We just bumped into each other, and now I'm leaving." She grabbed her bag from Julie. Nick took her arm.

"I'll walk you to your car." Of course he would, and it would be a waste of time to argue. Julie winked as they walked past her. Cassie and Nick would probably be gossip fodder at the resort Monday morning.

The employees were still at the bar, laughing and drinking. A few waved at them, and a few more watched with interest. Cassie didn't like people talking. Too much talk was why she'd had to leave Cleveland. That's how Don found her there. That's why her last name was now Smith. Nick nodded good-night to the group, then opened the door and held it for her to go out.

"You can go join the guys, Nick. I'll be…"

He looked down at her and continued to hold the door, his expression saying it all.

"Right. You're going to walk me to my car whether I need it or not."

"Now you're getting it." He followed her across the dark lot, and she tried to define the emotions swirling around inside her. It wasn't fear—she knew what fear felt like. But the jolt of adrenaline wasn't dissimilar. She was on edge. Anticipating, but anticipating what? That Nick would touch her again? Or that he wouldn't?

She resolved that question when she almost walked right past her car. She stopped so quickly that Nick bumped against her back, his hand resting on her waist to steady them both. But she didn't feel steady. He was usually quick to remove his hands from her, ever since that second training session when he let his fingers linger on her neck. But his hand wasn't moving now. In fact, she could almost swear his grip tightened just a little. And damn if she didn't lean into him.

"Cassie…" Nick cleared his throat, his grip loosening but not releasing her. "Isn't this your car?"

"Oh…yes. Sorry." She stepped away, proud of herself for being able to do it calmly and thanking the heavens for the dimly lit lot. He wouldn't be able to see her confusion. She reached in her bag for her keys.

"You aren't going to pepper-spray me again are

you?" She welcomed the wry humor in his voice. This was the Nick she knew how to deal with.

"No, you're too close for it to be effective." His brow rose in admiration, and she grinned. "At this range, I'd probably try running first, or maybe throwing something at you and screaming, since we're in a public place." She glanced around, trying to remember her lessons. "If you came any closer…" He stepped toward her, stopping just short of brushing against her chest. He was testing her, and she was ready. "Now it's heel time. I'd stomp on the bridge of your foot with my heel while simultaneously jamming the heel of my hand into the bottom of your nose." She mimicked the moves as she spoke.

Nick gave a short laugh. "You really are a good little student."

Cassie felt an unexpected burst of pride. It had been only a few weeks, but she was stronger. And smarter. She gave him what he was looking for, because he deserved it.

"I've had a good teacher."

"You have. But you also listened and followed through. That'll come in handy when we go rock climbing tomorrow."

Cassie stepped back, bumping into the car. "Excuse me?"

"Wasn't that the deal you suggested? I teach you to have a life, and you try to teach me how to sit still and read a book?"

"No, I wasn't serious…that was just… No. We're not doing that. I am *not* hanging from some cliff by a rope!"

He folded his arms across his chest.

"Fair enough. How about a simple hike up Gallant Mountain? There's a trail. We'll stop before the rock climbing part." His head tilted. "Let's see how all that elliptical work has helped your stamina."

A rough laugh escaped her. "That's a hard *no*. Not happening."

It was as if she hadn't spoken. "Blake has a conference call scheduled with the Barbados resort at two, so I'll pick you up after that. We'll still have enough daylight. It'll get chilly as the sun gets lower, so bring a sweatshirt or jacket. And good walking shoes."

"Did you hear me? Not. Happening."

"It's a lot of walking—wear thick socks or double up so you don't blister."

"Nick! I'm not doing that." What part of *not happening* did he not understand?

He reached behind her to open her car door. "Come on, get in. I want to make sure you get out of here safely. Text me when you're in your apartment."

"I don't have your number…"

He handed her his phone. "Send a text to yourself. Then you'll have it."

She stared at Nick's phone in her hand.

"Yeah, and you'll have mine." A total of four people knew her current mobile number. Amanda. Blake. Her mom. And an assistant district attorney in Milwaukee. Everyone else had the landline number at the apartment.

…I think you know in your heart you're safe with me…

She typed her number in and sent a short text, knowing he'd read it.

Not happening.

She handed the phone back. He read it but didn't react.

"Text me when you're inside, or I'll be driving over to check on you."

"Don't give that number to anyone."

Nick's head snapped up. This was a matter of life and death for her.

"I won't, Cass. You have my word." She thought about all the promises Don broke in the past. But Nick wasn't Don. At least, he didn't seem to be. It was too late to take the number back, so she finally nodded. What was done was done.

She kept her eyes on Nick in the rearview mirror as she drove out of the lot, his expression troubled in the glow of her taillights. He had questions. And she wasn't about to answer them.

Chapter Seven

Nick had never been the type to go after viral social media fame. But the look on Cassie's face when she opened the back door to her apartment Saturday afternoon was so priceless he regretted not capturing it with his phone. She clearly wasn't expecting him, judging from the unicorn leggings and oversize T-shirt she was wearing. Her hair was pulled up into some kind of messy twist on top of her head. Her feet were bare, showing off surprisingly bright blue toenails.

But her expression? That was the prizewinner. Her green-gold eyes were wide, and her mouth formed a perfect, pink-lined O. She seemed frozen there, her hand clutching the edge of the door. Cassie slowly took him in, and once again, her lingering gaze had the power to make his blood heat. She started with his well-worn hiking shoes, then on up to his cargo shorts and rugby shirt before her gaze finally reached his face.

"What are you doing here?"

"Uh… We're going hiking, remember?"

Her head went back and forth emphatically. "What I remember is telling you that I was *not* going hiking. So thanks for stopping, but you're on your own." She started to push the door closed, but Nick's hand shot out to stop it.

"Have you even stepped outside today?" He gestured behind him to the bright blue May sky and the maples leafing out on the other side of the parking lot. The air was fresh and rain-washed from the showers they'd had that morning. "You haven't, have you? You've been cooped up in this place all damn day." She opened her mouth to protest, but it was obvious he was right. "Come on. Go change, and we'll take a pleasant stroll on the mountainside—nothing challenging. You need to get some sun and exercise, and you'll love the views from up there." She still hesitated, so he offered a trade-off. "Look, you go for a hike with me today, and I promise to give you a day doing whatever you want. Including reading and sipping tea, if you insist."

Her eyes narrowed, but the corner of her mouth betrayed her amusement.

"Whatever I want?"

Nick had the sinking feeling he was getting the losing end of this bargain, but it was too late to back out now.

"Whatever you want." He held back a groan at her

obvious pleasure with his concession. "But it's late and it's gonna get cool as the sun gets low, so hurry up."

There was another moment of indecision before Cassie nodded. "Fine. Give me ten minutes. And this had better be a nice 'stroll' because I am not climbing any cliffs. Got it?"

"Yes, ma'am." He remembered how tense she'd been a few weeks ago when he went into her apartment to carry that box of mugs. "I'll wait for you in the Jeep." He tapped his watch. "Ten minutes."

The drive to the trailhead wasn't long, but it sure seemed that way with the silence hanging over the vehicle. Cassie had changed clothes in a flash, but she'd also withdrawn into Nick's least favorite of her personas—the quiet mouse. She was answering his questions about her day in single syllables, staring out the window instead of at him, huddled against the passenger door as if ready to open it at any second and throw herself out of the moving vehicle. He finally had enough and pulled off on the side of the mountain road.

"Tell me what's going on."

Her cheeks flamed, then paled. "Wh-what do you mean?"

"I know I coerced you into joining me on this hike, but the idea is for you to enjoy it. And you are definitely not enjoying yourself right now. Why?"

The color came back to her face and she straightened a little at his brusque question. "You can't just order me to have fun, Nick. I told you last night I didn't want to hike a mountain with you."

"And yet you changed your clothes and hopped into

the Jeep with me when I showed up at your door. What's happening? Do you want to go back?"

A slideshow of emotions played across her face. As a cop, he'd always been good at reading people, but this woman defeated him every time. He had no idea what she was feeling, and he had a hunch she didn't know, either. But the primary emotion he picked up from her body language was...fear.

"Are you *afraid* of me?" Her silence spoke volumes. "You have got to be freaking kidding me..."

He slammed the Jeep into gear and did a U-turn. He wasn't kidnapping the woman, for God's sake. He was only trying to help her get out more. Had she really been too intimidated to refuse him? The thought gave him pause. How many times had Jada warned him about his "steamroller" approach when he thought he was right? Was that what he'd done to Cassie? He'd driven only a mile or two back toward town when Cassie sat up straight and spoke.

"Stop, Nick. Turn around. I don't want to go home."

This woman gave him emotional whiplash.

"Are you sure?" She nodded, and he pulled into the next driveway and turned back up the mountain. "Are you going to tell me what the problem is?"

She chewed on her lip for a moment, then turned to face him, her words coming out in a rush.

"I haven't been alone in a car with a man in a long time..." When her words trailed off, he took his eyes off the winding road just in time to see a single tear spill over. Damn. He hated when women cried. She hadn't told him much of her story since that day in the gym.

She'd been attacked in a parking garage. Maybe the guy dragged her into a vehicle? *Shit.*

"When you were attacked…"

"No, not then." Her hands twisted in her lap. "I just haven't been alone in a car with a man driving in a really long time, and it freaked me out more than I thought it would." He turned away to focus on driving, and was thankful when she continued. "I tried to work through it in my head, but I couldn't get past it. I thought I'd be relieved when you turned the car around, but I wasn't. It felt like surrendering, and I don't want to do that."

"You're a fighter." His words were low, almost unintentional, but she heard him and gave a soft snort of laughter.

"You've said that before, but I'm *not*. I'm a mess." She gave a gasp of surprise when he turned off the pavement and started up the steep dirt track. "Where are we going?"

Nick was thankful for the change in subject. "We're going up the mountain. In the Jeep for as far as we can. Unless you'd rather walk?" The truck rocked as it hit a dip on the path. She grabbed the door, but she no longer looked like she wanted to escape. In fact, she was smiling and leaning forward, watching the brush sweep the sides of the truck. She laughed when the wheels spun in the mud from last night's rain, finally catching hold of solid ground and catapulting the vehicle forward.

He had his hands full with the driving, but he soaked in the sound of Cassie's laughter and held it in his heart like the precious thing it was. He couldn't help stealing a glance at her, and her smile had him letting up on the gas pedal and nearly driving into a tree.

It was the first *real* smile he'd seen on her. Oh, he'd seen her smile. The warm-but-professional smile she had for Blake Randall. The conspiratorial smile of friendship she shared with Amanda or Julie. The cool, polished smile she used with employees and visitors. And the involuntary smile of frustrated amusement she occasionally sent his way when he'd been teasing her over something.

But this smile... He glanced over again, and she laughed, one hand on the door and one braced on the dashboard as they climbed the rutted path... *This* smile was really something. It was...uninhibited. Genuine. Uncensored. Unguarded. All of Cassie's protective shields had come down, and he was seeing his new, most favorite version of her ever. He was seeing Cassie unfiltered.

"Is this what they call four-wheeling?"

They reached the small clearing where the path leveled off. A wooden gate with a no-trespassing sign blocked their way. Nick turned off the truck, glad to be able to face her now without putting their lives at risk.

"Not exactly. Four-wheeling is usually done on four-wheelers, but I guess sometimes it's with trucks. And that was actually a pretty decent track to drive up—not exactly off-roading..." Nick stopped abruptly. He was babbling like a nervous schoolboy. And Cassie was still smiling at him. In fact, she may have even giggled—something he wouldn't have thought possible before now.

"That was fun! I'm so glad we turned around!" Yeah, so was he. She looked around at the thick woods surrounding them. "Will you have room to turn here?"

"Eventually, sure. But first, we hike."

She looked at the gate and the posted sign and arched her brow. "You want me to go trespassing with you to take a hike I didn't want to take in the first place? I don't think so."

He grinned at her last-ditch attempt to avoid hiking and opened his door. "It's not trespassing if you have permission from the owner. And Blake Randall told me it's just fine."

Cassie was pretty sure her calf muscles were tearing apart. The burning pain had her wincing as she followed Nick up the steep path. She wondered if she'd ever walk without pain again. A "nice stroll," huh? This was more like climbing Kilimanjaro with no training.

A few weeks on the elliptical were no match for Gallant Mountain. She could ask Nick to stop, but she'd just asked for a break a few minutes ago, and that was the third one. She hadn't missed his amusement or his sigh of impatience when he'd glanced up the trail. She vowed not to stop again. Surely they'd be stopping soon. He'd *promised* her there would be no rock climbing, and she could see a wall of rugged gray getting closer.

Too bad her legs would be destroyed beyond repair by the time they got there.

Nick glanced over his shoulder and slowed. She knew he was already taking this hike much slower than he usually would, so she gave him the brightest smile she could muster.

He frowned. "You okay?"

No, I'm dying. Literally dying.

"I'm fine! Great!"

I'm in agony, and you know it, you bastard.

His brow rose. "Really? You're feeling great?"

How much longer are you going to torture me?

"Sure, great! Absolutely!"

He shook his head, and she was pretty sure he was laughing at her, but she couldn't prove it, since he was climbing up the trail again. She stuck her tongue out at his back and bit back a groan of pain as she followed. If only they'd stopped their little adventure after the truck drive up the mountain. That was fun.

She'd never done anything like it, with the engine growling, the tires searching for traction and the Jeep rocking back and forth like some amusement park ride. She'd been so inside her head when they left the apartment, fighting off her unease at being alone with a man who was literally in control of the vehicle and, therefore, her. But once Nick confronted her silence, and then was willing to take her *home* rather than make her uncomfortable, she'd finally set her fear aside. Nick was right—it was a gorgeous day and she'd been missing it, sitting inside with her book.

When he'd turned the truck onto the steep dirt road—all rutted and muddy—she was so surprised that all she could do was laugh. Never in a million years had she ever pictured herself bouncing around in a Jeep going up a mountain. And it was…*fun*. She couldn't remember the last time she'd had actual fun doing something. Not that she hadn't had moments of happiness or laughter since leaving Milwaukee, but to *do* something that was fun, instead of just laughing along while someone else did something… Yeah, she hadn't done that in years.

Even this hike, with all its pain—and she was in serious pain—was almost fun in a weird way. She was so far outside her normal comfort zone that she was pretty amazed at herself. And proud. She slowed for a moment, thinking about that last word. She was *proud* of herself. Pride was that odd, unrecognizable sensation she'd felt over the past few weeks as she pushed herself to become stronger. As she started taking responsibility for protecting herself. For standing her ground.

She tried to remember the last time she'd felt proud of herself. High school? She'd always had good grades, but reading and studying had come easy for her, so it wasn't a big challenge. College? Her social awkwardness as an introvert made it hard to fit in with any of the cliques and clubs, but she had worked hard to stay on the dean's list every semester. That was something to be proud of, right?

"Cass? Seriously, are you okay?" Nick was right in front of her now, snapping her out of her thoughts and back into the present. The present where her legs were in flames. She blew out a long, slow breath and tried to keep her face as neutral as possible.

"I'm great, Nick. Don't stop for me."

He gave her a crooked smile. "I didn't stop for you. I stopped because we're here."

She looked around in surprise. They'd reached a small, grassy clearing. To her right, a giant boulder—the size of a city bus—sat at the base of the rocky summit far above. To her left was a view of Gallant Lake that took her breath away.

The mountains around the lake glowed with the bright green of new growth. The clear blue sky above was reflected in the calm waters of the lake, creating a palette that screamed, "Spring!" Cassie walked toward the rocky drop-off, mesmerized by the view. Nick gently stopped her with a hand on her shoulder, releasing her as quickly as he'd touched her.

"After yesterday's rain, let's not chance the slip-factor on this cliff, okay?"

She didn't respond right away, staring at the view. Then she spun to face him.

"We did it! We made it to the top of the mountain! And my legs aren't cramping anymore… Well, not as much, anyway…"

His quick flash of amusement vanished. "Your legs were cramping? Here, drink some water." He reached around and pulled a metal water container out of the small canvas pack he had slung over his shoulder. "You're probably dehydrated. You didn't say you were getting leg cramps—that's nothing to mess around with."

She took the water and drank deep. It was cold and refreshing. Then she handed it back with a wide grin. "Thanks." She gestured toward the view. "This made it worth it. I can't believe I climbed to the top of a mountain!"

He chuckled, his laughter warm and deep. "You didn't 'climb' a mountain. You hiked up a mountain path after I drove halfway up here. And we're not at the top." He looked over his shoulder. "But I can get you a little closer to it. Come on." He took her hand and gave a gentle tug. It felt oddly right to have her hand in his. He led her to the bus-sized boulder and she discovered there was a little path to the side that allowed her, with minimal climbing skills, to scramble to the top of the rock.

"Here," Nick said, tugging her back to the cliff wall. "From back here if you look out, it's like you're standing at the edge of the cliff with nothing below you. Without the risk of falling a few hundred feet down the mountain."

He was right. If she put her back to the rocks, the boulder was wide enough that it hid the grassy opening and trail, showing nothing but the lake and mountains.

"It's like flying." She barely whispered the words, but Nick nodded in agreement.

"That's what it's like when you climb a peak. You're on top of the world, and it feels like no one has ever been there before you."

There was something magical about standing here, sharing this moment with him.

"You've only been here a month—how did you find this amazing little secret up here?"

"It's not exactly a secret. Blake said it's a pretty popular spot for the locals, because it's such an easy walk…" She huffed out a laugh and he grinned. "Easy for the kids who like to climb up here, anyway. They call it the Kissing Rock."

She didn't answer right away. Gallant Lake seemed to inspire a lot of romantic names for places. Amanda called Cassie's apartment a love shack, and now she was standing on the Kissing Rock.

"It's a stone with a view," she said. "What makes it a Kissing Rock?"

Nick shrugged, and the movement caused his arm to rub the length of hers, pointing out how close they were standing. She could step away. But she didn't.

"I guess it's been called that for generations. People came up here with picnic lunches, and maybe the view, um...*inspired* them. Or maybe they came up in the evenings and watched the sun setting, like it's starting to do now, and they were alone at the edge of the world like this..." He looked down at her, his eyes dark and his emotions hidden. Was he pressing more tightly against her? Or was that her leaning in? "And I imagine a young couple might feel their inhibitions disappearing up here. No one would see them. No one would know if they stole a kiss or two."

They were facing each other now. She wasn't sure how that happened, but they'd both turned, so it was mutual. The sun was warm. A soft breeze rustled the young leaves in the trees that lined the view toward the lake. There were birds singing, but it felt like silence. Like a warm, safe cocoon of silence and...safety.

...you know in your heart you're safe with me...

They were so close she could feel the vibration in his chest when he spoke.

"It's a little like Vegas, I guess. What happens on Kissing Rock stays on Kissing Rock."

His hands were resting on her waist. How had that happened? And hers were on his biceps. His strong, hard biceps. This was an afternoon for new sensations. First was fun. Then pride. And now? Now she was feeling something she hadn't felt in…maybe forever. Sure, Don made her want to be with him. He'd paved the way to make it feel inevitable. But she'd never felt this pool of warmth deep in her belly as she flexed her fingers against Nick's arms and saw his nostrils flare in response. She'd never felt the tingle of excitement that had moved her so close her pelvis brushed across the zipper of his shorts, earning a low, strangled sound from him as his grip tightened on her.

He turned, putting her back to the rocks. Blocking the sun. Blocking everything but this new kind of burn. Not one of pain, but one of need. She whispered his name, and he closed his eyes, holding them tightly closed as if having a battle with himself. She said his name again, and he shook his head. His eyes didn't open until he started to speak in a voice filled with gravel and deep with emotion.

"This isn't why I brought you here. I didn't plan this…" He cupped her cheek with his hand. "There are a hundred ways this can go wrong…"

She rested her hand over his on the side of her face. "I can't believe you're the one being timid right now. *You.*" He smiled at that, but he didn't make a move. Oh, God, why wasn't he making a move?

He closed his eyes again, shaking his head slowly.

"This is a mistake." He stepped back, moving his hand away from her face and running it through his own hair. "We're coworkers. We hardly know each other. We've both got baggage. You're not…"

A chill ran through her veins. Nick didn't want Cassie. Of course he didn't. He was a cool, confident ladies' man, and she wasn't his type. She was a timid bookworm who jumped and flinched at everything, and big, bold Nick West, hero cop, didn't want someone like her. Nick wanted a fearless woman who swung from cliffs and rode a mountain bike. A woman who didn't need self-defense lessons. She straightened and moved out from between him and the rock face.

"Of course. You're right. I'm sorry." Damn it to hell, there she went, apologizing again. Apologizing for this *mistake*. Apologizing for being who she was.

Nick reached for her, but she tugged free, moving to the spot where they'd climbed up onto this stupid Kissing Rock. The sun was getting lower, and they really should get back to the Jeep and back to reality. The reality where she understood her place and knew her limits. She took hold of a small tree and put her foot on a root that had acted like a ladder rung on the way up here. But her heel couldn't grip that damp, round root the way her toes had earlier. Before she knew it, she was falling, her butt hitting the rock hard and catapulting her forward on her hands and knees on the ground. The fall, and abrupt halt, stunned her into silence. But it had the opposite effect on Nick, who was scrambling down while calling her name and cursing.

"Cassie! Are you okay? Damn it, Cass, say something!" He hit his knees next to her just as she sat back and rubbed the palms of her hands on her jeans, wincing a little. The mud softened her landing, but her wrists were still sore. And her knees. And her butt.

Nick's hands were running down her arms now, and then her back, before running up her neck and holding her face from each side. "Are you hurt?"

"Other than my pride? I don't think so." She gently pushed his hands away, not ready to fall into that temptation trap again. She stood, and he rose with her, one arm around her waist to steady her. The pain in her hip, where she slammed into the rock, made her grimace. "I'm such a klutz. I bet you've never seen your mountain climbing buddies do that move. As you know, my hand-eye coordination is subpar at best..."

"Cass, I once missed a cleat on a rock face and fell twenty feet before the rope caught me. But my harness was too loose and I ended up hanging upside down fifty feet in the air, swinging back and forth like a pendulum, with my ass exposed to the whole world."

She couldn't help a short laugh. "I would have liked to have seen that."

"Oh, you can. My buddy caught it all on his phone, and it briefly went viral on the rock climbing forums." His hand ran down her back, stopping at her hip when she flinched. "Yeah, I thought I saw you bounce off the rock right there. You'll have a hell of a bruise. Do you think it's any more than that?"

She took a few steps. She was sore, but that was probably as much from the climb up as from the fall. "I'm good. We should get back before it starts getting dark." He nodded, but he didn't head for the trail. Instead, he walked straight to her. She put her hands up and he stopped, his chest brushing against hers. "Wh-what are you doing?"

He stared at her hard, then slid his arms around her. She didn't resist when he pulled her up tight to him. "I'm doing what I should have done up on that damn Kissing Rock. Or maybe what I shouldn't have done. I don't know. I only know there's no way in hell I'm leaving this mountain before I've kissed you." Her fingers twisted into his shirt, just to make sure he didn't change his mind again. He didn't move, waiting for her consent.

She tugged on his shirt and lifted her chin.

"Well, what are you waiting for?"

And just like that, his lips were on hers. His kiss was firm and commanding. In control without making her feel overpowered. And skilled. Oh, so skilled. She parted her mouth and his tongue was inside her in a flash. She melted against him, trusting him to hold her upright, and he did, with a low growl of approval. Their mouths moved as one, in a dance as seductive as a tango. He took and she gave, then she rose on her toes and took from him, and his fingers gripped her waist and held her there. Her hands were eager to be part of the game and slid up so she could clutch the back of his head. Their teeth clicked together and apart and together again, and it wasn't enough for her. She wanted more, and she stretched even taller to meet him. To have a moment of control all for herself. As if knowing what she needed, Nick bent his knees, then lifted her up so her head was above his. The kiss never broke, but now she was the one being demanding. She was the one taking over. Her hands cupped his face. He stared up at her with a fire that mirrored hers. Startled, she pulled back.

Nick let her slide slowly down to her feet, his eyes never leaving hers. He kissed her again, but this kiss was different. This wasn't the experienced player using his skills to leave her legless. This was a kiss with more uncertainty in it, as if he was exploring some new territory where he'd never been before. Tender, cautious and slow. He drifted from her lips to her chin, then down her neck and up to the tender skin below her ear, then back to her lips. She was drunk on him. Drunk on Nick West. And she was hopelessly dependent. Craving her next fix before this one even ended.

Then his lips were gone from hers. He'd set her at arm's length from him, staring at her in bewilderment, then turning away.

"Holy shit, Cass." He shook himself as if to shake off whatever spell had come over them both. "What the hell was that?"

"Uh…a kiss?"

"Baby, that was a lot more than just a kiss."

Baby? Cassie did her best to ignore the endearment. It didn't seem as if Nick was using it that way anyhow.

He stared at the ground, then looked out to the lake, and the sun lowering beyond it. He kept his back to her.

"We should get back to the truck before it gets dark. Can you walk?"

What just happened? That kiss had seemed *electric*…until Nick flipped off the switch and pushed her away. But then again, Don always told her she was a boring lover.

"I'm sorry…" Every time she said those words, it burned her. But this time they felt appropriate. Clearly, she'd had a different experience than Nick had. "I'm not very good at that stuff. Kissing. Sex. All of it…none of it…whatever…"

Chapter Eight

Nick stared at Cassie in confusion. What the hell was she apologizing for? She'd just rocked his world with a kiss that would forever raise the bar on any future kisses that came his way. And did she say she wasn't good at *sex*? No way did he believe that. Not after a kiss that had him turning away to hide the erection tenting his shorts. If he didn't get her off this mountain, they'd be joining the decades-long list of couples who'd consummated their relationships on the Kissing Rock. And as much as his body wanted that to happen—*right now*—Nick knew Cassie deserved better. This wasn't where or how he wanted it to happen. *If* it happened. And it probably shouldn't happen. But *damn*…

She turned away, her head hung low. He had to fix this, and fast.

"Cassie, I don't know who the idiot was who told you that you weren't—" he raised his fingers into air quotes "—'good at this,' but he was wrong. Like, *really* wrong. Like, he couldn't have been *more* wrong." He walked toward her. "Did you not feel how great that was?" How could she not have felt that?

Her cheeks flamed. "I did think it was pretty…great. But then you stopped…"

He chuckled softly. "Uh… I had no choice. It was either put some space between us or embarrass myself like some middle school teen. You had me thinking some very impure thoughts, Cass, and if we'd stayed that close, you would have felt just how strong those thoughts were."

Her brows furrowed, then rose in surprise.

"Oh…"

Nick wouldn't have thought it possible, but the color in her cheeks deepened even further.

"Oh!" Her mouth lifted into a slightly proud smile. *Damn straight, girl.* "Oh. I thought…"

"You thought, once again, that you'd done something wrong. That's always your first response, isn't it? Why is that?"

Her smile vanished, and he kicked himself for speaking his thoughts out loud. But instead of avoiding the subject, she looked at him and nodded.

"It's generally my go-to. I… I had a lot of years of someone telling me I was doing everything wrong. Apologizing becomes habit after a while." She ran her fingers through her dark hair, smoothing the ponytail that had been mussed from her fall, and then from their kiss. "And you seemed to be…fighting it. Up there…" She glanced up to the top of the rock. "We were so close, and you started listing all the reasons we shouldn't…"

Nick couldn't help laughing. "That little speech up there? The list of all the reasons kissing you was a mistake? That was me giving myself a verbal cold shower." He ran his hands down her arms and caught her hands. "Being that close to you had my blood rushing to places it had no business rushing to. Not in the middle of the day on the side of a mountain. Rattling off that list cooled me down enough to step away and gather my wits."

He squeezed her hands. "But when you got upset and tumbled down the side of the rock trying to get away from me, I knew 'space' wasn't what I needed. Or at least, it wasn't what I wanted. But if I thought being close to you was a turn-on, *kissing* you was… Well, like I said. That was more than chemistry. That was a whole damn laboratory fire going on."

She held his gaze, and he could see her mind racing and stalling and crashing. Yeah, he should have just kissed her again before she had a chance to overthink things. She swallowed hard.

"But you weren't wrong… It's a mistake. We *do* work together. And we *do* have baggage. And we *don't* know each other that well…"

He let her pull away, sensing her rising panic.

"*Now* who's taking the cold shower?" He grinned, and she did her best not to grin back, but failed. He shook his head. "First—I think we know each other pretty well. I'd like to think we're friends, even. We may not have shared our life stories yet, but that can be remedied over dinner some night. Second—everyone has baggage. That's an empty excuse. And third—yeah, we work together. But I'm not aware of any rules against fraternization at Randall Resorts International. I'm not your boss, and we didn't kiss in the office." He shrugged. "Honestly, so far all we've done is have a stellar kissing session at the Kissing Rock. I'd like to have *another* stellar kissing session with you somewhere else, but that's your call, Cassie."

"I... I'm not good at this..." She held up her hand to stop his objection to the way she always put herself down. "That's not self-pity, Nick. I mean I'm not...experienced...at dating, or relationships, or kissing guys on mountains. I don't know how to navigate what happens next."

"Okay. Executive decision time." He took her hand and tucked it in the crook of his arm. They headed for the trail. "Let's stop worrying and get away from this damn rock. What happens at the rock, stays at the rock and all that." Cassie snorted in laughter. He liked all her laughs, even the snorting ones, so he kept lying to her. "No, really. No one has to know, and our friendship doesn't have to change. On Monday, we'll have a normal day at work, and a normal gym session afterward, like today never happened. And if one of us decides we need to pursue this—whatever this is—we'll discuss it like adults. Deal?"

She glanced his way quickly, careful to also watch where she was stepping as they went down the trail. He wasn't fooling anyone. Nothing would be the same between them, and the thought made him sad. He'd enjoyed the teasing and fun they'd shared. Watching Cassie gain new confidence and strength as they worked out together. He didn't want to lose that. As tempting as it was to pursue more kisses, or perhaps more than just kissing, he didn't like the thought of anything changing their existing relationship.

"Of course. That makes sense." She was playing along. "Nothing needs to change… Oh!" She stumbled on the trail, but Nick caught her waist and kept her upright, resisting the sudden and unexpected urge to pull her into his arms, bury his hands in her hair and kiss her senseless.

Bad idea… Too complicated…baggage…coworker…

"Exactly. Nothing needs to change. Nothing at all."

"Cassie-girl, where *are* you this morning? Nora called your name three times to tell you your cappuccino is ready."

Cathy set the foam-topped mug in front of Cassie on the window table inside the Gallant Brew. "Is everything okay? You haven't heard from Don…?"

"No, Aunt Cathy. It's not that. I'm just tired. I overdid things a bit yesterday."

That was the understatement of the century. She'd not only agreed to hike Gallant Mountain with Nick West, she'd also *kissed* the man. More than once. And she'd *liked* it. A lot. Definitely overdone.

"What'd you do, honey? Is Blake working you too hard up there at the resort?"

"Uh…no. He's not." Amanda Randall walked in. "Why would you ask that?"

Nora walked over with a plate of ginger cookies and a sly smile. Over the past few weeks, Cassie had given in to Amanda's pestering about becoming a hermit and started joining the cousins and Aunt Cathy for their before-the-Sunday-rush coffee in Nora's shop.

Nora set the cookies on the table and grabbed a chair. "Cassie said she overdid things yesterday and Cathy was worried. But I don't think it was Blake who kept her busy." Nora winked at Cassie, and she felt a sense of dread. "I think Nick West might be the one 'over-working' her these days."

Amanda sat quickly, putting her elbows on the table and her chin in her hands. "*Really?* Do tell, Nora!"

Cathy's eyes narrowed. "Nick West? That guy who was in the shop a few weeks ago and followed you upstairs? Cassie, what's going on?"

Amanda laughed. "I *told* you that apartment was a love shack! Come on, Nora, spill what you know."

"Hey, wait!" The last of the cousins, Melanie Lowery, rushed into the shop, smoothing her hair with her hand and looking flustered. "No spilling anything until I get some espresso and join in. I'm always missing the good stuff!"

Nora sighed and went behind the counter to make Melanie's coffee. "Maybe if you weren't always late to the party, Mel, you wouldn't miss everything."

The tall brunette waved a dismissive hand. "Honey, my fiancé's been on the West Coast for a week. By the time his flight landed, we had a lot of…um…catching up to do, if you get my drift." She took a cookie and sighed as she took a bite. "Oh, I love my gingers."

"Got it, Mel. Sweet ginger cookies. Hot ginger fiancé." Amanda fixed her gaze back on Nora as she rejoined them, delivering Mel's espresso with a flourish. "Spill it, girl."

Nora glanced out toward the empty sidewalk, making sure there were no customers heading their way, then leaned forward, lowering her voice dramatically.

"Well, I just happened to set some trash outside the back door yesterday afternoon to keep it from stinking up the kitchen. I always clean out the fridge and the display on Saturday afternoons to make way for the fresh Sunday baked goods..."

Amanda rolled her eyes. "Yes, yes, we know you're the queen of organization. Get to the good stuff."

"Seriously?" Cassie interrupted, glaring at Amanda. "Is this the 'magic of having girlfriends' you told me I needed?" No one paid any attention, all eyes fixed on Nora.

"Well," Nora said. "Imagine my surprise when I saw Nick sitting in his Jeep out in the parking lot. Before I could set the trash down and wave, I heard footsteps on the back stairs, and there was Cassie—" all four heads swiveled in Cassie's direction "—trotting down the stairs and over to the Jeep and hopping right in. Then they drove off together. On a Saturday afternoon. Almost like a date or something."

Three sets of eyebrows rose, but Cathy was scowling. "Cassie, you don't know this guy. Don't you think it's a little soon to jump right back into a relationship?"

Being the center of attention put Cassie on the defensive. "One kiss doesn't make it a relationship."

Oh, damn her filter-free mouth when she was nervous...

There was a collective gasp of delight from the cousins. Melanie rested her hand on Cassie's arm.

"You *kissed* Nick West?"

She bit her lip, upset that she'd blurted that out, but also wanting the advice of women she trusted and admired. She hadn't lied yesterday when she told Nick she had little experience at this. After college, Don had pretty much been her only relationship, and that was hardly the measuring stick she wanted to use for future ones.

Amanda's voice softened. "Hey, guys, it's a big deal to move on after what Cassie's been through. If she doesn't want to talk about it..."

"Actually, I think I *do* want to talk about it."

"Oh, thank God! Tell us everything!" Amanda's laugh made Cassie smile.

She gave the women a summary of the Nick-and-Cassie story. Their disastrous first meeting when she threw the stapler at him. Pepper-spraying him. Agreeing to let him help her with self-defense and fitness training. The playful teasing they did at work, with him hiding her stapler and her scattering reports across his desk in an untidy array that annoyed him every time. The bar Friday night, where she told him she would *not* go hiking with him. Nick showing up at her door anyway. The hike she thought would kill her. The kiss that nearly did. And finally, her and Nick's agreement to not allow it to change anything. There was silence for a moment when she finished, then Amanda spoke.

"So you think you and Nick might be friends, and you don't want to screw that up."

She thought about that. She looked forward to going to work when Nick was there. She never knew what she'd find on her desk or where her stapler might be. He always dropped some off-the-cuff comment that made her smile. He drove her crazy with that stupid foam basketball. He also did his best to make sure she felt secure, while pushing her to try new things. She'd never had a big brother, but if she had, she had a feeling that's what their relationship would be like.

She nodded at Amanda's guess. "I like Nick. I mean, like him like a friend. A fun coworker. He's a good guy who annoys me to no end, but he's also..."

"He's also someone you want to climb like a tree?" Melanie lifted her coffee mug in a toast. "I think we've all been there, right, ladies?"

The three cousins laughed and agreed, but Cathy wasn't amused.

"Keep it in the friend zone, honey. If you get attached and have to..."

Cassie nodded. The go-bag sitting by her door upstairs was a constant reminder that she could end up running again. Changing her name again. Starting over again. It hadn't been that hard to leave Cleveland, but leaving Gallant Lake? This move was going to hurt if it ever came. And getting involved with Nick West would make it that much more complicated. He didn't strike her as the kind of guy to just let her leave. He'd want to rescue her, and the thought of him going up against someone as flat-out evil as Don made her shudder.

"It's not easy to do." Amanda sighed. "Blake and I were friends, and I worked for him, but after that first kiss… Well, as hard as we tried, the friend zone was toast." Nora and Mel nodded in agreement, dreamy-eyed and smiling.

Cassie finished her coffee, trying to block the memory of yesterday's kisses. Going down that path would only lead to heartbreak.

"Aunt Cathy's right. I can't let this change things. Yesterday was a surprise. And yes—" she rolled her eyes at Amanda's snicker "—it was a nice surprise. It's nice to know I can still feel desire for a man, and that a man might desire me. That I could melt like that…" And there she went, oversharing again. She needed to get better at this girlfriend thing. Nora stood as a group of customers walked in, dressed in their Sunday church clothes.

"I gotta run," Nora said. "But if that man made you 'melt,' you should think twice before passing him up."

Chapter Nine

"Man, that climb was turbocharged today, Nick! Was there a race that I didn't know about?" Terrance Hudson took a long drink from his water bottle, then poured some on the edge of his shirt and wiped the sweat from his face. Nick, Terrance and the rest of the Rebel Rockers climbing club were sitting atop the Arrow Wall at the Shawangunk cliffs, known locally as the Gunks. "Shit, man. For someone who's never climbed this sucker, you were on fire. I ain't never seen a guy go up this wall that fast!"

Nick took a swig from his own water, pouring the rest of it over his head. The sun was high and hot today. He nodded to his climbing partner, whom he'd met only a week ago at his first meeting of the Rebel Rockers at the Chalet in Gallant Lake.

"Sorry for the pace. I tend to climb quick. That last part of the climb—what do they call it, Modern Times? That was pretty intense for a 5.8 rating. I just wanted to get it over with and get up here to relax." Also, he was running from the memories of yesterday's kisses with the not-so-shy-after-all Cassandra Smith. But Terrance didn't need to know that.

"Yeah, that last stretch is a challenge, but man, the views, right?" Terrance nodded toward the valley that stretched out hundreds of feet below them. It was impressive, but it had nothing on yesterday's view of Gallant Lake reflected in Cassie's golden eyes right before his lips touched hers. He shook off the memory. So many reasons not to do that again. And so many nerve endings humming in his body, begging for more.

Terrance turned and started chatting with another climber—Sam something—leaving Nick to consider all the options with Cassie. As much as he'd dismissed the coworker issue, he knew how messy workplace flings could be. He'd seen the damage done at the precinct back in LA when two of his fellow detectives had a quick affair. She'd ended it, but the guy didn't want to take no for an answer. Things got so ugly they ended up transferring the woman across town, which never sat right with Nick. She wasn't the one causing problems.

And he and Cassie would probably end up being a quick affair. They had nothing in common, other than driving each other crazy with office pranks. He was still finding new places to hide that blue stapler every morning. He'd even snuck into the ladies' room to set it on the sink in there. And ever since he told her how much he valued organized files, she'd started coming into his office and shuffling his folders or scattering them all over his desk.

But other than the office high jinks, what did they have? Well…hot chemistry, for sure. But besides that, what was there? He was restless and liked to be physically active. He hated sitting around, and that was her favorite thing to do—sit with her tea and a book. As much as she was improving her strength and fighting skills in their gym sessions, she was still jumpy and quick to take on blame. Always apologizing. He tucked his water bottle back in his pack.

She was a victim. He thought about Beth Washington going back to her brute of a husband over and over, until Nick shot the man dead. After Earl Washington had murdered his partner. Beth's refusal to leave the man, to protect herself, had directly led to Jada's death.

The fire of his physical attraction to Cassie started to cool as common sense prevailed. If she was one of those perpetual victims, then she wasn't right for him long-term, and short-term wasn't really an option when they worked in the same damn office. Problem solved. Sharing any more kisses was a no go.

"You ready for the return trip? Got your lines ready?" Terrance stood, his dark skin shining with sweat. He was sure-footed and relaxed, just inches from the cliff edge. Good climbers respected the mountain but were never intimidated by it. Nick stood and checked his gear.

"I'm ready if you are."

"Cool. Let's not race this time, okay? We won't be back here until next month, so try to enjoy it, man."

Nick nodded. His little self-talk had him settled down now where he could focus. From this point forward, he and Cassie were friends, and that kiss was an aberration that wouldn't be happening again.

"Nick, I swear to God, you're driving me crazy! I need my stapler!" Cassie slammed her desk drawer closed. She'd checked her desk twice and Blake's desk once. She'd looked on the coffee counter and the storage cabinets and the empty office by the door. She'd pulled the curtains completely open, and checked under the air-conditioning unit. She'd gone through Nick's office once while he was meeting with Tim in the surveillance room and was ready to toss it again, whether Nick was in there or not. And he was. Smirking at her from his desk chair, twirling his pen innocently.

She stood in the doorway and folded her arms, glaring at him. He'd upped his prank game this week to whole new levels. The stapler, of course. But, with Blake out of town and just the two of them sharing the office suite, he'd gone all out. Her desk phone went missing on Monday, hidden behind the drapes. On Tuesday her tape *and* the stapler *and* her notebook were sitting on Blake's desk. Her wireless keyboard was tucked behind the coffeepot on Wednesday. Yesterday the stapler was *inside* the empty coffeepot. And today, when he knew damn well she had to put together presentation packets for Blake's investor meeting this weekend, the stapler was nowhere to be found.

"Is there a problem?"

"Yes. A big, stupid problem who needs to get a life. Where. Is. My. Stapler?"

He tossed his pen in the air and caught it. That devilish grin made her heart jump. Damn, he was sexy. And annoying, she reminded herself. An annoying friend and coworker who was like a big brother and she wasn't attracted to him at all. Nope. Not one bit. She hadn't been attracted to him yesterday in the gym when he taught her how to use her elbows to break free from being grabbed from behind. Which meant he'd had to grab her over and over again, insisting that she get it right. Nope. Not attracted at all.

He'd been cool as a cucumber all week. He'd brought up the kiss first thing Monday morning, assuring her that it wasn't going to be a problem between them, and they should forget it ever happened. It was nothing more than a Kissing Rock spell that had been broken as soon as they left the mountain. She'd felt a sting of disappointment that he could set it aside so easily after telling her he'd had a hard-on after kissing her, but his actions seemed to support his words. He'd been the same Nick he'd been the weeks before—joking, teasing, playing basketball with the foam ball, teaching her, clowning around with the staff.

It seemed Nick had moved on from their kiss with nothing more to show for it than a renewed enthusiasm for his job. And driving her crazy. He tossed his pen again, almost to the ceiling, and had to lean back to snatch it out of the air when it came down. She bit back a sigh of frustration. He'd wait her out until the offices closed if he had to.

"Where is it, Nick?"

"Where have you looked?"

Her eyes narrowed on him. She was done playing. She reached for his desk and tried to take his cell phone, but he was too quick for her. He held it over his head and laughed.

"Seriously? You thought you'd outmaneuver a cop?"

"You're not a cop anymore, Nick. You're just the jackass who won't give me my stapler."

A frown flickered across his face. He didn't talk about his days on the LA police force. Amanda told Cassie last week she'd learned the beautiful woman in the wedding gown in the photo behind Nick was his former partner. And that she was dead.

He summoned a fresh smile and shook off whatever he'd been thinking about. "Check the coat closet. You might have to work for it this time."

"Wonderful. As if I'm not already working." She turned and went to the closet. She didn't see it at first. She looked up and saw the edge of the stapler barely peeking over the top shelf. She called over her shoulder as she rolled a desk chair to the closet. "Nice job, Nick. There's only an eighty percent probability this thing will bonk me on the head when I try to get it."

She was just putting her foot on the chair and praying it would stay put when she felt Nick's arm around her waist, pulling her back. "Are you actively trying to kill yourself? You can't stand on a chair with wheels." He sent the chair rolling back to the empty desk. "I'll get it. I didn't think about it hitting you, but you're right…" He stretched and worked the stapler off the shelf with his fingertips, while still holding her waist with his other arm. Her skin was tingling, but he seemed unaffected. "If it was going to happen to anyone, it'd happen to you. Here." He handed her the stapler, then rubbed his knuckles in her hair. Like she was his kid sister. Like she was a puppy. Like he had no desire for her whatsoever. And it ticked her off.

She swatted his hand away. "Here's an idea—stop hiding the damn thing! You're not a twelve-year-old, Nick, and this isn't grade school. What's next? Putting gum in my hair? This is an *office*. You said you wanted to keep things professional between us, so why don't you surprise me and actually *act* professional for once?"

"Whoa…easy!" Nick held up both hands in surrender. "What just happened?"

It was a fair question, but she wasn't in the mood to answer it.

"Nothing. I've just got actual work to do, Nick. And I'm pretty sure you do, too." She brushed past him and went back to sit at her desk. He closed the closet door and studied her, but she refused to make eye contact. She didn't trust her feelings right now, especially with the traitor tears threatening to spill over. What was *wrong* with her? Hadn't she decided that being friends was better than trying to follow up on that kissing business and possibly ruining everything? Wasn't that exactly what she'd agreed to on Monday—pretend the kiss didn't happen? Nick not being attracted to her was the best possible scenario. Besides, apparently the kiss really *had* been just a fluke for him, and that whole "chemistry lab on fire" that made him want a cold shower was a momentary phenomenon that had clearly passed. She was no longer the woman whose kisses made him hot and bothered. She was just a girl he liked to tease, whose hair he liked to noogie.

Nick walked over and sat on the corner of her desk, facing her. "Come on, kiddo, what's going…"

Kiddo?

She was on her feet in a flash.

"I'm not your *kiddo* or your *grasshopper* or anything else." And that was the truth. She wasn't anything else to him. And that was a *good* thing, damn it.

"What the hell is wrong with you today?" He took her arm, but she pulled away. She was losing it. She needed to get away from him before she burst into tears or threw herself into his arms. Either one would be a huge mistake.

"I need to go." She looked at the clock on the wall. "I'm taking an early lunch."

"Early lunch? It's not even eleven…" She glared at him and he stepped back, shaking his head. "Okay! Early lunch. Maybe we can talk this out later."

She nodded mutely, grabbed her purse and headed out the door.

Chapter Ten

Cassie headed for the lakeside path, hoping to avoid other humans for a while. It felt like something had just snapped inside her back in the office. Something that had been simmering since Saturday when she and Nick kissed up on the mountain that now rose above her, reflected in the water. When he slid his arm around her waist by the closet, everything she'd felt on Gallant Mountain had come rushing back. The heat, the liquid desire, the way his lips felt on hers, the sensation when he lifted her into the air and she'd looked down into his eyes, with the lake beyond him.

How could Nick deny what happened up there? How could he just continue to tease and taunt and touch her as if nothing had changed, when she knew she'd be forever changed? If nothing else, she'd learned she was capable of feeling not just desire, but as if *she* was *desirable*. Not a trophy on a shelf like Don treated her. But a woman who could appeal to a man like Nick West. Could make him want her. And damn it, she *knew* she'd made him want her, even if only for that moment.

To her, the sensation had been new and transformative. But Nick had kissed plenty of women in his life. She'd probably just been one more on a long list of fun little interludes he could easily forget. She slowed her pace, pausing to stare out over the water.

If that was the case, then it wasn't fair to be angry with him. He'd moved on because he'd had practice at moving on. And if he could do it, so could she. It would just take her a little longer. Like forever. She laughed softly to herself. *Stop being melodramatic.*

She was getting stronger. Smarter. Tougher. And Nick was the guy who'd helped her get there. Even when he didn't mean to. Sure, he taught her self-defense. But he also gave her noogies and hurt her feelings and kissed her senseless and hid her damn stapler. It seemed that *everything* Nick did made her stronger. And she couldn't be mad about that. She turned to head back to the resort. All she needed to figure out now was how to explain her little meltdown to Nick so they could continue as…friends. Wise, experienced, worldly friends who kissed one afternoon and were strong enough to move on without causing a ripple in their relationship.

Nick was gone when she walked into the office. Her stapler sat in the center of her desk, next to a vase filled with hydrangeas. They looked suspiciously similar to the blue hydrangeas near the back veranda of the resort.

Stolen daffodils had gone out of season. She picked up the note he'd left, in his usual hurried scribble that made it seem the words were ready to dash right off the page.

Your stapler looked sad, so I thought it might like some "borrowed" company. I forgot I have that meeting with the staffing firm in White Plains this afternoon. Let's start fresh tomorrow, and I'll give you a proper apology? —Nick

She smiled. He was a hard man to stay mad at. She'd forgotten all about the meeting in White Plains. They used temporary staff for large events, and Nick was training the company on proper security procedures. He'd be there all afternoon. Maybe it was for the best that they were going to have a little time apart. It would give her a chance to get her mind straight and put Nick firmly in the friend zone again. If he could move on from that kiss, well, then, so could she.

"Hey, Cassie! I'm so glad you're here." Julie came into the office. "Blake called a little while ago, but you and Nick were both gone." Julie gave her a pointed look, and Cassie rushed to set her straight.

"Nick's on his way to a meeting. I took an early lunch." She should have made sure the office was staffed. It wasn't like her to forget such a basic thing as making sure calls were handled. "I'm sorry. I should have let you know I was stepping out. What did Blake need?"

Julie looked flustered. "His flight is delayed, so he won't be here until almost midnight, and the welcome reception for the investors is tonight. Amanda offered to play hostess for dinner, but he wanted us to help her out for a few hours. He figured the group would go party on their own at the bar after that. Can you join us?"

Cassie frowned. A party with a bunch of powerful people she didn't know was not her idea of a good time. But she owed it to her friends and her boss to do her best. Besides this was new, improved Cassie—she was strong enough to do this. She put her hand on Julie's arm.

"I'll run home later and change into something dressy, and I'll be back in time for dinner."

Julie grinned. "You're a champ, Cassie! And after dinner, maybe you and Amanda and I can have a few Friday night cocktails together."

"Yeah, maybe." She had no intention of doing that, but Julie seemed so excited at the idea that Cassie didn't want to burst her bubble. She was sure she'd be so exhausted from pretending to be an extrovert and entertaining important investors over dinner that she'd beg off later with an excuse and head home.

But it ended up being a more relaxing evening than she'd anticipated. The four representatives from the investment firm were older, extremely professional and actually pretty interesting. The one woman in the group, Margaret Ackerman, was a book lover like Cassie, and they ended up discussing their favorite women's fiction while Amanda and Julie talked sports and travel with the three gentlemen. It made for an enjoyable meal. When the dessert plates had been cleared and the investors had gone off to their rooms to rest up for the early round of golf Blake had arranged for them, Cassie found herself with no viable excuse not to join the other women at the bar. After all, that's what girlfriends did, right?

Besides, she was eager to shake off her emotional morning with Nick. As happy as she was with her new plan to follow his example and just be buddies, there was a restlessness humming inside her. Her senses were on high alert, sending images of Nick's intense dark eyes through her mind. She could hear the breeze rustling through the trees up on Gallant Mountain, and the low growl in Nick's chest as he kissed her. She could feel his hands on her waist, lifting her into the air without breaking their kiss. She could smell the pines…

"Can I have another?" She blurted out the words as the bartender, Josie, passed by.

"Easy, girl! You're already on your second Gallant Lake Sunset." Amanda laughed.

Cassie shrugged. "Hey, it's just orange juice, right? And a little honey liqueur?"

Julie held her empty wineglass up to let Josie know she needed a refill. "And vodka. Don't forget the vodka that's in there. But don't worry, I can drive you home later."

Amanda looked at Julie's wineglass. "Isn't it customary for the designated driver to abstain from alcohol? Cass, there's always a room open at Halcyon, and it's right next door." Amanda and Blake lived in an actual castle, built on the lake over a hundred years ago. The place had at least ten bedrooms. But she didn't feel drunk at all. She checked her phone.

"It's only nine thirty, ladies, and this drink isn't that strong. I'll stop at three drinks and be done. Now, Julie,

finish telling us about this old farmhouse you bought."
Julie was more than happy to oblige, describing the adventures she'd already had with the old house outside
town. Cassie sat back and sipped her drink. This was
part of the girlfriend game that she could get used to.
Listening to women laugh and share their joys and frustrations together. It was much nicer when *she* wasn't the
topic of conversation.

She was halfway through her fourth Sunset by the
time the conversation started to wind down. The drinks
were sweet and tasty and proved very effective at helping her forget all that earlier confusion about…what's-
his-name. They helped her be better at girl talk, too. She
giggled at Julie's stories about the leaky roof and sagging floors at the old house she'd bought. She laughed
at Amanda's description of her young daughter, Maddie, throwing a tantrum at preschool because their nap
time was on yoga mats, not "real" beds with lacy canopies like she had at home.

"That's one of the reasons we wanted her in preschool as early as possible," Amanda explained. "We're
not *intentionally* spoiling her, but the kid lives in a castle, and Blake and Zachary dote on her every whim."

"And you don't?" Cassie winked at Julie, who was
holding back laughter.

"No! I mean…not on purpose. But you guys, she's
so damn cute. And smart. Way too smart." Amanda
yawned. "And that busy brain likes to wake up early,
so I'd better get home. It'll be midnight by the time
Blake gets here from LaGuardia, and he won't want to
get up with her. Cassie, you're coming with me, right?"

They all stood, but Cassie was the only one who had to reach out and grab the edge of the bar to steady herself. The room wasn't exactly spinning, but it wasn't staying still, either.

Julie shook her head. "I tried to tell you mixed drinks will get you every time. Stick to wine or beer, girl. I'll drive her home, Amanda. I switched to water a while ago." Amanda looked skeptical, but Julie closed her eyes and touched her fingers to her nose while standing on one foot. She didn't stop until Amanda gave in.

"Fine! Text me once she's inside, since I don't think *she'll* remember to do it."

Cassie frowned. Her face felt funny, almost like she couldn't quite feel her own mouth moving. "*She* is standing right here between the two of you. I know I had too much to be able to drive, but I'm not exactly wasted." She turned and gave Amanda her most serious look, which, for some reason, made Amanda giggle. "And I *will* remember to text you when I'm home. Mom."

"Yeah, yeah, laugh all you want at the responsible adult trying to keep everyone safe. That's fine. I'm outta here." Amanda gave them each a quick, fierce hug and headed out of the bar. Halcyon was a short walk up the hill, and Cassie saw Bill Chesnutt heading toward the boss's wife to escort her up to their home. She'd be fine.

"I have to get my stuff from the back office," Julie said, "and hit the ladies' room. Meet you by the staircase in five minutes?" Julie side-eyed Cassie as they headed out into the lobby. "Are you going to throw up or anything? Because my car has leather seats, and…"

"I am *not* going to throw up! I'm not drunk. I'm... tipsy. And I'm very much enjoying this rare and precious little buzz, so you buzz on out of here and do whatever." She looked across the lobby. "Maybe I'll go get a cup of tea."

Nick watched the two women from the top of the lobby stairs. He couldn't believe it. Cassie Smith was *drunk*? No, not drunk. *Tipsy*. She called it a "precious little buzz." Cassie was damn cute when she was buzzed.

He'd spent the afternoon in meetings and training sessions, but she'd been on his mind the entire time. She'd been really upset with him that morning. Things had been so good all week, after they agreed to pretend that kiss on Saturday never happened. He might have been a little more of a pest than usual, but he was only trying to show her that nothing was going to be weird or awkward just because they'd slipped up and kissed a few times. By accident. When he'd given her that little noogie today, it was just to emphasize how totally cool they were. But something had set her off, and she'd hissed at him like she'd done that very first day, when she sent the stapler flying at his face. And then she'd... well, he was pretty sure she'd almost...cried. Over *him*. It had bugged him all afternoon.

He tucked his planner under his arm and descended the staircase. The planner was more an excuse than anything else. It was a reason to paddle over to the resort tonight. Via the kayak he was thinking of buying.

The short, sturdy kayak he'd brought from Califor-

nia was designed for white water. And while there was
some of that around, especially farther north in the Ad-
irondacks, it wasn't the best for lake paddling. On lakes,
the longer kayaks gave a faster, smoother ride. The only
problem with this one, which the hardware store owner,
Nate Thomas, was selling, was that it was a little *too*
long. It was a two-person kayak, and Nick wasn't sure
he wanted that, even if the extra seat could come in
handy for carrying a cooler or other supplies. But he
wasn't planning on paddling out on a three-day trip anywhere. And it wouldn't sit on the Jeep very well if he
ever wanted to travel with it. He'd pretty much talked
himself out of buying it before he put it in the water.

But the sleek vessel had cut through the water like a
hot knife through butter tonight on the journey from his
house to the resort, and was stable and easy to handle.
He just never expected the trip to end with Cassie giggling and weaving across the lobby in front of him. At
eleven o'clock at night. He frowned. How were these
two women planning on getting home?

Her hair was pulled back, as usual, but tonight it
was held in place with sparkly clips behind her ears.
She was wearing a dress instead of her usual slacks
and sweater. The dark gold dress, swirling above her
knees, was loose and fluttery. The fabric followed her
curves when she moved. Her smile was a little crooked,
and a lot adorable, as she watched Julie walk away. She
headed for the coffee bar—definitely a good idea in her
condition—and swayed only a little.

She was so intent on opening her tea bag packet and

actually getting the bag *inside* the cup that she jumped when he walked up behind her.

"Pulling an all-nighter, Miss Smith?"

"Nick! What are you doing here? And why are you dressed like…"

She gestured to his attire, which he'd forgotten about. Battered cargo shorts and a well-worn T-shirt from Yosemite. A ball cap sat backward on his head, and he quickly grabbed it off and ran his fingers through his hair, tucking the cap in his back pocket.

"I'm more interested in why you're so dressed up. What was the occasion?"

Her brows furrowed, then she looked down at her dress.

"Oh! This? Uh… Blake's flight was delayed and Amanda needed Julie and me to help entertain some investors who arrived today."

"And how exactly did you entertain them?" Had she been hanging out at the bar with sleazebag bankers all night?

She rolled her eyes. "We had *dinner* with them, Nick. No self-defense moves required. Then we decided we deserved a girls' night out and went to the bar. And I had my first Gallant Lake Sunset. Well…" She smiled and shrugged. "I had my first four Gallant Lake Sunsets."

"You had *four* drinks? And you think you're driving home?"

She turned away from him, finally managing to get the tea bag inside the cup. She filled it with hot water and added her usual three packets of sugar. Her voice turned prim. "That's not really your concern, is it? After all, we're just coworkers. Just friends. So go on and do whatever it is you're doing, and don't worry about me."

She said "just friends" as if it was an accusation. It was what they'd *both* agreed to Monday morning. Unless maybe she wanted more? That possibility had Nick once again reciting all the reasons they shouldn't. Coworkers. Baggage. And… What was the last one? The memory of how she felt in his arms was short-circuiting his ability to focus. He forced himself to be the responsible one.

"I heard somewhere that friends don't let friends drive drunk, so I have every right to ask how you're getting home."

She heaved a dramatic sigh. "Fine. If you must know, Julie's driving me."

Nick couldn't help laughing. "The same Julie who was drinking with you and Amanda? Where is Amanda, anyway?" The last thing he needed was for the boss's wife to get in trouble under his watch.

"She went home. And before you ask, no, she didn't drive, and yes, Bill walked her to Halcyon. There he is right now." She gestured toward the main entrance and took a sip of her tea.

Bill saw them and headed their way at the same time Julie did.

"What's up, boss? I just walked Mrs…"

"Yeah, I know. Thanks." Nick fixed his gaze on Julie. "Are you in any shape to drive?"

"Sure. I had water for the last round, so I should be

good." She pushed her short brown hair behind her ear and gave him a confident smile.

"But the multiple rounds before that were not water, right?"

"Yeah, but it was only wine. I wasn't pounding the cocktails like Little Miss Cassie here. That's why I'm driving her home."

Nick looked at Bill, who sighed and nodded in agreement with the unspoken request. He turned back to Julie. "No, you're not. Even if you feel sober, there's no way you'd pass a Breathalyzer, and Dan doesn't seem like the type of cop to let that slide." Nick had met the local sheriff's deputy, Dan Adams, for lunch last week to discuss security measures at the resort. The guy seemed like a stand-up cop who cared about his community, and the community returned the sentiment. Everyone called him Sheriff Dan. "Julie, Bill's gonna drive you home."

She opened her mouth to object, but thought better of it.

Cassie spoke up. "What about me?"

"I'll get you home." He didn't mention it would be via kayak, but once they got back to his place, he'd put her in the Jeep and drive her to her apartment. Just like any good friend would do.

It was a sign of how much alcohol she'd had that she followed him out the back door of the resort without question. It wasn't until they were halfway down the lawn that she realized where they were headed.

"Wait. This isn't the parking lot. Where are we going?"

"I came here by boat. It'll only take a few minutes to get to my place and the Jeep."

"Oh. Okay. A boat ride sounds fun."

It wasn't until they got to shore and he pointed her in the direction of the long kayak that she balked.

"That's not a boat, it's a canoe!"

"It's not a canoe, it's a kayak."

"It has no motor!"

"*I'm* the motor. Don't worry about it. You sit up front and I'll have us back to my place in no time."

"Will it hold both of us without sinking?"

"It won't sink, trust me."

"But it's pitch-black out there! No one will see us if we drown. Will it tip over?"

"Not if you behave yourself. Come on, slip your shoes off and I'll help you get in."

That effort was a little tricky between her dress and alcohol consumption, but he finally got her settled and pushed off the beach, hopping in behind her. She squealed when the kayak rocked, and made a move to jump out.

"Sit!" He barked out the word, and she froze. "Stay still and trust me, okay?"

She didn't answer, but she did settle back into her seat, tense but curious.

"So you've done this before? Kayaked in the dark?" She hesitated. "With a girl?"

"I've competed in white-water kayak races, and I've kayaked in four different countries. And yes, I have been out on some waters with just the light of the moon to guide me."

She turned so quickly he had to steady the craft with the paddle. "But have you been with a *girl* after dark?"

Was shy little Cassie *flirting* with him right now? He needed to get her tipsy more often.

"I've been with plenty of girls after dark."

"But in a *kayak*?"

"No, sweetie, you're my first."

She did a fist pump that had him resting the paddle in the water again to steady the vessel.

"Yes! I'm your first!" A weird something fluttered in his chest.

"Turn around and sit still, will you? I'm trying to keep this thing upright."

She turned as requested, dropping her hand to run her fingertips through the moonlit water. But she wasn't done being playful.

"Are you really worried you can't keep it upright, Nick?"

He swallowed hard and didn't answer. This woman would have no problem keeping him "upright." He was almost there now. He put a little more effort into paddling, and the kayak started slicing through the water. The light on the back of his rental house was glowing bright. He angled them toward shore.

Cassie sat back, looking up at the moon as her fingers traced in and out of the water. Her voice was low and soft, as if she was talking to herself.

"It's beautiful out here."

Another big swallow for Nick, his eyes never leaving her. "Yes, it is."

She was so quiet the rest of the way that he thought

she might be nodding off. The alcohol was probably catching up to her. He wasn't prepared when, as he was nearing the shoreline, she sat up and moved to leave the kayak.

"Oh! We're here! I'll help pull the boat in…"

"No! Cassie!"

She didn't do a bad job of holding her body up and swinging her legs over the kayak before dropping into the water. The problem was, even though they were only fifteen feet offshore, the water was still over four feet deep. Cassie's eyes went wide as she kept going, not hitting bottom until the cold water was up to her chest. She grabbed at the kayak, tilting it wildly. He struggled for a moment to keep it steady, then realized he had no choice but to get wet if he was going to get her safely out of the water without flipping the boat. He emptied his pockets and dived in, grabbing the kayak line with one hand when he came up and Cassie with the other.

"Come on, you goofball. Out of the lake and inside the house."

She was sputtering and starting to shiver.

"I thought you were driving me home?"

"Yeah, well, that was before you decided to take us for a chilly swim. We both need to get warm and dry first." She didn't argue, the night air cold on their wet skin. He pulled the kayak up and onto the lawn, then took her arm and led her inside.

Chapter Eleven

Most of Cassie's alcohol-induced glow popped like a bubble when she hit the cold water of Gallant Lake. She'd watched Nick wade several yards offshore at the resort in knee-deep water. When she saw how close to shore they were at his place, she figured she'd be helpful—the level of her helpful ability probably inflated by cocktails—and bring the kayak in. It wasn't as much the cold as it was that moment of terror as she kept going and wondered if she'd ever hit bottom that sobered her up in a hurry. By the time her feet hit bottom, she was soaked up to her breasts, the gold dress clinging to her and turning nearly transparent.

She followed Nick up the steps to the deck behind his cute little rental house. As soon as they were inside, he grabbed a blanket from the back of the sofa and wrapped it tightly around her.

"Hang on and I'll get some towels." He saw her head-to-toe shiver and frowned. "On second thought, maybe you should go take a hot shower to warm up. I've got a shirt you can put on after, and some sweats."

She shook her head sharply. "I can shower at home."

"I know that." He took her shoulders and turned her toward the hall. "But you're cold and wet *now*, and we're not heading to your place right away because I am *also* cold and wet. Go on, and I'll bring you dry things. I'll shower in my room." He gave her a light push toward the bathroom door, reaching in front of her to turn on the light.

And just like that, she was alone in the bathroom. She waited for him to return with dry clothes before peeling off her cold dress, then locked the door and stepped into the shower. The blast of hot water killed any remaining intoxication, but she still felt…something. To be here in his house, naked, even if it was behind a locked door, felt exciting. Which was silly. But she couldn't deny what she felt. It was the same sensation she'd had on the mountain last weekend. It was desire. She moved the washcloth slowly over her skin, closing her eyes and pretending it was Nick's hands she felt. And really… What harm was there in that? She'd been without male company for a long time now, and her own fingers could do only so much. She was ready for more. And maybe a little sexy time with a player like Nick West was the solution. He'd just bragged about how many women he'd been with after dark. Why couldn't she be one of them?

And then this itch would be scratched and maybe *then* they could be just friends.

She lost track of time as she let the hot steam seep into her skin. It was after midnight, but she felt wide awake. Maybe she could come up with a plan to keep Nick from taking her home tonight. Eventually she turned off the water and dried off. She slipped into Nick's sweats and shirt, both woefully too big on her, and stepped out of the bathroom. The house was quiet, and she had no sense of where Nick might be. She checked the kitchen and living area first, but it was empty. She headed farther down the hall, finding an empty guest bedroom and then Nick's room.

The only light was from the attached bathroom. Nick was on the bed, as if he'd stretched out there to wait for her. He'd showered, because his hair was rumpled and wet. He was sound asleep, one arm behind his head, the other resting on his bare chest, rising and falling in slow, deep breaths. She shook her head and sighed. So much for her big plans. He'd had a long day, and it had clearly caught up with him. She pulled his blanket up to cover him, but not before admiring his chest, cut with muscle and highlighted with a fine layer of dark hair that trailed down to vanish beneath his shorts. She wanted to reach out and touch him, but she was afraid of waking him, so she covered him and went to stretch out on the sofa to sleep.

Nick woke her two hours later. "Cass, what are you doing? Are you okay?"

"Uh…yeah. I was sleeping. Are *you* okay?"

He ran his fingers through his dark hair, leaving it

standing even more on end than it was to start with. "Did I fall asleep while you were showering? Damn, I'm sorry. Why don't you use the spare room and I'll run you home in the morning. Or I can take you now if you want…"

Cassie shrugged off the blanket and stood. She'd been dreaming about Nick and now he was there in front of her. The hum she'd felt before was still moving under her skin. She put her hand on Nick's chest, sad that he'd slipped on a T-shirt before coming to find her. He sucked in a sharp breath.

"What are you doing?"

"What do you think I'm doing?" She moved closer, and his eyes darkened. "Let's face it, Nick. The whole 'just friends' thing isn't going to work if we're both wondering what we'd be like together. That kiss last Saturday promised some things that don't fit in the friend zone."

He set his hand over hers. "Cassie, you've been drinking, and…"

"That was hours ago, and the dunk in the cold lake pretty much took care of it. Any liquor left in my system after that was washed away in the shower. I'm perfectly sober." She was also tired, and steadfastly ignoring that ever-present "be careful" voice in her head. If she woke up too much…if she thought about this too much… She'd never go through with it. She pushed onto her toes and pressed her lips against his. He didn't react at first, but it wasn't long before he let out a low sound and slid his arm around her, pulling her tight as he took over the kiss, pushing his way into her mouth to let her know he was on board with this plan of hers.

"Are you sure?" he asked softly as he left her mouth and trailed kisses along her jawline.

She made a sound of some kind. It wasn't a word, really, but he understood it was her assent. He looked down at her with a crooked smile. "Here or in my bed?"

The sofa had been fine for sleeping, but she wanted something a little more special than a thirty-year-old pine-and-plaid sofa that had clearly been included in the lease. She took his hand and started down the hall with him obediently behind her. She could feel his amused smile, and who could blame him? It was pretty rare for her to take charge of anything, especially sex. After all, with Don…

She stopped so fast in the doorway that Nick brushed up against her, resting his hands on her shoulders. Her bravado was fading fast. If tonight was just an attempt to erase Don's hold on her, it wouldn't be fair to Nick. Could something ever be good if it was done for the wrong reason? Doubts started a whispering campaign in her head. What if it wasn't good at all? What if she couldn't please him?

Her mind was racing and blank all at the same time. This was it. The moment of truth. She focused on the electricity she felt through Nick's fingertips on the bare skin at the base of her neck and took a deep breath, still staring straight ahead.

"Nick, I want this. I really do. It's just that…" Her shoulders sagged as she felt her confidence waning. "I'm not exactly experienced… I mean, I've only been with two men in my whole life." She gave a short laugh. "The first was my college boyfriend, which was hardly memorable. The second was…well…memorable for all the wrong reasons… I'm not very good at this sex stuff. I don't want to disappoint you…"

Before she could continue, Nick kissed the back of her neck, setting her body on fire.

"My beautiful Cassandra…" She tensed at the name. Nick didn't know it wasn't really hers. There was so much he didn't know. He continued to softly kiss her neck and shoulders as he spoke. "I have two important things to say to you. First, nothing that's happened before tonight—before right this instant—matters at all. Second…" Nick's kisses moved up her neck and toward her left ear. Cassie tilted her head to expose more of her skin to his lips as he continued. "Second… We are very definitely *not* having 'sex stuff' tonight. That's what teenagers do the in the back seat of their dad's Buick. If you walk through that door, I am going to give you a night like you've never experienced before."

With that, Nick gently turned Cassie so they were facing each other. He rested his forehead on hers and spoke again, staring straight into her wide eyes. "But Cassie, you're going to have to walk through that door on your own."

She felt every cell in her body singing to her to make the move.

…nothing that's happened before tonight matters at all…

She smiled and turned, lifting her chin and stepping through the doorway with determination. She walked to the center of the room, near the foot of the bed, and turned to face Nick. He was still in the doorway, with his hands resting on each side of the door frame. His coffee-colored hair fell across his forehead. His gaze was intense, his eyes so dark they were nearly black. He looked so damned sexy she thought she'd swoon right then and there.

Cassie didn't flinch from the desire she saw in his eyes. When he stepped into the room, Cassie let out the breath she didn't realize she'd been holding. He walked to her slowly, and she didn't back away. She felt no fear, had no second thoughts. She wanted this.

He folded her into his arms and kissed her. She gave as good as she got, standing on tiptoe to push against him as their tongues teased and danced together. Nick reached down and lifted the hem of her borrowed sweatshirt. She stepped away to allow him to pull it over her head, shimmying out of the loose sweatpants at the same time.

Maybe she should have felt insecure as she stood naked before him for the first time, but...no. She felt self-assured. She felt beautiful. Nick made her feel beautiful, with his dark stare and the upward curve at the edge of his mouth. He was already making love to her with his eyes, and she reveled in it.

With one smooth motion, he peeled his shirt off over his head. Cassie was more than happy to have another chance to admire his broad shoulders and the sharply defined six-pack. He was one fine specimen of a man.

He lifted her into his arms. She embraced his neck and placed her lips on his. The kiss was full of lust and need. He laid her on top of the sheets, then stepped away to shed his shorts. Nick walked to the bed and placed one knee on the edge of the mattress. He looked into her eyes and she knew he was looking for permission. She granted it with a barely perceptible nod.

She could feel his gaze sweeping across her skin, and it made her blood burn with need. When his eyes reached hers, he fell on her like a starving man falls on an all-you-can-eat buffet.

They were consumed by the heat of their desire. Their hands ran over each other's bodies frantically. Nick's kisses began on her forehead and ran down her neck and chest. He paused along the way to trace her breasts with his lips, as light as a whisper, before he went across her abdomen, then ever lower. Cassie's nervous anticipation of everything that was to come had her writhing in excitement before he even reached his goal. His fingertips were tracing the same trail around her breasts that his lips had just followed. She moaned, her eyes closed as his mouth settled on her most private and sensitive place. She tried to resist letting herself go too soon, but failed. Loudly. He was too damned good at what he was doing, and she fell hard.

Now it was Nick's turn to moan as he continued, ignoring Cassie's pleas for mercy as she continued to move under his onslaught. He stopped only to tear open a condom wrapper grabbed from the nightstand, then he followed his own trail of kisses back up to her lips. Her legs curled around his torso, and she cried out his name when he entered her. She dug her fingernails into his back, causing him to grunt in response. His muscles rippled under her fingers.

They both felt a driving sense of urgency. The sheets wrapped around them as they moved across the bed. At one point, Nick grasped Cassie tightly and rolled so that she was astride him. She braced herself with her arms beside his shoulders. They stopped moving momentarily and she looked down at him. Her hair fell wildly around her face. She felt giddy with power.

Nick smiled up at her. "You seem pleased with yourself, ma'am."

Cassie gave a throaty laugh. "Oh, I am very pleased indeed. I'm even *more* pleased to see that I'm pleasing you."

"Oh, you are definitely doing that, babe."

They smiled slyly at each other as if they were both in on some very special secret. Nick put his hand securely on her back and rolled so that she was lying under him again, without breaking their bond. He kissed her gently and began to press into her at an increasing pace. Cassie felt the room spinning as her body responded yet again. She closed her eyes and arched her back. As she did, Nick slid his arm under her and lifted her lower body up into the air as he rose to his knees. And that was it for her. She cried out and let herself fly.

Nick shouted her name roughly and dropped her back to the bed, setting his teeth on the tender skin at the base of her throat as he drove on to his own release. His face dropped over her shoulder into the pillow beneath her. They lay in that position for several minutes, their deep breaths the only sound in the room.

As Nick's body weight pressed down on Cassie, she finally had to react. She tapped the front of his shoulder and softly said, "Nick, you have to move."

"No." He muttered it into her hair without flinching. "You destroyed me. I can't move."

"Yeah, well, I can't breathe, so you're going to have to move or listen to me suffocate."

Nick groaned loudly and rolled to lie at her side, with one arm draped over her ribs as he got rid of the condom with the other. Cassie put her hand on her chest and felt the sheen of sweat on her skin. Her heart was pounding.

Nick covered her hand with his. She turned away from him, pressing her back against his chest. He pulled her tight and kissed the base of her neck.

"I'm a shell of a man right now. I knew we had a physical attraction going on, but...damn, girl! That was some wickedly world-class sex."

Cassie smiled in contentment. "I didn't even know there *could* be sex like that, Nick. If this house were on fire right now, I wouldn't have the strength to move, much less stand or run."

Nick laughed softly, his mouth near her ear. "Then we'd burn together, babe, because I can't move, either. Now go to sleep. You're safe in my arms. Just go to sleep..." His voice was fading as he spoke.

When she woke, the digital clock on the side of the bed read 4:28 a.m. She'd rolled over onto her stomach in her sleep, and someone's fingers were lightly tracing up and down her spine. She lifted her head and Nick, propped up on one elbow, smiled down at her softly.

"So," he said, "it wasn't a dream."

Cassie stretched like a cat, turned on her side to face him and returned his smile. "Felt pretty dreamy to me."

He reached out and brushed Cassie's hair behind her ear. "There's only one problem. It left me wanting more."

"Really? I seem to have the same problem…"

Cassie leaned forward and kissed him, sliding her arm around his neck. Without saying another word, they made love again. But this time, it was less frantic, less desperate. They took things slow and easy. There was no crying out of names, only sighs and whispers and soft moans as they caressed each other, exploring each other's bodies with their fingers and lips. Eventually they brought each other to a sweet and tender release that left them both trembling. Cassie fell asleep clasped tightly in Nick's embrace, and she felt more secure and protected than she'd ever felt in her life.

It couldn't last, of course. She'd kept secrets from him. Big ones. They were just two grown-ups scratching an itch and all that.

But Cassie couldn't shake the illogical but powerful conviction that here, in Nick's arms, was exactly where she belonged.

Chapter Twelve

Nick slipped out of bed shortly after dawn. Cassie turned and murmured something unintelligible, then settled back to sleep. He watched her for a moment, then walked away. He needed to clear his head.

He thought maybe last night would be a resolution of their "chemistry" issue. But he'd been a fool to think one night with Cassie would ever be enough. He'd seen enough addicts on the street to know that for some, all it took was one time—one hit—and they were hooked. That's how he felt. Just one night with Cassie, and he was toast. Her kiss had ruined him for all other kisses, and making love with her had destroyed him for all other women.

What did it mean, though? Was there any chance in hell of them having a relationship that wouldn't make a mess of both their work life *and* their friendship? Was she even interested in a relationship? Or was last night enough for her? Maybe she'd explored their chemistry and found it wanting. Would that be a good thing? Or would it make the ache he felt in his chest just that much worse?

He took his cup from the coffee maker and gulped half of it, anxious to clear the fog in his head. He glanced around for his phone, then remembered he'd taken it out of his pocket before diving in the lake last night. Hopefully it was still in the kayak. He headed outside, where a gentle mist rolled across the smooth surface of the water.

The phone screen was lit up with messages, and something else was buzzing in the boat. Cassie's purse was still there, and her phone was going off, too. Had something happened at the resort? His phone chimed with an incoming call. Blake Randall. He frowned. *Something* was happening, that's for sure. Blake wouldn't call him this early on a Saturday morning otherwise.

"Blake? What's up?"

"I don't know, man. You tell me."

"I…what?"

Blake let out a sigh. "Just tell me if Cassie's with you, wherever you are."

"I… I'm home." Nick stalled. "Why are you asking about Cassie?"

"Julie said you were giving Cassie a ride home. But she's *not* home. Are you saying she's not with you?"

Blake's tone sharpened with concern, and Nick had to come clean.

"She's here."

"Thank Christ." Blake's voice grew faint as he spoke away from the phone. "She's okay. She's with Nick." Amanda's voice was muffled in the background. Blake came back on the phone. "Did something happen? My wife's been texting and calling her all damn night. She was getting ready to call Dan Adams and report her missing. Was she scared to go home or something? She's not running, is she?"

"Running? Running where?" Nick grabbed Cassie's purse and headed back into the house, trying his best to catch up with this conversation.

"From Don. The asshole who almost killed her a couple years ago. Damn. She hasn't told you that yet, has she?" Blake paused. "Wait. If she wasn't scared to go home, then why is she at…?" Another pause. "Aw, hell. Are you two a *thing* now?"

Amanda's voice was much louder now. "I knew it!"

Blake shushed her. "So she's at your place because *why* exactly?"

Nick wasn't used to being grilled by his employer about whom he did or didn't sleep with.

"No offense, Blake, but I don't see how that's your concern. I'm sorry you two were worried, but Cassie's safely asleep and this won't affect our job performance on Monday."

Blake digested that for a minute, then agreed. "Fair enough, but I call BS on the job bit. It'll affect you at work, one way or the other." Amusement crept into his voice. "Just do your best to keep things cool, and don't hurt that woman or you'll have to deal with my wife *and* her cousins. Trust me when I say that won't be pretty."

"O-kay." This was one of those small-town things he'd have to get used to. People knew your business and took sides. In LA, they were too busy to care. Blake's voice dropped.

"Nick, now that my wife is out of the room, let me say one more thing. Cassie and Amanda have some stuff in common from their pasts, and you need to know about it before you go much further. If you're serious about her, you need to talk. If you're not serious about her, well… You're an idiot. She's a hell of a woman."

"Yeah. I know. Thanks."

After the call, Nick sat on the sofa and watched the lake wake up with Saturday action. At this hour, it was primarily local fishermen, drifting or trolling with their lines in the water, occasionally pulling in a fish. A blue heron strolled calmly along the shoreline, watching for minnows.

So Cassie had secrets. As a former cop, it bugged Nick that he didn't know that. Of course, he knew she'd been assaulted in a parking garage, and the incident made her hypervigilant. Maybe that's all Blake had been referring to. But Nick suspected there was a lot more to it than that. It was something Amanda had in common with her, but that information wasn't helpful, since Nick didn't know Amanda's past. Had she been a victim of some crime, too? Was everyone at the resort hiding some dark past, or was it simply overblown small-town drama?

"Good morning." He turned to see Cassie standing near the kitchen. She'd pulled on the sweatshirt he'd given her last night, and it fell off one shoulder to reveal a swath of white skin he suddenly hungered for. Secrets or not, he wanted her again.

"Good morning." He stood and headed into the kitchen to start breakfast. Keeping busy would settle his mind and make the situation less awkward. "Scrambled eggs and sausage okay?"

"Um, sure. Or I could go…"

"Do you want to go?"

She stared at the floor and shrugged. Insecure Cassie had returned. "I'll do whatever you prefer. I don't want to be in your way."

He'd learned that a blunt approach tended to snap Cassie out of this timid persona that always made him angry. Angry *for* her, not with her.

"What I'd prefer is you naked on the sofa while I cook, so I can enjoy the best view in town."

Her mouth dropped open and her face colored. Then she laughed, and he saw the spark of confidence return to her eyes.

"And what about *my* view? What would I get out of this deal?"

"I don't think nudity and frying pans go together very well, so you'll have to wait for your special view."

"Yeah, well—so will you. I'm going to go freshen up and see if my dress is salvageable. I left it hanging in the bathroom. I don't suppose you have any tea?"

"I think there's a box in the cupboard on the end."

Cassie found the green box and smiled. "English Breakfast. My favorite."

"I don't have a teapot."

"Don't need one. I'll run water through the coffee maker without putting a pod in there. That's how I do it at the office." She dropped the tea bag into a mug, pressing the button with a grin. "I'm very resourceful."

The conversation was neutral. Normal, even. They were just a couple of adults, standing in the kitchen together. He had no shirt. She had no pants. Making breakfast. It was nice.

A sizzle from the stove brought his attention back to cooking, and by the time he looked up again, she was gone. She returned as he was plating the food, wearing a wrinkled, but dry, dark yellow dress. Her hair was pulled back into her usual ponytail. Her skin was radiant. Nick frowned. *Radiant?* Since when did he start using words like that? She took her plate to the small table by the windows. Since he met a woman like Cassandra.

They were almost done eating breakfast before he thought to tell her that Blake had called.

"Oh, God, I was supposed to text Amanda last night! I completely forgot. Where's my purse?" She jumped up from the table.

"Relax. She knows you're here and you're okay." He carried the plates and utensils to the kitchen, nodding at her purse as he passed it.

"Amanda knows I'm *here*? Oh, no. That means they all know…"

"They?"

"The cousins. Amanda, Nora and Mel are basically one unit. What one knows, they all know." She groaned. "I hope Nora didn't tell Aunt Cathy…" She scrolled through her phone, then hurriedly typed a message. It chirped a minute later, and her shoulders relaxed. "Amanda said Cathy doesn't know and she's off today anyway. She also said I have lots of 'splaining to do. Tomorrow's coffee meeting should be fun."

"Coffee meeting?" This was the problem with having a casual breakfast conversation with someone you didn't know all that well. There were too many blanks to fill in. Which reminded him that he had a few blanks he needed filled in sooner rather than later.

"We have coffee early on Sunday at Nora's café, before the after-church crowd starts filling up the place. Amanda insisted I join them, because she thinks I need friends." She frowned, and he had a feeling she'd said more than she'd intended.

"You don't have friends?" Nick finished cleaning the cooking pans and put them away. Cassie shrugged, looking everywhere but at him. "Cass?"

"Well… I'm fairly new to town, and it's not always easy to make new friends. Especially when you're a homebody like me."

"What about your friends in Milwaukee?"

She stiffened. "There weren't many. Not *any* that lasted past me leaving town." She gave him a bright, tense smile. "Like I said, I'm a homebody. Give me tea and a book and I'm happy."

"But you had a job there. Didn't you make friends at work?"

Nick knew how to read body language, and hers was screaming that she didn't want to have this conversation. He moved closer and put his hands on her shoulders, tipping her chin up with his thumbs.

"Hey, it's me. The guy you had wild-and-crazy sex with last night." The corner of her mouth twitched toward a smile, but her eyes were clouded. He bent over and kissed her.

It was supposed to be a quick kiss to jolt her into trusting him, but as soon as his lips touched hers, he forgot all about his motivation. He wanted more. His hands slipped behind her head and he kissed her hard and long. And damn if she didn't kiss him right back, matching him beat for beat. Her fingers buried in his hair, and she pressed her hips against him, creating an instant response. He pushed her against the wall and dropped his hands to cup her behind and hold her against his now-aching body. She hooked a leg around his, as if afraid he'd move away. Not a snowball's chance in hell. He lifted her up and slipped his hand under her dress, quickly moving past the lacy underwear he encountered.

She moaned his name, long and slow and rough, and he slid his mouth down her neck to nip at her throat, all the while moving his fingers inside her. She was grinding against him, and he was ready to lose his mind. It was broad daylight. They'd just had breakfast. He was supposed to be taking her home because everyone was so concerned about them being together. It was a mistake to keep this going. They worked together. They had baggage. She was keeping secrets. The back of her head hit the wall with a thud as she arched her body against him. That cold-shower list of excuses didn't work anymore. He knew what sex with her was like now, and when she shuddered in his arms and cried out as she came for him, he knew where they were going to end up.

"I want you. In my bed. Right now."

She dropped her head to his shoulder and nodded against him. It was all he needed. He scooped her into his arms and carried her down the hall. There was a flurry of clothing hitting the floor. He was so desperate to be inside her that he almost forgot protection. She laughed when he swore at the foil package, which didn't open anywhere near as fast as he needed it to. And finally, *finally*, they were connected and moving as one. It was fast and hard and hot and they both made the same strangled sound of ecstasy when they reached their goal together. He stayed over her, unable to look away from the sight of her hair splayed out on the mattress beneath her like a flame.

She pinched his side. "You gonna stay there all day?"

He bent down and kissed her. "Would you mind if I did?"

Her smile lost some of its light. "Real life is going to catch up with us sooner or later."

He nodded. "Yeah, this was a very nice but unexpected detour on our morning." He reluctantly left her softness and slid off the bed. "I'm going to shower, then I'll take you home. After we talk about what comes next."

Chapter Thirteen

What comes next...

Cassie tried to sort out her poor, abused gold dress for the second time that morning, but it was hopeless. Somehow, it had been torn both near the neckline and under one arm. She couldn't blame Nick, because he hadn't undressed her. No, that was her, in a frenzy to get naked, who had torn the most expensive dress she owned. It was bad enough she'd be doing the walk of shame to her apartment in broad daylight, but to do it in a rumpled, water-stained and torn dress? With hopeless bed hair, kiss-swollen lips and a general haze of good-sex vibes in her eyes? Ugh. If the cousins saw her like this, she'd never hear the end of it.

...what comes next...

She glanced at the bedroom window. She could probably escape the upcoming conversation by climbing through it, but she had no idea how to get home from here. Like it or not, she was going to have to talk about "what comes next" with Nick. Sex last night was beyond her dreams. She'd thought she was going to have a night with a guy who kissed her senseless, and then she'd be able to move on. Easy-peasy. Sure, she'd expected it to be good. But being in bed—or against a wall—with Nick was more than good. It was…transformative. There wasn't a chance in hell either one of them would be able to pretend last night, or this morning, didn't happen.

So…what? A relationship? Bad idea. Despite her best efforts to pretend it wasn't the case, her life was a mess. At any moment she might have to pack up and run. If she and Nick were going to be more than just one night—and morning—he needed to know that. He needed to know everything.

She did her best to tame her hair back into a ponytail and found a clean black T-shirt in Nick's dresser. She pulled it over her dress and tied it into a knot at her hip. Not exactly a fashion statement, but it concealed the torn fabric and most of the wrinkles. She grinned at her reflection. If she pulled her ponytail over to the side of her head and teased it a little, she'd look like a flashback to *Flashdance*.

Nick apparently thought the same thing. He gave her a wide smile.

"Nice look. Are you off to the disco later?"

"I did the best I could. Maybe we should wait until after dark to take me home." It was bad enough the cousins knew she'd spent the night with Nick. The whole town would know it if she tried to sneak into her apartment in the center of town in an outfit straight out of the 1980s.

"That's your decision, babe. But first…" He patted the sofa cushion next to him. "We need to talk, Miss Smith."

"That's not my name." Not exactly the way she wanted to start this conversation, but the words just blurted out. Nick leaned forward and frowned.

"Your last name isn't Smith?"

She twisted her fingers together. She was in it now, and Nick deserved to know the truth.

"My last name isn't Smith. It's Zetticci. And my first name isn't Cassandra. It's Cassidy."

"Your name is Cassidy Zetticci. For real." He started to smile, as if he thought she might be pulling his leg. When she didn't respond, he realized it was no joke. "How did you manage to get past the resort's background check?"

"Really? *That's* the first question you have?"

He stared at the floor for a moment, his foot tapping anxiously. "I looked at your employee file." He glanced up and noted her surprise. "I look at *everyone's* files, Cassie. It's my job. You picked the most common surname in America to make yourself harder to find. Who's looking? Don?"

Now it was her turn to be surprised. "How do you know about Don?"

"Well, I didn't hear about him from *you*." He stood and paced by the windows. Carefully avoiding her.

"Blake mentioned the name this morning, and it's not that hard to put together. He's the one who assaulted you, right?"

On which occasion?

"Yes."

Nick stopped, his brows furrowed.

"And now he's stalking you?"

"Yes."

"You were in a relationship with him?"

He was in full cop mode now.

"He was my husband."

Blake didn't move, yet Cassie could feel him backing away. His eyes went icy cold. His hands curled into fists, then quickly released. His mouth slid into a disapproving frown.

"You stayed married to a guy who beat you." He was no longer asking questions. He was accusing. And she didn't like it.

"I said he *was* my husband. Past tense."

"Did you leave the first time he hit you?"

"Am I a suspect in some crime here, Officer?"

He rubbed the back of his neck, his jaw sawing back and forth. He turned away, staring out the window toward the lake. She waited, not willing to give him any more information until she knew what he was thinking. Of all the reactions she'd anticipated, anger with *her* hadn't been one of them. He shoved his hands in his pockets and let out a long breath.

"I wasn't ready to hear that you were a victim of domestic violence. I thought it was some stranger..."

"Does it matter?"

"It shouldn't."

"No kidding. But it obviously does." She shook her head. "In the interest of full disclosure, he was a police officer. A patrolman."

Nick turned. "He was a *cop*?"

"Yes, Nick. He was a cop. Believe it or not, cops do bad stuff, too. Or are you going to stand behind your 'blue line' bullshit and deny that?"

They'd completely traded places now. She was the angry one, while Nick seemed chagrined.

"The blue line is a brotherhood, not a blindfold. It doesn't protect criminals."

She scoffed at that, remembering the lost friendships and lack of support from the police in Milwaukee after Don was charged. The roadblocks that were thrown up time and again as the district attorney put the case together. The mishandling of evidence that led to the retrial now pending. While Don remained free.

Nick took a step toward her, and she tensed. He stopped, reaching out to take her hands gently.

"Okay, let me rephrase that. It *shouldn't* be used to protect bad guys. I'm sorry. I... I have some history with domestic abuse victims as a detective. Some bad history." He gave her hand a squeeze and she looked up to meet his gaze.

The coldness was gone. She was once again looking at the man who'd whispered kisses across her ear when he thought she was asleep last night. The man she trusted. The corner of his mouth lifted into a half smile.

"Last week we agreed we both had baggage, Cass. I brushed it off as no big deal. But I'm beginning to suspect the things that led each of us to be in Gallant Lake are a little more connected than we imagined." He lifted her hand and pressed a kiss to her knuckles. "We had a deal that if you went hiking with me, then I was going to owe you a day of sitting quietly. Today's that day. Let's sit and talk."

"Actually, I think you said you owed me a day of doing whatever I wanted, and you're crazy if you think I want to talk about this."

"You can have the rest of the day to boss me around. But right now we need to talk. No assumptions. No grilling for answers. Okay?"

Her voice dropped to almost a whisper. "It makes me feel weak. Vulnerable. Stupid."

"Hey." Nick tipped her chin up with his finger. "I saw from the first moment we met that you were a fighter. Not weak. Not vulnerable. And definitely not stupid. So get those words out of your vocabulary. That's *him* talking, and you need to kick that asshole out of your head. Now I understand why you apologize and doubt yourself all the time, and that needs to stop."

"It's not that easy."

He pressed a soft kiss on her lips, and she welcomed the warmth of it. "Nothing worthwhile ever is."

They settled onto the sofa. She sipped her fresh cup of tea, stalling for time. Nick waited patiently, and she finally had to fill the silence with something. So she started at the beginning.

She told him how she'd always been a shy kid. Her parents had a volatile marriage and an even more volatile divorce. To avoid their arguments as a child, she'd stayed in her room and lost herself in books. She was good with numbers and awkward with people. Don was the opposite—outgoing, with the ability to charm everyone he met, from children to little old ladies.

She was working at an insurance company when Don came in to discuss an accident investigation involving one of their clients. She'd been fascinated by the handsome, blue-eyed blond in uniform. He looked like a Nordic god, and he paid attention to *her*. He was ten years older and had the kind of calm confidence she'd craved. She couldn't believe it when he asked her out for coffee.

He made it easy to want to be with him. He took her mom to the ballet, and he took her dad fishing on Lake Michigan. He was the first thing in years that her parents agreed on—they adored him. He treated Cassie like a princess, and if he was a little controlling, he'd always explain that it was only because he loved her so much and wanted the best for her. And she'd believed him. She'd married him, ignoring the little warning signs leading up to the big day.

"What kind of warning signs?" Nick reached over and took her hand.

"He made *all* the decisions about the wedding. Where. When. What I'd wear. Whom we'd invite— which did *not* include any of my friends from school or my coworkers. He started distancing me from my former life, told me I was 'too mature for that crowd.' He pressured me to be like the other, older police wives. I was so eager for his approval that I threw myself into it, not noticing I was leaving my life behind for his." She took another sip of tea, delaying the words that made her cringe with shame. "We'd been married a year when he hit me for the first time. I had a flat tire one night. A coworker changed it for me, but I was late getting home. Don accused me of lying and told me I must be cheating on him. It was so ridiculous that I laughed, and he slapped me. Hard."

Nick didn't say a word, but his grip tightened on her hand as she told him the rest. About Don's tearful apology. That time, and the next time, and the next time after that. The way he subtly made everything her fault. If only she wouldn't "provoke" him, he wouldn't lose control. The episodes were sporadic at first, and she thought he really meant it every time he said he'd never hurt her again.

But when he was passed over for sergeant, things took a darker turn. It was all her fault, of course. She'd distracted him because he had to "keep an eye on her" all the time. She'd embarrassed him with her appearance, her words, her behavior. She was flirting with everyone. She didn't listen. She finally worked up the courage to walk away after he tried to push her down the stairs in their home one night. But leaving didn't make her safe.

"He's the one who assaulted you in the parking garage?"

She nodded. "I'd gone out with a bunch of people from work to celebrate my birthday. It felt so good to be with people my own age, relaxed and laughing. No one there to criticize my every move. It was the first night I'd felt *free* in ages. It was a new beginning. On the way back to my car, he jumped me and just started punching, over and over, telling me what a whore I was. He broke my cheekbone and five ribs. Punctured a lung. Slammed my head against the cement so hard that I was unconscious for two days."

"Jesus…" Nick's voice was thick with emotion.

"Yeah."

"So the bastard's in jail?"

"Not exactly." She shrugged. "He went to trial, but there was some mysterious mix-up with the evidence or procedure or something, and the judge declared a mistrial. His new trial is coming up. Meanwhile, he's on probation and isn't supposed to leave Milwaukee or contact me in any way. I moved to Cleveland to put some distance between us, but he tracked me down. Got my phone number. My address. Called the office where I worked. Started texting me with threats from a burner phone or something, telling me he was watching me. The DA's office said that wasn't possible, but it freaked me out. Don had never met Aunt Cathy, so I called her, changed my name and came to Gallant Lake."

Nick stared out at the water. She could tell he had a lot of questions, but he was trapped by his promise not to grill her. He was tense. Angry. With her? He said he had a "bad history" with domestic violence victims, but she had no idea what that meant. Police went on a lot of those calls, of course. And they tended to be fraught with danger because they were so unpredictable. Did something happen? She reached out to touch his hand, but he flinched and she pulled back, hurt and confused. Never one to stay still for long, Nick got up and started pacing again. He rubbed his neck in agitation, coming to a stop but not making eye contact.

"I should probably get you back to your place." Her heart fell.

"That's all you have to say?"

He finally met her gaze, and she was shocked to see his eyes shining with…tears? She stood, and he blinked away from her as if he knew what she'd seen. This wasn't about her. This reaction of his may have been triggered by her story, but it wasn't about *her*. It was about someone else.

His voice was gruff. "I know I'm being a jackass right now, and I'm sorry. But I need a little time to digest this."

"Was it the woman in the photo? Your partner? Was she abused?"

Cassie knew his partner was dead. Had she been murdered by her spouse?

His mouth hardened. "Jada wasn't abused. She would never have put up with tha…" She did her best not to show how much that hurt.

Nick shook his head. "Shit, I don't mean it like that. I just…" He stared up at the ceiling. "Jada was killed on the job. By a guy who beat his wife."

Cassie sucked in a sharp breath.

…the things that brought each of us to Gallant Lake are a little more connected than we imagined…

"Nick, I'm so sorry."

He gave a short laugh, but there was no humor in it. "I haven't even said those words to you, have I? I didn't tell you how sorry I am for the hell you went through.

That's how far in my own head I am right now. Look, I need to process this…"

They stood there for a few minutes, neither of them moving or speaking. He was wound so tight she thought he'd snap. She knew what that felt like. It was her normal. But Nick—this strong man who kept people safe for a living—didn't know how to deal with the fear of losing control. It wasn't until she saw a small shudder go through his body that she knew she had to help him. And she had a crazy idea that might snap him out of his melancholy.

"So the plan is for us to spend today doing what I want to do, right?"

Nick finally took his eyes off the ceiling and looked at her.

"I don't think that's a good idea, Cass. I'm feeling a little…raw…right now. I won't be good company. Let me just take you home, okay?" He walked to the sliding glass doors but froze when she placed her hand on his shoulder. She hated to see him in this kind of pain.

"What I have planned will help you relax. Come on."

He pulled the door open, still not looking back. "I don't think…"

"You don't have to think. You just have to do what I say. That was the deal, and you're a man of your word, right?"

She peeked around his shoulder to glimpse up at his face and saw the quick, reluctant smile.

"I'm a man of my word."

"I thought so. Get moving."

"Where are we going?"

"My place. I have everything we need there."

"Need for *what* exactly?"

She gave him a push to propel him through the door. "You'll see when you get there."

"That's wrong. I told you what we were doing last week."

She laughed. "You told me it was going to be a *stroll*. That was a hell of a lot more than a stroll."

He turned, his gaze heated. "Yeah, it was a lot more than a stroll."

She shoved him again, knowing he was referring to that red-hot kiss that ultimately led to them falling into bed together last night. "Go on. You climb rocks to unwind. I'm going to show you how I do it."

Chapter Fourteen

"You expect me to take a *bubble bath*?"

Nick stared, stupefied. No way in hell was he getting into that tub full of sweet-smelling foam, surrounded by candles. *Candles!*

"You expected me to climb a mountain, so yes, I expect you to take a bubble bath. It's decadent and a lot like being in a sensory-deprivation capsule. The world just falls away, and you can't help but relax." Cassie looked pretty proud of herself.

He never saw this coming. He'd tried to bail on her, but she had a stubborn streak a mile wide, and she was determined this was his Day to Obey. When they got to her place, they'd sat in the living room of her funky little loft above the coffee shop for a while. He didn't think anything of it when she excused herself, figuring she'd gone to change. She *had* changed, into a simple top and jeans, but she'd also created…this.

After she'd dropped that bombshell on him earlier about having a crazy ex-husband who nearly beat her to death, he'd been having a hard time pulling his thoughts into line. The story filled him with rage. Rage that someone had hurt her. Put her on the run. Made her feel like a lesser person.

He already had an endless slideshow running on a loop in his head 24/7 from that night two years ago. Beth Washington admitting she'd let Earl move back into her house. His partner, Jada, who had always wanted children, carrying the Washingtons' baby down the hall to put her to bed. The sound of a shotgun blast.

Now those familiar images were mixed with new ones from his imagination. Cassie being slapped hard across the face. Cassie at the top of a long flight of stairs, fighting for her life. Cassie being brutally attacked in a deserted parking garage. Maybe he did need the distraction of whatever silliness she was going to subject him to. But a bubble bath?

"If you think I'm going into that tub, you don't know me very well."

"I *don't* know you all that well, Nick. But I know you're taking this bath, because you're a man of your word, remember?"

"With the emphasis on *man*. I don't do bubble baths."

She was unimpressed.

He resorted to begging. "Come on, Cass. I don't want to do this. It won't be relaxing, it'll be…embarrassing. Annoying."

She folded her arms and arched a brow high.

"I distinctly remember telling you I did *not* want to go hiking. It was hard, and exhausting, and I was embarrassed when you had to keep stopping for me. I was pretty damn annoyed by the time we got to the top of the trail. And I was in pain."

He grabbed her waist and tugged her close. "Yeah, but look how much fun we had once we got up there. That made it all worth it, didn't it?"

The sound of her light laughter made his chest feel funny. "And who's to say you won't get a nice surprise later today..." She pushed away from him and reached for the door. "*After* you get in that tub." She gave him a wink. "Man of your word, remember?"

He groaned, knowing he'd been outplayed. She flipped off the lights and closed the door behind her, leaving him in the candlelit bathroom. It was a big tub, framed in large marble tiles. She'd told him Nora had remodeled the downstairs bathroom before Cassie moved in.

Cassie's voice called through the door. "I don't hear any splashing in there! Don't think you can bluff me, Nicholas West. I'm going to deliver a glass of wine in a little while, and you'd better be chin-deep in bubbles."

Nick shook his head. May as well get it over with. Besides, the idea of Cassie bringing wine sounded pretty damn good. Maybe he could convince her to join him after all, and restore his manly pride. He shed his clothes and stepped into the not-quite-scalding water. As he settled down into the tub, he tried to remember the last time he took an actual bath, other than soaking in some hotel hot tub. He had to have been a kid, and there were no bubbles involved that he could remember.

What was he supposed to do? Scrub behind his ears? Or just sit here and wait? He felt ridiculous. But Cassie was right—she'd hiked a mountain last weekend when she really didn't want to, and he'd made a deal. He finally leaned back and let himself settle into the water a bit. The warmth felt pretty good on his muscles, tired from a night of lovemaking, and the flickering yellow light of the candles was almost hypnotic. He closed his eyes. That hideous slideshow was still playing in his head, but the images started to shift as he inhaled the perfumed suds.

He saw Jada, but she was at her wedding now, kissing her wife, Shayla, under an arbor of ivory roses. Laughing in the car on a stakeout, teasing him about his "obsession" with healthy eating while she devoured a bacon double cheeseburger. He saw Cassie, but she was trimming the daffodils he'd given her, bending over her desk to inhale their scent and smiling to herself. She'd had no idea he'd been watching her, or she never would have let on how much she liked the stolen goods.

There was a soft tap on the door, and Cassie stepped in. Her eyes lit up when she saw him in the water, chin-deep as ordered. And the hell if he didn't feel relaxed and sated. He didn't even bother trying to deny it.

"I could do without the actual bubbles, but I gotta admit—this feels pretty good."

"Now you know another of my secrets, Nick. I do this a few times a week, just to relax and feel pampered." She handed him a glass of wine, and he was glad to see she'd brought one for herself. That meant she was staying. To her, bubble baths were about feeling pampered. *He* wanted to be the one to make her feel that way. He wanted to be the one who kept her safe and spoiled her rotten and made her forget anything bad that had ever happened to her.

She sat on the corner of the tub, her hair falling loose over one shoulder. The candlelight made her skin glow as if from within. She was the prettiest thing he'd ever seen.

He crooked his finger at her, ignoring the white bubbles that drifted away from the movement.

"Join me."

Her smile was playful. "That defeats the purpose of pampering *yourself*. You're supposed to be relaxing alone."

"And I was doing that…until you walked in. Which makes me think maybe you really want to join me in here before the water gets too cool."

Her mouth opened, then closed again and she stood. "Soak up a little more warmth and relaxation, and I'll see you in the kitchen when you're ready." She moved to walk past him, but he reached out and grabbed her hand. She was the only comfort he craved.

"Don't go, Cass. Being alone with my thoughts is not… It's not relaxing."

She sat again, this time behind his shoulder. "Why don't you tell me about it. Tell me what happened in LA."

"Not much to tell. My partner died because of me."

"I don't believe that." Her answer was quick and sure.

"It's true. I made a bad call, and she paid the price. Jada was shot. Killed. Because of *me*." Her fingers traced patterns through his hair, her words barely a whisper.

"Tell me."

He told her about the night that replayed in his dreams over and over again. When he'd heard uniforms were called to Beth Washington's house earlier that night, he'd felt sick. He and Jada had been there a dozen times in previous years, but, with their encouragement, Beth had dumped her bastard of a husband. Nick and Jada had been there the day Earl moved out, to make sure there wasn't any trouble.

"Let me guess," Cassie said. "She took him back, because he promised he'd change?"

"She seemed like such an intelligent woman, but…" Nick glanced up at Cassie and grimaced. "Sorry, I didn't mean to say you aren't intelligent, but at least you left and didn't go back. I don't understand how someone can go back to a guy who does that. He broke her freakin' arm *twice*, and she still took him back."

Cassie sighed. "I had plenty of opportunities to leave before I finally did it. Abusers are very good at convincing you they'll change. They're the world's best apologizers. They play head games better than anyone else. They make you think *you* were the one who caused it, so if you just behave the way they want, things will be fine. But things never are."

Nick couldn't imagine forgiving someone for beating on him. But he'd heard all the science supporting what Cassie was saying. His head knew she was right, but his heart couldn't get past that night at Beth Washington's. Couldn't get past Jada paying the price.

"Jada and I drove by the house a few hours after the patrol unit responded to the call. The report said a neighbor had complained about a loud argument and crashing sounds next door. Of course, Earl gave them some BS story. He said they'd been watching a movie with the volume way up, and that was what the neighbor heard. His wife and kids backed him up, so the patrol told him to keep the volume down and left."

"But they weren't watching a movie, were they?" Cassie's fingers stopped moving. She knew what was coming next. Too bad *he* hadn't been smart enough to see it. It was only supposed to be a wellness call at the end of their shift. Jada had already taken her vest off. They'd argued about that constantly—she hated wearing a vest.

"We knocked on the door and Beth answered. I told her we were just checking on things, and she told us the same movie nonsense. But there was something about the look in her eyes. In the eyes of those kids lined up on the sofa. Jada took the youngest girl down to her room, and I asked Beth where her husband was. She said everything was fine. Kept saying we needed to go."

And just like that, Nick was back in that living room again. Nice house. Nice neighborhood. No sign of the horrors that had occurred. No warning of the horror to come. Jada returned from putting the baby to bed, stopping at the end of the hallway. Nick was lecturing Beth about how they couldn't protect her if she wouldn't protect herself. Beth looked up at him, tears and terror filling her eyes. That moment was his first clue that something was *wrong. Really* wrong. The hair on the back of his neck stood on end when she grabbed his shirt, hissing that Earl had a gun. He'd said he was going to kill them all, and if she couldn't get Nick and Jada to leave, he'd kill them, too.

"I looked up at Jada. We both reached for our weapons. There was a shotgun blast, and Jada…" Cassie stroked his head again. "When she fell, Earl was right there behind her, reloading the shotgun. I shot him in the chest, then grabbed the two kids and Beth and hustled them out the door. Everyone was screaming. I went around to the back door to get the baby from her room. The neighbor took a picture of me running out of the house with the screaming kid in my arms, and the media went nuts, making me out as some kind of hero cop. It was all bullshit." He swallowed hard. "I did everything wrong, and my partner…my friend…died in my arms. Because of me. My colleagues on the force knew it, too. I could see it in their eyes when the story hit the news. I could see it at the funeral. The way they looked at me. The way her wife, Shayla, looked at me. They all knew."

"Nick…" Cassie waited until he turned to look up at her. "Are you sure you weren't just projecting your own guilt into their eyes?"

Cassie watched Nick consider her words. He weighed them, almost gave in to the temptation of believing them, then dismissed them, opting to hang on to his pain.

"Good cops don't let their partners get shot in the back. That was on me."

"That's a lot of weight to carry around." He shrugged, staring at one of the candles that were burning low. She'd almost forgotten where they were. What a bizarre place to be having this conversation. "It's why you left LA."

"I was done being a cop. I didn't have the fire for it anymore. I started blaming the victims for putting themselves…"

Cassie nodded. "You blamed them for putting themselves in danger. For being victims." It certainly explained why he'd reacted so angrily to discovering her ex-husband had assaulted her.

Nick raked his fingers through his hair. "I know it's bad. It's wrong. And it sounds even *worse* when you say it out loud. But the fact is, if Beth hadn't taken Earl back, Jada would still be alive."

"So now you're saying it's Beth's fault that Jada is dead, not yours."

"Don't twist my words. It was *my* fault. I walked us right into the middle of a disaster."

"Did Jada not want to go? Do you think she had any idea what was going to happen when she took the baby and left you alone in the living room?"

"No, of course not."

"Then how is this all *your* fault? You both stopped at the house out of concern, and Jada agreed to it. Neither of you expected to run into a lunatic. Something terrible happened, but I don't see how you made any huge mistake that led to it." She tugged at his hair gently until he looked up at her, his dark eyes troubled with memories of a night too horrible to imagine, much less witness. She leaned forward, resting her forehead on his. "Nick, if you and Jada hadn't stopped that night, that whole family would be dead. Those innocent children would be dead."

He closed his eyes. He didn't *want* to feel better about it. He wanted to hurt.

"Shayla tried to tell me that, but it doesn't help."

"Because you don't want it to?"

He pulled away, looking at the bathtub with a flash of surprise, as if he'd forgotten he was in there. She didn't want to push him any further. They'd both shared a lot, and he was probably feeling as raw and wiped out as she was. She stood and handed him a towel.

"I imagine that water's pretty cold by now. I'll make some grilled cheese sandwiches and warm up some tomato soup, and we'll sit and relax for the rest of the afternoon. That will square us up on the deal we made."

He stared at the towel before reaching for it, avoiding eye contact with her.

"It might be better if I head home."

"And I think it would be better if we both had some food and took some time to recover from all the soul-baring that's gone on today. And since this is *my* day to call the shots, you don't get a vote."

He looked up, one brow arched, his mouth sliding into a devastating grin. And then he stood, glistening wet and completely naked. A small cluster of bubbles slid slowly down his chest, and she watched their journey in fascination. He sounded amused.

"I think I liked you better when you were timid.

This bold-and-bossy Cassie makes me think I've created a monster."

Cassie licked her suddenly dry lips. Her mind was empty of coherent thought. The bubbles were below his ribs now, gliding towards…

"My eyes are up here, babe."

She blinked and looked away from him, which finally freed her tongue. "I know where your eyes are. They're right above your smart-ass mouth. Get dressed and…"

He stepped out of the tub. The combination of hard male body and floral-scented bubbles was frying her brain cells. Nick chuckled.

"Are you sure you want me to get dressed? Or did you mean to say you want me just like this?"

Oh, yes. She wanted him alright. Just like this. Just *exactly* like this. The crooked grin. The mischievous light in his eye. The vulnerability he'd shown earlier. The tenderness when he'd held her in his arms. The strength of those arms, the safety she felt when she was with him. It was all so new.

Nick was her friend. He was her safety net. The man she'd made love to. No—had sex with. No. Made *love* to. The man she was falling for. Freefalling for. She had no right to. She was a fool if she did. But it was too late. He was her everything. And she was falling in love with him.

The realization caught her by such surprise that a nervous giggle bubbled up. She covered her mouth to keep from blurting the words out loud, since this man always left her thoughts in chaos and her mouth with no filter whatsoever. She giggled again as she, for some reason, remembered a Sun Tzu quote from her self-help book.

In the midst of chaos, there is also opportunity...

Chapter Fifteen

Nick was standing naked and wet in a bathroom with a woman who was giggling at him.

It wasn't exactly great for his ego, but he tried not to take it personally. She seemed as surprised by it as he was, the way her hand came up and covered those soft lips. The way her eyes went wide. The way her cheeks flushed pink. He cleared his throat loudly.

"So the sight of me standing like this makes you laugh, huh?"

"I'm sorry. I really am. It's been such a...*day*... Hasn't it?" Her hands went wide. "I don't know what we're doing, Nick. I don't know what's happening, or what comes next, or how to..."

"Shh." He put his fingers over her lips this time. "Let's not overthink this, okay? One day at a time seems like a good place to start. Let's take it a day at a time, together, and we'll figure it out as we go."

Her eyes went more gold than green, her brows furrowed. "But shouldn't we have a plan?"

She'd been on the run for a year now, planning for all kinds of contingencies. All sorts of what-ifs, ready to flee in the middle of the night. Letting their relationship simply play out was clearly scaring the daylights out of her. But he needed time to sort through his own feelings, and he couldn't do that while laying out some master plan of how this might work. He decided to distract her.

He kissed her softly, his hand pushing her hair back from her face. She trembled when his lips touched hers. And that was it.

That little tremble was his moment of truth. He was falling for this woman. Not *because* she trembled at his touch. That was just his wake-up call. He was falling for her because she was strong and tough and kind and funny. Because she made him want to be a better man. Made him want to be her protector. Forever. He'd known lots of women. But only one made him think of forever. And it was this woman. Right here. Right now.

"You're naked." She said the words against his mouth, and he felt her smile. He'd gotten her to smile again. And it made him feel like a god. He grinned.

"I am. It's generally the way to bathe, or did I do the bubble bath thing wrong?"

She shook her head. "No. You did it just right, Nick." She was still smiling, but there was something else going on behind those eyes. Something deep. She blinked and straightened. "I'd like to think we can do more than hop in bed every five minutes, though. So let's eat and sit and have that quiet afternoon together, okay?"

He didn't want her thinking they were just bed bunnies. He knew now that he wanted more. He wanted all of her.

"This is your day and I'm at your command." He kissed the tip of her nose. "And I *know* that we can do more than hop in bed every five minutes, Cass. We're more than that."

She looked into his eyes intently. He wasn't sure what she was looking for, but she seemed to find it. She nodded and relaxed against him. Then, remembering his nakedness, she pulled back and gave a nervous giggle. Glancing down, she noted his physical response to their close proximity. It was pretty tough to hide while naked, and he didn't bother trying. The corners of her mouth tipped up. "Who knows? Maybe I'll decide on some bed hopping later."

"Whatever you want, babe."

The rest of the day passed in quiet, peaceful time together. They were both exhausted—emotionally from all the sharing they'd done, and physically from a night full of activity. Nick was shocked at how much he enjoyed settling onto the flowered sofa and having another glass of wine while he watched Cassie read her book in the armchair by the window. She'd explained that the furniture all belonged to her landlady, Nora, who owned the coffee shop downstairs. Much of the main floor of the apartment was open to the beamed ceilings two stories above. There were metal stairs leading to a loft where Cassie slept every night. He wanted to see that loft, but, surprisingly, he wasn't in a rush. It was nice to be here with her, each lost in their own thoughts, but together. And the together part felt really good.

He glanced toward the door and frowned at the duffel bag sitting there. The only dark spot of the afternoon had been when Cassie explained it was her "go-bag," packed and ready to grab if Don ever tracked her down here. Nick wanted to tell her to unpack that thing and forget about leaving, but he could sense the security it gave her to feel...prepared somehow. They'd discuss it some other time, when he'd convince her it was no longer needed, because she had *him* to protect her now. Now and forever.

Damn, that word kept moving through his thoughts. *Forever.* They'd had one night. One night, even one amazing night, couldn't possibly lead to a forever. Could it?

He dozed off for a while, and when he woke, the lake outside the windows was peach colored from the setting sun. Cassie had fallen asleep, too, her book open in her lap, her head back against the corner of the wingback chair. He got up as quietly as he could and took the brightly colored throw from the back of the sofa, wrapping it around her. He figured he'd leave a note and slip out before she woke. They both needed the sleep. But as soon as he straightened, her eyes swept open and she stretched, yawning before smiling up at him.

"Whatcha doin', Nick?"

"I figured it's time for me to head to my own bed. We're both wiped out."

"Stay." It wasn't a question. Just one simple word that could lead to a whole lot of complications.

"Are you sure?"

"I'm sure I don't want to go to bed alone tonight. Do you?"

She had him there. He knew he'd be reaching for her in his dreams.

"No, I don't." He helped her to her feet. "But be sure, Cass. Because one night together is…one night. *Two* nights is a relationship. Even if it's not a long one, it's a relationship. It means something." This already meant something to him, but he wasn't certain where Cassie's head was. If they were doing this thing, they were doing it. All or…nothing? He didn't even want to think about what nothing might feel like.

Luckily, he didn't have to worry about it. Cassie took his hand and led him up the long flight of steps to where a huge iron bed sat, facing the arched windows on the top level of the loft. She turned to face him by that bed, repeating the only word he needed to hear.

"Stay."

Cassie smiled into her tea, staring at her computer screen, struggling to focus on work. She and Nick had settled into a happy routine over the past few weeks. Most of their free time was spent at Nick's house, to avoid the prying eyes of Nora and Aunt Cathy. Nora and the cousins were delighted over their being together.

Amanda reminded Cassie that now the apartment really was an indisputable "love shack."

Aunt Cathy, on the other hand, was not delighted. She worried that Cassie was jumping into a serious relationship too soon. That Nick was "smothering" her by being around all the time. Cassie tried to explain that the difference between this and her former marriage was that she *wanted* Nick around. Cathy reminded her that Nick was a cop, just like Don. But that wasn't fair. There were thousands of honorable police officers out there, and Nick was one of them. Cathy had finally agreed to reserve judgment until she had a chance to get to know Nick better. Which would be happening that weekend.

Here at work, things were easier than she'd anticipated. They made a deal to stay focused on the job while at the resort, and, for the most part, it worked. Nick still hid her stapler every damn day, just like always. They continued to have sparring sessions in the gym like always. He continued to *borrow* flowers for her desk. Other than Blake, no one would ever know things had changed. Unless they saw Nick pull Cassie into his office for a lunchtime make-out session.

Blake wasn't exactly enthusiastic about the new office dynamic, but he didn't post any objections, either. Other than a quiet warning that first Monday to keep it professional and to save their personal life for their personal time, he'd stayed quiet.

A foam basketball went whizzing past her head, bouncing off the window and up into the air. She jumped and squeaked in surprise, then turned her chair to see Nick leaning against the door frame to his office, looking very pleased with himself.

She rolled her eyes. "Are you bored?"

"Hey, you're the one who said nothing should change at work. So this is me, not changing." He picked the ball up from the floor and flipped it into the air, catching it behind his back with a flourish. "I thought maybe we'd take the kayak out after dinner tonight, and watch the sunset from the water."

"You really think it's a good idea to put me back in a kayak?"

He bounced the foam ball off her desk, snatching it from midair in front of her face. She did her best not to flinch. He grinned, impressed.

"I don't know. You in a kayak worked out pretty well once before."

She tried to hold back her laughter, but failed. "Fair enough. I'll give it another try, and I'll try to stay inside the boat this time."

And she succeeded. Nick rowed them out toward the center of the lake that night, where they drifted on the calm water and watched the sun slide behind the mountains. Nick had come prepared, with cookies and wine. She teased him about drinking and rowing. But when she insisted on trying to row herself, they ended up going in circles, so she finally conceded and let him take them home. Neither of them got wet, but they still ended up in bed later, wrapping themselves up in each other after making love.

Aunt Cathy arrived for a cookout on Saturday wearing a healthy dose of skepticism. Nick laid on all of his charm, but Cathy was tough. She'd been through a lot of men back in her day, and most of them had been bad apples. But as the afternoon went on, and Nick presented flawless grilled steaks and veggies, sharing stories and treating Cassie like a queen the whole day, Cathy seemed to relax. Cassie thought maybe they'd won her over, so she was blindsided when her aunt leveled a look at Nick across the picnic table.

"So what are you going to do when Cassie has to pack up and leave Gallant Lake?"

There was a beat of silence. Nick looked at Cassie, then back to Cathy. His voice strong and sure.

"That won't happen."

"Really? Don found her once. What's to say he won't find her here?"

"Aunt Cathy…" Cassie didn't want to talk about this today. Especially after getting two hang-up calls this week from a Milwaukee number she didn't recognize. But that could have been anyone. She hadn't mentioned the calls, because talking about them gave them more weight than they probably deserved.

"No, it's okay, Cass." Nick looked her aunt right in the eyes. "I didn't say Don wouldn't find her. But that's not what you asked. You asked about Cassie leaving, and *that's* not going to happen. Because I'm here, and I'll keep her safe."

It wasn't the first time he'd said that this week, and it was beginning to grate on Cassie. She didn't want him thinking he had to protect her all the time. After all, that's why he'd taught her self-defense.

"I'll keep *myself* safe," she said. Nick and Cathy both

turned to look at her in surprise. "One way or the other, I'll keep myself safe."

Cathy frowned. "Your go-bag is still packed and ready."

"And it'll stay that way." She cut off Nick's objection. "Until Don's in jail, I need to be ready to go. It's not just me he'll be looking to hurt. He'll go after anyone near me. I'm not saying he will find me. I've been careful. But he has connections. He's smart. And I've got to be ready, just in case."

Nick's jaw worked back and forth.

"Don't you leave me, Cassie. You call me, no matter what, and we'll face it together. Promise me you'll call me before you do anything." He reached out and took her hand. "Promise me, babe."

She hesitated, then nodded. "I promise." He stroked her hand with his fingers, the way he often did when they were sitting together, and they gave each other a warm smile.

Cathy looked back and forth between them.

"Well, I'll be dipped. There really is something going on between you two."

Cassie scrunched her brow. "Uh, yeah. That's why you're here, remember?"

Cathy waved her hand in dismissal. "I don't mean the shacking-up part. I wasn't crazy about you two playing with fire when you were in such a precarious position, honey. But you're not *playing* with the fire. You're already dancing in the flames, aren't you?"

Nick looked as confused as Cassie felt.

"Aunt Cathy, what are you saying?"

Her aunt sat back, pushing her pewter-colored braid over her shoulder. She looked at the two of them, then started to chuckle lowly.

"You don't even know it yet, do you? Okay." She stood, and Nick scrambled to his feet, reaching out to help Cassie extricate herself from the picnic table. Cathy shook her head. "I had my doubts about this, and it could still all go down like the *Titanic*, but one thing I know after today. Whatever's happening here is real. And real lo… I mean, real…well…you deserve a chance to make it. If you want my blessing, you have it. But remember one thing." She fixed one last glare on Nick. "I know where you live now. And if you hurt this girl, I will be paying you a visit. Got that?"

"Yes, ma'am."

After her aunt left, Cassie looked at Nick. "What on earth was she talking about?"

"Damned if I know. She's *your* aunt."

"Ugh. I need a cup of tea. You want anything?" These days, Nick's kitchen was fully stocked with tea, sugar and wine for Cassie, along with her favorite cereal and cookies. He'd teased her about her sweet tooth, but she shut him down fast when he suggested she try baked kale instead of a cookie. She didn't mind getting herself in better shape. She didn't mind the new curves and muscles she was developing, or the stamina she hoped would get her up Gallant Mountain tomorrow with less huffing and puffing than the last time. She didn't even mind cutting her carb intake a *little*. But trade cookies for kale? Nope.

Her phone buzzed in her pocket. She pulled it out,

and a shadow fell on her happy afternoon. It was the Milwaukee area code again, but a different number this time. She quickly tucked it back into her shorts. If it was someone she knew, or someone from the DA's office there, they'd leave a message. If it was the random hang-up caller, there wouldn't be any message. Was it Don? One of his pals? But how would they have her number? Maybe it was just a fluke.

"Cass? Who was it?" Nick was frowning at her. "What's wrong?"

"Nothing. Just one of those telemarketing places that got my number somehow."

His forehead creased. "How would they get that number? I thought you said only a few people had it."

She shrugged, heading to the house. "Who knows? Probably on some random list out there. If I don't answer, they'll give up." She hoped. Especially since she knew, deep in her heart, that it was not a random call. It wasn't fair that, at a moment when happiness was finally staking a claim in her life, her past was trying to kick down the door.

The calls didn't stop. She received three more the next week. She answered one of them to see if the caller would speak, but they hung up immediately. The fourth call came the following Sunday, while she and Nick were coming home from the crazy-high cliffs he'd climbed with his buddies, called the Something-Gunks. She'd stayed at the base with a handful of nonclimbers, male and female, who agreed their respective significant others were insane for clambering up the sheer rock face. But when Nick came back down laughing with his pal Terrance a few hours later, he looked energized and happy. As long as he never expected *her* to do anything like that, she was cool with being an observer.

The call came just as Nick was driving down the hill into Gallant Lake. She looked at it, bit back a sigh and moved to put her phone away. But Nick grabbed it from her, glaring at the screen.

"Why didn't you answer? Who is it? Why do they keep calling?"

She bristled at his tone. "Don't use your cop voice with me. You know I don't like it."

His voice softened, but she could see from the set of his chin he was agitated. "Cass, you've been getting these calls for over a week now that I know of." She started to speak, but he cut her off. "And don't give me that telemarketer BS. What area code is that? Milwaukee? Is it Milwaukee? Is it Don?"

She didn't answer. She couldn't, not with him pressuring her like that. Firing off questions that sounded more like accusations. She shrank back in the seat, hating herself for feeling vulnerable right now. With the guy who was supposed to make her feel safe. Nick muttered something under his breath as he pulled into the parking lot behind the apartment. Even in his anger, he'd remembered she wanted to pick up some more clothes. He put the Jeep in Park and sat back against the seat with a sigh.

"I'm sorry. I don't mean to give you the third degree. But I'm worried. I see the expression on your face when those calls come in. The way your whole body goes tense. Something's going on, and you're keeping it a secret for some reason."

"Okay, okay. I've had a few calls from a Milwaukee area code. I don't recognize the numbers, and they're not always the same. They always hang up. Maybe it's just somebody with a wrong number."

"Somebody in *Milwaukee* with a wrong New York number? That's quite a coincidence, don't you think?"

Cassie shrugged. She didn't want to tell him that's how it started in Cleveland, too. Random hang-ups until one night it was Don's voice on the line. Nick thought she was a fighter. He'd given her the tools to take care of herself. She didn't want him thinking she was just another helpless victim.

He didn't ask about the calls again, but he started hovering more than usual over the next few weeks. He was hanging around if she worked late, even after she told him she'd meet him back at the lake house. He jumped to attention every time she looked at her phone, even if she was just checking the time. Maybe she should be more appreciative of his desire to protect her, but instead, she found it annoying. She didn't tell him about either of the two new calls that came in, for fear he'd overreact and start insisting on driving her everywhere like some damn bodyguard.

A few months ago, she'd have given anything to have a big, strong bodyguard. But that was before she learned to protect *herself*. Before Nick pushed her to be stronger, smarter, tougher. And now that she was finally seeing herself that way, he suddenly wasn't.

Chapter Sixteen

The final straw came when she and Julie went to lunch the following Wednesday at the Chalet to celebrate Julie's birthday. The place was crowded with noisy tourists and locals.

"You're different now," Julie said as she finished up her cheeseburger.

Cassie picked up her taco. "Different in what way?"

"I don't know." Julie studied her for a moment. "You're calmer these days, almost mellow, and it's not just because you're shagging Nick West."

Cassie coughed and sputtered, trying not to scatter taco crumbs everywhere. "What are you talking about? I'm not…"

"Oh, please, everyone in town knows you two are together." Julie waved her hand. "I know you're trying to be discreet at work, but no one can miss those sizzling looks going on between you two. But that's not why you're different. No…" Julie reached over and pinched Cassie's bicep, then nodded. "You're leaner. Stronger. You're not as jumpy and timid. You make eye contact with people. You even *walk* different, with that don't-mess-with-me vibe. It's a good look on you, girl. You came out of your shell."

They moved on to talk about the new proposal Blake was working on, trying to build vacation condos on the water. But Cassie kept rolling Julie's words around in her head. If other people were noticing how much she'd changed, why couldn't Nick?

When they walked out to Julie's car, Cassie couldn't believe her eyes. Nick's red Jeep was pulling out of the parking lot. She recognized the climbing sticker on the back door. Had he *followed* her? Her eyes narrowed. This wasn't a coincidence any more than the Milwaukee calls were a coincidence. He was following her, just like Don used to. Not for the same reason, of course. But it still ticked her off. She didn't say anything to Julie, but she was fired up when she got back to the resort.

Nick's head snapped up in surprise when she stomped into his office and closed the door sharply behind her. He quickly smiled and came to greet her.

"Hey, babe, what's up? Did you miss me…? Oof! What was *that* for?" He rubbed his upper arm, where she'd punched him. Hard.

"Did I *miss* you? How can I ever miss you when you never let me out of your sight?"

"What…?"

She held her hand up flat in front of his face. "Stop! Don't tell me you weren't at the Chalet just now. You probably know what I ordered, what I drank and what time I went to the ladies' room. I didn't get rid of one stalker just to pick up another!"

"Whoa. I am *not* stalking you, for Christ's sake. I know you're worried about those calls you refuse to talk about, and I want you to feel safe!"

"But isn't that what all the self-defense classes were for?"

"Well, yeah, in case you're alone and in trouble. But you don't have to be alone anymore. You've got me to protect you."

She dropped her head in frustration. He cared about her. In fact, there were times when she saw the spark of something in his eyes that looked a lot like how she felt for him. A lot like love. But she couldn't let this obsession keep going. She met his gaze. His expression was somewhere between amusement and worry. Damn the man for making her feel this way.

"Nick, I love…how much you care." Whew, that was close. This was no time to blurt out that she loved him. "But you have to trust me to handle myself. You've given me the tools. I've got the moves. Let me have a chance to use them."

He rested his hands on her shoulders. "Today was a fluke, I swear. I had to run up to the sports shop in Hunter. I drove by the Chalet, saw your car and remembered you were going to lunch with Julie. I knew there was that mountain biking event in town. I knew you were in there with a bunch of testosterone-loaded adrenaline junkies, so I figured I'd just…make sure…" His words trailed off, and he had the good sense to look embarrassed. "I don't want you to *have* to use those skills I taught you, Cass."

"I'm not saying I want to put myself at risk. But you can't always follow me around. What about when you're gone this fall to visit the other resorts? I'll be alone then, so why can't you let me be alone now?"

Nick scowled in thought, then gave her a begrudging nod. He cupped the side of her face with his hand and leaned in to kiss her.

"Be patient with me, babe. I'll try to do better. It's just… I tend to lose the people I care about… And I don't want to lose you."

Her eyes went to the photo of Jada on the bookcase, and her chest tightened. He was fretting because he cared. She had to remember that.

"Okay. You try to do better—and I mean *really* try. And I'll try to be patient. But you have to understand that having someone watch my every move brings back bad memories. We *both* have baggage, remember?"

Nick tugged her into a warm embrace, and she rested her head on his shoulder. He really was her safe place. They just had to figure out how to keep him from also being what she wanted to run away from.

A soft knock on the door forced them apart. Nick opened it, and Blake walked in, stopping short when he saw Cassie there.

"Oh…uh… Am I interrupting…?"

"No, we're done." Cassie blushed. "I mean, we're done *talking*. Just talking. And now… We're done."

Nick started to laugh. "Quit while you're ahead, Cassie." He pulled her in for a surprising kiss in front of their boss, and whispered into her ear. "I'll see you at home tonight, and you can show me some of those moves you've got."

She knew her face had to be flaming. She didn't answer, but she also couldn't keep a straight face when she passed Blake and went back to her desk, thinking about which self-defense moves would translate best to the bedroom.

Her muscles were still protesting her successful efforts the next day when she joined Nora and Cathy at the Gallant Brew to help them take inventory. The coffee shop was too busy on weekends to do it, so Blake had given her Thursday afternoon off to help her aunt.

"Hey, Cassie, should I start looking for a new tenant upstairs?" Nora winked at her. "You two don't seem to be spending much time there these past few weeks."

Cathy barked out a sharp laugh. "They prefer his place, where no one's watching their comings and goings. You must be moved in there by now, right?"

Cassie waved her clipboard with one of Nora's infamous checklists attached, and stared at the two women in mock exasperation.

"It's a little early for me to be permanently taking up residence there, and I still have clothes and a toothbrush upstairs, so don't evict me yet." She and Nick hadn't formally discussed their living arrangements, but it was true they seemed to be unofficially living together. And last night they'd managed to christen the few rooms they hadn't already made love in, including the shower in the master bath. Yeah, that was fun. She bit back a triumphant grin. "But I did not come here to be quizzed on my love life, ladies. I came here to help with inventory, remember?"

Cathy glanced at the only occupied table in the place and lowered her voice. "Closing time was half an hour ago. They've paid, but they don't seem interested in leaving. Should I say something?"

Cassie looked at the teens sitting near the window. They were involved in an intense discussion, or at least the shaggy-haired boy was. He was leaning forward, his blond hair hiding his face. But his head jerked as he spoke, his shoulders rigid. The girl couldn't be more than sixteen. She didn't do much talking, just nodded, her head down and shoulders rounded. She was closing in on herself, in a protective stance that Cassie recognized immediately. That girl was afraid of him.

"I'll take care of it." Nora and Cathy looked at each other and shrugged.

The girl startled when she saw Cassie approaching, then brushed her dark hair back over her shoulder and looked away. There was a yellowed bruise on her wrist. The boy sat up and looked at Cassie with a contempt she was sadly familiar with. It was like staring into the eyes of a younger Don. And, just like Don, he quickly smoothed a cool smile onto his face to conform with expected polite behavior.

Cassie looked him straight in the eye and returned the thin, insincere smile. "Hi, guys. Is there anything else you two need today? I don't want to chase you away, but we're doing inventory and we'll be shutting down the coffee machines."

The girl rushed to apologize. "I'm so sorry. We're ready to go." She glanced across the table, suddenly uncertain. "Aren't we, Tristan?"

He sat back lazily and shrugged before slowly standing. "I guess so. If we're gonna be thrown out." There was challenge in his eyes, and Cassie didn't blink.

"I'm not throwing you out, but we do need to shut down. We won't be able to serve you."

He jerked his head toward the girl and she leaped to her feet as if he'd tased her. He turned his back and tossed his words over his shoulder as he opened the door.

"Whatever. This place sucks anyway."

The girl hurried to follow, whispering a quick "I'm sorry" as she passed Cassie. They left, and Cassie stood by the door, filled with regret. That girl was in trouble, and Cassie hadn't done anything to help. She went outside to the sidewalk, but they were gone from sight. She'd missed her chance. She rejoined Nora and Cathy.

"Is there any kind of shelter for abused women around here?"

Cathy shook her head. "Not in Gallant Lake. But there's a place over in White Plains, probably half an hour or so away. Why?"

"I was just wondering. It's too bad there's not someplace closer." It would have been nice if she could have at least handed that poor girl a number to call for counseling. She'd have to check out the shelter and learn more about it. Maybe even volunteer. She didn't help that girl, but maybe she could help someone else.

Nora lifted the trash bag out of the bin behind the counter and Cassie reached for it. She needed the distraction.

"I'll take it out, Nora. You two get started counting cups and spoons and whatever else we have to count."

She was barely three steps out of the back door when she heard a frightened cry.

"No, Tris, stop! That hurts!"

The boy's voice was rough and angry. "It oughtta hurt, you stupid cow! I heard you apologize for me to that bitch in there. Don't you *ever* make apologies for me again, you got it?"

It was the kids from the coffee shop. He'd yanked the girl around the corner of the building and pushed her up against the empty bakery two doors down. Cassie dropped the trash bag and headed toward them. He continued to berate the girl, and was raising his arm in the air when Cassie reached them.

He never saw her coming, and let out a yelp when she grabbed his wrist and twisted his arm behind his back before releasing him with a shove that sent him stumbling a few steps.

"What the hell are you doin', you crazy..."

Cassie nodded toward the girl, now wide-eyed and silent. "Go!"

Tristan avoided Cassie's grip, keeping his distance as he glared. "Shut up! Daynette, don't you listen to her!"

Daynette looked between Tristan and Cassie, crying and confused. Cassie kept her voice level.

"Daynette, this isn't the first time he's hurt you, is it? I saw the bruises on your wrist. Let me guess—he always says he'll never do it again, right? And then he does?" Cassie took a step toward her. "And then he makes it your fault, right? Blames *you* for making him mad?" She could see in the girl's eyes that her words were hitting home. "He's never going to change, Daynette. I've been where you are, and I can tell you he's never going to change. Get out while you can."

Tristan sneered. "And who's gonna stop me from chasing after her? *You?*"

Cassie ignored him. "Daynette, do you have someplace safe to go? Is home nearby?" The girl nodded. "Okay. Go there. Talk to someone about this. And stay away from this jerk."

The boy stepped forward. He was thin, but solid, and Cassie knew she'd have her work cut out for her if he got physical.

"Don't you leave, girl. Don't you walk away from me."

Daynette hesitated, then looked at Cassie, searching her eyes for the promise of something better. Cassie nodded toward the street.

"Go."

Tristan moved to grab Daynette when she ran off, but Cassie elbowed him hard in the ribs. He grunted, then jumped away.

"Lady, you are batshit crazy!" He grabbed her arm, and Cassie could hear Nick's steady voice in her head. *Lower your center of balance. Don't try to outpower him, just go after the pain points.* She didn't try to pull away, surprising him by stepping into his grip, coming close enough to bring her heel down on the top of his arch. He cursed and let go of her arm. Adrenaline was pounding through her veins. She should walk away, but she wanted to push him onto his ass and kick the living daylights out of him right there in the parking lot. Before she could decide between the two options, she was shoved aside.

By *Nick*.

All Nick saw was red. He was driving back to the resort when he saw some punk kid drag a girl around the corner and into the lot behind Cassie's apartment. It took him a minute to turn around and swing back there to make sure the girl was okay. The last thing he expected was to see this guy grab *Cassie* and yank her around. Nick jumped out of the Jeep so fast he wasn't even sure if he'd put it in Park. Cass was fighting back—he saw her stomp on the guy's foot. The kid didn't have time to straighten before Nick grabbed the little piece of garbage and slammed him against the brick wall.

He looked like he was ready to soil his underwear when he got a look at Nick pulling back his fist. He started talking, and fast.

"No, man! You got it all wrong! My girl and I had a little fight, and this lady thought I was going to hurt Daynette, and I was explaining that I'd never do that! We're cool! Everything is cool, man, I swear!"

Cassie pushed past Nick, wagging her finger in the boy's face.

"Liar! You've been using that girl as a punching bag,

and that's going to stop. You don't own that girl, and you don't put your hands on her again. Got it?"

"Cassie, damn it, get back! I got this."

"No, Nick, I *had* this before you got here. And why the hell *are* you here?"

The teen struggled, and Nick twisted his shirt up at his throat.

"I'm gonna let you go now, and you're gonna apologize to this lady and walk away. And whoever you were using as a punching bag? You stay the hell away from her. Got it?"

"Yeah, yeah, I got it. I'm sorry, lady." He took off like he was on fire.

Nick turned to Cassie, trying not to think about how many ways this scene could have gone wrong. "Are you okay? What the *hell* were you thinking, going after that guy?"

"Why do you keep insisting on being my knight in shining armor?"

"Most women *want* a knight in shining armor, don't they? Why are you mad at *me*?"

"Because I don't *need* your help, Nick! Wasn't that the whole point?"

"The whole point of *what*?" Nick raked his fingers through his hair.

"Of *us*!" Cassie gestured angrily between them. "I was your little pet project, right?"

"What the hell are you talking about?"

"Come on, Nick. You wanted to be a hero for teaching me a few self-defense moves, and you got a little fun between the sheets on the side. Big man, right?"

She stepped back and looked him up and down, hands on her hips, eyes flashing with emotion. "Well, I don't want to be your project anymore, Nick. I'm an independent woman and I can take care of myself!"

Nick's mouth fell open, but he couldn't form any words that he trusted. But Cassie didn't have that problem.

"I've already been with a man who controlled my every move. And *he* tried to tell me it was for my own good, too. But it *wasn't*. It was all for *him*. To make him feel like a big man. And you're doing the same thing. You've got some kind of hero complex…"

Anger rushed through his veins, white-hot. "I am *nothing* like your ex."

"You're *exactly* like him!" She threw her hands in the air. "You're trying to tell me what to do and how to think and where to be…"

"I would never hurt you!" His voice echoed off the brick wall. There was a time when shouting made Cassie flinch and stammer. That time was apparently long gone. Now she stepped right up to him, shaking her finger in *his* face this time.

"You hurt me *today*, by not trusting me!"

Guilt punched him hard in the gut, but he pushed it aside.

"I'm not Don. I'd never put a hand on you."

She blinked, lowering her hand slowly. Maybe she was finally hopping off the hissy-fit train. Her voice steadied, but there was still fury and hurt in every trembling word.

"Fine. You'd never hurt me physically. But the broken bones weren't the worst thing Don did to me, Nick. Stealing my self-worth, sucking away my confidence, changing who I was—*that's* the most serious damage he inflicted. And now you're doing the same thing."

"Cassie…"

She spun away, her shoulders so tight and straight he thought she'd snap. And he'd made her that upset. But how? By wanting to keep her safe? How could that be so wrong?

He scrubbed his hands down his face with a growl, staring at the ground. *Damn it.* She accused him of stealing her self-worth? He'd taught her how to defend herself and stand up for herself. Sucking away her confidence? She'd climbed a fucking mountain with him. Change who she was? He'd made her a better person…

His shoulders dropped. But was it his place to do that? She said he had a hero complex. Jada used to say the same thing. She'd died because of his hero complex. And look what he was doing to Cassie now. Christ, he was such a screwup. He looked up and found her staring at him. And he couldn't help defending himself, because…screwup.

"I thought I was helping. I thought that's what you wanted. I thought you…"

I thought you loved me.

But he couldn't say that out loud, not when she was staring at him with so much anger and hurt. This wasn't the time to tell her he was in love with her. He might be stupid, but he wasn't *that* stupid. He couldn't throw those words out there when there was a very good chance she'd stomp on them and fling them back in his face.

Cassie's arms wrapped tightly around her own body, as if holding herself together. He wanted to be the one to do that. He started to step forward, but she shook her head sharply, stopping him in his tracks.

"Don't. I can't…" She shook her head slowly. "I… I don't trust my feelings right now, Nick. Maybe I'm mixing you and Don up in my head. Maybe I'm lashing out at you because I never had the chance to lash out at him. Or the *courage* to lash out at him. Or maybe you deserve every bit of it because you built me into something you don't seem to like very much."

"That's bullshit, and you know it."

"Is it? You didn't want me to be a victim anymore because you don't like victims. But victims are the ones who need a hero's rescue. So if I'm not a victim anymore, you no longer have a role to play. I don't need you to save me, because you taught me how to save myself. You taught me that I don't need a hero. So where does that leave us?"

His mouth opened, but he had no idea what to say to her convoluted logic. If he *loved* her, it was his job to protect her, right? But then, why had he taught her how to protect herself? His brain was spinning faster than tires on ice, and his frustration boiled up again.

"You've got all the answers, Cassie. You've clearly psychoanalyzed me and come to your own rock-solid conclusion. So why don't *you* tell *me* where it leaves us?"

Her eyes hardened.

"So now the big, bad cop is refusing to take a stand. Who's the victim now?"

He bit back the angry words begging to be said. They'd reached the point in this argument where someone was going to have to walk away before they burned down any hope of repairing the damage already done. His jaw tightened. It galled him to be the one walking. It galled him to quit before a winner was declared. But he could see it in her eyes. She was drunk on her newfound ability to take a stand, and she wasn't going to back down.

He got it. For years, she hadn't landed even a glancing blow on her asshole of an ex. She was going to stand and fight now just to enjoy the adrenaline rush of getting her punches in. But it wasn't in his nature to be someone's punching bag.

They could finish this conversation when they were both more reasonable. He turned for the Jeep, his parting words spoken over his shoulder to the woman he loved.

"I think we're done here."

Chapter Seventeen

I think we're done...

Those words rolled around in Cassie's mind on an endless repeat cycle as she stared into her morning coffee.

We're done.

She hadn't slept at all, tossing and turning until the sheets were in a twisted heap. After Nick left, she'd sent a text to Cathy, saying she had a bad headache and begged off from the inventory. Then she'd quietly gone up to the apartment to assess what just happened.

Done.

She didn't know where all that rage had come from. One moment she'd been standing there, feeling like an Amazon warrior after setting Tristan back on his heels. And the next, it was as if Nick had snatched all of her power away. After teaching her those skills, he'd been furious when she'd used them. And something inside of her had just…snapped.

She brushed a fresh wash of tears from her cheeks. How many tears could a human body produce, anyway? She'd been crying all damn night.

All the hurt and rage of a decade had risen to the surface like lava in a volcano yesterday, and she'd unleashed it on Nick. It was frightening to be so completely out of control, with no ability to hold back words she wasn't even sure she believed. Wasn't sure if they should be aimed at Nick or at Don. Or perhaps even at herself.

The one person who could help her sort it all out, and the only person whose opinion mattered to her, had ended things yesterday. She sniffed back the tears threatening to drown her again.

I think we're done here.

Just like that, after she'd attacked him one too many times, he'd walked away.

We're done.

The man she was in love with, the man she *thought* loved her back, had declared them over. In a way, it may have been best that he'd left, as the argument had been racing toward a flameout. She'd kept throwing his words back at him over and over, until he finally said the one word she didn't have the strength to repeat.

Done.

Had Nick truly given her strength only to resent her for having it? That might not be fair. He came upon the situation with Tristan and Daynette without knowing what had happened. If the first thing he saw was Tristan's hand on Cassie's arm, it wasn't unreasonable for him to assume the worst. He wasn't wrong to want to protect her. But it *felt* wrong. It felt like he didn't want her to step up and be strong, even though that was all he'd been talking about since they met.

Her coffee had turned cold enough to make her grimace when she took a sip. A sad realization pressed down on her. Nick might never be able to see her as anything other than a victim. If she was going to start a new life as a new Cassie, she might have to do it somewhere other than Gallant Lake. Somewhere where no one knew her past. Where people would know only brave, strong Cassie. She glanced at her dusty go-bag by the door. She wouldn't be running away. She wouldn't be hiding. She'd be looking for a place to blossom and grow and be her best self. That would be a good thing. So why did the thought of leaving Gallant Lake, of leaving *Nick*, make her heart hurt?

Another one of those damned Sun Tzu quotes came to mind, and it stung.

Who wishes to fight must first count the cost...

Was losing Nick really a price she was willing to pay?

Her phone started vibrating across the stone counter, making her jump so high she almost fell off the kitchen stool. It wasn't Don, thank God. It was Blake Randall. She glanced at the clock and swore. She was late for work. She looked down at the sweats and cami she was still wearing. Whom was she kidding? She wasn't going to work today. She couldn't possibly face

Nick in the office until she had some kind of control over her thoughts. Until she had some sort of plan. Or at least until she stopped crying.

Blake's call was on its third ring before she swiped to answer.

"Um…" She had to clear her throat and dislodge the tears. "Hi, Blake."

"Hi, Cass. Did you have a Friday off I'd forgotten about?"

"No. I should have called, sorry. I know I took time yesterday, but I need a personal day. Will that be a problem?"

"Of course not. Well, it's always a problem when I have to take care of my own damn self, but…" He paused, waiting for her to laugh at his little joke, but she didn't have it in her to even try. "Are you okay? Has something happened?"

"Yes. I mean… No, nothing's happened, and yes, I'm fine." She cursed the shaky breath she took and hoped he couldn't hear it. "I just…need a day."

"Just a wild guess—does this *need* have anything to do with the dark bags under Nick's eyes this morning and his general air of stay-away-or-I'll-stab-you?"

Cassie's chest tightened. Nick had been the one to end things, but at least he was paying a price for it right along with her. Was it wrong if that knowledge gave her a small dose of satisfaction?

"Cassie?"

"Oh…um… What?"

"Yeah, that's what I thought." Blake sounded resigned. "Is this going to be a problem?"

Does a broken heart qualify as a "problem"?

"At work? No, of course not. I just need a day, okay?"

"Don't be surprised if you have company shortly." Was Nick on his way over? Why? He'd said they were finished. She started to rise until Blake continued. "Amanda took one look at Nick this morning and managed to deduce everything in about five seconds. She scares the shit out of me when she does that, because she's never wrong. She called Nick a few choice names and flew out of here a few minutes ago. Odds are she's headed your way."

As if scripted, there was a sharp knock at the door.

She opened the door to find Amanda standing with hands on hips. She gave Cassie a quick once-over and stepped in for a sneak-attack hug. Cassie didn't bother pretending she didn't need it right now. She even returned it, and felt Amanda flinch in surprise. They stood in the doorway like that, and Cassie did her best to hold back the tears that threatened yet again. It was Amanda who stepped back first, wiping something from her face before meeting Cassie's gaze.

"How bad is it? Do I have to hire a hit man? Should I make Blake fire him? Banish him to Bali? Tell me and I'll make it happen."

Cassie couldn't stop the laugh that bubbled up. She'd never had a friend who had her back like this. It eased the pain, if only for a moment.

"Bodily harm won't be necessary." Although, to be honest, she had no idea how she'd be able to face Nick at work every day. "Let's face it, this was inevitable. I was never going to be able to trust Nick not to hurt me somehow, and he was never going to be able to see me as anyone other than a victim. It's better for both of us that it happened now instead of..." The words choked her into silence.

Instead of after I told him I loved him.

"That's a load of bull. You two are crazy for each other. And if it makes you feel any better, he looks even worse than you do, so there's no way he's thinking this is a good thing. Come on, pour me some coffee and tell me what happened."

Nick called and texted Cassie a dozen times with no response Friday. Ignoring him was childish, and it irritated him. Sure, the fight was bad, but pulling the silent treatment on him was ridiculous. He sent another text near the end of the workday, basically saying exactly that. Half an hour later, the boss's wife walked into his office and made it clear that he'd be putting himself in mortal danger—from *her*—if he bothered Cassie again for at least the next twenty-four hours.

"I get that you already regret breaking up with her," Amanda said, "and you *should* regret it, but leave her the hell alone for a few days. That kind of hurt doesn't go away with an *I'm sorry*. And as far as I know, you haven't bothered to actually say you were sorry yet." Nick frowned, going over his texts and messages in his mind. He'd apologized. Right? He must have apologized. Or had he just talked about how they "needed to talk" before he started chastising her for not responding? Damn, he was really bad at this relationship business.

Blake appeared in the doorway, an amused smile on his face as he slid his arms around his wife.

"Is there a problem here, honey?"

She twisted her neck to look up at him, then leaned back into his embrace. Nick felt a pinch of pain in his chest at the look of intimacy between them. It was the same type of look he and Cassie had shared more than once.

"Nothing serious, dear. Your idiot of a security chief made an ass of himself and hurt the woman he loves, but he's going to make it better. Right, Nick?"

...you already regret breaking up with her...

"Wait…did you say I *broke up* with her? We had a fight, and it was ugly, but…" He tried to rewind their argument. They both said hurtful things, sure, but not *that*. "Did she tell you I broke up with her?"

It was the first look of hesitation he'd seen in Amanda's blue-eyed glare since she'd spotted his unshaven, disheveled appearance that morning, then looked to Cassie's empty desk and lit into him for obviously being the reason for her absence. She tipped her head to the side, her eyes narrowing again.

"Are you telling me you didn't tell her you two were 'done'—" she lifted her fingers into air quotes "—before you stormed off?"

"I…" Nick's mouth stayed open, but no more words came out. *Had* he said that? No. Well… Yes, he had. But…

"I didn't mean it that way." He knew that sounded bad, and Blake's sharp laugh confirmed it.

"Dude. You told the woman you love that you were

done in the middle of a fight, but you 'didn't mean it'?" Now it was Blake's turn to do air quotes. "How does done not mean *done*? There aren't that many ways to interpret the word."

"I meant the *argument* was done. I was done *fighting*. I figured we needed to stop before it got worse, so I declared an end to it." He knew without hearing Amanda and Blake's sharp intake of breath that he sounded like a controlling asshole. Kinda like the guy Cassie had accused him of resembling last night. He scrubbed both hands down his face in aggravation. "Okay. Maybe I was wrong." Amanda's brow lifted sharply. "Okay, I *was* wrong. But damn it, how could she think I'd end us like that?"

Amanda started to answer, but Blake rested his hand on her shoulder.

"Let me field this one." He sat in one of the chairs in front of Nick's desk, pulling his wife onto his lap. He gestured for Nick to take the other chair. "You're in love with a woman that…"

"Okay, why do you two keep throwing the *L* word around here like it's some foregone conclusion? I've never told you I'm in love with Cassie."

Amanda bristled, but Blake chuckled and held her tight.

"It's okay, babe. I was the same damned way. I refused to admit the truth about my feelings for you. I didn't ever *want* to be in love, so I clearly *couldn't* love you. Don't you remember?"

Her eyes softened and she patted his arm. "We both had a lot of denial going on back then."

Blake nodded. "And that's where Nick is right now. He doesn't *want* to need anyone, so he won't admit he needs that woman more than he needs air to breathe."

Nick straightened. "'He' is sitting right here."

"Yeah, you are. And she's sitting alone in an apartment in town. And you both feel like shit. I've been there, Nick." Blake glanced at his wife. "*We've* been there. You ask how Cassie could believe you'd end it, but the question is—why would she believe you *wouldn't*? Have you told her you love her?"

Nick didn't need to answer that. They all knew he hadn't.

"Okay. Have you thought about her past?"

"I'm the one who taught her self-defense, remember?"

"That's nice. But have you *really* thought about it? How deep it goes?" Blake sat back and sighed. "Look, I knew about Amanda's past, and her issues with trust, once we got involved. We'd talked about it, and everything was cool in my mind. What's done is done, right?" Nick saw the flash of pain that crossed Amanda's face, and Blake must have sensed it, because he pulled her close again. "Then Amanda thought I'd lied to her about something. I hadn't lied, despite all the evidence to the contrary. I *told* her I didn't lie, but her past taught her that men weren't to be trusted. I was so butt-hurt that she wouldn't believe me that I got pissed off and left, basically proving she was right—men couldn't be trusted." Blake shook his head, lost in the memory of what was clearly a bad time for them.

Cassie had accused Nick of having a hero complex.

Of refusing to see her as anything but a victim to be rescued. That he wanted to rescue her and simultaneously resented her need for rescue. How twisted up his beliefs were with what happened to Jada. He glanced at her photo on the bookshelf. If Jada were here right now, she'd kick his ass six ways from Sunday for being such a lunkhead.

He frowned. She'd kick his ass for a lot of reasons. And at the top of the list would be the guilt he'd carried around for two years. The way he'd avoided Shayla since the funeral. The anger he'd been carrying toward Beth Washington. The way he ran from LA, trying to flee all those memories. The way he'd projected all of that baggage onto Cassie, when she was already carrying a full load. He stood, but Amanda jumped up before he could bolt out the door.

"Give her some space, Nick. You're both exhausted and hurting right now. Spend a little time thinking about things, and give her time to do the same." She turned to smile at Blake behind her. "Those days we spent apart were brutal, but, looking back, I think we needed that space to decide if we were both willing to change. Tomorrow you'll be thinking more clearly and can come up with a way to win her back."

He looked at Blake. "Is that what you did? You won her back?"

He was hoping for a few pointers, but Blake laughed. "Nope. She beat me to it. Chased me down and basically dared me *not* to be in love with her." He shrugged. "It worked."

Everything in Nick was telling him to run to Cassie,

but he resisted. He looked at Jada's photo again. He was no good to Cassie if he couldn't confront his own demons. He slapped Blake on the back and tapped Amanda under the chin with his finger.

"Thanks, you two. I'm still new in the corporate world, but I'm pretty sure this conversation is way above and beyond what's expected from an employer. I appreciate it."

Amanda smiled, but there was a steeliness in her eyes. "That's great. Just make sure you know what you want. And don't hurt her again, Nick. Or you'll be dealing with me."

Blake laughed again. "Okay, Rocky, let's go. Good luck, man."

Nick went home and sent one last text to Cassie.

I'm SORRY. We're NOT done. Let's talk when you're ready.

He was frustrated, but not all that surprised, when she ignored that text, just like she'd ignored the others. For all he knew, she'd turned her phone off after he'd kept hounding her earlier. Saturday passed without a word, but he didn't text her again, even though he checked his phone at least fifty times.

He poured a glass of whiskey and sat on the deck Saturday night, watching the sun setting over Gallant Lake. The ice cubes were almost melted before he finally picked up the phone and dialed. Shayla's voice was surprised and guarded.

"Hello? Nick?"

"Hi, Shayla." Silence stretched taut while he watched a blue heron walking on the lakeshore, pausing every other step to stare into the water, looking for dinner.

"It really is you. Is something wrong?" He pictured Shayla, her hair long and wild with curls, the way Jada liked it. Shayla was the light and energy to Jada's practical and, yes, controlling ways. Jada had been all business, the consummate professional police officer, while Shayla was the free-spirited dance teacher. They'd both had to compromise their ways to make the marriage work, and they'd done it without a second thought. At least it seemed that way.

"Hello? Look, Nick, if this is a drunk dial, I don't have time for it. I've got a recital tonight at the school…"

"I'm not drunk. I mean… I'm drinking, but it's my first one of the night. Do you have a few minutes?"

He heard her snort of laughter. "If you're gonna *speak*, I got an hour. If you're just crying into your whiskey, I ain't got the time or temperament for it, Nick. I haven't heard from you in more than a year…"

"I'm so sorry, Shayla."

There was a beat of silence. "Sorry for *what*?"

The heron was on the other side of the dock now, frozen on one leg, head tipped to the side as if he was waiting for Nick's answer, too.

"For every damn thing. But mostly for taking Jada from you."

There was a sharp intake of breath on the other end of the call, then he heard a rustle of fabric as if she was sitting down.

"Earl Washington took Jada away from me. From us.

I told you at the funeral not to listen to those idiots at the department, didn't I? That you weren't to blame?"

"If I hadn't gone to that house…"

"If you hadn't gone there, Beth Washington and those kids would be dead. Is that why you haven't called before now? Is that why you left LA? Because you think you're responsible for me being a widow?" She paused. "I absolved you of that two years ago."

His short laugh had no humor in it. "It didn't take, Shayla."

"Clearly. Where are you?"

"I'm in the Catskills. I took a security job for a chain of resorts based here."

"Putting that master's degree to work, eh? And today, out of the blue, you sat down with a drink and decided to beg my forgiveness for Jada's death?"

"Pretty much, yeah."

"Why?"

Nick smiled. Shayla had picked up some of Jada's directness in their brief time together.

"Someone… Someone's been pushing me to face my past."

"In other words, you've met a woman who called you on your bullshit?"

The heron struck out, its head diving under the surface of the water, coming up with a wiggling minnow. Nick chuckled. "You sound just like Jada. Straight to the point."

"That's why you were so good together. You didn't take any shit from each other, and you almost knew what the other one was going to do before they did it. Jada said you two were like one person when you worked together."

Nick thought back to the years he and Jada worked together. Once they'd hashed out their initial power struggle, they really were like a well-oiled machine. They broke up a sex-trafficking ring. They moved a drug gang out of a residential neighborhood so children could feel safe playing on the sidewalks. They solved dozens of murders. Probably hundreds of crimes. As weird as it might sound, they'd had a great time doing it. It just worked.

Until it didn't. Until he saw Jada falling from the blast of Earl's shotgun. Once Nick had everyone out of the house, he'd rushed back in to hold Jada in his arms. The sound of her rattling breaths drowned out the screams of the children and the wail of approaching sirens outside.

"Her last words were about you."

"I know, Nick. You told me. You came to me and repeated every word she said, just like she'd asked you to do." The tremor in her voice betrayed her tears. "Are you sure this isn't a drunk dial?"

He shook his head and took another swig of whiskey.

"You listen to me, Nick West. Jada's death is. Not. Your. Fault. She was a police officer following up on a domestic violence call. That's as unpredictable and dangerous as it gets. She knew that as well as you did. She used to tell me all the time that sometimes bad shit happens, and you can't always control it."

"She didn't have her vest on."

"That's not on you. She hated that vest. We used to

argue about it all the time. Jada did whatever the hell Jada wanted, and she wasn't going to be bossed around by you or me or anyone else. The vest was her choice. And as high as the shot was, it may not have saved her anyway. Nick, you gotta let go of the guilt. It's too much to carry."

Cassie had told him basically the same thing. *Too much to carry.* Maybe he needed to start listening to the women in his life. He heard a rustle on the phone… Tissues? Shayla sniffled, then her voice steadied again.

"What if the situation was reversed?"

"What do you mean?"

"What if you were the one killed, and Jada survived? Would you have wanted her to be burdened with guilt over it? Would you want her quitting the force, running away, torturing herself over some made-up idea of being responsible for controlling your actions or the actions of a madman with a gun?"

He didn't answer right away. He couldn't. It was too much truth to take in. If Earl Washington had come in the front door, behind Nick, it would have been *him* shot in the back. And Jada would have been the one watching in horror. He'd trade his life for hers in a heartbeat, but that's not what happened. Earl came in from the back of the house, behind Jada. And there wasn't a damn thing Nick could do to roll back time and change it.

"Nick? What would you want if it was reversed?"

He drained the whiskey, welcoming the sharp burn of it sliding down his throat.

"I'd give anything for it to have been me who died that night. I'd want Jada to be alive, you two to be together, having that baby you dreamed about. But no, I wouldn't want her feeling responsible for me."

"Because...?"

"Because sometimes bad shit happens, and we can't always control it."

Neither of them spoke for a moment, then Shayla sighed.

"I've gotta go get the kids ready for this recital tonight. But Nick, you should know that I'm adopting a little girl. It's what Jada and I always wanted. Tamra's four years old, and I swear to God she's a reincarnation of Jada." Nick smiled at the thought. "She's all spit and fire and power, and she's gonna take over the world by the time she's ten if I'm not careful. I miss Jada every single damn day, but seeing love in this little girl's eyes keeps Jada with me in a *good* way. I honor her memory by loving someone the way she loved me. You should do the same. Maybe with this woman who's got the brains to tell you to straighten the hell up."

Chapter Eighteen

Cassie scrolled through Nick's messages for the who-knows-how-many-eth time. It was Sunday afternoon, and she hadn't heard from him since Friday night. His final message said they *weren't* done, but it sure felt that way from the silence. On Friday, silence was exactly what she'd wanted. He'd been driving her crazy with all the texts and messages. Just like he'd driven her crazy trying to run her life.

She stared out the window of the apartment—the *love shack*—as cars passed below on Main Street. She wasn't being fair. He said they'd talk when she was ready. He was giving her control. He wasn't intentionally trying to run her life. Or maybe he was. She dropped her head back against the overstuffed chair. The whole thing was such a confusing mess!

On one of their hikes a few weeks ago, Nick had pointed out a small whirlpool in a mountain stream. A maple leaf was swirling around and around in the water, unable to break free. That's what she and Nick were like. Neither could break free from their individual whirlpools.

Whoa. That was deep.

She grinned to herself as she reached for her wineglass. Teatime had ended yesterday when she declared it sadly ineffective. Last night's bubble bath was equally unrewarding, since it only reminded her of Nick standing in a tub full of bubbles. Not productive at all.

Wine was doing a much better job of freeing her mind to drift, as well as dulling the pain when she bumped up against a painful memory. Every kiss. Every moment between the sheets. Against the wall. In the tub. On the sofa. In the Jeep. On the mountain. In the gym. She took a sip of wine. Okay, maybe a gulp of wine. It was more effective than tea, but not effective enough.

She was going to have to go to work tomorrow, and Nick would be there. Nick, who hadn't reached out since Friday. Amanda said he was a mess then. Was he still a mess? Awash in guilt and regret? Anger? Or was he tucking it all inside, as he so loved to do, ignoring the truth? Would he pretend everything was fine, the way they tried to do after their first kiss? Would he confront her and defend his controlling ways?

She frowned. Not fair again. And it had been especially not fair for her to compare him to Don. Those mysterious hang-up calls had put her on edge Friday.

Then she saw Tristan and Daynette, and Cassie just flipped. And it felt *good*.

It felt good to help someone instead of being the victim. It felt good to see Tristan back down. Yes, he was just a kid, but she'd been drunk with power at that moment, and she wasn't seeing Tristan anymore. She'd been seeing Don. She'd been imagining making *him* back down. Making *him* stop hurting her. Following her. Stalking her. Frightening her. Having power over her.

And then Nick robbed her of all of that by swooping in to the rescue. And she was so damned angry that he took her power away. Except… He hadn't. Not really. Not on purpose. Don worked at making her powerless. Nick did the exact opposite. He wanted her to be strong. Did she really expect a man, especially an ex-cop, to *not* rush to help if he thought the woman he… Cassie closed her eyes. She was so sure he loved her. Just as sure as she knew she loved him. Of course he'd leaped to the rescue.

And what had she given him in return? All that rage that she'd been holding on to for Don. She'd just spewed it all at Nick. He hadn't deserved it. Yeah, he was over-protective. But he'd watched his best friend die in his arms. He'd convinced himself that Jada's death was his fault. It made sense that he'd react by wanting to protect the people he cared about from any chance of harm.

Cassie stared at her wineglass. Damn, this stuff was making her pretty smart today. Maybe after she had another she'd have the courage to call Nick and tell him to come over so they could work it out. Better tonight than tomorrow in the office, with Blake and Amanda watching them and playing matchmaker.

But that third glass of wine only made her sleepy. Or perhaps it was the fact that she'd hardly slept in two nights that made her fall asleep in the big chair. The apartment was dark when she heard her phone ringing on the counter. By the time she woke up and got to it, the ringing stopped. Her heart jumped. Was it Nick? She didn't recognize the number, but she knew the area code. Milwaukee. She ignored it and checked the time. Almost eleven.

She and Nick would have to figure things out tomorrow after all. It was too late and she was too tired to do it now. Her phone chirped with an incoming text. It was from the same mystery number that had just called. That was new—she hadn't received any texts since leaving Cleveland.

Cute little place you found there.

No. It couldn't be. A dagger of ice hit her heart.

She didn't touch the phone, willing it to stay silent on the counter. It chirped again.

Nice little waterfront tourist town.

Don couldn't have found her. Not now. The comments were vague, though. Maybe he was just fishing for information. She picked up the phone, hoping he was done. Several minutes passed before the final chirp.

Gallant Lake sure looks pretty in the moonlight.

Cassie dropped the phone onto the counter. Don was *here*. In Gallant Lake. He didn't mention her apartment, but if he was in town, it wouldn't take long for him to find her. She glanced at the go-bag by the door. She didn't want to run. But if she didn't, Don would ruin everything. Again. And he might hurt the people she cared about. Aunt Cathy. Nora. Amanda. Blake. A chill swept over her. Don would kill Nick. There wasn't a doubt in her mind of that. There was only one way to keep everyone safe. She grabbed a jacket, leaving her phone in the kitchen. If he was tracking her with it, she had to leave it behind. She'd buy a burner phone and call everyone tomorrow, once she was safe. Once *they* were safe.

She went to the door, picked up the duffel bag and flipped off the lights. It looked like she'd be making that fresh start in a new place after all. But this time she would go there unafraid of the shadows. She wasn't the same person anymore. She'd found her strength. She'd found her heart. She blinked back tears as she locked the door behind her. That heart wouldn't be coming with her, though. Because she'd given that heart away.

Nick knew walking into the office on Monday morning that the day would be tough. Cassie was probably still angry with him. After all, she'd never responded to his final text. Maybe he really *had* ended things, simply by being an idiot. He stood outside his car and gave himself a stern lecture.

He loved her, and he'd do whatever it took to make sure she understood that. He'd earn her love in return if it took him the rest of his days to do it. He'd make sure she knew how much he respected her. How strong he knew she was. How willing he was to let her stand on her own without him hovering around like a body-guard. Although that last one would be tough. But he'd do it for Cassie. She said he'd taken her strength away, and he needed to give it back.

It wasn't until he started walking toward the resort that he noticed her car wasn't there. He stopped behind her parking spot and frowned. It hadn't occurred to him that she wouldn't show up. Blake would have let him know, wouldn't he? Nick checked the time. His sleep-less night had him up and moving earlier than usual. It was barely seven o'clock. She'd be here. And when she arrived, he was going to bring her into his office, close the door and kiss her senseless. Then they'd talk. It was going to be fine.

But three hours later, Cassie still hadn't arrived. Wasn't answering her phone. Wasn't answering *any-one* on her phone. Amanda and Blake were in his of-fice, looking as worried as he was. Amanda called Nora, who said Cassie's car was gone. Blake didn't wait for Nick to ask.

"Go. I'll call Dan Adams and see if he's heard… anything."

He didn't want to think about what the deputy sher-iff might have heard. Maybe there'd been an accident. Or maybe she'd had car trouble somewhere. Maybe she was at the auto shop out on the highway. Maybe she'd broken down on the way to work.

"Nick?" Blake was holding the phone, staring at him. He'd been frozen in place as his brain tried to solve the mystery of Cassie's disappearance. Nick gave Blake a quick nod and left.

Cathy and Nora were already in the apartment when he arrived. The police-detective part of his brain was annoyed that people were traipsing around, possibly destroying evidence of what happened. Where Cassie went. But then Nora motioned to the phone sitting on the kitchen island.

"We didn't touch anything, Nick. I knew you'd want to see everything the way we found it. She left her phone. And…she took her bag."

He spun to look by the door. Her go-bag was gone.

"That doesn't make sense." He refused to believe she'd go without a goodbye to anyone. To him. "That was her panic bag. Why would she take that instead of packing her stuff and talking to someone?"

Cathy folded her arms. "You *know* why."

Thinking she was referring to Friday's argument, he held his hands up in innocence. "It was just an argument. We'd have worked it out. She wouldn't have run away because of a fight."

Cathy's eyes narrowed. "I wasn't talking about any argument, but I'd definitely like to hear more about that. I was talking about that crazy ex-husband of hers."

"He's in Milwaukee," Nick said.

"Is he?" Cathy walked over to the phone.

"He's on probation. A restraining order…"

"And those always work, right?" She twirled the phone and slid it across to him. "Her pass code is 1111."

Nick grimaced. "Original."

"It's her birthday."

"It's four ones. Not a very secure passcode."

Nora threw her hands in the air. "Oh, my God. Stop debating cybersecurity and unlock the phone!"

It opened to Cassie's text screen. It was a number he didn't recognize, and the words chilled him to the marrow of his bones.

Gallant Lake looks nice in the moonlight.

Innocent words on their own, but on Cassie's phone, from a Milwaukee area code, they dripped with danger.

Don had found Cassie somehow. And he'd managed to convince her he was in Gallant Lake. And she *left*. Nick walked to the windows and looked down to the street. If someone *had* been out there watching, she would have been an obvious and vulnerable target fleeing in the middle of the night. Although she'd certainly give Don a better fight now than a few months ago.

But something didn't feel right. His instincts told him Don was still in Milwaukee. That the bastard was playing head games with Cassie for his own amusement. He could have an accomplice, of course, but that didn't feel right, either. Don was in it for the game. He wouldn't want someone else to have the fun. Abusive husbands didn't hire out their dirty work. Like Earl Washington, they wanted their victory all to themselves.

Cathy walked up beside him. "She said if she ever

had to use the bag, she'd buy a throwaway phone the next day and call to let us know she was okay."

"She promised she wouldn't leave without me."

"I know, Nick, but we don't know what happened. All we can do now is wait."

He nodded mutely. Waiting wasn't his thing. But he had no idea where she'd go. Farther east? North to Canada? Catch a flight to the West Coast? None of that felt right. And she would have left in the middle of the night, so how far could she have gone? As a detective, he'd always trusted his gut. And his gut was telling him she wasn't far away. He turned and strode to the door.

"I'm going to drive around and see what I can find."

Cathy's hand rested over her heart. "What you can find? You think Don…?"

Nick shook his head, but it was Amanda who answered, walking through the door with her phone in her hand and looking ticked off.

"Don's not in New York," she said. "I just talked to the sheriff. He called and talked to Don's probation officer in Milwaukee. The probation officer went to Don's place with the police. He was at home. They found three burner phones he was making calls from. The idiot had them sitting right there next to his chair, along with a bottle of scotch. They're charging him with violating his probation, among other things."

"So Cassie's not in danger? Thank God." Cathy sat at the kitchen island. "Maybe my heart can start beating again."

Cassie might be safe from Don, but she didn't *know* that. She was on the run.

He headed for the door. "I've got to find her."

Amanda turned to walk with him. "I'll pick up Blake and we'll head west if you want to go east."

Nora walked over and gave Nick's hand a squeeze. "I have to get back down to the shop, but my husband, Asher, knows the area really well. I'll have him head north toward Hunter. We'll find her, Nick."

Nick hadn't prayed in a very long time, but he did his best to plead his case with whoever might be listening as he drove out of Gallant Lake. He was desperate for some clue of where she might be. He passed the mountain road that led to the walking trail up Gallant Mountain. It didn't make sense that she'd hike up the mountain alone at night. But he couldn't ignore the nagging thought that he'd find her there. After driving less than a mile farther down the highway, he pulled a U-turn and headed up the winding road. He turned onto the rutted track that led to the base of the Kissing Rock trail.

His head told him her little car probably wouldn't have made it up here, but his heart told him he was getting closer to her. Sure enough, when he pulled into the clearing by the gate, her compact car was there, covered with mud. It was empty. He smiled and looked up the trail. She was on Gallant Mountain.

He took his phone out of his pocket as he grabbed his small pack from the back seat, texting Blake. No sense in everyone else searching. Even if he didn't have eyes on her yet, he knew Cassie was here.

Got her.

As he went through the gate, he thought of her going up the trail in the dark. It was a decent path, but steep, and through dense woods. She might be here, but was she okay? He'd just picked up his pace when Blake's response came.

I'll let the others know. Amanda says make sure you KEEP her this time.

Nick shook his head. He deserved whatever Amanda threw at him. And whatever Cassie threw at him once he found her. He'd been an idiot, and he'd almost lost her. But that would never happen again. He tapped a quick reply as he hurried up the trail.

Tell her to count on it.

Chapter Nineteen

Cassie had watched the sunrise from the top of the Kissing Rock. Actually, she watched the effects of the sunrise, since it came up behind her. It cast the shadow of Gallant Mountain on the lake and the smaller mountain on the opposite side, but that shadow receded slowly as the sun climbed higher. Pretty soon she'd be warmed by its light, and she wouldn't mind that one bit.

In her panic, she'd left everything in the car before climbing up here in the silver predawn light, including the go-bag with her jacket in it. It was amazing she'd made it here in one piece, but someone must have been watching over her as she did her best to remember the trail and not walk smack into a tree.

She stretched her legs in front of her. There was water and granola bars in the bag, too. The bag that was in her car. She really should have thought this through a little bit better. She didn't dare go back, in case Don somehow found the car. Highly improbable, but even if he *did*, he'd have no idea where she'd gone. Unlike Nick, Don *hated* the outdoors. She'd left the apartment in such a mad blur of panic after Don's texts. Then heartbreak took over as she drove out of Gallant Lake and away from Nick. She couldn't leave him. She couldn't bring herself to *go* to him, either. She'd said some awful things to him. His last text said they *weren't* done, but… What if they were?

Her flight out of town had been horrible. The road out of Gallant Lake led past the resort and the large estate called Halcyon, both on the lake. She'd slowed by the resort, filled with regret that she wasn't going to be able to say goodbye. At two in the morning, the lake had been black as ink beyond it. She didn't want to wake Blake and Amanda at that hour. What would she say?

Hello, I'm an idiot who chased off the only man I've ever loved and I don't know how to fix it. I thought I was tougher now, but I freaked out when my ex tried to scare me. So clearly I'm not tough. I'm just stupid and I don't know what to do... Help!

She could imagine the expression on their faces if she woke them up with that little pity party in the middle of the night. Amanda would do her best to make her feel better, but…no.

Cassie was so afraid Don would find her that she panicked every time she saw headlights. She'd finally turned off the main highway and started on the twisting mountain roads. It wasn't long before she was hopelessly lost, with no cell phone to call for help. By some miracle, she'd recognized the road Nick used to get to the Kissing Rock trail. She slowed until she found the opening in the trees to the dirt road leading up the mountain. Up to the place where she and Nick had kissed for the first time. Where they'd made love under the stars just last week. Where she'd felt like she was on top of the world. Invincible. If there was any place on this earth where she could figure out what to do next, this was it. And Don would never find her here.

The first hint that she wasn't alone made her pulse jump. She heard footsteps. Rustling branches. Was it Don? Maybe a hiker? A bear? She glanced up the rock wall behind her. She had no idea how to climb it, but if a bear strolled out of those trees, she might just give it a try. She scooted across the rock, wishing there was more cover, and knowing if she stood she'd be even more visible. She caught a glimpse of blue in the trees. Not a bear.

Nick stepped out from the shadows and stopped, looking straight at her as if he wasn't the least bit surprised to see her. She rolled her eyes at herself—duh, he'd seen her car, of course. But how had he known where to look? And what was that expression on his face? Anger? Relief?

"Do you mind having company up there?"

She shook her head, straightening against the cliff again. "Not if that company is you."

He climbed that little path up the side of the rock like it was nothing. He hesitated, then sat next to her, with his legs out in front of him like hers were. He looked out at the lake. Not at her. Her heart fluttered in her chest. They sat like that for several minutes before he spoke, his voice like honey and electricity in her veins.

"Don was never in Gallant Lake."

"I got texts. He knew where I was."

"I saw the texts. He knew about Gallant Lake, but he's not here."

She turned to him in surprise. "You opened my phone? How?"

"Seriously?" He gave her the first glimmer of a smile. "Your password is 1111. It wasn't that hard. He's not here, Cass. He's in Milwaukee. They arrested him there this morning and found the phones he's been using. You're safe."

She didn't answer. All that panic. For nothing. She was overwhelmed with exhaustion.

Nick nudged her shoulder with his. It was an innocent move, but the contact instantly had her nerves on end. His eyes met hers.

"That was pretty smart, hiding up here. But it doesn't surprise me. You're a pretty smart lady. You can take care of yourself." He grew more solemn. "You've always been able to take care of yourself, Cassie. You never needed me. Not now. Not before."

She let those words settle in. She hadn't realized how much she needed to hear them. She thought she could dismiss their argument and forgive everything. But forgiving wasn't the same as forgetting. It meant a lot to know he'd *heard* her on Friday.

"Thank you for saying that. I'm sorry about what I…"

He put his finger to her lips. "You were right. About

everything. I mean, yeah, you twisted me up a little too closely with Don, but I get it." His words came out in a rush. "I was all tangled up with my guilt over Jada and the anger I hadn't dealt with… And then I fell in love with you and it scared the daylights out of me. The stronger my feelings got, the more I kept thinking that I couldn't lose someone *else* like that. I couldn't stand having you out of my sight, and I smothered you. I know that now. I see how it could make you think I was doing it for all the wrong reasons…"

Cassie moved his finger aside so she could speak.

"Say that again."

His brows rose.

"All of it?"

"The only part that matters." She needed to be sure she'd heard him right. He looked at the ground for a second, rewinding his rambling speech. Then his mouth curled into a smile, his eyes deepening to the color of hot, black coffee. He cupped her face with his hand and leaned in, repeating the words against her lips before he kissed her.

"I fell in love with you."

She sighed and let him kiss her. Let him pull her onto his lap and tip her back and kiss her until she was dizzy. When he lifted his head, she was clinging to his shoulders. Then she released her hold, fell back and grinned up at him as she stretched her arms out wide. It felt as if she was dangling over the edge of the mountain, with the lake glistening blue beyond them. Nick was bemused.

"Whatcha doin', slugger?"

"I'm letting you take care of me, Nick." She glanced up at him before gazing back out at the dizzying upside-down view. "I *am* able to take care of myself. And I *will* take care of myself. But it's okay to lean on the arms of the man I love and trust him to keep me safe."

Nick pulled her upright so fast she gasped, resting her hands on his arms.

"Say that again." His voice was thick with emotion.

Their smiles mirrored each other.

"All of it?"

"Just the part that matters."

"I love you, Nick. And I trust you." He kissed her again, scattering her thoughts until all she felt were his lips and his hands sliding under her shirt and up her back.

"God, Cassie, I love you so much. Don't ever leave me again. You promised you wouldn't."

She pulled away, pinched with guilt at the pain she saw in his eyes.

"I'm so sorry. I didn't know where we stood after that horrid fight. I was afraid I'd blown everything. When I saw that kid grab his girlfriend and threaten to hit her I…kinda lost it. The mistake was that I lost it with *you*." She gave him a quick kiss. "I got a little carried away with my newfound independence and daring-do, and it went to my head. Then the text came through last night and…"

He placed his lips on her forehead and stayed there, as if reveling in the moment, before he answered.

"I went all caveman on you. I took your victory away. I get it. But from now on…"

She snuggled into his arms and finished the sentence. "From now on, you and I will talk things through and trust each other. I'll trust you to take care of me without making me feel helpless…"

"And I'll trust you to make the right decisions for yourself, even if they aren't the decisions *I'd* make." He kissed her. "I'll trust you to love me, even when I'm an overprotective husband."

"*Husband?* Did I miss a question somewhere?"

"The question won't come until there's a ring in my hand, but trust me, it's coming."

"O-kay. Then I'll trust you to love me, even when I'm a stubbornly independent wife."

"Sounds like we may be having a few…um…fun discussions down the road."

"Maybe. But as long as we remember the love-and-trust part, I think we'll be okay." She cupped his face with her hands. "You were wrong earlier, Nick. You said I didn't need you, but I do. I need you as much as I need the air I'm breathing. When those 'fun' discussions come up in the future, and I'm sure they will, we have to remember that need. That promise to love and trust."

He pulled her close. "We'll write it into our vows." He grinned. "I'm sorry, that sounded bossy, didn't it? I *suggest* we put it into our vows. Only if you agree, of course."

She chuckled against his chest. "I think that's a very good 'suggestion.' And now to a more important question…"

He looked down at her, one brow raised, waiting.

"Do you have food in that pack of yours? Because I am starving!"

Nick laughed and reached for the pack while cradling her in his other arm.

"You know I do. And water, too."

"I can always count on you, Nick."

With a quick twist, he laid her back on the rock and rested on top of her, his hand running down her side and around to her buttocks, pulling her up against him.

"Yeah, you can always count on me, babe. Don't ever forget that."

She knew what he was thinking, and frankly, she was thinking the same thing.

"What if someone hikes up to the Kissing Rock this morning?"

"On a Monday? Highly unlikely. I think we're safe." He kissed her. "Well, I don't know if *safe* is the right word. I never feel safe with you, because you make me crazy." He kissed her again. "I love you, Cassidy Zetticci. And I'll never stop loving you. You still hungry?"

"Oh, I'm hungry, alright. Hungry for you. I love you, Nick West."

"Don't ever stop loving me, Cass. It'll break me."

"I couldn't stop loving you if I tried. Always."

He kissed her.

"And forever."

* * * * *

We hope you enjoyed reading

One Touch of Moondust

by *New York Times* bestselling author

SHERRYL WOODS

and

A Man You Can Trust

by JO McNALLY

Both were originally Harlequin® series stories!

From passionate, suspenseful and dramatic
love stories to inspirational or historical,
Harlequin offers different lines to
satisfy every romance reader.

New books in each line
are available every month.

HARLEQUIN

SPECIAL EDITION

Believe in love. Overcome obstacles.
Find happiness.

Harlequin.com

SPECIAL EXCERPT FROM

HQN

Journey back to Rendezvous Falls, where, with a little luck, one fake relationship might actually become the real deal. Even as they tell themselves it's only make-believe between the sizzling glances and toe-curling kisses…

Read on for a sneak peek at
Barefoot on a Starlit Night *by Jo McNally.*

I'll explain later, but I'm ruined if you don't play along. My career. My visa. Please…I need you.

When she didn't respond to his begging, Finn had started to step away, defeat dulling his eyes. But she'd stopped him. She had no idea why.

She should have slapped him in the face, right there in front of his boss and her customers. He'd *lied* about her. He'd humiliated her. She should have screamed obscenities at him and thrown him out of the pub. Out of *town*. That's what she *should* have done. What she *would* have done without hesitation if it was anyone else but Finn. She'd looked into his desperate eyes… It would have felt like kicking a puppy. Besides, her nana and Father Joe were watching. She couldn't make a scene in front of them. At the very least, she'd give Finn a chance to explain. To fix this. Whatever *this* was. There had to be an explanation.

I need you…

She fluttered her eyelashes up at him like a playful coquette. "Well, if Nana knows…*darling*, then there's no sense hiding our love any longer, is there?" Finn's eyes widened. Warming to her role—and to making him squirm—she lifted her hand and waggled it near his face. "And now I can finally wear that big, beautiful *ring* you promised, sweetheart."

He finally found his voice. And the hint of a relieved smile. "'Tis true, *dearest*. But didn't we agree 'twas dangerous for you to be cooking with a great rock on your finger?"

She leaned into him. Tomorrow they could call it off. For tonight, she'd have fun letting him twist in the wind. "Oh, don't worry, *baby*. I'll be careful. I mean…you *did* say I deserve the best."

His smile deepened enough for a dimple to appear. "Oi, you're a minx, Bridget McKinnon." He tapped his finger under her chin. "Life will ne'er be dull engaged to you, will it?"

For an instant, she could imagine it, like a quick video playing out before her. Laughing with Finn. Marrying Finn, surrounded by her family. Raising a family... She blinked and looked away from his damnable eyes, which had darkened as if he was seeing the same ridiculous fantasy.

"You know, O'Hearn—" Greer cleared his throat "—I'll admit I had some doubts when you told me you two were engaged, but now that I see you together, there's no doubt at all. You may as well seal the deal with a kiss."

Bridget recoiled. Kissing hadn't even occurred to her—outside her fantasies, that is.

A cheer went up around them. To her horror, nearly everyone in the place was looking at her. At her and Finn.

Everyone hooted and hollered and shouted for them to kiss. What. Was. Happening? Finn turned her slowly to face him, muttering an apology under his breath before his lips touched hers. Her ears registered the pandemonium going on in the Purple Shamrock, but every other sense was strictly focused on her mouth, now held captive by Finn O'Hearn.

He started by just pressing his lips against hers. It was an act, just to make everyone happy. A quick press of lips together, and then they'd pull apart and figure out how to end this engagement farce without him losing his job or her breaking Nana's heart. Fine. Get it over with.

Except...Finn didn't pull away. His arm tightened around her back and drew her in. Her hands rested on his shoulders, but she didn't push at him. In fact, her fingers curled into his shirt and held on tight. His head turned slightly, and his lips moved ever so gently. There was a gentle sound of surrender, and she realized it came from her. Her mouth went soft and pliant, and she pressed against him. He gave a low growl and ran his tongue along the seam of her lips. And she let him in. God in heaven, she let the man kiss her senseless, right there in front of the whole world. She didn't want him to stop. Ever.

Someone whooped near them, and Finn drew back as if stung. He looked around, his face reddening.

"I...I'm sorry..." He mumbled the words, his face close enough to hers for the words to be private. "That's not what I expected...I mean... intended. It won't happen again." The corner of his mouth tipped up. "But damn, woman. You're good at this."

Don't miss what happens next in...
Barefoot on a Starlit Night *by Jo McNally!*

Available now wherever HQN books and ebooks are sold.

HQNBooks.com

⬢ HARLEQUIN
SPECIAL EDITION

**Believe in love. Overcome obstacles.
Find happiness.**

Save $1.00

on the purchase of

ANY Harlequin Special Edition book.

Available wherever books are sold,
including most bookstores, supermarkets,
drugstores and discount stores.

- ✄

Save $1.00

on the purchase of ANY Harlequin Special Edition book.

Coupon valid until January 31, 2021.
Redeemable at participating outlets in the US and Canada only.
Not redeemable at Barnes & Noble stores. Limit one coupon per customer.

52616785

5 65373 00076 2   (8100)0 12463

BACCOUP91877